THE RINGS OF HESAURUN

BOOK ONE

A NOVEL BY

PETER HARRETT

Praise for The Rings of Hesaurun

"*The Rings of Hesaurun* is absolutely riveting. With vivid imagery and a compelling tale, the author does a phenomenal job of drawing you into this mystical yet oddly familiar world. Your greatest challenge in reading it will be putting it down. Brilliant."

- Heather Valeria Eder

"*The Rings of Hesaurun* put the fun back into sci-fi for me. This story needs to be a movie! It's hard to find any story with such great character development, soul, action, and adventure, but this is all of them. Compares to classics like The Hobbit and Dune, but a lot more fun. It had me laughing, crying and left me wanting more. A great read! I can't wait for BOOK 2, The Ring Bearer."

- Marcus Hill

"*The Rings of Hesaurun* is a grand feast of the imagination and a triumphant return of Epic Sci-Fi! Peter Harrett's story unfolds and wraps itself around your brain with knife-edge suspense and haunting originality. This is the novel most authors only dream of writing!"

- Sam Sevren

Book design by www.delaney-designs.com

ISBN: 978-1-63848-522-3 (Paperback)

PROLOGUE

Hesaurun— Time Indeterminate

Hesaurun's binary stars scalded the dead planet with heat and radiation, so intense nothing survived. But it hadn't always been that way. The rich biosphere that once included sentient life had been stolen, ripped away, reduced to nothing, leaving only deep gouges and devastation as evidence that there had once been something more, something thriving and flourishing.

Now Hesaurun and its previously-inhabited moons lay barren, devoid of the raw materials that fuel life. Other than the Boecki, few species could survive more than a few minutes in this harsh reality—which was one more reason the Boecki were the most numerous and successful species in the galaxy. They were also the most ruthless. No world had ever stood against them and lived to tell the tale.

The Boecki Dominion was mired in an unrelenting quest for resources. An interplanetary wrecking machine that swarmed on star systems like locusts, devouring everything in their path, leaving nothing of value. Their flawed procurement system was untenable, but that didn't deter them, for their way had become survival or ruin. Resources being finite, they risked overreaching themselves. They saw no alternative, so they continued overrunning star systems harvesting those worlds, stripping them of anything of value without regard for life.

No one was spared. The Dominion had institutionalized brutality so thoroughly that equity had become an inscrutable concept. The fortunate inhabitants of "harvested" worlds died early, however the unfortunate survivors were relegated to slavery or stockpiled for consumption. The Boecki had a thousand worlds to sustain and feed. The Hesaurun system had been just one more crop to be gathered before moving on to the next resource well.

Stripping planets of their eco-systems heedless of their inhabitants was something one harvest ship commander considered unconscionable. Bitterness at the barbarity of the very society that bore him caused this officer to reject it in its entirety, to abandon his command, and oppose his own kind. He refused to be part of it anymore, making him both a renegade and a target.

The Dominion would never know they had unintentionally alienated one of their greatest assets, spawning an opponent who would someday be instrumental in knocking them from their imperial perch. However, the wasteland that was Hesaurun made it the last place the Dominion would ever look for him. Secreting themselves there made perfect sense, so Commander Osomarío built a life for himself and his collaborators on this ruined world. They sought not solace on Hesaurun but a place to plan the monarchy's downfall.

Despite the Boecki's best efforts to appropriate the entirety of Hesaurun's assets, a hidden treasure remained concealed: The Preservers, as they referred to themselves.

The five rings of Hesaurun, ancient sentient mechanoids, witnessed the Boecki ravage their world and its inhabitants and were outraged by it. However, the Preservers were ineffectual without a host. They needed a capable aide, a ring bearer. Albeit, this ring bearer must be pure and dedicated to their cause, or the power they shared might be abused, employed for selfish reasons. The Preservers found what they had long-awaited — a worthy cause and a conduit in which to accomplish their goal of ridding the galaxy of the Dominion; a Boecki defector; Osomarío.

So the Preservers bonded themselves to their new host. Infused with immense energy provided by the five rings, Osomarío now had the power and the means to stop the Dominion and save a multitude of inhabited worlds from extinction. All he needed was a plan, one that would make amends for his past errors. But Osomarío could not accomplish it by himself for fear he would draw unwanted attention from the Dominion. He needed a non-Boecki ally, a vassal. So the Preservers sent Osomarío on a quest to seek out one such as himself. He found what he was looking for in an unlikely place — Earth.

The human child woke from her dreams to find herself in an alien world. Startled and confused at first, she lay silently on the ground, wondering at the strange surroundings, gathering her nerve. Looking up, she saw the creature's four-armed sinewy frame towering above, but she was no longer afraid; she felt its presence in her mind, and it was good.

The creature reassured her she was safe, handed her a gift, a cat, and asked her to share Hesaurun's view with him without a word being spoken.

Too small to reach a hand, the little one cradled the animal in one arm and wrapped the other arm around a spindly leg for support. The odd couple stood at the edge of a precipice surveying the scene of Hesaurun's desolation. Deep furrows scarred the surface in a criss-cross pattern, punctuated by enormous boulders heaved up from the depths. It was a world of gashes, chasms, and blowing dunes punctuated by blistering heat.

But there was more: an immense device, a ring-shaped articulated machine with five images, hieroglyphs, pressed into its base. Another four of the strange instruments were scattered among the rubble, each producing a thrumming that shook the ground beneath their feet.

As the thrumming intensified, the ground shook violently, and the five rings loosed themselves from their foundations, showering the surface with boulders and gravel. The onlookers watched as the rings rose slowly from Hesaurun's ravaged surface and into the air until they floated silently above them, blocking out the twin stars' light. Then the rings began resizing, shrinking until they were too small to be seen. It seemed they had disappeared until the creature saw they had attached themselves to his hands.

Osomarío shifted his eyes to the purring cat, then turned his attention to the child. Although young, he had great expectations for her. But his chiseled features framing the reflective mirrors that were his Boecki eyes betrayed no hint to his thoughts or emotions.

The child peered up at the creature curiously, searching those dark orbs for a sign. But she saw only her own image reflected in them. And yet, little Valerie Dunne wasn't afraid because she knew they were alike. Despite their differences, these two were kindred spirits bound together by a power shared. Together they were a force to be reckoned with, one that would one day be unleashed upon an unsuspecting enemy, powered by the Five Rings of Hesaurun.

Chapter 1

Pearse— January 2431 BCE

An hour before dawn on a freezing February morning, the family of five slept comfortably together in a warm bed of woolen blankets. The night fire had burned down to smoldering embers, leaving the interior of the stone house icy-cold and in absolute darkness.

The man was awakened by a distant reverberation, a rumbling, the sort of thing one feels in the bones before hearing it. It was unlike anything he had ever felt or heard. With his eyes wide and breath held, he lay unmoving in his bed, waiting in silent anticipation for any clue that would reveal the source. He glanced at his wife and children, who were still dozing, but he was prepared to fight if he sensed danger to his family.

As the rumbling became audible and grew, he sat up, listening with rapt attention. His first impression was the sound of an approaching wildfire, although he knew that was out of the question. A wildfire would be impossible with temperatures well below freezing and deep snow blanketing the entire region. Maybe, he reasoned, it was the sound of a windstorm; but when a sonic boom detonated in the atmosphere, the thought perished.

Leaping from his bed, he threw on his boots and coat in one swift movement, then burst through the door to investigate. His eyes scanned the horizon, but he found no danger there and no visible reason for alarm. Yet the sound continued to grow in intensity. He stared at the heavens, realizing something unknown to him was tearing through the atmosphere.

Winter's predawn horizon was barely visible beyond the snow-covered ridge where Pearse made his home. The River Nore, now ice-bound, wound its way through a grassy flood plain in the distance. A ragged strip of charcoal gray gave evidence of mountains distant. Behind them, dawn threatened to ignite the murky sky.

Now the growing rumble echoed through the river valley. Pearse stared in that direction, but the sound offered no clue to its source or the cause. Lauryn, his wife, and their three children joined him on the high bank, all searching the murky sky as one. A mixture of wonder and dread of the unknown filled their hearts.

As it neared the ground, the sound grew exponentially, roaring, snapping, popping, and shaking the bones of the small group of onlookers. Then the low-hanging clouds began glowing, radiating yellow light on the snow-covered grasslands as if the sun was falling to earth.

When a fireball broke through the glowing clouds and streaked to the ground, they stared in horror. As it struck, the object threw up a frightening plume of earth and snow, followed by a deafening boom. The concussion wave that followed sent them reeling. They struggled for balance as their world shook violently and snow fell from the trees around them. Lauryn held their youngest child to her breast as it wailed inconsolably.

Pearse studied the growing debris cloud in wonder as Lauryn tended the children. The little family huddled together as they attempted to understand what had occurred. The event they had witnessed was beyond their scope of knowledge or experience. But they were certain whatever happened had laid waste to their little valley.

When the air cleared enough to expose vague details of the devastation, they were awestruck. Through the smoke and mist, firelight was visible. Then as the smoke dispersed and the air cleared, they were able to make out the outline of a crater with a shimmering shape at its center.

"What is that—*thing?*" Lauryn asked her husband, with wonder in her eyes.

"I don't know," Pearse whispered, "but I'm going down there to find out." Once he had set his mind on investigating the scene, he began barking orders.

"Lauryn, you build a fire while I get ready to go."

"Tierney," he called to his eldest son, "go get ready, you're coming with me. Get something to eat and gather overnight supplies for two. We're leaving as soon as we're ready."

"Aedan and Saoirse," he ordered the younger ones, "go help your brother."

Tierney, the thirteen-year-old, was always eager for an adventure. As he ran excitedly to the house, his siblings followed closely on his heels. The three youngsters wasted no time collecting the supplies needed for cold-weather travel in deep snow. Once they had gathered everything together,

Tierney took stock of the piled provisions. There was no room for error once they were out in the weather; it had to be right the first time. Their lives depended on it.

The kit included a two-day supply of food and water with fire-starting stones, tinder, knives, a long-handled ax, and enough skins to build an overnight shelter. Once satisfied, they bundled it all together in waterproof skins with sewn-in shoulder straps. When finished, Tierney felt satisfied he had completed the task his father had commanded. He stopped to eat only when he was sure they were prepared to travel.

Pearse put his hunting gear on, threw his pack over his shoulder, then noticed the air had cleared, allowing better definition of the glimmering mass in the crater. A peculiarity caught his eye. The fires seemed to shine rather than flicker as expected. Moreover, those strange fires appeared to surround the object spaced at even intervals. When he realized the fires shined without flickering or emitting smoke, Pearse's apprehension of the thing increased, and with it, his curiosity.

Straining to see more in the dim light, he wondered if his eyes were playing tricks on him. The improbability of the scene filled him with a sense of foreboding. Nothing was ordinary about any of what he saw there. The longer he stared, the more questions arose. Everything about the scene was strange, unknown, beyond his understanding. As he inspected the devastation, he probed his people's history, collective memory, and own experience for answers but found nothing comparable. This strange object was something he would have to see for himself and try to understand.

Despite being keenly interested, he was a cautious man. He was not about to allow curiosity to jeopardize his safety or that of his son. Pearse was determined to approach the thing with caution, vigilant, and weapons at the ready. There was no way for him to know what to expect, so he would go in expecting the unexpected.

Pearse said goodbye to Lauryn and his children, assuring them he would be careful and intended to return before dusk. Then he and Tierney set off on what he estimated to be a three to four-mile walk through the knee-deep snow.

Once they had made their way down the high bank and crossed the River Nore, Pearse and Tierney made good time following a game trail across the snowy flood plain. The thick cloud layer blocked out most of the morning light without offering the slightest hint of its location in the sky. Since their footfalls were silent in the dry fluffy snow, all was quiet except their steady breathing. Pearse and his son were the only things moving in the desolate valley that morning.

Dense forest replaced the grasslands as they trudged up the incline leading into the surrounding hills. Snow was piled high under the trees, shaken loose by the morning's strange event. The tall trees were free of snow for the first time in months. Now forced to crawl through loose deep snow, the pace slowed considerably.

Soon the investigators found themselves confronted by masses of downed trees and thick branches blocking the way at the top of a ridge. Although relieved to be out of the loose snow, they now faced the arduous task of scrambling over the big logs one by one. Many were as big around as they were tall, making the going difficult. Now progress slowed to a crawl.

"Father, why are the trees broken like this?" Tierney wondered aloud.

"I cannot say, boy," Pearse confessed, panting from the exertion. "Do you want to turn back? I think we are close."

Tierney considered the offer for a moment before answering. "If we are close, let's keep going. I want to see it," the boy bravely declared.

Rubbing his son's shoulder affectionately, Pearse said, "Alright, but be careful climbing over these trees. I do not want to carry you back!"

As the boy and his father fought their way to the top of a ridge, they came to a viewpoint that revealed the entire crash site. The destruction seen there was stunning, stopping them in their tracks. Below lay a half-mile-wide clearing devoid of anything more substantial than a pebble. The cleared depression was surrounded on all sides by enormous trees, all lined up in neat rows in every direction. The landscape appeared as if a giant hand had combed those trees into place around the impact crater. An earthen wall encircled the strange glittering object placed perfectly at the crater's center.

The gleaming silver shape shone brightly against the earthen backdrop, with its nose partially buried in the ground. Sensing the boy's tension, Pearse put his arm around his son's shoulder. He noticed how the lights were evenly spaced along its smooth flanks, just as he had seen from his home on the high bank of the River Nore. His curiosity increased as he realized they must be lamps but wondered how they burned without making smoke.

Bewildered, Pearse and Tierney sat together on a log resting from the hard climb, studying the unearthly sight. The area was eerily silent, with nothing moving on the ground or in the air. Beyond the affected area, thick snow covered the forests as far as the eye could see. Furthermore, everything within a half-mile diameter of the crater was swept clean of both trees and snow. The destruction was complete, yet the mysterious object lying at the crater's center dominated their attention.

Pearse stared at the object intently. He could only compare it to that of a fish, although he knew no fish could ever be as large. But it was not a fish, and it certainly was not alive. The shiny surface made him think of glass. Pearse had seen glass at the summer gatherings. In his estimation, the thing appeared to be similar to that glass.

"Father, what is that?" Asked the boy, his finger pointed at the indescribable object.

"I don't know. But it seems to be made of glass."

"What is glass?"

"See how it shines? Glass shines like that," Pearse explained. "Remember when we saw glass last summer, outside the conclave lodge? A man had a table with white and black glass for sale. It was smooth and shiny. White, just like that thing."

"Oh, yes, I remember. But that man only had a few pieces, and they weren't as bright as that." Tierney cocked his head curiously to the side, then added, "Do you think there are people inside?"

"I do not know," his father sighed. "Maybe we will find out when we get there."

The possibility of people inside the glass fish was something Pearse had not considered. The thought troubled him. *The thing seems to be constructed rather than naturally occurring. There is no question it is large enough to hold many people,* he reasoned. *If there are people inside, are they dangerous?*

"Can we eat now?" Tierney asked, giving a hopeful glance at his father's bag.

Pearse smiled. *Teenagers,* he thought to himself. *They are always hungry.* Without answering, he opened his bag and removed two long strips of dried meat, one for each of them, which they ate in silence. The boy attacked the simple meal as if he had not eaten in a week. After the meat was gone, they shared a handful of dried camas root and water from a skin bottle. When they had finished eating, they stared in silence at the extraordinary scene of devastation with the gleaming silver object laid out before them.

"I wonder if it's dangerous," Pearse said absent-mindedly, unaware he had spoken the words aloud.

"It doesn't seem to be dangerous, and it is not moving," the boy observed. "I do not see anything that looks like trouble about it. But..." he thought for a moment, then said, "why did they build a wall around it?"

"I do not think anyone built it. I think it happened when that thing hit the ground. Do you know what happens when you throw a rock in the river?"

"It makes a circle where the rock went in?"

"That's right. I think it happened the same way," Pearse said. "But the rock is a lot smaller than that big glass thing over there," he observed. "That thing is a lot larger than a rock, and so is the circle."

Tierney nodded his understanding. "That thing is greater than the conclave hall!" He exclaimed.

"It's big," admitted Pearse. "I think someone made it, and the makers might be inside. It is large enough to hold many people. If there are people inside, we need to be careful not to anger them."

Tierney nodded. Meanwhile, Pearse's mind was assaulted by a myriad of questions. Logic dictated that people had built the thing, that it was not something naturally occurring. Pearse assumed that if people made it, those same people might still be inside. But that possibility troubled him because if people were inside, that meant it was a vessel. And if it was a vessel, who could build such a thing? Undoubtedly anyone strong enough to make something that big to ride in might be dangerous.

We have probably seen enough, although I wouldn't mind getting a closer look at that glass fish. But is getting closer to it worth the risk? The last thing I want to do is put the boy in danger.

Pearse's gut told him he should turn around and go home. That would be the safest thing to do. But if he were to go back now after getting so close to the goal, he feared his son might believe he was afraid, which was something he could not allow. Plus, Pearse wanted answers, and he would not find them if he turned back.

"Let's get going, boy. Just remember, this is like hunting. Be careful, and be ready for trouble."

Pearse slipped his quiver over his shoulder and readied his bow to establish the seriousness of the situation. Then he took the knife from his belt, a large killing knife, and handed it to the boy. When the man locked his gaze on his son's eyes, he saw fear in them. But he considered that a good sign: *He understands the risk we are taking.* As Pearse hardened his stare, the boy glowered back at him bravely despite the danger, searching his father's eyes, refusing to blink.

It was a proud moment for Pearse; the boy was becoming a man, someone he believed he could count on when he needed it. At that moment, he knew there was no turning back. *Nothing here to be frightened of,* he told himself. Then he turned and began creeping warily toward the earthen wall with the boy mirroring his every move.

When they arrived at the base of the berm, they were relieved to find it climbable, approximately twenty feet high, with a moderate grade. Once they had reached the summit, they found the crater's inner surface as smooth and shiny as a polished marble floor. However, Pearse's heart sank as he realized the smooth surface provided no protective cover for them. With nothing to conceal their approach, they would be easily seen by anyone or anything within half a mile.

Crouched atop the mound, Pearse saw that nothing moved in the sky, on the ground, or about the ship. The silence was eerie. Pearse guessed the impact had either driven the birds and animals away or killed them outright. As he assessed their surroundings for threats, he found no reason for concern other than the object itself, which gave no sign of danger.

Before moving forward, Pearse inspected the overcast sky to determine the time of day. He was worried about being out past dusk without a visible moon or stars to guide them home. He decided it must be close to midday, which meant time was limited. The wind was picking up, and the low-hanging clouds threatened snow. If they did not keep moving, they would be forced to spend the night in the cold, which Pearse wanted to avoid.

"I see no reason why we should not get a closer look at it," he said to the boy. "But keep your guard up. Let's go; we need to hurry if we are going to make it back before nightfall," warned Pearse.

The approach to the glass fish was visually deceptive. As the adventurers drew closer, they found themselves dwarfed by its size. Being a lover of storytelling, Pearse wanted to be able to relate his experience accurately. Pacing off the vessel's width and length, he discovered it to be thirty-five paces wide and one-hundred-twenty paces in length and guessed the height to be just less than the width. Then he paused to evaluate the object in greater detail.

First impressions being what they are, he did not expect the assumption that the thing was a glass fish to hold true. He never believed it was a fish; it just happened to look like one. Like a fish, it was longer than it is wide, with protrusions not unlike fins. As expected, the skin was smooth, just like glass, brilliant in the diffused light of the winter day.

Pearse scratched his head, puzzled at the nature of the ship's skin. He wondered how something so large could have hit the ground with such force and yet remained so clean and smooth. He concluded it must be the nature of the glass, so he reached out to touch it.

The instant Pearse's skin contacted the glass fish, a bolt of energy hit him, hurling him to the ground. He was laid out flat, unmoving, as a whisper of smoke escaped from his clothing. The boy rushed to his father's side, shaking him, praying for a response—anything! But his father didn't move, and he wasn't breathing.

"Father! Father!" the boy called repeatedly, but the man remained lifeless in his arms.

The horrified boy felt hopeless, deprived of any basis for understanding as to what had happened. Now he was left alone, without answers or any help, desperate to do something to help his father. Tierney did not know what to do. Confused and terrified, the boy cradled his father's limp body in his arms and wept bitterly.

Pearse and Tierney were not the only ones interested in investigating the unusual sights and sounds occurring that morning. Four men, hunters, watched every move Pearse and Tierney made from their vantage point on the opposite side of the crater. As hunters, these men were instinctively cautious, satisfied to let others go about the seemingly dangerous job of assessing the strange object.

Crouching and hushed to protect their position, they watched as the man and boy approached the ship. Anticipation built among the hunters as the man reached out to touch it, then gasped as one when a flash of light erupted. The air wavered briefly around the man; the strange silence was broken as the man was hurled roughly to the ground. The boy ran to his father's aid, crying out in alarm, but the truth was immediately evident. Smoke rising from the man's unmoving body could only mean one thing: lightning struck him. The man was dead.

Rattled by the unearthly scene, Jotham, the youngest and most impulsive of the four hunters, jumped to his feet, about to run for his life. But Amon, leader of the group, wrenched him roughly back to the ground by the arm.

"Stay down and be silent," Amon growled. "I will tell you when it's time to move. Have you no courage at all?" He accompanied the insult with a pointed finger and a stern look of disapproval to reinforce the reprimand. The other men were frightened too, but their leader stared them down, his face a stony mask of silent condemnation.

Jotham turned away angrily. He was not one to be insulted by anyone, let alone by one he considered to be a feeble old man. Being pushed around and chastised was an offense Jotham was not about to let go unanswered. Although he obeyed Amon for the moment, rage simmered silently within.

Unaware of Jotham's growing malice, Amon's dark eyes continued surveying the scene with instinctive cunning born of experience. The seasoned hunter's gaze took in every detail, scrutinizing everything, missing nothing. Rather than being fearful, he was intrigued by what he saw. Experience told him that whatever was going on here wasn't over yet, and they should expect more to happen. Amon regarded patience and caution as assets born of experience. *Only fools like Jotham disregarded such skills,* Amon reasoned.

Although Amon thought the man was dead, nothing else had changed. The big shiny object remained where it was. As long as it stayed put, Amon believed anything could happen, and he was not about to miss what came next. There was nothing left in the area to hunt, and they were not in a hurry. So why move? He had no intention of missing it, even if it meant spending the night in the snow without a fire.

Amon ordered the men to dig in, set up tents to shelter them from the cold and do so quietly. As they worked, the hunters took turns keeping watch over the strange scene in the crater. All were eager to see what would happen next, including Jotham.

Chapter 2

Valerie Dunne— March 2009 CE

Stone's skin felt prickly. He felt his ring's yearning; it craved being reunited with the rest of its kind. Its whispers had grown more persuasive in recent days. He did not know why, but Stone understood the five rings were created to be together in one person. He wanted to be that person, which was why he was at war with his fellow ring bearers. The Hesauranaki had fought over the rings for four thousand years, so it was nothing new. Nor was it a secret. The rings made keeping secrets between them impossible.

Although widely separated, the rings shared an undeniable connection. The closer they came to one another, the stronger their urgings became. Stone saw it in dreams, felt it in his heart, and heard the whispers. His ring implied it was inevitable they would be reunited. But he scoffed at the notion because he knew the truth.

The Hesauranaki will never allow that to happen, he told himself. They were too greedy. They used their rings for selfish gain, becoming rich, powerful, and semi-immortal. The ring bearers would never give them up. They always wanted more. Too much of a good thing was never enough, and Stone was no different from the others. And that is why he was there that day. Egan Seamus Stone wanted more.

With nearly one hundred and twenty years behind him, he had enough experience to know what the tingling sensation meant. And what he was feeling now was a clear indication another ring bearer was in the vicinity. So, he viewed it as a warning of sorts. In this instance, it told him they were coming. It was about time because he had grown tired of hiding and waiting.

Grass clippings and stale gasoline contributed to the stale air of the tool shed. It was damp, dark, and crawling with bugs. For a man of his size, it was a tight fit. But the shed was the ideal hiding place for what he had in mind. While he waited, he busied himself by smoking and picking spider webs from his hair and clothing.

Headlights flashed in the darkness, alerting him to their arrival. Theirs was the last house on the tree-lined drive, so he had no doubt who was headed his way. The sound of the approaching vehicle became more pronounced as it drew closer.

The tool shed window was dusty; mouse droppings littered the sill. But it was clear enough to identify the black sedan as it turned toward the house. To keep from being silhouetted in the window by the lights, he moved quickly away from it.

From his vantage point behind the door, he was able to see the three occupants riding together in the car. He liked that because his job would be easier if they stayed together. Things could get messy if they separated.

Motion-activated lights bathed the car as it pulled up to the garage. He heard the doors open and close as they got out.

Peering between the door and the frame, Stone saw they were relaxed and unaware of his presence. He liked that too.

The couple began unloading the car and carrying groceries into the house. Their four-year-old daughter Valerie plucked up the family cat Orson, a big tabby, and carried it inside. *That cat is almost as large as the kid,* Stone thought. When she emerged, the cat tagged along right behind, bringing a smile to his lips. Now they were coming together. The time was right.

Got a little surprise for you folks! Stone chuckled to himself. *But you are not going to like it. Just hold still, and I'll have that ring when I am done!*

Stone stepped through the door, took a deep breath, felt a burst of anticipation, and summoned the power of his ring. It felt good; the ring's power warmed his bones as the power sought release. He was ready. But when the little girl turned to him, fixing her eyes directly on him in an unblinking stare, his blood instantly chilled. Even the cat seemed to give him a dirty look. The little one's eyes darkened, then her gaze became a stark glower that knocked Stone back on his heels.

Whoa! His mind thundered. *I am well hidden in these shadows! How could the kid have seen me? No way she could have known I was here unless—unless she has help. Must be a ring at work, but I don't see one on either of the folks. Could she be the one with the ring? Naw, who would trust a curtain-climber with something so powerful,* he reasoned.

Stone knew the rings of Hesaurun were not children's toys. They could be dangerous. *No one in their right mind would allow a kid to wield such a formidable weapon,* he decided. As unsettling as the little girl made him feel, Stone dismissed her as being insignificant and irrelevant.

Precious time had already been wasted on the child. As he refocused his attention on the adults, Stone cursed her for the distraction. They were nearly finished unloading the car. *The time to strike is now. Now or never!* Success depended on catching them outdoors, unaware, and close together, leaving no time to run, no time to panic, and no time to spare.

Stone paused. There was no sure way to know which one of them had the ring. With so little time, his best guess would have to do. But there was danger in that. If he were to strike the wrong person, the one with the ring might have time to retaliate before he could react. His timing had to be perfect, or the tide could turn against him.

Finally, the couple came together, standing side-by-side at the driver's side of the car, exactly as he had hoped. Their cheerful voices carried in the night air. The moment was perfect. As Stone stepped out of the shadows and into the light, they noticed the movement. Both heads turned instinctively toward him. They saw him and froze like statues, their voices cut off mid-sentence.

"What—what do you want?"

Out of the shadows strode a giant of a man, nearly seven feet tall, dressed entirely in black. In a heartbeat, they realized the truth. The hulking giant was there to kill them.

Transfixed by the startling sight, the couple wrapped their arms around one another. At twenty yards, the big man stopped, raised a hand as if gesturing for them to halt. But in their hearts, they knew he did not mean for them to stop. Holding each other tightly, they looked to themselves for answers but found none. The last thing the horror-struck couple would ever see was a flash of blinding white light.

The energy wave loosed upon the young couple erupted with a blazing flash, a bolt of blinding force, shattering their bodies on impact. The mixed remains of them, the car, and much of the yard were hurled high into the air. The tumbling shell of the car thundered and crashed as it slammed to the ground, over and over. Bits and pieces were flung all over the property. When what remained of the vehicle came to rest, it was unrecognizable as an automobile. The landscape was torn and littered with a grisly combination of twisted metal, debris, and gore.

The big man stared dumbly at the carnage, scratching his head in wonderment. A hubcap fell out of the sky, landed where the car had been with a *clank*, then rolled away into the darkness. Finally, all was silent, the air thick with the noxious stench of fuel, oil, and blood.

"Damn it anyway! Guess I over-compensated," he muttered. *Now everything is destroyed! How am I going to pick the Hesaurun ring out of that mess? It'll be like finding a needle in a haystack. Now I have to sort through a yard full of rubble and busted bodies to find it. Should've used a gun. Would have been a lot more sanitary. Better get at it—time's a-wasting.*

Stone scanned the devastation, wondering where to start looking. As he stepped into the debris field, something shiny caught his eye. As he bent to pick it up, he saw it was a quarter. "Cha-*ching!*" he chuckled, then shoved it in his pocket, happy to be ahead by a quarter-dollar. It wasn't much, but it lightened his mood.

When Stone noticed the sky start to glow, he was baffled. He looked up, expecting to find nothing but darkness and stars as he searched the heavens. Instead, the night sky continued brightening, taking on a purple hue. He watched in wonder as purple changed to orange— and then red. Soon the entire sky was a painter's pallet of blazing colors. The odd chill he felt told him something had gone wrong, terribly wrong.

"You hurt my mom and dad," said a small voice from behind him.

Startled, Stone whirled, and then the realization struck him. *You forgot the little girl!* As he turned to face her, he was surprised to find the child and the cat she carried splattered in blood. Some of it was her own, yet the little tyke didn't seem to care. She stood resolute, gazing up at him, her eyes boring into his soul, seemingly unafraid despite the carnage she had witnessed.

The look she wore startled him; his breath caught in his throat. But what worried him most were her eyes—mirror-like orbs, black as obsidian, perfectly reflecting his immense image. Seeing himself reflected in those terrifying eyes sent chills cascading through him like a winter storm. The kid wasn't dead, but her eyes were. At least he thought so.

His eyes searched the child but found no sign of a ring. He thought that puzzling, considering he had not seen a ring on her parents, either. *But I can still feel a ring's presence somewhere! What force is working on her if she doesn't have it?* Earlier, he had discounted her as being insignificant and irrelevant. Seeing those dead eyes instantly dispelled that notion. Stone sensed she was dangerous.

The sky also had a word to say about her. It spoke volumes as sparks began gliding down around him. The message was undeniable. Those embers provided all the proof he needed to know; the kid was both significant, relevant and that he had made a big mistake by writing her off too soon.

A firestorm was brewing in the heavens, spitting sparks at him. The hot embers seemed focused on him alone, and he was at the eye of the storm. Misjudging the girl had been an error, alright but underestimating her placid expression might be even worse. Although he could not read her eyes, Stone's gut told him she intended to make him pay for what he had done to her parents.

"What's your name, little girl?" Stone asked, trying to sound as friendly as possible.

"Valerie Dunne," she stated without emotion.

Stone almost laughed. "Your name is Valerie Dunne? Now there's a coincidence!"

Still, the girl stared up at him as if sizing him up, calculating her options.

The name Valerie Dunne is synonymous with the five rings of Hesaurun, he thought. *They are one and the same. But the Valerie Dunne I know of isn't a crumb-snatcher like this little one. That Valerie Dunne was the original keeper of the rings, not a snot-nosed brat. If she was alive—which she can't be—she would have to be thousands of years old, which disqualifies this pint-sized witch.*

As Stone burst out laughing, the wind picked up, swirling around him, and he immediately realized he should not have laughed. Hot cinders landed on his head and shoulders, and Stone rushed to pat them out. Now he was afraid because he knew what she had in mind.

Time's running out. You need to strike first if you want to live. Stone sized the little girl up, set himself, and summoned the power of his ring. But it was too late. Little Valerie Dunne struck first—or was it the towering four-armed stick figure standing directly behind her?

What's that? Stone croaked, then gaped in awe. Having never looked up at anyone his entire adult life, he stared up at the creature, slack-jawed. *Where did it come from, and what is it doing here?* The thing looked like a cross between an eight-foot-tall scarecrow and the bronze effigy of a Roman god, with a hairless pear-shaped head the size of a rugby ball. But what really terrified him was the creature's eyes; large, deep-set eyes, incomprehensible, obscure as obsidian—just like the awful little girl.

Stone realized he had seen enough and wanted no more of the kid or her friend. Panicked, he backpedaled, lost his balance, and fell to his knees. Paralyzed by fear and confusion, he pointed a trembling finger at the towering four-armed bronze creature. His mind swirled in chaos as his mouth moved wordlessly.

The girl stared menacingly, watching the man who had murdered her parent's babble. Pent-up anger and pain of her loss erupted from little Valerie Dunne in the form of a fireball, a conflagration the color of hot lava. The discharge of energy, amplified by the massive alien, hit the big man hard, hurling him high into the air like a blazing meteor shrieking all the way. When the big man hit the ground, a cloud of sparks detonated around him. High above, the sky stilled while the wreathing man's clothes burned like a torch in the darkness.

———————————

Valerie would remember little of what happened to her parents that day and nothing of her confrontation with their killer. The inner power used to defeat Stone that night was immature. It withdrew, locked safely away into the dark places beyond the child's knowledge and consciousness. Wiped from her memory, the source of her power remained, crouching in the darkness, developing, growing to maturity. It would wait to emerge from the darkness much as her antagonist, Egan Seamus Stone, had done.

The warm memories Valerie had of riding in the car with her parents, arriving home, and carrying groceries into the house with them that last time would be long cherished. Every detail of the surprise attack and the deaths of her loved ones seared into her consciousness, something she would never forget. Although hidden throughout her formative years, the mysterious power drawn on that day would continue developing, evolving, and shaping her character.

With the rage spent, the child's body and soul were drained of energy. Mentally, emotionally and physically exhausted, Valerie wobbled into the house and sat with the cat cradled on her lap, staring at the blank television screen. As she descended into shock, time was lost to her—until the phone rang. Although she didn't answer, the ringing telephone made her think of her Aunt Angie. As the ringing ceased, she picked up the phone, pushed a button, then began shaking.

"Hello?" Angie answered. There was no response, but the sound of the child's breathing was enough to identify the caller. "Valerie? Are you there?"

Moments of silence passed.

"A man hurt my mom and dad," the quivering little voice answered, then continued. "Can you come get me? I want you."

The shock and trauma in the child's voice were impossible to miss. Angie's heart leaped in her chest, pounding so violently she nearly blacked out. She was frantic. Despite that, she held herself together long enough to respond coherently.

"What happened, dear?" Angie asked, trying to sound as calm as possible. Then with her hand held over the mouthpiece, she shrieked at Jim, her husband, *"Jim, get in here- now!"*

"A man hurt my mom and dad," repeated the child.

Jim almost jumped out of his skin. Panicked, he flew into the kitchen like he was shot from a cannon. "What's wrong!"

"Valerie said a man hurt her mom and dad." Angie choked on the words. "Start the car; *let's go now!*"

Jim's face paled. As he snatched the car keys, Angie tightened her grip on the phone.

"Stay right there, honey," Angie cooed into the receiver, her voice cracking. "Jim and I will be right there. Okay?"

"Alright," Valerie replied, then hung up without saying goodbye.

Jim already had his car out of the garage when Angie vaulted inside, fear and grief surging inside her. The instant the car door slammed, Jim stomped on the accelerator so hard the tires screeched.

"My God, she's only four years old!" Angie cried.

"What happened?!" Jim repeatedly shouted, never expecting an answer.

Angie did not have to tell Jim to hurry; he drove like a maniac. With trembling fingers, she dialed 911 and told the operator what she knew. After giving Colin and Janet's address, she pleaded with them to hurry. Still, they beat the county sheriff there by ten minutes.

Jim and Angie were horrified by the destruction they found in front of the home. Twisted car parts were mixed with what was left of their loved ones. The front yard was obliterated. The devastation was so complete they never considered looking for survivors. Evidence of their macerated bodies was distributed over more than an acre of ground.

The yard looked as if it had been pummeled by a wrecking machine. Fences, landscaping, even the concrete driveway were all demolished. Trees were either snapped in half or uprooted. Jim and Angie assumed an explosion had occurred; no other possible cause made sense.

Jim began picking his way through the field of debris while Angie ran straight for the house to hunt for Valerie. "Valerie? Valerie, honey!" she cried out in anguish. Once inside, she found her unresponsive with the cat on her lap. The girl was staring at the blank television screen, shaking like a leaf; her gaze locked in a thousand-yard stare. Blood ran from a nasty gash on her cheek and onto her shirt. Angie guessed correctly that the little girl was in shock but did not know what to do about it. The best she could do was put pressure on the wound and offer comfort until help arrived.

Upon closer inspection, Angie was horrified when she noticed the child's blood-spattered clothes. Globs of sticky red goo were stuck to her shoes, tiny dress, and in her hair, but only on her left side. *That's odd*, Angie thought. She speculated that whatever had happened narrowly missed Valerie but was thrown back on her when it smashed into Colin and Janet.

Valerie's cat, Orson, meanwhile posted himself on the girl's lap, staring into her face like he was in a trance, his large blue eyes locked on hers. At first, Angie thought it was sweet that the old cat cared so much for his person—but that abruptly changed when she tried pushing Orson aside to comfort the girl. Frustrated by his refusal to move, she pushed and then shoved, but it was no use. Not only did the animal refuse to budge, but it also seemed unmovable, hard as a rock, impossible to move.

Oh well. That cat's not hurting anyone, Angie thought, realizing there was nothing she could do. It was as if the animal was made of stone. Angie had never seen Orson—or for that matter, *any* animal—act this way or seem so unmovable. It seemed to her as if the cat had supernatural strength.

The old boy must be getting up there by now, thought Angie. Colin and Janet had been married for about ten years. Before Valerie came along, Orson had been Colin's cat, but for how long? *How long do cats live anyway?* She had never heard of one living longer than fifteen years. Orson had been a fixture in the family's life for as long as she could remember. But what was going on now was unexplainable, which gave her a chill.

Anxious for help to arrive, Angie felt relieved when she heard sirens approaching. The county sheriff arrived first, followed by an assortment of emergency vehicles and Washington State Police. While the medics treated Valerie, the Sheriff's Deputy questioned Jim. Soon, Jim had a small crowd of first responders gathered around asking questions he could not answer. Having just lost his brother and sister-in-law, Jim was not in the mood to talk, which led to a confrontation with one of the state patrolmen.

"My niece called and asked us to come," Jim repeated irritably, "so we rushed right over here. We found it like this."

"Why are *you* here?" the officer asked again.

Jim sighed, tired of being questioned. "My *niece*," he said again, more urgent, with an annoyed wave of his hand, "who is in the house with my wife, called us, so we came as quickly as we could. We live ten minutes from here."

"Tell me what happened and why *you* are here?" Officer Bob insisted.

Jim's face darkened. "You already asked that question, Bob," Jim responded with mock civility. "And I already told you. We live ten minutes from here. My niece called. We rushed over here. My wife is in the house with her. *Now get off my back!*"

"No! You never answered the question!" the patrolman shot back. "I stood right here and asked you four times. Tell me: why—are—*you*—here?"

"Maybe I'm not close enough for you to hear me—Bob!" Jim snarled, stepping forward until he was face-to-face, nose-to-nose looking down on the shorter patrolman. With balled fists and face beet-red, Jim yelled.

"I SAID MY NIECE CALLED! WE RUSHED RIGHT OVER HERE. WE DIDN'T TAKE THE BUS AND DIDN'T STOP FOR DOUGHNUTS! GOT IT?"

"Leave him alone, will ya, Bob?" interrupted Cheryl, the patrolman's partner, stepping into the fray. "The poor guy lost loved ones here. Give the man a break."

The doughnut comment galled Bob, who was prepared to take the argument to the next level. But he relented as Cheryl grabbed Jim by the arm and dragged him back a step, defusing the confrontation.

"Sir, why don't you go sit in your car until this is over," Cheryl advised.

Good idea, Jim thought, unballing his fists and agreeing with a nod. *I've had enough of being badgered.*

But before Jim made two steps toward the car, he was waylaid by two men wearing dark suits.

"Sir! Agents Rice and Timmons with the FBI. Can we have a word with you?"

Jim groaned and rubbed his head, wondering when the questions would ever end.

"Sir?" repeated Rice.

"Yes?" Jim sighed with a resigned shrug.

"Can you tell me what type of device was detonated here?"

"And we will need your name," insisted Timmons.

"It's Jim—I'm an attorney, not a demolition expert," he snapped, glaring at the agents. "Ask the bomb squad when they get here."

Then Jim turned and hurried to his car and was safely sequestered inside just as the KNOB-TV News mobile production unit pulled up. Before the camera-laden beast rolled to a stop, every door on the vehicle popped open, simultaneously disgorging its complement of smooth-faced talking heads and film crew. Jim was delighted when the TV crew shined bright lights in patrolman Bob's face and started asking him questions he could not answer.

Got out just in time, Jim thought. *Those KNOB's would have had me in a headlock for sure!*

Since everyone at the scene believed a bomb had detonated but was without evidence to support the theory, the interviews were brief. The only witness, Valerie, wasn't talking, so the investigation was stymied. The four-year-old was too young to be considered a reliable witness anyway. The investigators had no credible witnesses, no clues, and no leads to follow. All they had to work with was a yard full of debris and the widely broadcast remains of two local professionals.

There was no evidence of explosive residue anywhere. Furthermore, the windows and doors on the house were all intact. The authorities were even more confused when they noticed the funnel-shaped debris field.

"I don't get it," Agent Timmons grunted.

"Me neither," Agent Rice replied grimly, scanning the home. "Something strange about that kid, though."

"I know," Timmons agreed. "What do we do now?"

"Go back to square one," Rice said. "Whatever the cause, it's pretty clear the blast originated at a single point near the center of the yard."

Timmons nodded. Blasted wreckage and blackened earth all pointed in one direction. The affected area appeared to have been subjected to a shaped charge. Oddly, the demarcation line was razor-sharp, which was considered impossible by any means. The one thing they were all able to agree on was all evidence pointed to a focused explosion. Beyond that, answers were few.

If it wasn't a bomb, what happened? No one had an answer to this very fundamental question. Therefore, every piece of the car and the decedents was bagged, tagged, and sent to the FBI crime lab for further evaluation. However, no one was ever able to pin a label on the cause. In the end, it was ruled an accident for lack of evidence.

With the child suffering from shock, the medics recommended emergency transport to Arlington General Hospital. There she was given sedatives, cleaned up, and the gash on her cheek sutured. Valerie was admitted for observation and spent the night with Angie watching over her. The next day, Valerie and her cat Orson went to live with Jim and Angie permanently.

In the immediate days following the murders of Colin and Janet Dunne, Valerie continued to be reticent and aloof. Angie assumed she was unwilling to talk about the tragedy, although the truth was far different. The child was simply unable to remember much of what happened. The child's young mind had blocked out the most tragic events of the day. Ultimately, she remembered only what was safe for her to remember.

Fortunately, both families had agreed to exchange mutual wills naming each other as beneficiaries. Jim, a lawyer, prepared the documents, and the firm managed a trust account for the child. Their foresight relieved them of any legal entanglements regarding child custody, property, and investments.

His clothes burned and smoldering, Egan Seamus Stone survived the blast by escaping into the forest behind the Dunne's house. Staggering blindly through the trees, the remainders of his still-smoldering clothes trailed smoke and ash. He stumbled and lay twitching in the grass, his heart pounding, clutching at his wounds. Growling and howling like a wild animal, Stone struggled to his feet, his world one of intense pain and misery. Driven by the torment, he pushed on in a delusional attempt to outrun the agony and the evil thing that set fire to him. *I will get even with the little beast,* he told himself, over and over. *No matter how long it takes, I will find a way to make her and that bronze scarecrow pay for what they did to me!*

As he stumbled into a neighborhood, the big man blundered in front of a garbage truck. Startled, the driver stood on the brakes, sending the cumbersome vehicle into a sideways skid. The tires screeched as it slid to a halt inches short of flattening the smoking man.

For a moment, the startled driver was not sure of what had happened or what he had seen. His first impression was of Bigfoot stumbling in front of his truck. The sight of the smoldering creature lumbering across the road momentarily confirmed the notion. *Sasquatch must have caught fire and crossed the road right in front of me!* He would have sworn on a stack of Bibles a mile high he saw Bigfoot on fire until he noticed the shoes on the creature's feet. Last he heard, Bigfoot went barefoot, so the driver jumped from the truck to get a better look.

What he found there staring up at the front of the big truck wasn't Bigfoot at all. When he realized what he had nearly run over was a badly burned man, he jumped back in the truck and radioed dispatch for help. Alarmed, Stone took off running.

Soon after, another startled driver spotted the smoldering man and called 911. Ambulances were already in the area due to the Dunne murders. One arrived within minutes and took the still-delusional Stone to Arlington General Hospital, the same hospital treating little Valerie Dunne. However, both patients were sedated, preventing anyone from linking them. Consequently, neither of them would ever know they were in the same emergency room immediately after their first encounter.

Stone's burns were severe enough to require helicopter transport to a Seattle burn center. Surviving them would have been unlikely without his Hesaurun ring, which greatly enhanced his body's healing abilities. Typically, the burns he suffered would have meant months or years of hospitalization and skin grafts. But within a week, Stone was back on his feet and released ten days later.

Unfortunately, his scarred flesh would make him even more of an outcast than he had been previously, contributing further to his haunting appearance. People had always avoided him, and he avoided them, so Stone saw little difference in how he was perceived.

In truth, Stone did not care what people thought of him anyway. He never needed people or friends and had always gotten along fine without them. In his mind, caring about other people was for women and children. His parents had abandoned him, and the few people he'd ever cared for had either left him high and dry or tried to kill him. Stone was long past caring about anyone other than himself.

What he did care about, more than ever, was getting even with the little Dunne girl. *I'd already have the Dunne's ring if it weren't for her interference!* By his way of reasoning, the little imp had gotten in his way. He figured she must have known about it and may have even hidden it from him. Now his prize was either lost in the rubble or in that evil brat's possession. Either way, Stone blamed her for the loss. As he saw it, little Valerie Dunne had ruined everything.

He hated her for burning him, believing it was unfair and unnecessarily cruel. Only a witch would do such a thing. Admittedly he had killed her parents, although those deaths were quick and painless. They never knew what hit them; didn't that count for something? The girl had a right to be upset. But she had gone out of her way to burn him, a slow and painful penance to be sure. The malicious little terror needed to be taught a lesson. He vowed to see to it, and when he did, he would enjoy every beautiful minute of it.

Although he would never admit it to anyone, let alone himself, deep down, Stone was afraid of her. And what of the four-armed bronze scarecrow? Was that—*thing* real or a hallucination? And what happened to that evil cat that gave him dirty looks? He could only pray those were just visions or an aberration of agony.

Though Stone had not seen a ring on little Valerie Dunne, he was convinced she had one. *Just because I didn't see it doesn't mean it wasn't there!* He could conceive of no other way she could have loosed fire on him the way she had. For all he knew, she might have swallowed the ring or worn it on her big toe. But it was there somewhere, and he would find a way to get it.

As it would turn out, he was wrong about that, every bit of it. Other than his own, there never was a ring there that day. Valerie never possessed one, nor had her parents. The whisperings Stone heard and felt were his own rings, yearning to be reunited with the girl. He could not know that the ring he wore *was her ring*. Nevertheless, Valerie Dunne was an obsession from which he would never escape.

Colin and Janet Dunne were well-known and well-liked in the community. Janet had been a wedding planner and Colin, a city engineer, so almost everyone in town knew them. Both were born and raised in the area, making their loss a local tragedy.

The couple's memorial was held at the Magnolia Wedding Hall on a Saturday morning. More than three hundred people attended, leaving standing room only in the former ballroom. Friends and family sat on folding chairs lined up in neat rows or huddled together along the walls. Yet, one man stood alone, not because he was antisocial or didn't care about the decedents and their families. He cared alright, more than most, but had business to take care of and wanted to avoid being noticed.

Corell Paris had come in late, having driven all night from Southern Oregon. As he entered the hall, the mayor was eulogizing the deceased couple. Scanning what seemed like a sea of people, he eagerly searched face-after-face for the one he sought.

"It has been said that it takes a village to raise a child," the mayor's voice echoed in the cavernous hall. "Colin and Janet were born, raised, and married right here in Arlington, which makes them children of this village, and they will be sorely missed."

The room stirred as the weight of those heart-rending words hit home. The mayor's remarks weren't an exaggeration of the impact of the loss on the tight-knit community. Corell found himself nodding his agreement as his dark eyes anxiously searched the crowd of hundreds.

He found more than a few familiar faces but doubted they would remember him. They had grown old while he had remained unchanged through the years—just one more reason he wanted to avoid being identified. Yet he wasn't there for them, those older ones; he was there for the four-year-old girl, Valerie Dunne.

Corell ran his hand through his thick gray hair and breathed easier when he finally spotted Colin Dunne's daughter Valerie, seated in the front row between her aunt and uncle. Since learning of Colin and Janet's deaths, he needed to be sure Valerie had survived and that she was safe. Accepting someone else's word for it wouldn't do; this was something he had to see for himself.

Valerie Dunne's survival has driven my life for more than thirteen hundred years, Corell reminded himself. *Her survival isn't the most important thing in my life; it is the only thing!*

I got soft, he scolded himself as he crept closer to the girl's row. *I felt too comfortable, and look what happened. I should have known better, been more diligent, and maybe things would have turned out differently. Colin and Janet are gone, which is a tragedy, but it would have been catastrophic if the world had lost Valerie!*

Corell noticed his skin tingling for the first time since arriving, like an alarm going off that goes unheard until fully awake. He had been so focused on finding Valerie that he had ignored the sensation entirely. But that didn't surprise him; it was something he had lived with his entire life. He had grown used it, that and the whispers of his Hesaurun ring, whispers that always accompanied the tingling sensation.

Corell Paris had worn his ring for more than thirteen hundred years. He had been around long enough to know what it meant. It was always the same; the five Hesaurun rings craved being together—they yearned to be reunited, so they sent sensory messages to the wearer. Although that day, the feeling he experienced was different. And he knew why.

It's the girl, Valerie Dunne. My ring wants to be with her! Rather than desire, he felt recognition and delight from his ring. He felt its euphoria at being close to her, and this exhilaration was what warmed his bones.

As the Mayor continued the eulogy, Corell crept closer still. Little Valerie Dunne was seated between her newly adopted parents in the front row. She was the one his ring had sought for millennia. The ring felt her presence, purring and whispering joyfully. It recognized her and craved being with her. It did not matter that she was a child or that she had never laid eyes on Corell's ring. The ring belonged to her, and she to it. Somehow the ring knew that and whispered to her, seeking fulfillment, trying to draw her attention. But it would have to wait for another day. She never heard it because her time had not yet come.

Steeling himself, Corell Paris backed off. *I'm alright with waiting,* he thought, slipping back to the entrance. *The ring and I share the same goal.* As he watched the child from the back of the crowd, he wondered what she felt. Could she feel it? Did she sense the Hesaurun ring calling, whispering her name?

After all, it was her ring. Corell's job was simply to return it to her.

Chapter 3

Valerie Dunne—April Present-Day

She watched the moon rise over the mountains while feathery clouds floated past like windblown curtains. Silhouetted against them, Valerie Dunne sat cross-legged in the grass, scanning the star-studded sky hoping to sight a meteor, or perhaps a satellite or two. While there was never a warm spring night in the Seattle area, this one was comfortable enough for blue jeans and a sweater.

Her sleep had been interrupted by a recurring dream that troubled her deeply. Finally giving up on sleep, she wandered outside to a rise in the pasture behind the house. The place was special to her because of the view. The grey outline of mountains punctuated by snow-covered crags gleaming in the moonlight provided solace for the weary girl.

One hundred yards below, the river was close enough to hear the rush of water over the sound of traffic on the two-lane highway two miles distant. Day or night, traffic was always present there. Farms dotted the valley drawing irrigation water from the meandering little river. The lights of downtown Arlington were visible; traffic lights blinked in their usual rhythmic staccato.

While the dream itself never changed, it came to her predictably in bits and pieces, never progressing from beginning to end in any one episode. One segment could be mundane and the next terrifying. This night was one of those, making falling back to sleep impossible.

Valerie replayed the dream while watching the night sky. She saw herself panicked, running hard from a hulking man in a darkened building, a terrifying killer intent on murder. Hearing his dreadful voice call her name, then laugh at her feeble attempt to escape. Merely recalling the brute's evil laughter raised goosebumps on her skin, and she shuddered.

The man she dreaded would surely kill to take something from her, although she had no idea what *it* might be. She simply knew *it* was something terribly important, something she could never allow him to have. If he was allowed to have the *thing* she protected, terrible consequences would result. Plus, she would be dead. She just wished she knew what he was after. What a relief it would be to know that one piece of information.

As she ran from her antagonist, a second man shadowed her movements, providing hope of assistance. But help would not come from him; he stayed in the shadows even as the killer closed in. Panicked, Valerie's heart pounded in her chest like a sledgehammer. She ran as hard as she could but was unable to escape. An unknowable force pulled her toward her antagonist. But it was no use; that unknowable force was irresistible, relentlessly pulling her closer to her doom.

Each step she took away from the monster dragged her half a step closer. Her arms and legs grew heavier until she was barely able to move. Taking hold of a door frame held her in place for a moment, but the increasing force pulled harder until her feet lifted from the ground. Hanging sideways in the doorway, she heard him call to her. Fear shook her to the core.

"Valerie!" She heard her name echo in the gloom. "You can't hide from me; give up! You can't win!" snarled the mocking voice. Then came the evil laugh. But she knew she must continue fighting to the last ounce of her strength. She couldn't allow herself to stop now. Everything depended on her winning this desperate battle. Although in her heart, she knew she had already lost.

With fingers aching, Valerie began losing the tenuous grip on the door frame. She begged her fingers to hang on. Then to her horror, the door frame gave way. Shrieking as she sank into the unknowable darkness, she knew there was nothing more to do but die.

Valerie was wrenched from the dream when Orson, her cat, crept onto her lap, purring softly. "Orson, you big lug!" Valerie said with a startled smile. The big tomcat was one of the few constants in her life. Orson always seemed to appear when she needed him most. Fourteen years earlier, she had inherited the old tabby upon the death of her parents. The big cat loved to snuggle with her, licking her hands with his rough tongue as she wrapped him in her arms.

"Something the matter, Orson?" Valerie whispered, tilting the eyeglasses on her nose for a better view of the old cat's form. Orson purred his appreciation. *He always seems to know when I have been troubled by a dream,* she thought to herself, slipping her head to the grass to rest again. Moments later, the big tabby was asleep, cradled in her arms.

Although taller than most girls her age, Valerie would need time to fill out. Her body was lean and straight, although lacking the feminine curves typical of girls her age. Despite that, her symmetric features, clear skin, full lips, and silky black hair more than made up for any deficiency in curves. The eyes behind the glasses were light blue, shining with quiet intelligence and determination. The jagged scar on her left jaw added character to her features rather than a flaw.

Having turned eighteen recently, Valerie was preparing for high school graduation. Focus, self-discipline, and a 4.0 GPA earned her a scholarship to the University of Washington. She had made significant sacrifices to get there, postponing getting a car and avoiding frivolous social activities, viewing them as unnecessary distractions. There had been plenty of opportunities for boyfriends too, but she had passed on them, believing sacrifices were necessary to reach her career goal as a dermatologist.

At that moment, Valerie felt compelled to touch her old scar. While the scar was part of her persona, it was not (as Jim and Angie Dunne had pretended for fourteen years) a grim reminder of the car crash that killed her parents. Colin and Janet Dunne had not died in a car crash; they were murdered when she was four years old. But they hadn't lied; Jim and Angie couldn't know the truth because the only witness at the time, Valerie, had blocked much of the tragedy from her young mind.

The child was fortunate to have survived the attack. No one other than she and the attacker would ever know the truth of what happened that day. Single-handedly defeating her attacker at the tender age of four was wiped from her memory. Valerie escaped the carnage wrought upon her parents that day with minor injuries. Nevertheless, her life was irreversibly altered in a way that she would not understand for decades.

Later that morning, Valerie carried Orson downstairs, where she found her Uncle James and Aunt Angela at the breakfast table. Jim read the paper while Angie watched the morning news. Jim welcomed her silently with a nod from over the newspaper as she entered the room, although Angie was much more demonstrative.

"Good morning Valerie," Angie sang cheerily, then made a scene of hugging, rubbing her arms, and planting several loud kisses on her cheek. It was a warm household filled with love despite the loss they shared. Valerie giggled, grabbed a cup of coffee, a bagel, and cream cheese, then joined them at the table.

Jim smiled. He was tall, over six feet, thin with a pale complexion punctuated by a full head of black hair, like his older brother Colin, Valerie's father. However, the married couple could not be more dissimilar in appearance. In contrast, Angie was barely five feet tall, a natural blonde with a round buxom shape. Jim tended to be more serious, reserved, but caring, while Angie was outgoing, everyone's favorite aunt.

"We heard you up late last night. Is everything alright, honey?" Angie asked as she reseated herself.

"It was the dream again," sighed Valerie. "I couldn't sleep, so I went out back for a while. They are getting more intense," she admitted, staring absently at the bagel.

"I'm sorry, sweetie," Angie replied, placing a comforting hand atop Valerie's. "Are you going to be alright?" Angie was well aware Valerie was regularly tormented by the same disturbing dream ever since she had come to live with them. Her concern for Valerie was heartfelt, although she could do little for the girl other than offer comfort. Angie met her husband's eyes for a moment as they both knew Valerie's time was near. Was it any wonder that her dreams were getting stronger?

Valerie finished eating then rushed off to school with little more than a wave and a smile. "Bye, you guys!"

Angie forced a wave back, then turned to her husband. Since the couple was childless and Valerie was Jim's brother's only child, they loved Valerie as their own. Despite that, they preferred giving Valerie the freedom to form her own opinions about their family relationship. While they would have loved to be called mom and dad, it didn't appear their adoptive daughter shared that sentiment.

"Angie," Jim said as he folded the newspaper. "It's time we had a talk with Val. We have to tell her; she needs to know the truth."

"I know, Jim," Angie said sullenly. "I've worried about this for years, but—"

"No buts, it's time," Jim insisted. "We need to get on with it. She's eighteen. What if Corell Paris was to show up, and she didn't know? He will be back, and probably sooner than later. It will go a lot smoother for her if she knows what will happen and why. It's time to tell her," he repeated.

"Alright, Jim," Angie relented, her eyes downcast. "When?"

"Tonight."

Valerie left home early enough to meet her neighborhood friend, Darcy Ewen, who walked to school with her. Arlington High School was fifteen minutes on foot from her home in the Glen Eagle development. The two friends walked together down the smooth sidewalk in silence, enjoying the tranquility of the spring morning.

The sun, already bright in the sky, warmed their faces. The air was fresh with the pleasant scent of alder pollen swirling about. The best friends walked in silence, for words were not necessary. The girls walked to and from school together, shared a locker, had classes together, and ate lunch at the same table, marginalizing the need for conversation. Darcy was first to speak.

"You look tired this morning. Did you sleep alright?"

"No… I had a bad dream and couldn't get back to sleep."

"Same one?"

"Yeah, same one, only a lot worse than usual."

"Really? Worse? *That's not good,*" Darcy exclaimed. "Maybe you should see a doctor or something."

"Been there, done that," Valerie said as they hurried up the steps leading to the school's main entrance. Darcy could not help but notice the hopelessness in her friend's voice and feel sorry for her.

What seemed like a tidal wave of students flowed out of buses and cars and into the building. Inside, the school's common area was awash, with students streaming in every possible direction. A multitude of voices echoed off the high-peaked ceiling as the students began their school day.

Darcy called to friends and waved at more people than Valerie could count. It seemed Darcy knew everyone, and everyone seemed to know her. Though they were best friends, Valerie felt invisible walking next to her best friend.

"I don't understand how you do it." Valerie sighed.

"Do what?" Darcy said, raising her voice to be heard over the crowd.

"You're a social butterfly. You like everyone, and everyone likes you. I wish I were more like you that way." But Valerie's was just one small voice lost in a hall Among hundreds of others talking all at once.

"Got to go, see you at lunch!" Darcy called, waved, then rushed off to class, leaving Valerie standing in front of their shared locker feeling glum.

She hung her head against the locker door for a moment, staring dejected at the floor. Valerie wanted to be more sociable but just did not know how to do it. She was a loner at heart and knew it, which frustrated her to no end.

As she slowly closed the locker door, she noticed Jack Dylan, a boy she was friendly with, talking to a girl she didn't recognize. Valerie couldn't help but stare as they laughed and joked together and could not suppress the jealousy welling in her chest. She and Jack were about as close as friends could be without being a couple.

I wish Jack would talk to me that way, Valerie thought, straightening her glasses. *I have known Jack Dylan since kindergarten,* she reminded herself, eyeing the new girl. *You don't even know him! Who are you anyway?*

Valerie spun the dial on the lock then turned toward class, taking her past Jack and the girl he talked to. But when Jack noticed her eyeing him, he abruptly excused himself from the conversation and fell in beside her. Valerie smiled that he had dropped the other girl like a hot potato, which improved her self-esteem a notch.

"Hi Val, have a good weekend?"

"Yeah, but I worked through most of it."

"You work too much!" Jack exclaimed, flashing a bright smile. "Finn had a party on Saturday. You were invited, weren't you?"

"Yeah, but I don't care for him much, so I stayed home."

"Finn can be a jerk, but you should have come anyway. I was watching for you," Jack said with one eye on Valerie, hoping for a reaction. Valerie felt it and smiled but kept her eyes off him for fear of showing her true feelings.

"School's out in two weeks. You should get out more," Jack persisted. "What are you going to do this summer?"

"Probably work in my dad's office."

"More work, huh? See what I mean? You work too much!" Jack laughed.

Valerie grinned; Jack's laugh always dazzled her. He stopped in front of the Athletic Department door. "I have PE first period, so I have to go. You have my number, call me sometime, okay? I don't want to lose track of you after graduation."

"I will, I mean, I *won't*— "Valerie stuttered. "I won't lose track of you after graduation, I mean. And call you." Valerie blushed. Then she added, "We get our yearbooks today. Find me at lunchtime, and we'll look at them together."

Jack scratched his head and smiled with amusement at her awkwardness but left it at that. "Sounds good. Bye," he said as he pulled the door open.

That was nice, Valerie thought as she watched him go. *Right when I needed to feel good about myself, too. Was he asking me out? I hope so because if he does, I will definitely say yes. Heck, maybe I should ask him out myself!*

Lunchtime was a beehive of excitement as the students had received their yearbooks that morning. Few were actually eating; most were huddled in groups pouring over the pictures and talking. The students were up and down as they eagerly swapped yearbooks signing them for one another.

Valerie, Darcy, and their friends sat together at a long table, comparing pictures from the yearbook, talking, and laughing together. Jack, Finn, and their friends gathered around the girls' table and began sharing their yearbooks.

Jack sat down directly across from Valerie while Finn slid next to her on the bench, which irritated Jack. Finn was close—too close, intentionally invading her personal space in an overt attempt to be a nuisance. Finn, who loved to tease Valerie, found her yearbook photo, then made a show of laughing loudly, slapping his forehead, and pointing at it as if it were insanely funny.

"Dat girl so ugly. Oh, Lemme see that again!" bellowed Finn, loud enough to be sure everyone within hearing distance saw and heard, then resumed laughing obnoxiously.

Angry and embarrassed, Valerie's eyes welled up, then she slammed her book shut. Standing, she slugged Finn's shoulder, then left the table without a word. All eyes followed Valerie as she rushed from the lunchroom.

"Not funny, Finn!" Darcy cried then ran after her friend, who was already out of sight. Everyone left at the table felt embarrassed by association. Despite that, Finn seemed very pleased with himself and continued laughing.

Jack held his head in his hands for a long moment, struggling to control his anger, resisting the urge to hit Finn.

"We're done, Finn," said Jack pushing himself up. "Stay away from Valerie *and me*—or I will explain it to you with this," Jack growled, holding his fist under Finn's nose. Then Jack left the room, and a moment later, the table was empty.

After the last period, the girls met at their shared locker and walked home together, but they stayed off the subject of what happened during lunch. Instead, they gossiped about their girlfriends and how their lives would change after graduation day, well aware their care-free days as high school students were about to end. Would they stay in touch or drift apart? How different would their lives be in a year? Both girls hated the thought of losing touch with their friends.

Valerie entered the house through the kitchen, feeling blue. Her mood was lifted immediately by Angie's warm greeting. The little woman tended to dote on everyone, lavishing praise and love on them, Valerie more so than anyone.

"Sit down, honey," Angie said after a warm hug. Then she took Valerie's pack. When Angie reappeared instantly with cookies and milk, Valerie immediately became suspicious. Angie seemed worried; Valerie knew something was afoot. She could feel it. The little woman didn't appear to be angry, just nervous. Valerie doubted anyone they knew had died. *Whatever is bothering Aunt Angie must not be too serious,* she decided.

"How was your day?" Angie asked sweetly, clutching a hand towel to her chest.

"Good, now that finals are over. Most classes are pretty much a waste of time now," Valerie mumbled through a mouthful of cookies, petting her cat Orson under the table. She ate fast, thanked Angie for the snack, then carried the cat upstairs to her room.

Dinner that night was one of Valerie's favorites, homemade deep-dish pizza, topped off with spumoni ice cream. After doing the dishes, she was not surprised when Jim called the family together to meet at the dinner table.

"Val, we need to talk," Jim said with a hint of gravity to his voice. "There's something we need to tell you."

Valerie removed her eyeglasses and cleaned them with a heavy sigh. "I knew something was up, deep-dish pizza, spumoni ice cream—I'm adopted, right?" she joked. But it did not help; the folks looked unusually ill-at-ease.

"This involves your parents and the dreams you've been having," Jim said. Aware he had her undivided attention, he allowed a moment for her to prepare for what came next. Valerie knew something disturbing was about to be disclosed but waited for it wordlessly, her hands clasped tightly on the tabletop. Angie covered Valerie's hands with hers for support. Stress hung in the room like a dark cloud.

"There's something about your father's family you need to know," Angie said.

"Alright, what is it?" Now Valerie was worried. The subject of her parents had been seldom addressed. Even after fourteen years the topic was still too sensitive, still too soon.

"Well," Jim began, pausing as he gathered his nerve. "Several things, actually. First—your parents didn't die in an automobile accident; we told you that to protect you when you were little. Back then, we felt it was something you couldn't understand because the truth is— "He paused, swallowing hard.

"What? Just *say it!*" Valerie insisted, now visibly upset.

"It's a lot different than what we told you," Jim admitted. "You need to understand what I am about to tell you is a secret. You cannot divulge. You must not share this information with anyone. Do you understand? It's going to sound crazy, but it's all true."

"Alright—I do, and I won't," Valerie agreed uneasily.

"Val," Jim croaked, then took a deep breath, "your parents never died in a car crash. They were murdered—*a sorcerer killed Colin and Janet.*" Then Jim added, "I refer to him as a sorcerer because there is no other word for what he is."

Ridiculous as they sounded, Jim's words made Valerie nervous. "You're kidding, right?" she said, looking from one face to the other for any sign they were joking.

"I wouldn't lie to you, Valerie," Jim assured. "And this is something no one in their right mind would joke about."

Right mind?" Valerie thought, focusing on those two words. Her mind flashed on the scene at lunch. Finn sure didn't hold back from making her the subject of his jokes. Did that mean he wasn't in his right mind when he purposely embarrassed her in front of everyone today?

"How can you expect me to believe in sorcerers?"

Jim drew in a cleansing breath before continuing. "His name is Stone. Call him what you like—magician, sorcerer, whatever— but I assure you he is real, and he is dangerous. Stone has magic rings with tremendous power. He used that power to kill your parents. He nearly killed you, too, which is the real reason you have that scar."

Jim leaned forward now, searching Valerie's eyes. "There's more. We believe Stone will come for you. And that is why we are having this discussion."

"Me! Why?" cried Valerie, her face now a pale mask.

"Take it easy, Jim! You're scaring the poor girl!" scolded Angie.

"You're right. Sorry," Jim said, leaning back in the chair. "Why don't you tell her about Corell Paris."

Jim smiled at Valerie. She looked up and returned it, although weakly.

Enough! Her mind thundered. *This is enough!* No one had to tell her it was all true; she *sensed* it. The memories of her parents' deaths were like shadows that ran away from her whenever she searched for them. She didn't know why, but suddenly those shadows were dragged into the light where they could no longer hide.

"I know," Valerie admitted shaking her long black hair, which now concealed her face entirely. When she raised her head, tears streamed on her cheeks.

"I know it was murder; I can see it," she blubbered, feeling as if she was coming apart at the seams. "How could I have not known until now?"

The hurt in Jim and Angie's eyes said more than a thousand words ever could. A long pause passed between them as each reflected on what happened that fateful day.

"Repressed memories," Jim said, breaking the silence, "which is not unusual among trauma victims.

A trauma victim? Is that what I am? Valerie wondered. Once the wall collapsed, the truth came raging in upon her like a storm tide, uncovering long-buried memories. For the first time in fourteen years, Valerie recalled in detail the horrifying murders and resulting devastation wrought upon her family fourteen years ago. *The man in black. He murdered them. Then he was on fire!* Heartbreak weighed heavy on her chest as she recalled searching for her mother and father but finding only carnage where she had last seen them.

I remember, Valerie thought. *I can see it now. I felt something strange, so I turned and looked—a giant of a man dressed in black appeared out of the shadows. He saw me and stopped because I knew him—felt him. I knew what he was and what he wanted to do. But he paid no attention to me because I was just a kid. Then there was a splash of light, and everything went dark all at once.*

When I awoke, my family was gone. I knew what happened and why and that I would be forever alone. That monster took everything I loved away from me! Then laughed at me! I wanted to cry, but I was too angry to cry when he laughed at me. I wanted to hurt him more than I wanted to cry. But I don't remember anything more than that. But how could I ever forget the pain! The horrible pain of losing my parents!

"Alright," Angie said, trying to pick up where Jim left off.

"Val, do you remember Corell Paris? He drops in on us occasionally. Jim and Corell have a history. Without him, we would never have understood what happened and why. Corell has been a Godsend. Without him, we would be totally in the dark about all of this."

"Corell is a relative," Jim interjected. "You knew that—right? According to him, Stone thought your father had a magic ring. He wanted it and killed your parents for it. But the fool was mistaken. There never was a ring. Here is the problem; Stone thinks you still have it, so it's only a matter of time before he comes looking for you. And when he does," Jim sighed, "he would not hesitate to kill you for it."

Valerie paled noticeably.

"Honey," Angie assured her, "we're trying to protect you by sharing what we know with you."

Valerie continued with downcast eyes, sniffed, then nodded a silent reply. Angie handed her a napkin as she began pulling herself together.

"What makes him think I have this—this *magic ring* he wants?"

Angie turned to Jim expectantly, knowing he was best suited to answer the question.

"We Dunne's come from an ancient family," Jim began. "Five magic rings have been handed down through our family line for thousands of years. Paris says power-hungry Hesauranaki, such as Stone, are continually at each other's throats trying to steal one another's rings. The family has lost control of most of them long ago."

"Paris said your father Colin was next in line to inherit his ring, but Stone jumped the gun and killed him before he ever got it. Colin never said a word to me about any of this, so everything I know has come from Paris. But I believe every word of it. The story is just too fantastic not to be true."

"Hesauranaki?" Now Valerie felt like her brain was going to burst. "What's that?!"

"It's what the people with the magic rings call themselves," Jim replied.

"I still don't understand why he thinks I have a ring," Valerie cried.

"Don't you see?" Angie exclaimed. "You are Colin's only descendant, which makes you next in line to inherit Paris' ring."

Next in line? Me? "Oh!" Valerie gasped, realizing she had missed the obvious.

"Yes," Jim added, "and that makes you a target. You recently turned eighteen, so you are of age now. It's only a matter of time before Stone shows up again looking for the ring you will inherit from Paris."

All was quiet at the table as each contemplated the impact of Jim's warning.

"I know," Valerie admitted, breathing deeply, her heart pounding in her chest. "I dreamed of it just last night. Recently my dreams have been insane! I didn't know why, but now it's all beginning to make sense."

"You will have your ring soon, dear," Angie cooed. "We expect Corell to come to you soon. You can trust him."

"What if I don't want it? What then?"

"I asked Paris the same question," Jim conceded. "He said that you have no choice; it's your ring, it wants you, and it will seek you out. I asked him to explain that, but he said *you would tell us* soon enough. That sounded cryptic to me, but I couldn't get him to say any more about it."

"He said I would tell you? What does that mean?" Valerie asked, exasperated, throwing her hands up.

"I don't know! Paris planned to turn his ring over to Colin the day after the attack. Stone was waiting for them, which also means he was watching them.

"Here's another thing," Jim added, "Paris said he saw him—Stone, I mean—after the funeral. That's bad because that means he knows who we are and probably watches us, too."

Subdued now, Valerie nodded, picking nervously at the tablecloth.

"Angie and I were close to your family. We visited regularly. One day, as Colin and I left the Blue Bird Café, we ran into Stone—literally. He was going in while we were leaving. Colin told me he had seen Stone following him. This guy must be close to seven feet tall—I am six feet, and I was looking straight into his chest. I can tell you first-hand Stone is an intimidating character."

"Can you tell me more about this ring? I think it's part of what I have been dreaming about."

"According to Paris," said Jim, "it's the fifth ring. He made it sound like there is something special about it but never told me what makes this ring different from the others. You can ask him yourself; we expect to see him again any day. He said he would be back when you are eighteen."

"Val," Angie interrupted, "you've said your dreams have been getting worse. Would you like to tell us what they are like?"

"Well," Valerie said, gathering her thoughts. "They never run from beginning to end. The dreams come in bits and pieces. Some parts are okay, but other parts are—*scary*," she murmured, then took a deep breath before continuing.

"The part I hate the most is where I am running from the killer, but he uses something to pull me backward—toward him. He's like, using magnetism or something, against me. The harder I run, the harder I am pulled backward—towards him. If I stand still, I can maintain my distance from him, but it's a struggle, so I hang onto something—a door handle actually—to keep from being reeled in. The force pulling me becomes strong enough to pull me off my feet while I'm hanging hang onto the door for dear life."

Valerie paused, digging deeper into her memory. "The man trying to get me in the dream is huge, dressed in black, and with long hair. He is fearsome. He never moves, just stands there with his arm outstretched. Whatever he's doing pulls me closer, dragging me down a long dark hallway toward him. He calls my name and tells me to give up and that there is no use in fighting. That's what..." she stopped, sobbing again. Wiping her eyes with a napkin, she breathed deeply, then continued. "That's what scares me the most. It's so *real!*"

"That sounds exactly like Stone to me. That has to be him!" Jim insisted.

"One more thing I want to tell you," Valerie continued, "besides the big man in black—Stone, I guess—there is someone else, and Orson is with him! I cannot imagine why Orson would be in these dreams. It's just so weird, don't you think? Anyway, this man and Orson are there; they are watching this together but aren't helping me. Here's what's really strange; I get the feeling both of them want to help me, but for some reason, they don't, and I don't know why."

"I'm guessing, but that man might be Paris," Jim offered. These dreams seem to have a lot of meaning to them, but I cannot guess why your cat would be in them.

"He's always there!" Valerie cried. "I love Orson," she admitted, "He can be so weird! Sometimes I wonder if he is some kind of alien from a planet full of cats!"

Everyone laughed at that, which relieved the tension in the room.

"Valerie, how often do you have these dreams?" Angie interjected.

"Until recently? Maybe once or twice a month, but since my birthday, almost every night." Then she added, "The intensity of the dreams has become unbearable. I can't sleep!" She admitted, sobbing loudly. "I'm walking around like a zombie half the time because I can't sleep!"

"What can we do, Jim?" Angie turned to her husband, misty-eyed.

"I don't know, hon, but now that it's out in the open, I think we should hope for the best and prepare for the worst. I don't think this is something we can hide from. Maybe we should hire protection for her. I'm a lawyer; I know people," Jim suggested.

"I think that is a great idea, Jim! What do you think, sweetie?"

"A bodyguard?" Valerie said dismissively. "I don't want some creep following me around."

"I assure you we wouldn't hire a creep to follow you," Jim assured her. "That's not how professionals work. We would hire a specialist who would not be watching you; he would be looking at what is going on *around* you, looking for threats. You would never know he was there unless there was trouble. That's when he would be there for you."

A bodyguard. That doesn't sound so bad, Valerie thought. *I could live with that. And having a little extra protection wouldn't be such a bad thing, would it?* Considering the danger her guardians might be subject to, she thought it prudent.

She settled back in the chair and relaxed as she thought about it. Then Orson's piercing blue eyes caught her attention. Valerie noticed the cat's eyes moved from one speaker to the next, always following the conversation as if he understood everything said. *That's ridiculous!* Valerie reminded herself. Yet when his eyes returned to hers, she thought she saw his pupils dilate just before abruptly looking away as if she had caught him eavesdropping.

It made her feel odd as if she had been caught coming out of the shower naked. And this incident was not unusual; Orson *always* seemed to be watching her. *The darn cat likes getting attention from other people, but he doesn't watch them with the same focus or diligence that he watches me.*

Valerie's thoughts rattled on and on about the cat. The big tabby always seemed to be on his favorite perch halfway up the stairs, an undercover spy watching her every move, listening to every word. If Orson was snooping, he chose his post well since it was the only place in the house with a clear view of the entire main floor. His focus in life seemed to be that of a paid observer. Although Valerie was used to it and loved the attention, it still felt somehow odd, as if there was more to it than a cat merely looking at its favorite person. But what more could there be?

"The man I'm thinking of does this for a living," Jim continued, breaking Valerie out of her daydream. "I've worked with him, he's good at what he does, and I trust him. Would you be okay with that, Val?"

"I don't know... I guess so." Valerie said uneasily.

"I'll take care of it," Jim assured, squeezing her shoulder affectionately. "Let Angie and I know if you can think of anything else we can do to make you feel safe. Alright?"

Valerie nodded, warming to the idea.

"And tell us immediately if you see anyone suspicious, promise?" Angie added.

"I have a suggestion," Jim said. "Until further notice, let's keep our cell phones on us at all times. And make sure they are charged and with the ringer on. Sound good?"

"Alright," Valerie said. "Thank you, Uncle Jim, Aunt Angie. I appreciate it. Really," she added with a warm smile.

Valerie went to her room that night feeling much better, appreciative of her guardians' support and the kindness shown to her. She slept peacefully that night with Orson curled up and purring loudly by her side, the first good night's sleep in days.

The Law Offices of Dunne, Morgan & Associates occupied the top floor of a renovated 1920s-era department store in downtown Arlington. The following day, Jim arrived there an hour earlier than usual. He had Miles Bigelow, a private investigator and close friend on the phone within minutes. The private number rang just once before it was picked up.

"Hi, Jim. You're early. What's up?" said Miles.

"Up early for a good reason, Big. I have a job for you. What does your schedule look like?"

"That, sir, would depend on the three W's: who, what, and where."

"Actually—this one is personal."

"Really. Is everything alright?"

"It is, and we want to keep it that way. I would like to explain it to you personally. Can you stop by today?"

"Yeah. I'll be there in an hour."

Miles Bigelow climbed the familiar stairs to Dunne & Morgan's suite sixty minutes later. The hardwood framed glass doors led into the carpeted lobby. A sliding glass window provided a view of the support staff area. Miles went to the window and leaned on the counter but didn't have long to wait before an assistant slid the window open.

"Hi Mr. Bigelow, Jim is expecting you. He will be right out to meet you."

Miles seated himself, but before he could get comfortable, Jim opened the door to a hallway leading to the private offices and meeting rooms, inviting his friend in with a wave of his hand.

"Come on back, Big," Jim welcomed Miles in with a friendly smile, then led him to his office where they were seated.

"Thanks for coming," Jim said appreciatively. "Can I get you coffee or water?"

"No, thanks. I'll have white caps on my kidneys if I drink any more coffee. What's up?" He asked, getting right to the point. "Is everything okay with you and your family?"

"Sure, we're good, but we want it to stay that way, which is why I reached out to you," Jim explained, settling back in the big leather chair behind his desk. "How busy are you?"

"Not too busy to help you if needed."

"I appreciate that, but this might take some time, and it could be dangerous."

"What's going on?"

"We believe Valerie is in danger, that a murderer is stalking her." Jim let that sink in for a moment.

Miles' breath caught in his throat, and he frowned. "Really."

Jim sighed, then leaned forward in his chair. "I know that sounds crazy, but we have sound reasons for concern. In addition to being close to us, you have a concealed carry permit, which makes you our best bet. To be specific, I am asking you to observe her, watch for trouble, and be ready to step in should the need arise.

"This is urgent, Miles," he added. "We feel that if something bad is going to happen, and likely sooner than later."

"I don't understand," Miles said, scratching his bald head. "This doesn't make sense. How does a straight-laced, no-nonsense high schooler like Val become the target of a killer? What's the rest of the story?"

"Sorry, Miles, I can't tell you that. But that doesn't change the truth or her reality. I can tell you this: the guy has a record and should be considered extremely dangerous. You need to be safe, too."

"Tell me about the threat, Jim. Who is he?"

"All we have is a description and a name, Stone. He is white, unusually tall, close to seven feet. Forty to fifty years old with long graying hair. And one more thing, he always wears black, nothing else. I think he would be pretty hard to miss in a crowd."

Miles thought for a moment before answering. "Alright, sounds fun," he stated, smiling, leaving no doubt to his level of commitment, "When do you want me to start?"

"Yesterday. Last week would be even better."

Miles narrowed his eyes, rubbing his chin. "I'll have my calendar cleared by the end of the day. I can see this is going to require a lot of time, so I'm going to give you the good-guy discount on this."

"Oh—you don't have to do that," Jim insisted.

"Naw," Miles said, concerned. "This is personal for me. This thing could put a lot of time on the clock, and I want to keep the cost down for you."

"Alright then, bill it to the firm."

Miles smiled then got up to leave. "Oh, by the way," Jim added, "Valerie usually walks to and from school with her friend Darcy Ewen at around seven-thirty and leaves school just after three-thirty. I consider her to be highly vulnerable at those times."

"Got it," Miles agreed and shook his friend's hand. "Don't worry, Jim. I'll see to it Val stays safe."

"Thanks, Big, we appreciate it. Let me know right away if you see Stone."

"Will do," Miles said on his way out the door.

Four days later, Valerie left the house at the usual time and dropped by to pick up Darcy on the way to school. The fifteen-minute walk was uneventful. The two friends walked together along the smooth sidewalk, animatedly discussing upcoming graduation activities.

Neither girl noticed the man in a white minivan monitoring their movements for the better part of a week. His position in front of the unoccupied split-level provided him with an unobstructed view of the Dunne house and approach to the high school. Miles Bigelow observed the girls' movements and what was happening around them from behind darkened windows at the back of the van.

Neighborhood residents assumed no one lived in the vacant house on the corner. For as long as anyone could remember, groundskeepers and meter readers came and went, but no one seemed to live there, and no one knew who owned it.

What they couldn't know was that Corell Paris had purchased the house and another one directly behind it fifteen years earlier. An access tunnel between the two properties allowed supplies, equipment, and personnel to move between them undetected. No one in the neighborhood knew that the place was occupied 24/7 by no less than three Secret Service agents at any given time.

Paris had connections in high places, and this post proved it beyond a shadow of a doubt. The second floor was a showcase of cutting-edge electronic surveillance equipment. Everything that moved in the neighborhood was automatically tracked, recorded, identified, and cataloged. A drone was always in the air monitoring and recording everything that moved and some that did not. For fifteen years running, Arlington's Glen Eagle neighborhood had been the most secure area in Washington State.

"What's with the white minivan?" Paris asked, watching suspiciously as it pulled up to the curb outside and parked.

"That guy has been showing up here all week, watching the kids walk back and forth to school," Agent Flores responded with a knowing smile.

"We thought he was a degenerate at first," Agent Graham added with a laugh. "We expected to see the door slide open and hear him ask the kids if they like candy— but the guy checks out. According to the State Patrol database, the van is owned and registered by Bigelow Security, a private security firm."

"Miles Bigelow is a private investigator," Flores corrected. "According to QuickBooks, Jim Dunne hired him. Once we connected the dots, we knew Dunne hired Bigelow to keep an eye on the subject."

"Seems prudent," Paris observed. "After all, he isn't aware of this post."

"I would do the same if I were in Dunne's place. Smart move if you ask me," Graham conceded.

"You guys ready? It's about that time," said Paris.

"Yes, sir," Flores and Graham acknowledged simultaneously, immediately followed by a third resounding "Yes, sir!" through the sound system.

"Was that Agent Sevren? Who is in the nest today?" Paris asked, puzzled.

"Sevren here," the voice reported, again through the speakers.

That's good, Paris thought, satisfied knowing Sevren had the scope. *Sevren could shoot the eye out of a pigeon from half a mile.*

"Thought I left you at the farm yesterday, Sevren."

"You did. But I like you— I like you a lot, so I followed you here."

Paris chuckled. "Has there been any sign of threat?"

"Not so far," Flores reported.

"What are the other shifts reporting? Anything unusual?"

"Just one thing," said Flores. "But it might be a coincidence. Yesterday, the third shift reported seeing a State Patrol car—"

"Subject is on the move," Graham interrupted.

"Confirmed," Sevren reported.

Flores whipped around to his workstation facing four flatscreen monitors. Two seconds of tapping the keyboard brought up thirty-six images, nine viewpoints on each screen, all focused on Valerie and Darcy walking together.

"I have the subject and Ewen-3 on screen," Flores confirmed. "All assets are operational."

"We have a good overhead," Graham reported. "Drone on the move. Armed and ready."

Fantastic sound quality, Paris thought. *I never get used to it. Every sound the girls make, including their conversation, footsteps, breathing, even the rhythmic swishing of clothing, is audible. I'm surprised I can't hear what they are thinking!*

"You comfortable up there, Sevren?"

"Subject has a cookie crumb on her chin," Sevren joked.

The banter ceased as the team focused on their work. The room was silent, other than the chatter of the girls' conversation and their movements. Paris stood behind Flores and Graham, scanning the monitors for any sign of trouble.

Graham's aerial views encompassed an eight-block area around the Dunne residence, moving slowly, keeping pace with the girls. The cameras focused in and out as Graham scanned the streets, automobiles, and pedestrians for threats.

Meanwhile, Flores busied himself clicking between thirty-six separate camera angles. The cameras recorded Valerie and Darcy's every move, every word until they had safely crossed Highway 9 and walked under the covered bridge on Arlington High School's approach.

When the girls were out of range of Flores' cameras, he pushed his chair back and joined Graham, watching the drone's images on his monitors. Only after the girls were safely behind closed doors did the men relax.

"Now, what were you saying about that State Patrol car?" Paris asked, pulling up a chair next to Flores.

"Yesterday, third shift reported seeing a State Patrol car pass by the subject's house twice in a twenty-minute time frame. That may not seem noteworthy until you look at State Patrol's log. That same car was reported missing from the Marysville station. Then it mysteriously reappeared two hours later."

"Do they have surveillance cameras on the lot?"

"Not according to the report. Only inside the station."

"This is the twenty-first century!" Paris exclaimed, jumping to his feet. "You'd think they would surveil their own station, for God's sake."

"One would think so, sir," Flores agreed.

Flores and Graham's eyes followed Paris as he paced the room, hands shoved in his pockets, jaws tightened, clearly upset.

"That was no coincidence," Paris declared. "That had to be Stone."

He glared at the ceiling for a moment. *Stone's getting better at this game,* he thought. Although the big man had yet to make an overt appearance in the neighborhood, he knew it was only a matter of time before he showed up. He expected reconnaissance would come first, most likely from inside a vehicle. *And what better vehicle to use than a cop car?*

Some might judge Valerie's habit of walking to and from school as an unnecessary risk. However, Paris considered it a blessing in disguise. His goal was to bring Stone out into the open, where he could deal with him. He expected Valerie's carefree predictability to lull the culprit into a false sense of security, making anticipating his actions that much easier.

His biggest worry had always been that Stone might anticipate his plan to transfer the fifth ring to Valerie and get to her first. *If that happens, things could get complicated.* A hostage situation seemed plausible, but he doubted Stone could sneak past his security team. *But if he did, he was unlikely to kill her before he had her ring on his finger. Until then, Valerie Dunne is worth far more to Stone alive than dead, making early detection the key to her survival.*

Paris considered Stone's theft of a cop car as a shot across the bow. *The girl's eighteen now. It's time to take evasive action,* he realized. The time had come to remove the girl to a safer location, and he knew just the place. He believed he had the Dunne's support but knew a lot was being asked of them, especially of Angela, who would not be likely to allow Valerie to go without a fuss. Yet Paris knew he would win in the end because they were not ignorant of the risk Stone presented.

The decision was made. Paris intended to be inside the Dunne house and waiting for the girl when she returned home from school. He hoped to have her on the road within minutes. When Paris dialed Jim's cell number, he picked up on the second ring.

"It's time, Jim," Paris declared.

"I know, I'm nervous as a cow with a bucktooth calf," said Jim, his voice anxious.

"Valerie's usually home by three-thirty. Can you get off early today?"

"I'll go home for the day at lunchtime. I can talk to Angie about it then. She is going to have a hard time with this."

"I figured. We need to get Valerie out of here tonight," Paris insisted. "She needs to be relocated to a safer place. Don't let Angela talk you out of it, okay?"

"Don't worry, I won't," Jim assured.

"Good. But I will not tell you where that is for your own safety. If Stone gets a hold of her before she is ready, there's no question he will kill her. I can feel him. He's in the area."

Jim took a moment before responding. *Paris is right about one thing,* he thought, *Valerie is an easy target as long as she is allowed to walk to school unprotected.* That had to change immediately. He agreed with Paris on that point. He just wasn't sure he wanted to send Valerie off with Paris without knowing where they were going. No doubt this would be a key sticking point with Angie.

"We have a graduation party planned for next weekend," Jim admitted.

"Gee, I'd hate to see her miss the party!" Paris said sarcastically. "Do you really think we should hang around waiting until she graduates? I'll bet dollars to doughnuts that's exactly what Stone is waiting for. He must know she graduates next week. That's probably the only reason we haven't seen him yet."

"Alright," Jim finally conceded. "We'll talk about it this afternoon. Around 2 PM?"

"We will have her bags packed. See you then."

Hanging up, Jim retreated into his thoughts. He understood it would be best for everyone if Paris took charge of Valerie at this critical time. She needed a mentor and time to learn unhindered by outside threats. But he doubted Valerie would be willing to miss her party or graduation day with her friends. One more hurdle to cross was Angie, who Jim suspected would fight tooth and nail to keep her niece home as long as possible.

Jim wasted no time calling Angie to tell her he would be home for lunch. Once they had eaten, Jim broke the news to her of his conversation with Paris. Hearing the plan, Angie agreed wholeheartedly, which surprised him. Colin and Janet's violent deaths remained fresh enough in her mind that she was willing to make any sacrifice to avoid a similar outcome for Val.

Valerie arrived home that afternoon to find a black four-wheel-drive Suburban with blacked-out windows parked on the street in front of the house. Surprise showed on Valerie's face as she entered the Dunne home. Time stood still when she discovered her bags had been packed and were waiting for her in the entryway. Time resumed when voices in the next room alerted her to this new reality. No one had to tell her everything was about to change. As she came into the kitchen, she found Jim and Angie seated at the dining room table with a man she did not recognize.

"Val, come meet Corell Paris," Jim said, standing as she entered the room. Valerie put down her school bag, seated herself at the table, smiled widely, then focused momentarily on the visitor playing with her cat.

That's weird, she thought. The usually reserved Orson seemed to be so comfortable playing with this stranger as if they were old friends.

"So, where are we off to, Mr. Paris?" Valerie asked dryly. Everyone laughed at her directness, which melted tension in the room. Still, the question remained and required an answer.

"I can't tell you that," Paris admitted reluctantly. "I can't tell Jim and Angie, either. No one can know where you are going or when you will be back."

"Why not?" Angie objected, this having been an area of contention for the past hour.

"If you want Valerie to be safe, that is the way it has to be," Paris explained.

"We're not going to tell anyone, so why can't you tell us?" Angie pleaded.

Paris hardened his stare. "And if Stone was to show up? What then? You don't think he would know you were lying?" Paris' eyes glowered, looking to each of them for an answer. But they remained silent, knowing what he implied was true.

"Ignorance is not easily feigned," Paris added. "Your ignorance protects all of us."

"What about *us*? Who is going to protect *us* while you are gone?" cried Angie. Jim gave Paris a hard look, undoubtedly seeking an answer to the same question.

"I am concerned about that, too," Paris admitted. "So, I've taken steps to protect both of you. I cannot tell you exactly what, but you can rest assured that you are safer than you have ever been."

"Alright," Angie sighed, "if you can't tell us how we are safer than we've ever been, tell us why we should believe you."

"I have connections in high places."

"Really," Angie challenged, still pushing back.

"Yes, I do," Paris added. *"Very* high places. Do you understand?"

"I get it," Jim broke in. Then turning to Angie, he smiled. "Give it a rest, will you, Angie? He can't tell us that, either."

Angie nodded. "I'm sorry. I'm just scared, afraid for Valerie and afraid for us."

Paris understood. He spent the next few minutes presenting his plan and answering questions. Once Valerie understood the circumstances and what he expected of her, she surprised everyone by having no objections.

Why should I complain? Sure, graduation parties sound like fun, Valerie thought. *But I would probably feel like a wallflower the moment I arrived. So far as graduation day formalities go, I can take it or leave it. I care a lot more for Jim, Angie, and my friends than I do for that piece of paper with my name on it. Protecting them must come first. Anyway, the diploma will be valid whether it is handed to me or put in the mail.*

So, it was decided; Valerie would go with Paris, and nothing more was said about where she was going when she would be back or what steps Paris had taken to ensure Jim and Angie's safety. The issue settled, they set about agreeing on a cover story to explain Valerie's sudden disappearance. Teachers, friends, and neighbors would want to know where she had gone and why she disappeared. A plausible excuse was needed, one that was both simple and believable.

"Here's one," Valerie offered. "I got pregnant and went to live with relatives in Ireland."

Corell laughed. "That's a good one!"

"Really?" Angie said, taken aback, clearly against any such notion.

"Anything like that would raise more curiosity than we'd want," Jim asserted.

"Yeah, then everyone would want to know who the father is," Valerie moaned. "Hey! What if Uncle Jim got me an internship with a senator or something like that?"

"That sounds good to me," Angie exclaimed, turning to her husband expectantly. "I like it. Jim?"

"I like it, too," Jim admitted. "Just one problem, though. Things like that take time to arrange and require security clearances. Additionally, it's something we all would have been talking about, which we haven't been. That by itself casts doubt on its veracity."

"That's lawyer-speak, for he doesn't like it," Valerie said, elbowing Paris.

"That reminded me of something," Paris reflected. "I have a friend, a retired lawyer, and doomsday prepper. He moved to Montana recently to get away from people, and he took his grandson with him. They are both preppers, competitive shooters, and hunters, a couple of real Nimrods. The rest of his family is not at all happy about it because they don't know where his place is; he keeps it secret."

Paris thought for a moment, then continued. "What if we adopted their story for Valerie and me? I would be her grandfather. You could tell people Valerie's gone to Montana for the summer to stay with her off-the-grid, doomsday-prepping grandfather. And that's why you don't know when she will be back. And better yet, grandpa keeps the location a secret."

"I like it," Jim admitted, smiling broadly. "Val?"

"Works for me."

"Me, too," Angie said, sounding relieved. "It's a lot better than saying she got pregnant and moved to Ireland!"

Everyone laughed at that, but it was apparent Angie was relieved to have squelched that idea.

"Agreed then," confirmed Paris. "That's the story; just be sure to keep it straight."

Although the story seemed far-fetched, it was just strange enough to ring true. Nevertheless, fear of the unknown pressed in on Valerie.

Then Jim produced a legal-sized Dunne & Morgan Law manila envelope and pushed it across the table to Valerie, who immediately set about opening it. Inside, there were two sealed envelopes, which she shook onto the tabletop. The first contained a document. The second package was smaller but substantial enough to hit the table with a thud.

Valerie opened the document envelope first. Inside was a formal letter written on Dunne & Morgan Law letterhead, stating that Corell Paris was authorized to serve as Valerie's legal guardian. Although Valerie was eighteen and of legal age to go wherever she chose, Jim insisted on providing the letter and keeping a copy on file should the issue of guardianship arise at any time.

Valerie raised her eyebrows but didn't comment. Valerie picked up the other bundle after returning the statement to the envelope. Peering inside, she gasped at what she saw there—two thick wads of one-hundred-dollar bills. Each band indicated the amount as ten-thousand dollars.

"Uncle Jim, that is *way* too much money! I can't take it!" Valerie blurted out.

"You can and will take it," Jim insisted. "It was withdrawn from your trust. It's your money. Colin and Janet were diligent about investments and executing your trust— which," he added, "has grown the past fifteen years substantially. Now that you are eighteen, you have access to the account. You need to get by on your own and travel without being traced. The only way to do that securely is with currency. Credit and debit cards are too easily traced, so don't use them."

Concern colored Jim's face as he reached out to touch the girl's shoulder. "One more thing, Val," he continued. "We don't know when you will return. We want you to have enough cash to last you a while. Just take care, so it lasts. When it runs out, let me know, and I'll get more for you."

Valerie nodded, her eyes welling up again. At her feet, Orson purred. Rubbing away the tears, Valerie reached down and plucked the cat into her lap.

"I am eager to get going," Paris interjected.

"You're right," Jim agreed, then to Angie said, "we need to let them get going."

"Before we go, just one more detail," Paris added. "No communication between any of you until Valerie returns. Agreed?"

Valerie nodded. With the discussion over and decisions made, she hurried upstairs to her room, cradling Orson. She grabbed a few personal things and an animal carrier for the cat. But before leaving, she stood in the center of her room, surveying the things she was leaving behind.

This will never be the same for me, she realized as her throat tightened. Valerie felt saddened to think everything she lived for was in this house, in this room, and that she was voluntarily walking away from it. To think it might never be her home again hit her hard, but she hugged Orson tight, dutifully turned, and pulled the door shut on that part of her life.

———————————————

Downstairs, the adult discussions continued. "We shouldn't allow anyone to see Valerie getting in my Suburban or see her leaving," Paris said to Jim. "Do you mind if I back into the garage so we can load up with the door shut?"

"Alright," Jim said, "let me move my car."

Jim pulled his car out of the garage, parked it on the street, and then guided Paris as he backed the black Suburban into the garage. Jim closed the door and then set about helping Valerie, who had been dragging her feet, feeling glum about leaving her family, home, and friends behind.

Ever the doting Aunt, Angie loaded the travelers up with homemade cookies and brownies for the trip. Although her eyes were wet, she helped hurry things along and remained supportive.

"Valerie will be well taken care of. You can count on that," Paris assured as he shook hands, first with Jim and then Angie. Yet, in his gut, he felt like they were brushing him off. He saw the hesitation in their eyes and knew what was holding them back.

"Just remember," Paris reminded them. "There can be absolutely no communication between any of you until

Valerie returns. That means no phone calls, texting, or emails. Let's be specific—*nada communicion*," he said, gesticulating. "*Nikto, aucne, keiner, none!* Do we agree on this?"

No one answered. Jim, Angie, and Valerie stared at their feet, avoiding his gaze. All three remained silent as Paris turned from one to another seeking support.

"Come on—it's for your own good," he pleaded. "If Stone, or anyone else, was to ask you where Valerie is, you can honestly deny having any knowledge of her whereabouts. Actually, *not* knowing the truth makes your story more believable. Don't you see that? It's a good story, too!"

Paris's words were met with stone silence. But it wasn't long before he had everyone nodding in agreement, although reluctantly. Obviously, no one in the family liked it, but they all knew it was for the best, so they agreed to his conditions.

After a prolonged family hug and more than a few kisses, Valerie climbed in the Suburban and buckled herself in. Angie sobbed inconsolably on Jim's shoulder as Valerie waved goodbye from the passenger seat. As the big SUV rolled out onto the road, the garage door went down.

Chapter 4

Eagan Seamus Stone— November 1938 CE

"What?!" Stone answered the phone gruffly. "Say that again!"

"It's Chad Evers. I have a job for you. Can you be at my office in an hour?"

"It's five o'clock in the morning. What's the rush?"

"It's almost six, but who's counting," Evers said dismissively.

"It's *early*. This better be good, Evers," Stone warned, rubbing his bloodshot eyes and glaring at his watch. "I'll be at the Market Diner in twenty minutes," he barked, then slammed the phone down on its hook without waiting for an answer. Evers knew the place, and where it was, so he saw no need to say more.

The towering man in a well-worn black overcoat, hat, and boots tramped through the darkened streets like a man on a mission. Still, more than an hour before sunrise, the glowing tip of the Lucky Strike cigarette smoldering in the corner of his mouth provided the only evidence of his passing. Stone's eyes shot to his wristwatch, a devotee to time and punctuality. It said five minutes to six, which meant he still had a few minutes to spare. He was making good time.

The unevenness of his gait became more evident as he walked down the slope towards the Farmers Market, immense in the cold morning darkness. The big man limped visibly, the hitch in his step resulting from an old back injury worsened by time and the damp Seattle air.

Low hanging clouds diminished the city lights, magnifying the gloom. Situated within walking distance of the piers, the Farmers Market was vast, a multi-leveled arcade for local farmers, fishermen, and artisans. Seven days a week, fresh fish, meat, and vegetables were unloaded, unpacked, cleaned, cut, and prepared for distribution to the bustling city's restaurants, markets, and residents.

Stone heard voices through the gloom and mist, shouting instructions to workmen and the rumble of delivery trucks unloading their goods. As he turned on to First Avenue, he became merely one among many in a sea of men moving purposefully about their Monday-morning business.

A huddle of delivery men in oilskin coats clutched coffee cups in their gloved hands. Above them, the thirty-foot FARMERS MARKET sign was posted on the rooftop. Across the street, glowing like an open fireplace against the surrounding darkness, was the Market Diner. Open twenty-four hours a day, it was a closet-sized harbor of greasy food and Asian pastries.

Hungry as always, Stone turned at last, with pleasure, into the diner's familiar grease-laden atmosphere of frying eggs and bacon. *Evers isn't here yet,* he grumbled. The sparse little eatery had a row of booths lengthwise along one wall, metal tables, and chairs opposite. A timeworn Asian woman sat at the cash register, seemingly indifferent to anything or anyone. Two men in overalls had just vacated a table leaving an open booth. Stone maneuvered his bulk into the small space and sank into it with a grunt of satisfaction.

No need to order; he was a regular. The waiter placed a thick white mug of coffee in front of him, along with a pair of doughnuts. Within moments the doughnuts disappeared, replaced by his usual breakfast of bacon and eggs on an oval platter.

Already tired of waiting, Stone swallowed his food. Although exceptionally tall, broad, and rough-looking, he blended well with the steady flow of men making their way in and out of the diner. His high-domed forehead was punctuated by a broad boxer's nose, coarse brows, and long dark hair secured behind his head with a leather tie. The unshaven jaw covered in stubble, combined with his deep-set eyes, provided the merciless collector for bookies with an appropriate appearance, considering his occupation.

The big man had just started gnawing on bacon when Chad Evers, Deputy Mayor, slid into the bench across from him. The aspiring politician was almost as tall as Stone but rail-thin with a choirboy's complexion. His face had a strange asymmetry to it as though it had been punched one too many times—that being the only thing preventing him from being girlishly handsome.

"I've got a job for you," Evers said as he pulled off his hat, glancing around the diner suspiciously as if afraid of being seen.

"Want some food?" asked Stone through a mouthful of bacon.

"No," Evers said bluntly.

"Rather wait 'til you can get bread pudding and tea?" asked Stone, grinning widely.

"Up yours, Stone," Evers responded irritably.

Stone chuckled. He enjoyed needling the man, viewing him as a prissy paper-pusher who was pathetically easy to aggravate. He watched with disdain as Evers ordered tea and pastries with an air of insolence, beckoning the indifferent waiter (as Stone noted with amusement), "Oh sir!" *What is the matter with him? Doesn't he know this place is a hash-house?*

"Well?" demanded Evers, with the cup of hot tea in his long pale hands.

Stone continued eating in silence while Evers bristled.

"Depends. I'm a busy man."

No doubt, busy breaking legs thought Evers, knowing better than to say so outright to the enormous man. Stone had a dangerous edge to his demeanor and a well-earned reputation for violence. *Definitely, not one to provoke,* Chad reminded himself.

Evers fished in his overcoat pocket, brought out an envelope, then slid it across the table. Stone looked at it blankly as if a dead rat had just landed on his plate.

"Read it."

"Later," Stone grumbled without looking up from his breakfast.

"Alright. Call me then." Assuming the conversation was over, Evers got up and left, leaving Stone to finish his meal.

When he was certain Evers was gone, Stone opened the envelope and studied the letter, along with a handwritten note authored by Evers. After deciphering the first few sentences, he shoved both documents in his pocket, deciding to read them later.

Back at his room, Stone flipped on the overhead light, pulled the envelope out of his pocket, tossed it on the kitchen table, and then started a pot of coffee. The Vista Hotel suite was dated and poorly maintained. The room included a kitchenette, a small table with two chairs that didn't match, a private bathroom, and a bedroom that doubled as the living area. The only addition to the bed was a dusty overstuffed chair and a side table with a brown radio. The double-hung window pane permitted just enough filtered light through the grime to be considered a window.

After pouring himself a cup of coffee, Stone grabbed the envelope, then sank into the chair with a grunt. While sipping coffee, Stone contemplated his meeting with Chad Evers and the significance of the message. He unfolded the unsigned typewritten letter dated November 20, 1938, then read it.

Dear Mayor Langley,

Last Saturday night, in the Garden Room, I was at the Olympic Hotel for dinner. I saw you there with that woman. I also saw where you went with her afterward. Your wife is not going to like learning about this. Wire ten thousand dollars to the following account to prevent that from happening. You have until 5 PM Friday when the banks close.

Western Union account: 59924006

Stone folded the letter back inside the envelope, grinned, then eyed his watch; it was 6:57 Monday morning, which told him Evers received the letter sometime during the weekend, or it was a holdover from Friday.

Politicians don't work before 9 AM or on weekends, he thought. *Friday fit best as the day the letter was delivered. But if that is true, why didn't Evers call sooner? But he didn't, so I was either the first choice or the last. Not that I care either way, but if I was the last choice, that means my price just went up. I smell money, so I will gamble on me being the last choice.*

According to Evers' note accompanying the demand letter, he had a solid tip on the woman's identity seen with the mayor. Evers wanted him to tail the woman to see if he could catch her with Langley. He also wanted a photograph of them together. But the offer of one-thousand dollars per week, plus expenses, was hard for him to believe—and impossible to pass on.

Evers assured him Langley's opponents would love to have this little tidbit to use against him come election time. Once he had the woman's identity and pictures as proof, his instructions were to take that information directly to him and him alone, no one else. Evers also claimed he intended to turn it over to the mayor to protect him from a political scandal. Despite that, Stone knew better; he didn't believe a word of it.

I smell a rat, Stone thought. *None of it makes any sense for two simple reasons. First, all it would take to identify the owner of the Western Union account is ten minutes and a fifty-dollar bill to grease a palm down at the Western Union office. And two, one-thousand dollars a week is downright silly; far too much money for such a mundane task. I would have done the job for a hundred bucks and laughed all the way to the bank!*

Turning his eyes to the window, Stone stared outside, his mind still rambling. *This does not add up! Why spend days or weeks following some dame around town hoping to get a photo of her and the mayor together when there are faster, easier ways to get the job done?* Then he realized that if he could milk the job for three weeks, he could buy a house in Ballard with that much money!

Stone knew Evers as a climber, one who would stop at nothing to move a rung up the political ladder. In Stone's mind, everything Evers said was suspect. He had something up his sleeve. Stone knew it; he just didn't know what—yet.

After pouring himself another cup of coffee, he paced the room, trying to work the problem out in his mind. The one thing he could rely on was his gut, and it was telling him there was something fishy about the entire story.

As a debt collector, Stone was intimately familiar with the nature of people. In his experience, when someone threw a lot of money around carelessly, there was nothing careless about it. There was always a motive in play. Cash was hard to come by, so only people who didn't work for it wasted it. As he continued pacing, the pieces of the puzzle began to come together for him.

Evers must be planning to use the pictures and information to advance his own political career. The mayor would be just another casualty of his climb up the political ladder. By Stone's way of thinking, there could be no other reason. Nothing else made sense.

Essentially Chad Evers was willing to pay him an obscene amount of money for what boiled down to be a photograph of a woman. He also doubted the woman's identification, if there ever was one in the first place. If she existed, Evers must already know who she is. Stone considered that to be a matter of fact. He also knew that he must still be very close to the truth if he was wrong. So, he moved on to the next point, the money.

It appeared to him Evers had so much money he was in a hurry to waste it— a big hurry. If that was true, Stone reasoned, Evers must not have worked for it, which meant he either inherited the money, won a lottery, or stole it. Inheriting a sum large enough not to care how it was spent seemed like a long shot. He gave that possibility a low likelihood. Winning a lottery would have had everyone talking about it. If that were true, he would have heard about it, but he hadn't.

Chad Evers must have stolen his wealth, Stone thought to himself. *But where did the money come from? And how much was there? Heck, if I could find Evers' stash of cash and get my hands on it, I might be able to do a whole lot better than a house in Ballard,* he concluded, smiling at the thought. *Yes, lightening that prissy politician's pocket has a definite appeal.*

Stone sucked in air, then roared with laughter. It was decided; he would accept the job offer but planned to do it his way. Tailing his boss would be a lot more fun than following the mayor's skirt around town. This way, Evers would be paying him for following himself. Stone loved the idea, chuckling at the irony. It was a good plan. With the decision made, he picked up the phone and dialed Evers' office.

"City Hall, how can I direct your call?" came the switchboard operator's mechanical response.

"Give me Chad Evers' office," he demanded.

"One moment, please."

Stone did not like waiting, and if the operator had not put the call on hold so abruptly, he would have told her so. "One moment please," was the wrong thing to say to a man as impatient as him. It was against his nature to be forced to wait for anything. It wasn't long before he started counting the moments while staring at his watch. He hated waiting and hated time wasted. He also hated timewasters, and this lady was being paid to waste his time. When someone finally picked up the line again, more than a dozen moments had already been wasted, and that made him cross.

"Mister Evers Office," a female voice announced.

"Give me Chad Evers."

"Who may I say is calling, please?"

"E.S. Stone!" he growled.

"Let me see if he is in. Please hold."

Damn! Stone barked, glancing at his watch again. His patience was being tested to the limit. Time was being needlessly wasted. He hated that.

"The line is busy; would you like to hold or leave a message?"

Stone rolled his eyes, fatigued with having to jump through so many hoops to get that twerp Evers on the phone.

"Tell him Stone will be in his office in twenty minutes sharp," he snarled, then slammed the phone down with a bang. *At least I had that small pleasure,* he thought.

With no time to spare, Stone grabbed his coat and hat, slammed the door, and ran down the stairs. Once at the curb, he hailed a cab, then directed the driver to take him to Seattle City Hall on 4th Avenue.

Experience told him his destination was ten minutes from the Vista Hotel by cab. As the driver reached City Hall, Stone checked his watch and was relieved to see he had six minutes left. *Perfect.* He intended to teach that lady a lesson in time management by walking through the door to Evers' office precisely when he said he would be there. He liked people to know he was punctual and intended to prove it by bursting into the office door at straight-up twenty minutes after he had hung up the phone.

Wham! Stone threw the door open so hard it ricocheted off the wall, nearly torn from its hinges. At almost seven feet tall, the ceiling was too low for the big man. As he opened the door, he had to duck to keep from hitting his head on the door frame, which he didn't like. Once inside, his hat only cleared the ceiling tiles by a few inches, making it uncomfortably close. He didn't like that either. By the time Stone realized the waiting room barred entry from the main office, he was fuming. He hated waiting rooms, and he hated waiting.

Moreover, he did not expect to find direct entry to Chad Evers' office regulated by the smartly dressed brunette blocking his way. The nameplate on her large oak desk announced her as Mrs. Dreyer. The elegant lobby featured stylish carpet, opposing brown leather couches, end tables with lamps surrounded by smoked glass walls. A glass door provided entry into the rest of the suite—which was obstructed by Mrs. Dreyer. Stone didn't like fancy lobbies, and he didn't like Mrs. Dreyer either.

Stone stomped toward the woman like he intended to go right over her desk and through her. Only when her desk impeded his forward momentum did he stop. Then, leaning forward, he glared silently into her face for a long moment. Not to be intimidated, Mrs. Dreyer locked eyes with the burly intruder as she wordlessly waited for him to speak.

"Stone to see Evers," he finally growled, the veins in his neck bulging. The big man saw her as an unnecessary roadblock, which he did not respect. If he thought he could get away with it, he would have thrown her and her big desk aside to get through the door.

"Do you have an appointment, Mr. Stone?" Mrs. Dreyer asked politely, fully aware he did not have one because she had answered his call twenty minutes earlier. The fact that precisely twenty minutes had transpired since then was not lost on her. She would not soon forget he had slammed the phone down in her ear, nor how he tried to intimidate her by invading her personal space like an angry grizzly. In her opinion, no way declaring he would be there within twenty minutes qualified as an appointment.

"Yes," Stone stated gravely.

"I'll see if he is in—please be seated," the resolute secretary responded. When the big man did not move, she silently but sternly pointed at one of the sofas indicating nothing would happen until he obeyed her. Finally conceding to her demand, Stone seated himself, although reluctantly.

Once Stone was seated, Mrs. Dreyer rose from her desk, then disappeared behind the glass wall for several minutes, presumably to speak to her boss. When she reappeared, she sat quietly at her desk with her hands folded as if she were waiting for something. However, she was not; this was her way of getting in a jab at the cur.

When Mrs. Dreyer felt like she had made her point, she politely announced, "Mr. Evers will see you now. He will escort you in momentarily." She said, her tone dripping with polished insincerity only years of government service can engender.

Stone nodded, feeling his temperature rise. Seconds later, Chad Evers opened the door, visibly annoyed, then wordlessly waved Stone into the suite. Once inside, he led Stone into a spacious office with six matching oak desks occupied by his staff members. One by one, the office staff eyed the big man suspiciously as he stormed by.

Stone followed Evers down a long hallway lined with offices and meeting rooms. Evers' own office was at the end of the hall. The heavy oak door to the office was left open.

The Assistant Mayor seated himself behind his desk with a grunt. Meanwhile, Stone proceeded to drag a heavy chair in front of Evers' big desk without invitation then throw himself into it as if he owned it. Chad bristled at the impropriety.

"What made you think you could come barging in here?" he snapped, wasting no time in telling the lumbering fool what he thought of the unwanted incursion into his world.

Stone was furious at the insult but knew better than to respond.

"And tell me," Evers continued, "what made you think it would be a good idea for you to come here when I asked you to work secretly? Don't you realize that coming here exposes you as being personally associated with me? Can't you see that?"

"I accept your offer," Stone stated calmly, picking at his fingernails.

Evers was bewildered by Stone's cavalier attitude, reconsidering the ramifications of hiring the brut before responding. He knew the man got results, which was good. But could he be controlled? That was what bothered him the most about the coarse, ill-mannered bully. Stone was well-known as a callous enforcer, a man not taken lightly. But wasn't that why he offered him the job in the first place?

"Alright," Evers conceded after serious consideration. "But I want to put an agreement in writing, so there are no misunderstandings between us," he said uneasily. The last thing Chad Evers wanted was a disagreement with a leg breaker, such as this rough-hewn character.

"I'll write something up, but we will change the description of the job so it cannot possibly be associated with our real goals. I need to protect this office and myself from reproach. How does that sound?"

"Agreed, when can you have it?" Stone snapped with finality, his eyes glittering.

Evers stared, once again having second thoughts about doing business with a leg-breaker. "I want you to get to work immediately, so I'll have it for you by the end of the day," he said, then added, "I'll call you when it's ready. Marcia Dreyer, my secretary, *whom I believe you have met*, will have a package waiting for you on her desk today at four o'clock. We close at five, so if you want to go to work tonight, you will want to be here before then."

Once said, Chad pushed a button on his desk, which buzzed in another office. Then he stood moving toward the door in a less-than-subtle indication he considered their meeting over, and it was time for his guest to leave. At the door, he added, "Don't do anything until you have the agreement in hand. There will be a money order in it to get you started."

Stone remained seated, glowering defiantly as Chad held the door open for him. He regarded Evers as a self-important worm, but right or wrong this gig was too rich to miss, so he decided to play along.

"*Yes, sir,*" Stone muttered mockingly, then rose from the chair. What he wanted to say was; *You better sleep with the lights on, buddy.* Stone noticed Chad recoil defensively as he passed by him at the door and counted it as a small victory.

"And don't call me," Chad said. "Bill me, send me letters or telegrams, but don't come here again without an invitation. If you do, I'll call the police and have you jailed. If I want to speak to you, I will call you. Got it?"

"Got it, boss-man," Stone chuckled to himself, then followed Marsha Dreyer's lead out of the office.

As instructed, Stone returned to the Deputy Mayor's office precisely at four o'clock, snatched the envelope from Marcia's outstretched hand, then left without a word. Marcia breathed a sigh of relief the moment the door closed behind him. The truth was the huge tough-looking man dressed in black had frightened her more than she cared to admit.

Although Stone resented being forced to yield to Evers, he was pleased and a little excited. Back at the Vista Hotel, he opened the manila envelope. While sliding out the legal-size documents, a money order glided onto the tabletop. Studying it carefully, he saw two things that disturbed him.

First was the name of the payee on the check. Just two people on the planet knew his full name Seamus Egan Stone, his mother in Ireland—if she was still alive, that is—and Stone himself. He had traveled with his father by steamship to New York at a young age, then west to California. There, his father worked as a logger. When he was fifteen, his father died in an accident, leaving him to fend for himself at a logging camp high in the Sierra Nevada Mountains.

At that time, Stone was already large, towering over many of the workmen. The boss hired him as a choke setter, which was hard, dangerous work, especially for a youngster. When one of the men made fun of his Irish name, Egan Seamus Stone, he promised himself never to utter it again. He used only his last name from then on, thinking of himself as

Stone. He used his initials, E.S. Stone, but never again divulged his full name to anyone whenever asked to sign something.

By the time he was eighteen, the young man calling himself Stone was bigger, stronger, and meaner than any man in the logging camps. At the first opportunity, he killed the man who made fun of his name by rolling a log over him and making it appear an accident. Soon after, he left the logging camps, working his way north until he eventually ended up in Seattle. There he took on a variety of jobs. Due to his size and intimidating physique, it was not long before a bookie noticed him, and young Stone began working as a debt collector. He liked it because it was quick, easy money.

The second thing that bothered him about the check was the amount of the draft, $1,500—more than ten times what the job was worth. It just did not make sense to him. But, it was the sort of gravy train he was willing to ride for that kind of money. If he dragged his feet, he could make the job last for at least a couple of weeks, which meant he could get that house in Ballard by the end of the month. He saw the check as the beginning of a beautiful relationship.

Why is Evers so eager to throw his wallet at me? Stone wondered, scratching his head. *Is the outcome worth that much to him? What am I missing? Whatever it is, I can't see it.*

Stone played every possible scenario over in his head. *Evers sure has done his groundwork; there is only one way he could have known my full name. To get that little tidbit, he would have had to go to the trouble of tracking me to California, New York, and all the way back to Ireland, which would be time-consuming and expensive.*

That realization troubled him. *Why bother? Why would anyone go to the trouble of researching my background before hiring me to tail a woman around town? What could possibly be so important that Evers would pay ten times what it's worth to put names and faces on two people he had already identified? Surely his goal isn't money—he'd just proved he had enough of that. Is it the desire for more power? Probably,* Stone thought. *What else would a politician want other than power and money?*

When the truth struck Stone like a sizzling bolt of lightning, it all came together at once. *Evers is Deputy Mayor. This whole thing must be about creating a scandal damaging enough to take the mayor down!* If the mayor went down hard enough, Evers would be tapped to fill in as interim mayor! Once in office, Evers would protect his position by using me as his enforcer.

Stone laughed so hard he choked. *That's it!* Only this scenario answered the question as to why Evers had so thoroughly researched his past. No doubt, he needed someone to rely on to bust knees when needed—someone without a history, just like him. In his mind, Evers proved that true when he had the money order written to Egan Seamus Stone.

Stone considered the mystery solved. Just one question remained unanswered; where did the money come from? He intended to find out on Evers' dime and send him the bill for it. Stone loved the absurdity of making Evers pay to have someone investigate himself.

Chapter 5

The Dreamer—January 2431 BCE

Tierney laid his trembling hands on Pearse's body. Overcome with grief by his father's loss, the boy kissed him goodbye, then wept bitterly. Without him, he and his family would surely starve. It was only a matter of time. For Tierney, this moment marked the beginning of the end for him and his family.

Although devastated by the tragedy, he was also pragmatic. He knew he wasn't strong enough to carry his father's body all the way home without help. To do it alone would be beyond his physical ability. But that meant leaving the body behind in the freezing snow. With wild animals in the area, he was reluctant to do so. But as Tierney saw it, there was no other choice.

Reluctantly he began planning the grim task. Wrapping the body in skins before burying it seemed like the right thing to do. The work would be hard without a shovel, but Tierney thought he could do it using his father's big hunting knife. He planned to mark the place with a stick so he could find it when, with his mother, he would return for the body.

Before setting to work, Tierney placed a loving hand on his father's chest one last time. Then his heart caught in his throat—movement, he felt movement! It was faint, there wasn't much, and he wasn't sure, so he stayed with it. Although barely perceptible, there it was. He felt it again. His father's chest was rising and falling rhythmically. Hope ignited in him all at once. His father was still alive!

Overcome with a combination of hope and excitement, the boy leaped to his feet. "Yes!" he cried to the heavens, celebrating the joy and relief he felt. But on closer examination, he realized his father's skin had grown cold. He needed to remedy that immediately! Hurriedly, he laid out the waterproof skins and cocooned his father in them. When Tierney was finished, nothing was left exposed to the frigid air but Pearse's nose. Then he stayed by his father's side, talking to him, rubbing his head with one hand while monitoring the movement of his chest with the other.

Gradually Pearse began to warm up. As his body warmed, his breathing became more noticeable, finally strengthening to the point he breathed normally. Seeing his father stir, the boy knew he had made the right decision to wrap him in oilskins. He was proud to have made the right choice and knew his father would agree. But most of all, he was thankful his father was alive.

Pearse's eyes fluttered open momentarily, although without focusing. Then he laid still for a few more minutes. The next time his eyes opened, they stayed wide and focused on his son Tierney, who hovered like a bumblebee over a flower.

"Why am I hot?" Pearse croaked weakly.

"I saw that you were cold, so I wrapped you up in the oilskins," said the boy.

Without answering, Pearse closed his eyes again and rested quietly. Tierney was well aware of the danger of sweating in freezing weather. The risk of hyperthermia was always present, so he untied and loosed the oilskins as a preventative measure.

Although Pearse was alive clearly, he was in no condition to travel. Unfortunately, that meant they would be spending the night in the flattened crater, with nothing larger than a pebble to break the wind. Tierney saw no firewood or tentpoles anywhere in sight, which meant he would have to go over the wall to obtain the supplies required to make it through the night. Regardless, going over the berm alone and in the dark was a frightening prospect to consider. The approaching darkness and the presence of wild animals were unavoidable realities he would have to deal with.

The boy summoned his courage then woke his father by patting his cheek. "Father," he whispered, "I' am going to go over the wall to find firewood and tent poles. We are going to spend the night here. I will be back soon."

The hard landing threw the ship's crew and company into disarray. The vessel was immersed in darkness, the only illumination provided by sparks and flickering lights: acrid smoke and the strobing lights combined to produce an otherworldly effect on the bridge.

Once the vessel had settled in place, Guyidian Thetis, *The Dreamer's* human commander, sat up, cradling his right arm. Guyidian guessed correctly that the bone was broken above the elbow. His head throbbed from slamming the floor, and his arm ached. As he struggled to assess his condition, he heard moans and cries for help. Those voices were a call to action, helping to clear Guyidian's mind and set himself in motion.

Guyidian discovered he was just one among many of the multi-species crew injured and disoriented. Pushing himself from the floor with his good arm, he winced at the pain as he staggered to a nearby control console for support. Within moments his mind had cleared enough to begin contemplating a course of action.

Flickering images of others moving about the bridge scalded his vision. Lieutenant Borst was immediately identifiable for no other reason than his prodigious bulk. At six-foot-six and four-hundred pounds, Borst's form was unmistakable in the gloom.

"Borst! Help me out here, will you?"

"Commander Thetis?"

"That's right, over here at systems control."

Borst moved quickly between flashes of light. One moment he was invisible, obscured by smoke and darkness, then reappeared directly in front of Guyidian, his massive face too close for comfort, which startled the ship's commander. It didn't help that the big man's face was a mosaic of tattoos that made his image appear monstrous in the swirling smoke and flickering lights.

"Are you alright, commander?" asked Borst, looking down on Guyidian.

"A little banged up, but I'll survive. Let's see if we can get the lights back on."

Borst rattled around under the control console, came up with a solar torch, and lit it. Guyidian followed Borst's lead until the light fell on the ship's Navari navigator leaning against a wall keening. Her black carapace was nearly invisible in the darkness, even with the light shining directly on her. Cresson clasped her thorax with all six appendages frozen in apparent agony, which worried Guyidian.

"Cresson?" the commander called, but there was no response from the beetle-like creature. Guyidian knelt beside the Navarin navigator for a closer look. "What happened to her lights? Usually, she is lit up like a Christmas tree from top to bottom. I have never seen her go dark like this."

"Sir, this is common with an injured Navari; it's called effulgence," said Borst.

"How do you know, lieutenant?"

"I crewed on a Navari vessel. I've seen it before," Borst admitted. "When seriously injured, they go into effulgence, which is like hibernation. It allows them to focus their energy on healing."

Guyidian tapped the Navarin's head with a forefinger. "Hello? Cresson, can you hear me?"

"Sir, I would not recommend trying to wake her up!" Borst warned, backing quickly away.

"Why not?"

"You know what a hypnic jerk is, right?" Borst said from a safe distance.

"Sure, night jerks."

"Well, you have never seen a hypnic jerk until you wake a Navari from effulgent hibernation. Wake her up now, and you stand a good chance she will jump up and bite your head off— literally."

Oh, Guyidian mouthed silently with eyes wide, then stood and backed up beside Borst. The lieutenant touched his commander's shoulder gently.

"Let her be. The doc will take care of her," Borst assured.

"Sounds good," Guyidian agreed, exhaling hard. "Let's see what other surprises await." Then the pair moved on.

Together they scanned the battered vessel. Guyidian was stunned to find Kenzil, his Tholian systems engineer, lying in a pool of transparent blood, the apparent victim of a severe head wound. *Dear Lord, not Kenzil!* The man had been his friend, so Kenzil's death was a personal blow. Guyidian was staggered by the loss. Tears welled, but he wiped them away; there could be others. He could not stop to mourn now. Ship and crew had to come first. The time for mourning his friend would have to come later.

Guyidian sensed other crew members moving among the sparks, smoke, and flickering lights. Intercom chatter began to pick up, and workstation monitors shuddered back to life making the situation seem more manageable. *Slowly but surely, The Dreamer is coming back to life,* he thought.

As ship commander, Guyidian needed a vessel-wide damage assessment, and he needed it quickly. With so many systems offline, *The Dreamer* was immobile and defenseless. He could not wait; he had to take action. The ship and its company were far too important to go unprotected for another nanosecond.

"*Borst!*" Guyidian called as he slid into a seat at one of the workstations with a grunt. The big man's tattooed face mysteriously reappeared from the gloom and flashing lights.

"Sir?" Borst answered dutifully.

"What a mess, eh?"

"Yes, sir."

"Go to sickbay and see if you can get Dr. Ipekk up here," Guyidian ordered.

As Borst rambled off, the commander thought; *This is bad—real bad. The ship is damaged, and we don't know where we are. The Boecki could have brought us here, and we would never know it. We have injuries and deaths aboard.* Then his throat tightened—*and I have lost a close friend!*

Guyidian's eyes welled up again. He wanted to rub his aching head, but that was not possible while cradling a broken arm. Unlike the Boecki, his enemy, he was one pair of arms short of being able to rub away the pain.

In addition to being genuinely concerned for his ship and crew's safety, Guyidian was frustrated and angry. The mission he had bought into appeared simple at the outset; return the Ring Bearer and her entourage to Earth. That seemed easy enough. As expected, crossing the void had been unremarkable most of the way. However, days before arriving at destination Earth, every operating system, instrument, and control on the ship inexplicably locked up or shut down.

Although everyone seemed to have a theory, none explained what happened or what they could do to change their unfortunate situation. Course-plotting froze in place, navigation controls were unresponsive, and sensors all went dead at once. Even the ship's chronometer stopped working as if time itself no longer existed. It seemed as if they had entered a zone of darkness where everything ceased functioning, and time stood still.

And yet, *The Dreamer* seemed to continue on its previously-programmed course, decelerating toward its rendezvous with Earth. That, however, was impossible. Deceleration from faster than light speed was a factored computation. If guidance controls locked up or shut down for any reason, the ship would not continue decelerating at the preprogrammed rate.

Guyidian's conclusion? Something or someone must have been monitoring and managing the ship's deceleration and descent. Without control management, the ship would sail by Earth at near light speed or crash into it. There were no options; it was one way or the other. The only assumption that made any sense to him was this; someone or something had a continuing hand in the ship's guidance.

Yet, here he and his crew found themselves trying to recover from a hard landing. About the only thing they were sure of was they had landed on a planet. But which one? Where? Guyidian couldn't even confirm which solar system they were in, let alone which planet they were on.

The vessel was damaged, with injuries and deaths aboard. Guyidian saw it as a miracle anyone survived the crash. Was it luck? He didn't believe in luck. Starship commanders were pragmatists; they had to be. They didn't have time for luck or fate, and certainly not the sort of luck or fate that drove his ship without his consent or knowledge. So the questions remained. Who or what had controlled the ship's deceleration and landing?

Building frustration got the better of Guyidian as he punched a button on the console with his good elbow.

"This is Commander Thetis on the bridge," he said in a ship-wide announcement. "I need a damage assessment from each section manager immediately." Guyidian waited patiently for a response, but none came. The pressure in his head increased as he waited, all the while wondering if the ship's communications system worked on all levels. The commander waited a minute more, then tried again, this time raising his voice in exasperation—

"This is Commander Thetis on the bridge! Report!" he demanded. He waited. Still, no reply came. He finally received a response just before trying again.

"Commander, this is Hafian Tohm, in Medical! Give us a few minutes! The Ring Bearer and I are assisting the injured."

"Thank you, Mister Tohm," Guyidian said, his worst fears allayed. After a moment's thought, he asked, "Mister Tohm, can I assume *she* is uninjured?"

"Don't worry, Commander," answered Tohm, the tone of his voice filling Guyidian with almost indescribable relief. "Valerie is unharmed."

I needed to hear that! Guyidian thought as a wave of relief washed over him. *The last thing I needed to hear was that The Ring Bearer was injured—or worse. What would we do if we lost Valerie Dunne? One thing is certain; if we lose her, we are finished—everyone and everything is finished!*

Guyidian relaxed, relieved as he reflected on The Ring Bearer. This woman, her rings, and her iconic ship had been synonymous for more than a thousand years. *The Dreamer* had been built by renegade Boeckian sympathizers, specifically for The Ring Bearer. Valerie Dunne and her vessel had leveled the playing field for Earth and their allies the moment it appeared on the scene. Losing her was impossible to contemplate.

Recalling all she'd accomplished and what she meant to his people made his heart swell with pride. Guyidian and his crew of volunteers had been hand-picked from threatened worlds and survivors throughout the galaxy. Although selected from the ranks of the Boeckian Resistance Union, he and his team followed The Ring Bearer's orders exclusively. She and her ship were considered irreplaceable assets to be protected at any cost. Guyidian wasn't about to allow anything to happen to Valerie Dunne or *The Dreamer* on his watch. He wouldn't hesitate to put his life on the line for her or her ship, and he was far from alone in that consensus.

But recent events caused grave concern for her safety and that of his crew. Before encountering the blackout, an encrypted message came in from the BRU that chilled Guyidian to the bone. It warned that the Boecki Imperium had learned from prisoners taken that The Ring Bearer had been responsible, at least in part, for virtually every setback they'd suffered during the past millennium. BRU Command had evidence the Boecki were concentrating their forces in an all-out effort to eliminate her.

By his reckoning, taking prisoners for intel purposes was accepted as a given in any prolonged conflict. And yet, it was common knowledge that the Boecki considered themselves so far above other life forms they didn't care what inferior species know or don't know. The sad truth about that was they were right. Without help from their own scientists, BRU star systems would have been harvested by the Boecki for their resources long ago.

Guyidian looked around the ship with new eyes. *This new tactic was a wake-up call, a game-changer, with ominous implications.* The Boecki had never acknowledged their enemies, let alone cared what they knew. But now they were taking prisoners! This change in tactics was a significant shift in methods by an enemy that, until now, never changed anything. Their arrogance precluded them from change. They were above it.

BRU Command believed it meant the enemy was finally beginning to take them seriously, were desperate for resources—or both. It was a disturbing development when one understood there wouldn't be a BRU without Valerie Dunne and her unique vessel, *The Dreamer*. Many of their worlds would have been destroyed a thousand years prior without these two assets. Was it any wonder why The Ring Bearer was widely regarded as the savior of the galaxy?

What worried Guyidian most was that, according to the BRU message, the Boecki knew about The Ring Bearer and was now focusing their resources entirely on capturing her— alive. He didn't know why the enemy wanted her alive, but the thought chilled his blood. He was determined not to allow anything to happen to Valerie Dunne or her ship.

As additional status reports came in, most were encouraging. Damage to the ship was turning out to be superficial, and the crew was resuming their duties. Reassured by good news, the pressure in Guyidian's head backed off a notch. Despite that, the flickering lights continued indicating control systems were out of sync. A complete reboot would be required to reset the system. After moving to the vacant systems engineers' workstation, Guyidian made a ship-wide announcement of his intention to do the reboot.

"This is Commander Thetis. I am going to do a hard re-start on the power system. A reboot should solve the problem we are having with power fluctuations. In a moment, power will be off in its entirety for approximately thirty seconds. Please wait patiently while the systems restart."

Finishing his announcement, Guyidian pulled himself together. Although he'd done a credible job of projecting confidence, he wasn't nearly as confident as he sounded. In truth, he was desperate to get the ship operational and off the ground. He couldn't allow the crew to know the truth about the danger they were in or of the uncertainty he felt.

Guyidian considered the situation dire because he suspected the Boecki might have orchestrated the onboard instrument failures, controlled the ship's deceleration, and forced a hard landing. In his mind, there could be no other suspect. It seemed the Boecki were onto them, and as long as the ship was on the ground, on a potentially-hostile planet, they were vulnerable.

Guyidian flipped the switch, which plunged the ship into darkness for what seemed like an eternity. When Guyidian restarted the power system, lights and ship systems on the bridge sprang to life all at once. Ventilation came on, clearing smoke from the air and heat, for the ship had grown cold, causing Guyidian uncertainty about conditions outside the ship.

Every head turned as Valerie Dunne, The Ring Bearer, stepped onto the bridge. The room went silent as they stared at her appraisingly. When they were satisfied she was safe, the crew let out a collective sigh of relief. Without exception, everyone aboard needed assurance that The Ring Bearer was unharmed by the hard landing.

Eyeing the crew, Valerie gave them a lopsided grin. The old woman wore a flowing gown that descended to her ankles. Her long silver hair was pulled back into her characteristic ponytail. But it was the eyes that defined The Ring Bearer; mirror-like orbs that reflected her surroundings perfectly. That alone was enough to give them confidence that everything was as it should be and that the dire situation they were in was manageable.

The Ring Bearer was accompanied by the Proxian, Hafian Tohm, her personal aide. The hairless yellow man was immediately followed by Zena Ipekk, *The Dreamer's* doctor, all of whom wasted no time turning their attention to the wounded. Meanwhile, Guyidian asked Doctor Ipekk if she could provide him with an injury report.

"Commander, of the forty-eight aboard, we had two deaths and five seriously injured. Of those injured, three were life-threatening. But thanks to The Ring Bearer," she said, gesturing to Valerie, "most of them have already returned to work."

"Who did we lose?"

"Besides Engineer Kenzil here," she said, motioning to the deceased Tholian on the floor, "we lost Alesia Zama in engineering."

Poor kid! Guyidian's mind cried out. It took a moment for the pain of losing one of *The Dreamer's* newest crew members to subside. "Put them in storage; we will be taking them home with us," Guyidian ordered, then added, "Who do we have left in engineering?"

"Maxim and Barton," Ipekk said dutifully, then continued. "Maxim was one of those seriously injured, although he has already returned to duty."

"We're lucky we didn't lose two of our engineers," Guyidian exclaimed.

"What about you? Are you hurt, Commander?"

Wordlessly Guyidian shrugged. Ipekk noticed the Commander had a knot on his forehead and favored his right arm. She guessed the bone was broken, but the commander seemed steady enough, so she assumed for the time being that he was not concussed. Zena knew Guyidian to be the sort of man to put his ship and crew ahead of himself. She allowed him that privilege knowing he would have himself taken care of when the time was right.

"I'm alright. My arm hurts, but I'll live," Guyidian winced, then continued without pausing. "We need to do a structural integrity assessment as soon as possible. Since we're short on engineers, I want you to take the lead on that. Put a team together and report your findings back to me within the hour. We are vulnerable as long as we are on the ground. I want this ship off this planet as quickly as possible."

"Yes, Commander," she responded, then left the bridge smartly.

Guyidian turned his attention to The Ring Bearer, who attended Cresson, the injured Navari. He did so just in time to witness something he had heard about but had yet to see for himself. She was about to heal the wounded navigator.

Perfect timing! He realized. *Rumor has it that The Ring Bearer is a witch!* He acknowledged that she fit the part in some ways. Certainly, her eyes met that definition, but that was about all, in his opinion. So far as he could tell, she didn't walk, talk or act as one might expect of someone described as being a witch.

Guyidian noticed she wore her long gray hair pulled back in a ponytail, which seemed youthful, and out of place at the same time. In his experience, powerful women wore their hair short in a more androgynous way. *Maybe,* he thought, *that was a concession to power or the men they worked with.* The same was true of the clothes she wore. Again, women of influence typically wore form-fitting clothes or uniforms, but her choice of robes was a concession to nothing and no one, and he admired her for that.

He saw Valerie Dunne as confident, capable though serious, and pleasantly unpretentious considering her stature. He liked that she put on no airs. She was tallish for a woman and seemingly athletic for someone everyone described and an old witch. She had a reputation for staying fit, which he admired. Those who knew her well soon forgot her age, status, and position, which is how she liked it.

Then he spotted her rings, the Five Rings of Hesaurun, one on each finger and thumb of her right hand. The sight of them reassured Guyidian. Those rings were unique, a calling card no one could duplicate. Consequently, her name was synonymous with rings, any ring at all. Everyone anywhere knew of her and those five legendary rings. Her reputation was unmatchable, yet they puzzled him whenever Guyidian saw them. *They seem so unremarkable, so crudely made—so cheap,* he thought.

He was pretty sure the ring's recycle value was virtually nothing. They looked worthless. Rather than gold or silver, they appeared to be made of copper or bronze and were devoid of decorations and precious stones. He guessed that no one would bother bending over to pick them up if they found them lying on the ground. Although modest, in a way, they fit her because she was modest too. That modesty was the one feature that made her unique in a world where people fought for prominence. Guyidian couldn't help but like that about her.

In his opinion, the only physicality of any note was Valerie Dunne's eyes. Many people feared her because of them. While her face had soft feminine features, those dark mirrors of reflected images for eyes disturbed everyone until they became used to them. More than a few were intimidated, even fearful, when seeing themselves reflected in her gaze. Some referred to her as a witch, others an oracle, but Guyidian knew those opinions had no basis in reality. With so many believing one's eyes are windows to the soul, it was no surprise to him that many saw her as a witch.

Guyidian stood back warily, watching as the Praxian Hafian Tohm spoke softly to Cresson. The Navarian was still immersed in its strange hibernation, keening in a low-pitched tone. He wondered if Tohm knew that he was in mortal danger if he startled her. As Guyidian was about to warn Tohm, the keening stopped, the Navari luminesced and opened her eyes.

"It's okay, Cresson," Tohm quietly reassured her, then helped ease her to the floor until she was comfortable, in a resting position. Once he had her relaxed, Tohm asked her a few questions, then stood and faced The Ring Bearer.

"She says she impacted against something sharp when the ship set down. She is in a good deal of pain. I think there is internal damage," he said, pointing to the affected area. Then added, "And there may be internal bleeding."

Valerie squinted at the Navari, then nodded. She knelt beside the prone creature, whispering something undetectable to the onlookers, then took her time locating the wound with her hands. Then the navigator closed her eyes and tried to relax. To those watching, it seemed as if the two were praying together.

What does she know about Navarian anatomy? Guyidian thought. *Although it probably doesn't matter. She isn't a doctor, and what happens next isn't likely to have anything to do with medicine anyway. But this should be good.*

Again the Rings of Hesaurun flashed into Guyidian's field of vision. *There they are, all five of them on her right hand,* he thought excitedly. His eyes were riveted on them, his heartbeat quickened, and breaths came fast and shallow, anticipating, believing he was about to see something extraordinary. *Maybe they will glow or something.* He didn't know what to expect. But one thing was sure; he was about to be a party to something others only heard rumors of— witnessing The Ring Bearer's magic and the Rings of Hesaurun in action.

Gently Valerie Dunne pressed her hands into Cresson's chest. Guyidian was vaguely aware that she whispered something. Now the room shimmered as if a desert mirage swept through it, enveloping everyone there and carrying them away. Guyidian felt he was inside a moving bubble entirely out of his control. It seemed as if time had come to a screeching halt, stopped, backed up a while, turned around, then charged forward again. His mind spun; he felt dizzy for a moment—and just like that, it was done.

Guyidian blinked and rubbed his eyes. It happened so fast he wondered if he had missed something. Valerie moved a hand to Cresson's head as her eyes fluttered open. When their eyes met, Valerie smiled warmly. The Navari ran digits from all six appendages over the affected area as if to be certain The Ring Bearer hadn't missed something. When she was sure everything was as it should be, Cresson scrambled to her feet and nodded graciously. Guyidian guessed that if the Navari had human lips and hearing organs, she would have been smiling ear-to-ear.

"How do you feel?" Valerie asked.

"Strange," Cresson responded her voice a high-pitched chirp. "But it feels like nothing ever happened! Nothing at all!"

Valerie smiled, then turned her attention to Commander Guyidian. *"You're right,"* she said to Cresson while gazing at him with a wry twinkle in her eyes. *"Nothing happened."* Regardless, her penetrating gaze stayed where it was, those dark pools of obsidian locked directly on the commander's eyes. What she saw there, he couldn't know. For a fleeting moment, he felt like a child and remembered the warmth of his mother's embrace—and shivered.

Guyidian wanted to know how The Ring Bearer had healed the Navari, and she seemed to know that! He sensed she had given him a valuable clue as to how she had done it, but there was more—a strong sense of *déjà vu*. It wasn't like he had relived witnessing Cresson healed by The Ring Bearer. No, it wasn't that. It was her saying, "You're right. Nothing happened." Guyidian was certain he had heard her say those words to him before. But when?

Allegories and rumors, thought Guyidian, realizing he had personally witnessed what many considered nothing more than fantastic stories. Regardless of the circumstances, he regarded the experience as a privilege, counting himself lucky to have seen it. But he couldn't shake the feeling of *déjà vu. Did she know his thoughts, or had she merely picked up on his emotions?*

Guyidian's thoughts were interrupted by a message from Ipekk, who was outside the ship with an inspection team evaluating the ship's hull.

"Commander, do you have a visual outside the ship? You might want to see this."

"Give me a moment to bring it up," he said as he switched on exterior monitors. "Got it, I can see you. Is there a problem?" Guyidian asked nervously.

Guyidian's eyes scanned the monitors. Ipekk stood alongside three crew members wearing cold-weather gear. The wind wrestled with their clothing as they continued working with hand-held instruments pressed against the hull.

"Nothing significant," Ipekk hollered over the howling wind. "The hull looks good so far. I just wanted you to know there are people out here."

People out there? Guyidian's heart leaped in his chest. Horrified, he imagined waves of four-armed Boeckian raiders swarming toward the ship. Was his worst fear being realized?

"How many?" he managed to ask.

"Just a couple. They seem to be humanoid, about two hundred yards out on the port side. One of them is building a shelter. The area around the ship has been entirely cleared of vegetation by our landing. You should have no problem seeing them. It seems odd to me anyone would build a shelter so close to the ship."

"Do they appear dangerous?"

"I don't think so; they look like primitives to me. They've built a small fire. One of them is lying down while the other, a boy perhaps, is working on the shelter. Can you see them?"

As Guyidian panned the cameras, he saw the barren landscape and was shocked at the destruction. He had never considered what would happen if a ship the size of *The Dreamer* tried to land. *The Dreamer* was a starship intended to space dock, not land planetside. The ground had been cleared in every direction as if a tremendous blast had occurred. *Can a starship be safely landed?* had been answered succinctly enough. But so had the question of *What would happen if you tried it?*

"I can see them now," Guyidian observed. "You're right. That does seem odd—but don't let that slow you down. Complete your scan. We'll keep an eye on them from here."

"Thank you, Commander," Ipekk said, then went back to work with her team.

"That man is injured," Guyidian heard Valerie say over his shoulder. "I am going outside to see if I can help them."

Going outside? Woman, are you mad?! Guyidian's first impulse was to lash out at her for wanting to do something so foolhardy. But he caught himself in time to stop saying something he would later regret.

"Are you sure that's a good idea?" He said to her, carefully measuring his words. In his opinion, it was a fool's errand. *The Ring Bearer is far too important to be wandering around outside the ship in a snowstorm. What is she going to do, drop in on the natives for tea?*

"We don't know if they are dangerous," he continued. "And there could be wild animals in the area. I recommend against it."

"I'm sure," Valerie responded with a note of finality.

I'm sure? What kind of answer is that? Guyidian was baffled by her response. Was she sure they were dangerous or that there were wild animals out there?

In a flash, it hit Guyidian: he couldn't stop her, it was her ship, and it was his duty to follow her orders, no matter how dangerous or ridiculous they might seem. She had made her mind up, and this wasn't the first time he'd heard that tone in her voice. Arguing with her was pointless, so he relented.

"Alright," said Guyidian reluctantly, "but armed security personnel will be accompanying you."

Guyidian worried she would refuse his recommendation but was relieved when she didn't object. "Mr. Tohm," she finally said without taking her eyes from Guyidian, "let's take a look at the Commander's shoulder before we go."

Guyidian let loose a heavy sigh. *Great. I should have expected she'd notice my injuries. Oh well, let's get it over with.* Tohm asked him a few questions, checked the lump on his forehead, and probed his upper arm. Guyidian winced in pain at the Proxian's touch.

"The Commander's head wound seems superficial, but I suspect the upper humerus has a break."

"Would you like to be seated, Commander?" Valerie asked attentively.

Guyidian shrugged. "Uhm, sure. Thank you," he said, flashing an excited smile as he eased into the chair.

"Alright. Relax and stay still; I'll do the rest," Valerie said soothingly.

The Commander shrugged, then complied. He considered the opportunity to be healed by The Ring Bearer too good to be true. This was a story he was sure would be worth telling his grandchildren.

Guyidian immediately felt drawn in by the healer's eyes, which remained mirror-like as she softly touched his injured arm. Just then, he realized it was a first; she had never touched him before. As she leaned in close to him, he caught her scent as she whispered —

"I know you want to know how it's done, so I am going to tell you. But you must promise to tell no one; it will be our secret. Alright?"

Guyidian's eyes widened. *How did she know?* He nodded wordlessly, his mind still on her fragrance and the warmth of her touch, which he found unexpectedly sensual. Until that moment, he had never thought of her that way.

"It's about time," she explained. "I am going to turn the clock back to the time before your injury occurred. Just your shoulder, mind you; it won't be like what I did with Cresson. You may not have caught it, but everyone on the bridge was duplicated for an instant because of the time warp — *except you.* Your injury is different. There's no need to send your entire body back in time. Do you understand?"

Guyidian nodded again but didn't understand. How could there be two of him or anyone else for that matter? It made no sense. Although what she said about manipulating time explained a lot, including how she made entire fleets of Boeckian ships disappear on command.

"Good," she whispered. "Let's get to work then."

As Guyidian stared into her eyes, those transparent pools of darkness seemed to disappear, replaced by an all-encompassing warmth he felt all the way to his bones. Guyidian felt beads of sweat popping out on his forehead, and his heart pounded in anticipation. At once, the arm felt heavy, then light again, as if it no longer existed. There was a floating sensation for a moment, then nothing. It was done. When he began to feel the limb again, it felt normal. The experience was over in a matter of seconds.

Although thankful for being healed, especially by The Ring Bearer, a small part of him was disappointed. Guyidian knew it was silly, but he hoped to experience the air wavering and glowing and shimmering about as he'd seen when she healed Cresson. So far as he could tell, none of that happened, which was a slight letdown. He wondered why it had to be different for him. He decided the difference must be a matter of perspective. Rather than being on the outside looking in, he had been on the inside looking out.

"How do you feel?" the healer probed.

"Perfect. It's great, thank you," Guyidian gushed while rubbing the mended limb as a demonstration of its renewed vigor.

"Are we free to go now, Commander?"

"Of course," Guyidian agreed, "but you are going to need protection. Give us a few minutes to put together a security escort for you."

"Commander, I will be taking Mister Tohm with me and going out of the cargo dock," she said, raising her eyebrows as if her request was negotiable.

But Guyidian knew better and frowned, aware her request did not include a question. The only question requiring an answer was whether or not he cared enough to argue with her about it. He wasn't in the mood for it, so he gave up trying to keep the outing as simple as possible.

"Alright," he shrugged, "but keep it quick, and don't take any chances. We don't know what's out there. And return as soon as possible. As soon as we have a damage assessment and have made repairs, we are leaving."

"Yes, sir," she said with a wry smile.

Guyidian knew her well enough to know she had more on her mind than merely stopping by to say hello to the natives. *She's keeping something from me. But what?* He couldn't know her real intentions or what secrets she kept hidden from him, but things always seemed to work out for her, so he let her go without argument. Guyidian didn't tell her that the very moment she left the bridge, he intended to take additional steps to ensure her safety. Her safety was his job description, which he took very seriously.

"Hafian," Valerie ordered, "get changed into cold-weather gear. I'm going outside, and you're coming with me. See you on the loading dock in twenty minutes."

Tohm nodded, then left the bridge with her. Guyidian's eyes followed them until they were gone.

"That woman has something up her sleeve," he remarked suspiciously, then pushed a button on his console. "Security, The Ring Bearer, Mister Tohm, and two armed guards will be disembarking from the dock in twenty minutes. I want your two best men on this. The moment the doors close, I want an additional squad of four men standing by. Is that clear?"

"Affirmative," the security chief acknowledged.

Guyidian rubbed his chin thoughtfully. "I'm telling you, that woman has something up her sleeve," he repeated to the bridge staff. "I want weapons charged and every monitor on the ship watching their every move. If so much as a snowball flies out there—open fire. No questions asked—got it?"

A chorus of "yes sir's" immediately followed. His point made, Guyidian scanned the exterior monitors, his eyes remaining grim.

When Valerie appeared on the cargo dock, she was more than prepared for cold weather. She wore a thick coat, insulated pants, boots, a fur hat, and lined gloves. She also had two heavy bags and an animal carrier, which produced questioning looks and more than a few smirks.

"How long are you planning to stay out there?" Tohm inquired, puzzling at the bags and pet carrier. Peering inside, he noticed her big tomcat Orson purring as if he didn't have a care in the world.

"Oh, I thought I would bring them a few gifts, that's all."

"Really? Why the cat then?" Tohm said, gesturing to the animal in the carrier. "Is he some kind of peace offering?"

"Orson? Oh, he asked to come along, so I said alright, as long as he stays in the carrier."

Tohm rolled his eyes. "Why do I believe that?" he said.

"You asked," Valerie said with a chuckle.

"I should have known better," he retorted.

When the cargo doors opened, freezing air blasted them in the face, sucking their breath away. Swirling snowflakes filled the air as they walked down the ramp, followed closely by two well-armed guards. Once on the ground, they made their way around to the ship's port side. In the distance was a small shelter, its coverings flapping in the wind, a light thread of smoke emanated from a fold in the roof.

"That shelter is barely large enough for two people. How did they ever fit a fire in there?" Tohm shouted over the wind, not expecting an answer. Drawing nearer, they saw a well-built shelter of animal skins, a stack of firewood by its side.

Upon reaching the campsite, Valerie signaled with a hand for them to sit a few feet away from the tent, then called out in an unfamiliar language. *How can she know what language they speak here?* Tohm wondered. Valerie surprised him so often he'd made it his policy never to miss an opportunity to be at her side. Still, how could she possibly know the language of this planet?

Valerie waited for a response, but nothing happened, so she called again, using the same strange tongue. A moment later, a boy stuck his head out of the tent. The boy's eyes widened at the sight of them; four strangers sitting together huddled against the wind. She watched his eyes darting back and forth between the guards, Tohm, and herself.

The boy stared long and hard at Hafian Tohm, the Praxian, no doubt questioning what he saw there. Tohm's yellow skin tone, enormous blue eyes, hairless face, and head were not expected. But then his gaze settled on her, and immediately she knew why. It was always the same, something she had come to expect. And when his mouth fell open in wonder, she knew the boy had noticed her eyes and that he was afraid.

Inside the tent, Tierney was startled to hear a woman's voice call his name. Who could it be? Who knew where he was other than his mother and father? But he was looking at his father, who was barely alive, and he was sure he hadn't heard his mother's familiar voice. Then he heard it again, a woman's voice crying out his name.

The boy slowly stuck his head out of a tent flap and was surprised to find four very strange people there, a woman and three men. Two men appeared to be soldiers, but they seemed somewhat unremarkable other than their distinctive uniforms. Then again, the other two, a yellow man and a tall woman, had his heart racing.

The yellow man had him questioning his sight. Was the blowing snow and wind playing tricks on his eyes? He was sure two men were soldiers, but he was uncertain about the yellow one. He guessed he was looking at a man, but he had never seen or heard of anyone so unusual. The yellow skin, hairless head, and enormous blue eyes peered at him unblinkingly, sending shivers down Tierney's spine.

These strange people were unlike any he had ever seen. Although they carried bags with them, he didn't see them as travelers or hunters, and they definitely were not clansmen. Tierney guessed the yellow man must be very sick. What else could cause one to turn yellow? The woman that called him by name greeted him with a disarming smile, but those dark eyes drove him back inside to the safety of the tent.

"Son, who is outside, and how do they know your name?" Pearse croaked out. His voice was feeble, barely audible over the howling wind and flapping tent skins.

"Father, there is an old woman and three soldiers out there. But the woman is the leader. *She is scary*," the wide-eyed boy exclaimed.

"There are three soldiers out there, and you tell me you're afraid of the old woman?"

Tierney saw his father's meaning, but that didn't change what he saw or how he felt about it. In his mind, he had good reason for fearing the woman who knew his name. *She must be a spirit, or an ancestor returned from the dead. How else could she know my name? And what of the yellow man? How can I tell father about him? He won't believe me,* Tierney thought.

"Hello, Tierney?" they heard the mysterious woman call again. "Please come out and speak to us! We aren't going to hurt you!"

"Son," Pearse said weakly, "if they were here to hurt us, they wouldn't ask to talk."

"Yes, father," the boy said, suddenly embarrassed by his fear. Once he had gathered his courage, Tierney stood determined to act like a man even if he wasn't. The boy put on his war face, shoved his father's big hunting knife in his belt, then exited the tent with a confident stride. Then Tierney seated himself directly in front of the strange old woman with dead eyes and did his best to look dangerous.

"Who are you, and why are you here!" the boy demanded, his adolescent put-on mask of courage glaringly obvious to the visitors.

Valerie stifled a smirk as she watched the boy with his hand on the hilt of a big knife, trying to appear as threatening as he could manage.

"My name is Valerie, and these are my friends," she offered, gesturing to the others. "Your father is hurt," she said cocking her head in a challenging way, "and I am here to help him."

Tierney studied the old woman carefully as he considered her words. She seemed to have noticed his unease about the soldier's presence. *The old woman called them "friends,"* he thought, *but that didn't mean they weren't dangerous.* And he wasn't about to take her word for it. He needed more information.

"Are you travelers?"

"We're from the ship," she said, gesturing at *The Dreamer* for emphasis. "We saw your father is hurt. I am a healer. I am here to help him."

"What is a ship?" asked Tierney, well-aware that *ship* must be her word for the big glass fish that hit the ground hard that morning.

"That," the old woman said, pointing again at *The Dreamer.* "It's like a flying boat. Do you know what a boat is?"

"Sure," Tierney said, "we see boats at the summer gatherings, but I never saw one made of glass, and I never saw one that big!" he added, pointing at the ship with a wide grin. Valerie was happy to see that the boy seemed to be warming up to her.

"You are Tierney; is that correct, young man?"

"Yes, Tierney," he said, savoring the fact that the woman had referred to him as a man, although he knew that he wouldn't be a man for another two summers. Nevertheless, she made him feel like a man the way she said it, and he liked that.

"Tierney, I am here to help Pearse, your father. He is sick. I am a healer. I can help him," Valerie repeated.

Tearney stiffened when he heard the woman call his father by name. *How is that possible?* he wondered. "How do you know our names?" he countered.

"Old people know stuff." A look of melancholy shaded the old woman's face, then she continued. "May I go in to see your father?"

Old people know stuff? What does that mean? Tierney raged. Pushing the dread aside, he reasoned, *I am not a child. I know about the Cailleach Bhéara—witch! We have never seen these people or their big glass fish before, but they already know our names? How can that be? I am not about to allow that witch near my father until I am satisfied these travelers are what they claim to be!*

I have plenty to worry about, thought Tierney, *fingering the handle of his father's knife. First, this big glass fish crashes to Earth then my father is badly injured by it. Then these strange people appear, claiming to be here to heal my father? And yet this strange woman expects me to trust them? It's all too much!*

A dead silence lay between the two of them. Tierney's gut rumbled with fear. "I do not understand. Tell me, how do you know our names?" he asserted again, still gripping his father's knife.

"I'm sorry," Valerie apologized, silently scolding herself for the slip-up. She should not have let on that she knew their names. Had she just confirmed in the boy's mind that she was a witch? She decided to come at him from another angle.

"We have an expression, 'Old people know stuff.' I was referring to the wisdom of the elders. You understand the wisdom of the elders—yes?"

Tierney narrowed his eyes. Slowly he nodded.

"Do your people have elders?"

Tierney nodded again.

"I am an elder among my people, and I know many things that others do not know, including your names," Valerie explained. She knew her explanation was lame, but it was the best she could come up with on short notice and hoped the boy would buy it.

Still fingering his father's knife, Tierney slowly began to relax. Although not satisfied with her answer, he was eager to see if the old woman could help his father. Pearse was unable to move anything below his neck and struggled to breathe. Even though his father was alive, their family was sure to starve if he remained in his present condition.

Tierney saw no other choice. He needed help. If there was any chance she could heal his father, he knew he had no option other than to accept.

"I will ask him first," Tierney told her, then went back inside the shelter, eager to report back to his father.

Tierney shared with Pearse the conservation he had with the woman but purposely left out two key points: the visitors claimed to be from inside the glass fish, and the mysterious old woman already knew their names. Despite their odd appearance and that the woman was probably the Cailleach, he didn't want to take the chance that his father might find a reason to refuse her offer. Tierney needed it. He needed hope that his father could be healed and didn't care how or who did it. Sure it was a gamble, but it was one he was willing to take.

Well aware of what was at stake, Pearse nodded his approval. He was in serious trouble if his condition didn't change, and soon. His family would suffer unless he recovered fully, so he was anxious to see if this strange woman could heal him.

"Father said for you to come in," Tierney called from the tent to the old woman. "But I will stay outside because there is only room for two."

Valerie quietly entered the smoky tent, then knelt beside Pearse without speaking. His was a patriarchal society, so she waited for the man to speak first.

Pearse studied the old woman closely, taking in her every detail before speaking. A sudden chill rushed through him. Now he understood why the boy feared her. Tierney had been correct in his description. He agreed with the boy; her eyes were precisely that—*scary.* In his estimation, her long silver hair and eyes as dark as midnight pools marked her as the Cailleach Bhéara. He had no reservations about that. But Pearse found nothing threatening about her other than her appearance. He didn't believe she was a threat, just a witch.

"Woman," he croaked. "You are the Cailleach Bhéara, yes?"

"I am a healer," asserted the old crone. "My name is Valerie; I am here to help you. Tell me what happened."

Pearse wasted no time in telling her his story. "It was the glass fish," he said. "I touched it, and it bit me. Now I cannot move."

"I know." The witch said soothingly. "May I touch you now?" she asked, her wrinkled hand hovering over him, anticipating his response. But Pearse didn't answer.

I know? How does she know? The Bhéara wasn't there when the glass fish bit me. How could she know what happened to me? She could only know what happened if she did what only the Cailleach Bhéara could do—something evil. With this realization, fear overcame Pearse. He wanted to leap to his feet, grab Tierney, and run away. The thought of being touched by a witch was now more than he could bear.

Staring at the hovering hand, Pearse shook his head. "No. No!" he pleaded, his voice frayed and eyes wild with fear. "Do not touch me—Bhéara!"

"It's alright—don't be afraid," whispered Valerie. "I only wanted to help you relax," she reasoned with Pearse, holding both hands up where he could see them. "Don't worry. I don't need to touch you to heal you," she promised.

You do not need to touch me to heal me? What kind of witchcraft is this? Pearse's eyebrows raised, and he relaxed just a little bit. But he didn't take his eyes off the old woman for a moment. He was too afraid to blink.

"I can show you; you don't even have to close your eyes. Just watch, and it will be done in a moment. It's easy. Then you can walk again," the witch said soothingly. She waited patiently for Pearse's answer as he weighed his options.

Pearse felt pulled in two different directions. *I hate the thought of being touched by the Bhéara,* he realized. *People say they worship evil spirits, eat children, and should be killed. This one looks like the Bhéara but claims to be a healer. What can I believe? Can she be trusted?*

Immediately he pushed those thoughts aside. *My life is over—unless I can walk again, my family will surely starve! I cannot move or feel anything below my neck. But this woman who claims to be a healer has been delivered to my doorstep. Do I turn her away? Or do I believe she tells the truth? Does it matter? I am already dead!*

Pearse listened to the howling wind outside the little shelter and the sound of the bucking tent skins. An occasional snowflake made its way into the smokey space, and he knew that time was short. The Bearnán Éile ridge and his home was a hard day's march distant, but he couldn't walk. *I will die here unless something can be done. I must accept the woman's help.*

The shelter shook and shuddered as the wind whistled through the tent. Pushing aside his fear, Pearse nodded his approval. She was close now, just inches away. He saw his image reflected in her eyes, dark pools of flowing nothingness that grabbed hold and drew him in. He let go and felt her take control, and his bones suddenly warmed as blackness enveloped him. But only for a moment.

The wind abruptly died outside the tent, and the shelter lay still. The hollow silence of the deep rushed in, washing him away in its irresistible current. Pearse felt himself sinking, his body becoming heavier, then nothing at all. For a frightening moment, all physical sensation faded away as if he no longer existed, drawn into the midst of the ebullient depths. For one terrifying moment, Pearse felt as if he had been released from the bonds of existence, freed of the constraints of reality, and then—

And then everything rushed back in on him like the crash of a broaching wave. Pearse knew he had returned when the howl of the wind resumed its loud grappling with the tent. The healer backed away, waiting silently for his reaction. Feeling returned, first to Pearse's hands, then to the arms, and finally his legs. Although left with a strong sense of *déjà vu*, he felt good, normal, as if nothing terrible had ever happened. Pearse was thrilled, amazed, and relieved all at the same time.

He lay still for a moment blinking his eyes, savoring the moment his body came back to life. Feeling better now, he sat up, testing his fingers and toes for sensitivity. *I feel rejuvenated!* Pearce had been fearful of permanent paralysis or a long recovery, so being instantly healed came unexpectedly. In his mind, the only explanation he could relate to was magic, but it wasn't anything malevolent. He could see that now.

The woman wielded a magic unknown to him, but he believed she had been truthful with him. Pearse understood the woman was indeed a healer, not the Cailleach Bhéara as he had assumed her to be. Any remaining doubts about her authenticity had evaporated the moment the feelings returned to his extremities.

Sheepishly Pearse eyed the healer, remorse stabbing at his gut for the harsh accusations hurled at one he now saw as an innocent, a healer, his savior, just as she had claimed to be. The embarrassment he felt for the terror he had shown colored his face. Pearse judged himself harshly, choking back the vile flavor of cowardice, which in his world smacked of an inexcusable breach of manhood.

Now the healer had his respect and admiration. Pearse wanted to express his gratitude for saving his life and, inadvertently, the lives of his loved ones. He wanted to thank her but couldn't find the words. At that moment, he vowed never again to call the woman a witch and sing her praises to anyone who would listen.

The old woman smiled, put her hand on his forearm, gripping it tightly, then wordlessly left the shelter and reseated herself opposite the boy. Tierney looked at her expectantly, but she remained silent. *Tell me,* his mind pleaded. *Please tell me my father will be alright!*

"Well? Have you healed my father?" Tierney asked impatiently, his watery eyes filled with fear.

Still, the old woman remained silent. Tierney was thrilled when, a moment later, his father appeared from the shelter. The boy jumped up and hugged him hard for a long moment as the visitors exchanged satisfied glances between them.

Carefully Pearse sat beside his son and gathered his thoughts before speaking. "You are a great healer, old woman. I thank you," he said, bowing his head, offering her honor and appreciation.

"My name is Valerie, remember?" she said, seemingly amused by being referred to as an "old woman."

"Valyri," he allowed, "our people can use a good healer such as you. Will you stay?"

Yes, stay, Pearse thought. *Although you are an old woman with dead eyes, please stay!* He and his people would have to get accustomed to such a frightening sight as this, but Pearse was sure it would be worthwhile. The benefits of having a capable healer in the clan definitely outweighed the awful presence of those dead eyes.

"I know, Pearse," Valerie agreed. "The ship will be leaving soon, but I will be staying here with you." Once said, the healer turned and repeated those words to Hafian Tohm in English, who immediately recoiled.

"What!?" Tohm exploded, jumping to his feet. "You can't do that! This planet is hostile. You must return with us!"

"Tohm, don't you realize? We *are* home," Valerie fired back.

"What do you mean, home?" he said, looking wounded. He had known her far too long not to recognize one of her riddles when he heard it, but this one had him both puzzled and deeply concerned.

"Just that, Hafian. We are *home*—on Earth, but nearly seven thousand years in the past. I brought us here, and I will see that you get back home safely. But I am staying here."

"Seven thousand!" Tohm gasped. He grabbed his head, then dropped to the ground as if his legs had failed him, a stunned look on his face. The guards gaped at each other as if they should do something but knew better than to try to force The Ring Bearer to do anything she didn't want to do. Their assignment was to protect her, nothing more.

"Then why did you bring me here?" Tohm demanded.

"You are a loyal friend, Hafian. I needed a witness. A lot of people are going to be asking questions and looking for me. I need you to tell them what happened and why."

"Alright, tell me. What happened and why," he snapped, the hurt in his voice evident.

Valerie stared, then drew in a deep breath. She rose and began pacing, which helped her gather her thoughts. "Last week," she began, "Guyidian received a message from the BRU indicating the Boecki have begun taking prisoners. They've never taken prisoners because they are so arrogant they never care what other species know or don't know. But now that has changed. In addition to taking prisoners, they interrogate them, which changes everything. The BRU believes it is a sign they are desperate for resources."

"What amazes me is we've kept them in check for over a thousand years, but only now are they finally getting the picture they need to take us seriously if they ever want to expand the Dominion into our sector of the galaxy."

As if she was dream-walking, Valerie kept pacing, immersed in her own thoughts. "This change in strategy is significant, a departure from—"

Tohm interrupted. "So, what's that got to do with you staying here?"

Realizing she had gone off-topic, Valerie ceased pacing, returned to Tohm's side, sat back down, and was silent for a moment before responding.

"The Dominion has mobilized its entire fleet. For the first time, they know who to look for and where. They are determined to hunt me down and eliminate me. We can hide, but it's only a matter of time before they catch us."

Tohm stared at her, speechless. He couldn't disagree; the implications were stunning. If the entire might of the Imperium was looking for them, they were surely doomed.

"I'm more than three thousand years old," she continued. "I'm getting close to my end, but I'm safe here in this time. I can help these people, and I can protect you and the crew at the same time. I'm staying, and that's that," she said firmly.

Tohm rubbed the back of his neck as he weighed the facts. Although this news was hard to swallow, he couldn't argue because he believed what was said. They couldn't defend themselves against a massed force of Boecki ships. Drastic action was in order, such as what The Ring Bearer intended to do now. Her plan was genius; it would be impossible for them to find her if she was hiding in the past— which made him wonder, what if she hid in the future?

"I agree, hiding in the past is brilliant. But why not hide in the future?"

"Because the Hesaurun Rings come to me from the *past*, not the future."

Tohm gulped. "What?"

"Back in the 21st century, I fought for and won the rings. If I hid in the future, I might never receive them from my ancestors. It would be a time paradox; in other words, if I kill my father before I'm born, I fail to exist, right? These people sitting here with us now *are* my ancestors. If I'm right—and I believe I am—I will be reborn in the twenty-first century and receive the rings once again through these people sitting right here."

She turned to Tohm, who was staring at her indecisively. "Don't you see? That's why I need to stay here. Do you understand?"

Tohm gazed at her, wide-eyed. He felt his face grow hot. "Let me get this straight. Do you plan to be reborn in the twenty-first century? How are you going to pull that off—if you're *dead!*"

"I don't have to pull anything off. This is the past, our past, remember? Nature will take its course. I will live out the rest of my life in this time frame, and when the time comes, I will be born again. Just like I was the first time."

"That is a big gamble," Tohm argued.

"I don't think so. I think it is a sure bet."

"What makes you think that?"

"It's an absolute. I have confirmed my assumptions by calling on my past and future self. Plus, I have left enough Easter eggs along the way to avoid every significant mistake I ever made. I have all the proof I need to know that I am right. I wouldn't try it otherwise."

"Do you know what's wrong with all of this?" said Tohm. "I actually understand it," he laughed. "I just hope you are right!" With a smirk, he then added, "Guyidian is going to be furious, which makes it worth doing all by itself."

They laughed together, then Valerie stood, eager to get going. The old friends hugged, then she kissed his cheek.

"I will miss you dearly, Hafian," she said, her eyes wet now, and she meant it.

"Me too," he said. "Just one thing. Why are you bringing your cat?"

Valerie turned her eyes to the animal crate, mustering a sly smile. "I'll tell you later."

"I hope so," he said thoughtfully, ending the embrace. Then Valerie instructed Tohm and the guards to stay put until they were over the crater wall.

"We need to leave before Guyidian figures out what's going on and comes after us," she announced.

Pearse and Tierney wanted to avoid offending their new friends, so they sat quietly during the debate between the healer and her companions without understanding a single word. Nevertheless, the gist of the conversation was obvious—when the healer told them she would be leaving with them, the yellow man objected.

Valerie quickly explained a simplified version of the conversation to Pearse and Tierney in their language.

"Pearse, we're going to go to your home now," Valerie proclaimed.

"But we cannot make it before dark," he protested.

"Yes, we can," she assured him, then knelt and reached into one of her bags, removing three solar torches. Valerie stood holding them out for Pearse and Tierney to see.

"These torches will light the way for us," she declared.

"Torches?" they exclaimed as one, their gazes darting between the healer's dark eyes and the gadgets being offered.

The connection between those small silver rectangles and the firebrands they were familiar with was entirely lost on them.

"Take them—they won't bite," Valerie said, handing the torches out. Pearse and Tierney stared at their devices as if they might indeed bite. Tierney held his up for closer inspection, squeezing it lightly between thumb and forefinger, frowning as if it was something foul.

"It's alright," she insisted. "Let me show you."

Valerie flipped the torch over in her hand then pushed a button that turned it on. The device clicked on, producing a brilliant beam bathing the entire area around the tent in sunlight.

Startled at first by what they considered sunlight in a box, Pearse and Tierney laughed nervously, then eagerly clawed at their devices to turn them on. Once they had their solar torches lit, they laughed as the intense light beam played on the ground, in the sky, on the tent, and—much to the dismay of the men still sitting on the ground—in their eyes. Soon Pearse and Tierney were dancing about joyfully like a couple of wild aboriginal tribesmen. Valerie got into the game by showing them how to make rabbit ears and bird shadows on the side of the tent.

"What's going on out there?" Guyidian's voice chirped over the guard's communicators. "Looks like a damn light parade!"

"They're just having a little fun with solar torches, Commander," the guard replied with a laugh.

"Well, tell The Ring Bearer to knock it off and get back in here. It's dusk, and I do not want her out there after dark. It isn't safe," Guyidian barked.

"Yes, sir!" the guard responded sheepishly.

"Party's over, Valerie," Tohm hollered, calling an immediate end to the fun they were having with the lights. "Guyidian is getting impatient. If you are going to go, you best get on with it."

"Party pooper!" Valerie laughed, then explained to Pearse and Tierney that they needed to get packed and ready to go as quickly as possible. Valerie said her final goodbyes to Tohm and the guards as they packed up. When Pearse and Tierney were prepared to go, she grabbed her bags and Orson's crate, and they set off for the crater's wall.

Alone atop the berm, Valerie turned for one last look at the gleaming ship in the distance. The day's fading light played on its silvery skin. Inside the crate, Orson gave out a high-pitched wail. The bitter wind grappled with Valerie's clothing and stung her face. Her throat tightened, and her chest swelled as she regarded the *Dreamer* wistfully. The vessel had been her home for so long she could barely remember when it hadn't been. To say she was about to leave part of herself behind would be an understatement.

The ship had served its purpose well and would continue doing so long after she was gone. She found solace in knowing it would outlive her and was confident she would see it again—*Although, in another life,* she told herself. Still, walking away from it was one of the most difficult decisions she would ever make. But she considered change the nature of things and steeled herself.

Needing one last look, she glanced around. Tohm and the guards were still visible in the growing dusk, sitting beside Pearse and Tierney's former campsite. She admired them for that. They waited there patiently, obediently, devotedly, just as she had asked. Their fierce loyalty was the only thing holding them there, which they proved by obeying her final request.

Valerie knew it would be hard for them to let her go, especially for Tohm, who had been her constant companion for more than thirty years. But he knew a time such as this would come; they'd discussed it together on multiple occasions. Now it was a shared reality, a pain shared, they would be forced to deal with separately.

Poor Hafian! she murmured to herself. She had thought seriously about asking Hafian to join her in this new adventure but knew he would accept, which wouldn't be fair to him. Hafian Tohm had his own life to live, and she couldn't deprive him of it. She believed he knew that and hoped he wouldn't hate her for it.

Then she recalled the many loved ones she had left behind during her long lifetime. However, there were too many to count and far too many names and faces to remember. The hurt of their loss would linger in her heart and mind forever, their memories a burden she would endure every day of her life. Leaving good people and loved ones behind was the brutal reality of outliving them. *Valerie reminded herself that it was always the same*; there was no choice, and this time was no different. She was getting good at it, a fact she hated to admit.

From his crate, Orson wailed sadly again. Valerie raised an arm to wave goodbye to her friends. In the distance, she saw the three men rise to their feet, returning the gesture enthusiastically. Elated, she waved harder, returning their enthusiasm. Then she realized she waved goodbye, not just to Tohm and the guards but also to *The Dreamer* and those within it. Then joy turned to tears as she turned away, stepping into the howling wind and the next chapter of her life.

The hunters did not have long to wait before Amon's hunch that there would be plenty more to see turned out to be spot-on. They watched in amazement as an aperture at the side of the spacecraft slid open, revealing a brightly lit corridor inside the vessel. Amon clucked and nodded his head knowingly; he had been right to wait.

Moments later, a detachment of four identically-uniformed crew members—three men and a small woman—appeared in the doorway. When the team stepped outside, the hunters noticed they immediately huddled together as if they were already cold. The hunters laughed and elbowed one another, scoffing at these people for their assumed weakness. Irritated by that, Amon gestured angrily at them to be quiet and stay down. Being detected by these strange people could mean trouble.

Any fool could see why these people got cold so quickly, thought Amon. *The stranger's clothing was thin and skin-tight.* In his experience, these uniforms broke every rule for cold-weather clothing. He could not guess why anyone would dress so foolishly in cold weather. *And those bright colors! Are they trying to attract bears?*

Amon didn't know what to make of the strange vessel either. He did not understand it, so he pushed thoughts of it aside until he had more information. Instead, he focused his attention on the people outside of it. Amon correctly identified these people as foreigners unfamiliar with their surroundings, judging by their unusual clothing and demeanor, which did not make them weak—it made them strangers.

In his estimation, these people were soldiers, but the woman appeared to command the men, which puzzled him. He knew why men were leaders and why other men followed them. Amon was a leader and expected to lead, not due to privilege but because of his strength, experience, and decision-making abilities. He knew how to stay alive in the wilderness and keep others alive by sharing his knowledge and skills.

But he was mystified why a small woman like this one had authority over the soldiers? *Surely,* he reasoned, *any one of these men should be able to best her in a fight. So why would they follow the small woman's lead?*

After some discussion, the woman separated the group into two pairs. What happened next caused the hunter to question these strangers' sanity.

One team took long sticks and proceeded to rub the top part of the vessel with them. The other team, a pair of soldiers, used shorter sticks to do the same thing on the vessel's lower sections. In this way, the two teams moved methodically along both sides of the ship, rubbing every part of it thoroughly. Once the inspectors completed their odd rubbing of the starboard side, they moved to the port side and beyond sight of the hunters.

"What are they doing, worshiping it?" Hethe wondered aloud.

Amon did not answer. When the first team was out of the hunter's line of sight, they assumed the show was over, and it was time to go home. The men began getting ready to travel, but Amon stayed put. *What were those people doing?* he wondered. He believed too many unanswered questions remained about these strangers and their peculiar ways. He wanted to know more, so he intended to stay.

"These people must be crazy!" Amon asserted to the others. "We need to wait and see what they do next."

"We need to *go!*" Jotham groaned, his face flushed, exposing his contempt for Amon.

Amon disagreed. "Darkness will come soon. We will camp here tonight. Pitch your tents; we're staying."

Jotham threw a look to the heavens and snarled. His next objection went unheard when a metallic clank pierced the air, followed by the whirring sound of motors. The four hunters hit the dirt all at once, awestruck as the huge clamshell-shaped cargo doors at the rear of the vessel were separated, opened, and ramp-lowered. When the sounds of moving metal stopped, four more people—three men and a woman—marched down the ramp carrying armloads of packages.

Amon stared in disbelief. Once again, his intuition had proved to be true. Although this group dressed more sensibly, the three men—soldiers Amon assumed, were again led by a woman. *How odd!* he thought. *Why would these men, soldiers apparently, allow themselves to be mastered by women? Were these men slaves? If true, what power did these women hold over the men? And why did the strangers only appear in companies of four?*

Amon was surprised when this group made straight for the boy's tent rather than rubbing sticks on the vessel. No doubt this group wanted to visit with the boy, or he assumed, help him bury his father.

Then Amon noticed this second woman was much different than the first. In addition to being as tall as the soldiers, she carried herself with dignity, and the men gave her obeisance. He then realized the truth—these men were not slaves; they respected the woman. Amon then concluded this woman must rank considerably higher than the first much-smaller woman. He did not know who or what she was, but he determined to learn her secrets at that moment.

The four hunters lined up on the snowbank like crows on a tree branch, observing the procession moving toward the little tent. Once there, the strangers huddled together next to the tent. The tall woman spoke to the boy, and then the woman entered the tent. A few minutes later, she left and sat with her companions. Confusion reigned when the hunters witnessed the man they all saw dead of a lightning strike, followed the tall woman out of the tent, and sat with them.

Baffled by the dead man's unexpected appearance, Amon and his men were dumbfounded; they could not believe what they were seeing. *The tall woman went into the tent, and a few minutes later, the dead man walked out of it—alive! How could this be?* Soon muted whispers turned into a heated argument.

"Isn't that the man who died?" Abiah exclaimed, his voice shrill. "How is he walking now?"

"I saw the smoke! That man was dead a few minutes ago!" Jotham bawled.

"That man doesn't look dead to me," Hethe scoffed.

"The man is dead—and now he is a spirit!" Jotham insisted.

"No, he isn't!" Hethe maintained. "If he were dead, he wouldn't be walking around. Look—he is talking to those people from that big shiny thing, whatever it is, and yet they are not running away yelling and waving their arms in fear. They are *happy*. Look at the boy, hug his father!"

"That man *was* dead! We all saw it!" argued Abiah.

"Will you empty-headed dogs be quiet?" Amon groaned.

The men continued arguing, expressing their deepest fears. All were certain of the facts. Lightning had struck the man as he touched the big shiny thing in the crater. They had witnessed the man's death. After the lightning strike, the body smoked, a sure sign he had perished. Even as the boy dragged him away, the man never moved. And here he was, walking and talking as if nothing had happened. Unbelievable!

It was a mystery, but the unspoken truth was they all believed the tall woman had performed a resurrection on the dead man. Although this belief was unanimous, it remained unsaid for fear of the unknown. Although the word *magic* was on the tip of each man's tongue, the word went unspoken, and the belief that they must have this strange woman who gave life to the dead was unanimous.

This same thought burned in Amon's brain. *Our people suffer from sickness, disease, and injury. Under the circumstances, weren't they obligated to capture her for the benefit of the clan? Wouldn't they be hailed as heroes for taking her?*

Yet fear also gripped Amon's heart. *What if the tall woman is a spirit or a witch?* Some believed that witches were nothing more than something evil to be destroyed. Amon could see beyond fear and superstition because instinct told him more was to be learned about the tall woman. A lot more.

Jotham, however, did not care that the woman healed the man or that she might have resurrected him. All he saw was an evil thing, like a fire to be stamped out. Whatever apparent good she might have done changed nothing. From his point of view, the woman was a worker of magic. And wasn't magic a dark vice to be rooted out and destroyed? Jotham knew what to do and steeled himself for it.

As soon as Amon saw the strangers preparing to leave, he gestured for his men to get ready to move. He did not need to tell them why.

Chapter 6

Corell Paris— May Present-Day

orell Paris was tense, his attention divided between the road and watching the rearview mirrors. The threat of being followed was a real possibility, one he could not ignore. Traffic was heavy, but he drove fast, tailgating and weaving in and out of the commuter lane. This way, anyone attempting to follow Corell and the girl would be quickly exposed. After the first hour, he relaxed and settled into the slow lane.

Valerie watched in silence as Interstate-5 rolled out in front of them. Since leaving Arlington, they had said little to one another. What was spoken between them was abbreviated and stilted. She didn't feel like talking anyway. Plus, her recently acquired, make-believe, doomsday prepper grandfather from Montana seemed to be satisfied driving in silence. Valerie did not like Corell's aggressive driving but understood his concern about being followed, so she didn't object.

Although she didn't know much about Corell Paris, she felt she could trust him. A faint voice, one she relied on, told her she truly could put faith in the man, so she didn't question it. She didn't know why, but Corell Paris felt somehow familiar. *Perhaps it is the shape of his eyes, that high forehead, and his long straight Irish nose,* she thought. His hair was gray now but still held evidence of what once was thick, straight, and black, not unlike her own and her relatives.

She did not mean to stare, but Valerie felt the drumbeats of the distant past in this man's pale blue eyes. She did not realize it just then, but when Valerie looked at Corell Paris, she did not see a stranger; she saw one of her own. Something stirred deep inside, something that was always there but buried so deeply she could not know what it was. Somehow this man made her feel different. She knew there was more but just didn't know what it could be, and yet, it felt right.

Something else—that name, Corell Paris, Valerie thought. *Who has a name like that? It just seems so phony, so made up. If true, and his was an assumed identity, why not pick something more believable? If it were me, I would choose something more believable like Sheldon Cooper or Leonard Hofstadter— anything but Corell Paris. When he chose that name, was he in Paris eating off Corelle dinnerware?* The thought of it brought a smile to her lips, and she decided to ask him about it sometime.

She regarded him questioningly when he passed the Interstate 90 East exit rather than turning toward Montana. *Hadn't he said they were going to Montana? If Montana was not the destination, then where? Shouldn't he have said something about where they were going by now?* Still, she said nothing, realizing it didn't matter where they were going as long as they were safe.

Orson slept on Corell's lap as he drove. The two seemed so comfortable together, so familiar that it aggravated her. The darn cat had been glued to Corell ever since he arrived. She felt left out like she didn't matter. Annoyed by that,

Valerie disconnected from them, staring out the side window as Seattle's scenery slid by.

Corell noticed and studied her wondering about her mood. But he was sympathetic, seeing more than a few valid reasons for her petulance. In a single afternoon, the girl's life had turned upside-down and inside-out. Her home, family, friends, and graduation plans were all thrown aside without notice or proper goodbyes. No doubt, she grieved for them. He saw her struggling with it, so he intended to allow her as much time and space she needed to work things out for herself.

He also worried the girl might push back against his plan to remove her from the threat Stone represented. Despite saying nothing about it, she appeared to be on a precipice. What if she demanded to be returned home? He didn't know what he could say or do to prevent that from happening. He needed to say something but decided to give her a little more time. He would wait until they were through Seattle before breaking the silence.

As soon as the vast metropolis was behind them, Corell made his move. "Valerie, are you alright?" he inquired sympathetically.

"Sure," she said, with little conviction, firing a dirty look at Orson. "Can I text my friends?"

"Yes, but tonight only, and no phone calls, alright? If it rings don't answer. Cell phones can be traced, so power it down and give it to me when you are done texting. That will eliminate any temptation you might have to do more texting or answer it. We cannot give away our location under any circumstances."

"Really? I can't have my phone?!" Valerie shrieked. "That is not fair!"

"Yes, *really*, and you know why, so please don't act like I am being unreasonable. Your life, the lives of your family and friends, may depend on how well you make yourself untraceable. Understood?"

Sighing heavily, Valerie nodded, frowning. "That's harsh," she mumbled.

"Never forget that Stone is determined to get this ring," Corell said, holding up his right hand for her to see. "He would have no problem killing either one of us to get it. His only reason for living right now is to get this ring."

"He already has one, doesn't he?

"Yes, and he killed to get it; don't forget that. But he wants all five of them, which puts us on his shortlist. He thinks that if he were able to get all five, he would be immortal."

"Would he?"

"Almost. He would live for a very long time, but not forever," said Corell without taking his eyes from the road. In his lap, Orson reacted to the news with a loud purr.

"Now listen," Corell continued, "if you are going to text your friends, you need to remember your cover story. You are going to Montana with your grandfather and staying the summer. Grampa is a doomsday prepper who does not want people to know where his place is. You have no idea where it is other than Montana. You will be back in the fall at the UW and see your friends then. You will be off-the-grid, so your phone will be out of service until you return. That's the message you need to send."

Valerie considered his words staring blankly at her phone. She didn't like it but nodded her consent.

Corell placed a supportive hand on her shoulder. "Valerie, I know this is hard for you, but you must be sure not to give any indication of where you are. That includes restaurants, gas stations, and scenery. If you see a pink elephant, keep it to yourself. Alright?"

Valerie snickered at that, then decided it was for the best and began texting in earnest. She started with her closest friends, including Darcy, Jack, Emily, Jim, and Angie. But after those few, she was stumped. She knew many people but didn't feel like any of them were close enough that she needed to communicate this news to them. *My social circle is so small*, she thought, then went back through her contact list with a grim realization. *I have so few friends!*

Feeling alone and miserable, Valerie powered down her phone and returned to brooding. But it wasn't long before she made up her mind to pull herself out of her funk and reconnect with Corell. She wanted to know more about this mysterious man, so she decided to dig deeper.

"Are you, my grandfather?"

Corell gave her a hard look before answering, appraising the girl as if reluctant to answer the question.

"I guess that I am," he admitted, then turning his eyes back to the road added, "but many times removed. Too many to count. I am over thirteen hundred years old."

To his chagrin, Valerie snickered. "Really?" she exclaimed with raised eyebrows. She put a finger to her lips as if slyly thinking it over. "So— you were born in the eighth century?"

"The *seventh* century. But who's counting?"

Valerie sat back and rolled her eyes. *The seventh century,* she thought. *This story just keeps getting better! How deep is this rabbit hole anyway? Maybe I should ask him a question to test him, ask something that he would have seen or experienced back then. But what?*

Slowly it came to her that Corell might be telling the truth. *What was the world like that far back?* She remembered just one thing from her studies: a lot was happening in the Middle East. According to textbooks, the seventh century was all about Muhammad's wars and that he died about then. She thought hard but was unable to think of anything else. But being European, there was no way Corell would be part of that anyway. Finally, she gave up and decided to say what was really on her mind.

"I am sorry, but that's pretty hard to believe."

"Believe it," Corell shot back without a hitch.

"Then give me a reason."

Corell groaned, his hands tightening on the steering wheel. "Look, I *can't* prove I was born in the seventh century. Back then, we didn't have birth certificates or picture identification! But you don't need a reason, and you know it," he exclaimed.

"What do you mean?"

"I mean, stop asking questions about me and search yourself. Look at what's inside Valerie Dunne because that's where the answers lie. This is all about *you*—don't think for a minute any of this is about me."

Corell continued. "Ask yourself this, what happened when you were four years old? Sure, your folks died, but there was more—a lot more. Who saved you from Stone? Your folks were already gone, which left just you and Stone all alone together in the dark that night, and with no one to defend you. Who saved you? Think about that, then ask me again."

Geeze, I didn't mean to get him riled. Valerie thought. *But I see his point. I remember it like it was yesterday. The yard was all torn up, my mom and dad were gone, and that huge ugly man did it to them. I hated him for that—I still do. I remember he wanted to hurt me too—but that is it, there is nothing more than that.*

Valerie looked at Corell apprehensively. *He has a valid point. Who saved me? There was no one else there; I would have remembered that! So how did I ever come out of that alive? Is he implying that my four-year-old self pulled a rabbit out of my hat and saved me?*

Valerie laughed. "Sorry, you're right. I remember that day, but I just cannot remember anything that happened afterward. I just don't know how I avoided being killed, too."

"I have a sneaking hunch that you will remember—and soon," Corell insisted. "That's why I am with you now."

"How did you know about me, anyway?"

"Well," sighed Corell. "You and I are connected through the ring. You will see. I have been certain you are heir to the ring ever since Colin died."

Valerie scoffed at that. She didn't understand how Corell could possibly know that. It sounded impossible, just more nonsense. She did not believe in telepathy, either. But what he said made her feel uncomfortable because if it was true, what more might he know about her?

Then her thoughts turned back to the ring Corell wore on his right thumb. She could see it; the ring was on his right thumb as he drove. She had seen girls wearing thumb rings but never a man. It seemed out of place for an older man to wear a thumb ring. *Weren't older people usually more conservative about such things?*

The ring was a simple thing, a dirty brown band with five insignias pressed into its face. It looked like cheap dollar store jewelry, the sort of chintzy trinket one might expect to come out of a fifty-cent plastic egg. She judged it to be the sort of thing no one would bother to pick up if they stepped on it.

"So that's the fifth ring, right?" she asked, gesturing to Corell's thumb. "Are you going to give it to me?"

"That's the plan, but not immediately. You have a lot to learn before then," Corell said.

"Like what?"

"Like—take a look at this," he said, pulling a leather booklet from his jacket breast pocket and handing it to her. "Read it," he said, "then we'll talk."

Valerie took the book, opened it to the first page, then gasped.

"Why does it say it's from Valerie Dunne? I didn't write it!"

"Actually, you *did* write it," Corell insisted. "See the date?"

Valerie squinted hard, bringing the book closer so she could see it better in the dwindling light. "Yes, it says August 3, 2409, BCE. Do you mean it was written by a relative, someone with the same name as me? Right?" she said, her voice hopeful. But she already knew the answer.

"No. You wrote it in 2409 BCE."

"What does BCE mean?"

"It means before our common era or before Christ."

"Are you kidding me?" exclaimed Valerie, her face contorted into an unfamiliar mask. "That's crazy!" she insisted. "I didn't write it! I'm not a time traveler!"

"You wrote it more than forty-five hundred years ago."

"Come on, that's not funny."

"Read it. Ask yourself if you could have written it. Then decide if you think it makes sense."

"Alright, I will," Valerie challenged, holding the little leather-bound book up to the light. After scrutinizing both sides, she began leafing through a few pages.

Utterly perplexed, she put the book down. "There is no way this thing is 4500 years old. It looks brand new," she said skeptically.

"It's printed on materials from the fortieth century. You must have brought the materials with you."

"Now, I know you're messing with me," Valerie laughed.

But those words caused her to pause as she continued inspecting the little book. Its materials did seem exceptionally durable. The brown cover had the look and feel of leather, although her fingernail would not scratch it no matter how hard she pressed. The lightweight paper was bright white, fine-textured, and refused to crease when folded despite her best efforts. These unusual qualities piqued her interest, so she began reading in earnest.

Corell's black Suburban continued south in silence for the next hour as Valerie read the book. At the Oregon border, she closed it and wordlessly returned it to Corell. Once across the Interstate Bridge, Paris stopped at a truck stop to refuel. They went inside, grabbed hotdogs and coffee, then drove on. Still, she said nothing about the book or its contents.

Corell continued to be patient, waiting for Valerie to break the silence that had grown between them. He expected her to question him about what she had read, but the girl seemed to be holding back, working it out in her mind, so he gave her the time and space needed to ruminate on it. He reasoned that she would say so if she rejected the story outright, but she didn't, and he considered it a good sign. She remained silent, staring out the window for miles as they continued southward into the night.

When they reached Eugene, Oregon, Valerie finally spoke. "How far are we going tonight?"

"My place is still about an hour and a half out. But if you are tired, you are welcome to crawl in back and get some sleep—if you choose." Corell smiled thoughtfully.

"No, thank you, I'm good," she said softly.

"I think you'll like my place." Corell said, trying to keep her talking. "It's on the Applegate River near Jacksonville; you will have your own room. It's safe and secure. A doomsday prepper like you will love it!" he joked.

Valerie nodded, smiling at his reference to being a doomsday prepper. "You're the prepper, remember?"

"True," he admitted easily. "Just not in Montana."

"It's a strange story," Valerie mused, referring to the book. "It seems possible, but I don't see anything in it that would make me believe I ever had anything to do with it."

Corell gave her a polite smile. Then Valerie pulled herself up against the dashboard, her arms crossed as she searched Corell's features. "Unless you are trying to tell me I've lived twice," she said pointedly. The question was locked and loaded. Their eyes met for a moment as Corell considered his response, and Valerie waited, eagerly anticipating the answer.

"No," he said, returning his eyes to the road. "You have lived one lifetime. That is a fact," he assured her.

"And no, you have not been reborn, either. You are living the only life you will ever live. However, it seems your lifespan will be divided between two entirely different time periods thousands of years apart."

Valerie's face seemed frozen in an expression of dawning comprehension. "Think of it this way," Corell went on. "By going back in time, you created a time loop and essentially became your own ancestor. You did that for two reasons: first, so you could escape the aliens who would have eventually killed you and won the war, and second, so you could apply what you learned during your first go-around in the future. With that advantage, you expect to win the war this time."

In his mind, Corell saw the whole plan. "It was brilliant, really," he marveled. "Now you have begun your life. But it is not a rebirth; your future self has involved your former self in a time loop. Do you understand?"

Valerie stared dumbly at Corell as if he was speaking a foreign language. Her eyes blinked, her mouth moved, but no sound came out. Over-communicated and overwhelmed, she fell back in the seat, struggling to reconcile that concept mentally.

"I'll take that as a no," Corell chuckled. "And I get it," he admitted. "It's a complicated story because it involves the future, the past, and time manipulation. My father told me that you were from the distant future although you wrote the book in the past. According to him, you were more than three thousand years old when you wrote that book. For the record, you wrote one book for each ring. So, this book is unique. It is one of one."

"How could your father know that?" Valerie said skeptically.

"His father Amos received the ring from Pearse, who received it directly from an old woman named Valerie Dunne –*that's you, in your future*. The story is reliable; it's history. *You* will be that old woman in the distant future.

"And here is another mind-bender: there are only four ring bearers between you, now, and yourself 3000 years old. The line of descent begins with Valerie Dunne, then Pearse, Amos, Bede, and me. Now here you are again, and we are back to you. The span of time is roughly 4500 years."

Valerie closed her eyes and sighed. Corell could see that her head was swirling. *Time to spit the rest of it out now,* he told himself.

"The ring," he continued, "was passed down to me by my father, so I have had it for about thirteen-hundred years. He said I should expect you to appear in this time period. His account handed down through me is reliable because he knew Amos, who knew Pearse, who received the ring from you."

Corell sensed that poor Valerie's brain was about to explode. "So how did Valerie," she stopped, then corrected herself, "I mean, how did that version of me get it in the first place?"

"Get *them*," Corell corrected. "You started out with all five rings. Before your death, you gifted one ring to each of the five Pearse family members, knowing they would be passed down through the Dunne family line. As you have read, you did it that way to dilute the power and prevent any one person from becoming a tyrant."

"But that doesn't tell me how I got them. Where did those rings come from?"

"I'll explain in detail later, but for now, all you need to know is that you get the fifth ring from me. The fifth ring is the most important of them because it is the master of the five. It includes all the capabilities of the other four *combined*, plus its own unique abilities. It cannot be defeated by any other ring or combination of them. It works like a lens, magnifying the combined power of the five. Like the book says, only when they come together in one person, the rightful owner, does their power reach its full potential.

"But never forget the ring can still be stolen and that you can be killed for it. You will never be immortal or invincible. The ring, however, is both immortal and invincible. It cannot be cut, bent, melted, or altered in any way. It is indestructible. Throwing it into a furnace or hitting it with a sledgehammer will not affect it."

"How long did I live—when I was in the past—I mean, do you know what happened to me back then?" Valerie stammered, unsure she wanted to know the truth about her end.

"I'm sorry, I don't know. And my father didn't know, either. I asked."

Valerie sighed miserably. "I understand. You look like you are in your fifties. How old were you when your father gave it to you?"

"I forget the exact year, but I was in my early twenties. My father was a good man, an historian. I served him as an aid until his death."

Valerie sat quietly, thinking. "The name Bede sounds familiar; I seem to remember the name from history class. Was his last name Dunne? Is *your* last name Dunne?"

"Yes, to both," Corell confirmed. "The name Bede is well-known to historians, although the name Bede Dunne is not. He didn't use it, and neither do I."

"Why not?"

"Certain people know about the rings and would try to get them if they knew how to find me. Early on, one of the rings was stolen along with its booklet. That book was copied, so reproductions exist. In the wrong person's hands, a ring could be used to set someone up as a king or dictator. I have seen it myself."

Valerie's eyes glinted up at him, puzzled. Orson gave him the same odd look as Corell continued. "The booklet is a two-edged sword, vital because it provides the necessary information to the owner of a ring, but it hides nothing. We must be careful. Right now, only two of the rings are in the hands of the rightful owners, and Stone is our biggest threat with two of the rings. If he were to end up with all five of them, he could rule the planet for thousands of years."

"Two-edged sword?" Valerie's eyes narrowed.

"A metaphor for a powerful weapon. A two-edged sword cuts on both edges, so it cuts either way you swing it."

Valerie took a few minutes to run the story through her truth filter. She was pretty sure she remembered learning about an English historian named Bede in history class. Her thoughts swirled, then she thought Bede might have been her grandson, grandfather, or maybe both. In a flash, she realized if any of this was true, the same would apply to Corell. And what would that mean for her? Did that make her her own grandmother and granddaughter at the same time? This was too much! She covered her eyes with her hands, feeling like they just might point in opposite directions.

Paris was barely visible in the dark SUV, the only available light provided by the instrument panel. She focused on him while driving with Orson asleep on his lap. The man appeared to be completely normal with no outward clue to extreme age. Judging by his appearance, she guessed he could pass for fifty, sixty at the most, which made her wonder about the ring's effect on time and aging. She wondered about that, so she decided to ask.

"Can you travel in time?" Valerie asked tentatively.

"No," Corelle said bluntly.

"But Valerie could?"

"Yes, but remember, she had all five rings. It seems you are destined to acquire all five rings, completing the circle."

"Circle? What circle?"

"The time loop," Corell reminded her. "The one you created when you went back to live with Pearse and his family."

Creating time loops sounded like dangerous business to Valerie, if possible, something to avoid. But if that was her destiny, she decided she would have to prepare herself for that eventuality.

"Does that mean I have to go back in time to do what she did?"

"Not necessarily," he reasoned. "It is a problem you will have to solve yourself. Whether you go or do not go, I can see the potential for a paradox either way. You know what a time paradox is, right?"

"Yeah," she nodded, "That would be like, a butterfly effect. Like if I killed my own father, would I still exist— right?"

"Exactly," Corell confirmed. "You could change everything if you go—or if you decide not to go. It's a problem any way you slice it."

"When someone time-travels, are there two people, or one?"

"Good question. But no, just one. We're almost there," Corell informed her. "Let's get settled in tonight, then talk about it in the morning over coffee."

"How did you know I drink coffee?"

"Old people know stuff," he said with a sly smile.

"From the way Orson has been acting, I thought you were going to say the cat told you," Valerie quipped.

The Suburban exited the Interstate, then followed a poorly lit two-lane country road for ten minutes. Then it left the two-lane and pulled onto what Valerie thought appeared to be a seldom-used dirt track in the woods. She followed the headlights as they illuminated the way through the darkness thick with dense foliage and a mixture of tall trees and ferns. The SUV's headlights fell upon a large tree blocking the trail about one hundred yards in.

"There's a tree down!" Cried in alarm, pointing at the massive log blockade. "How are we going to get past that?"

"See this?" Corell said, a remote in his hand. "We're going to push this little button right here. It's a magic button—so don't be alarmed when you wake up in Kansas," he winked. A click of the button later, the big log split in half like a drawbridge with the two halves rising high into the air.

With the roadblock out of the way, the Suburban continued along the trail.

"I told you old people know stuff," he said as the big log returned to its original position behind them.

"That you do, old-timer," Valerie conceded with a smile.

Moments later, motion sensor-activated lights blazed, illuminating the forest around them. Now a high wire fence topped by razor wire blocked their way. A pair of uniformed guards dressed in camo-fatigues approached each side of the Suburban as it rolled to a stop.

Valerie's heart leaped in her chest as she realized the stone-faced sentry peering in her window held an automatic weapon, a lightweight thing with a skeleton stock and long curved ammunition clip hanging from it. The gun was camouflage, the same as the uniform. Her eyes widened when she realized the guard's finger rested on the trigger guard and that in a fraction of a second, it could be turned and fired.

"Good evening, Smithers," Corell said as he lowered his window. Valerie noticed the name tag on the soldier's uniform identified him as Eastman. Nevertheless, he did not look amused or respond until he and his partner had a thorough look inside the vehicle. Once satisfied all was in order, Eastman's eyes softened, then he smiled.

"Good evening, Mr. Paris. So, it's Smithers this time? Have you been watching the Simpsons?"

"No, but If I didn't call you something different each time, how would you know it was really me? I could be a phony!" he joked for Valerie's benefit.

"Good point, sir. Good evening, miss Dunne," Eastman said, welcoming her personally. "I hope you had a good trip."

"I did, thank you." Valerie smiled, relieved by the guard's soft eyes and pleasant voice despite his previously stiff military demeanor. She wondered how Eastman knew her name, finally deciding that the guards must have had advance notice of her presence. *But how?* she wondered. *I have been with Corell every second since I got home from school, and he never made a call or text to anyone. Was this just one of many side-tunnels in the rabbit hole?*

"Another pet, Mister Paris?" Eastman said, eyeing the big tabby sleeping peacefully on Corell's lap.

"He's mine!" Valerie fired back, a little more aggressively than intended.

Eastman said nothing more, then waved at someone in the guard shack. The gates clanked, then slid open, allowing the Suburban to roll through. Once past the gate, the sky above them opened up, revealing a large clearing with several buildings illuminated in the distance.

Now paved, the road was lined by vintage streetlights evenly spaced along the curbed drive's sides, leading to the main structure that Valerie assumed to be Corell's home. Corell parked the SUV in front of the main entrance.

As Valerie climbed out of the vehicle, she was happy to have the opportunity to stand and stretch her tight muscles. It had been a long day and a long trip. Valerie saw something that bothered her in the dim light beyond the house: the form of another armed guard walking beside a dog. From the car, she heard Orson snarl.

"Quiet, Orson, that dog's not going to harm you," Corell said, half-smiling.

"Security is so tight here," Valerie marveled. "Back at the gate, I saw a squirrel give you a dirty look."

"Figures. That one is no good. He throws acorns at me when I'm not looking." Corell said dryly.

The house was a large two-story, Dutch Tudor-style home with a mixture of red brick and off-white shiplap exterior siding and green trim. A high-pitched roof with several windowed gables overlooked the turn-around drive. Although the home and gardens were beautiful, they were not overly formal. Valerie liked that.

An athletic-looking woman in her early forties pushed the heavy wooden door open, then obligingly stood beside it as Corell, followed closely by Valerie, entered the foyer.

"Good evening, Corell, and welcome, Valerie. I am April," the woman declared, holding out a welcoming hand for Valerie to shake. "I've heard so much about you," she said warmly, although businesslike.

"And who do we have here?" April smiled broadly, referring to Valerie's big cat in her arms.

"April, this is Orson. Orson, meet April." Valerie held out one of the cat's forepaws for April, who took the cue and shook it. They both chuckled.

"Let me help you with your bags. I'll show you to your room." April invited.

"Thank you; it's good to meet you, April." Valerie returned, smiling warmly. "And thank you, Corell. Your home is beautiful," said Valerie admiringly.

As the two women turned to climb the stairs, Corell called to Valerie, "You're welcome! Make yourself at home. It's late, so I will see you in the morning."

April led Valerie into a room at the head of the stairs, a small suite with hardwood floors covered with thick forest green throw rugs, matching floral wallpaper, and furniture.

The room had an undeniably feminine feel to it. Warm night air drifting through the open dormer windows moved white lace curtains slightly.

April set Valerie's bags down inside a walk-in closet next to a full-size private bathroom, then provided brief instructions on how the heat, air-conditioning, and fixtures in the room worked.

"I am the house manager," said April. "Call me if you need anything—anytime. Just press #, then 1 on the phone to reach me. You can call up food from the kitchen 24/7 by dialing # 2. Dial # 3 for housekeeping. I can answer any questions you may have in the morning, so if you don't need anything more, I will say good night."

"Okay. Good night, April, thank you," Valerie called as April closed the door.

Valerie strolled the room, surveying and touching every surface with her fingertips to get a feel for the materials. It felt good. Next to the queen-size bed sat a desk, floor lamp, and an easy chair that looked like a comfortable place to study or read. So comfortable was it that Orson immediately hopped onto the cushion and snuggled in for a nap. She decided that the room had a warm feeling, like a new home. The house was beautiful, everyone she had met so far was friendly, and she felt safe. *What a relief!* she thought. If nothing else, Corell had been successful about one thing: she was now far more security-conscious than she had ever been.

Valerie readied herself for bed reflecting on the day's events. Although it had begun like most any other, it had ended with startling changes in her life. It seemed as if destiny had run her down from behind, tackled her, then carried her in a direction she could never have anticipated. It was all out of her control—and that is what bothered her most. It was as if she had no voice in any of it.

In a day, I left everything behind. Family, friends, school—my home! How did I ever let that happen? The rabbit hole! It is deeper than I ever could have imagined and just keeps getting deeper. What's next, the Mad Hatter's tea party? The Queen of Hearts and the Jabberwock?

Valerie's throat tightened when she remembered school. *Teachers! Uh-oh. What will they think when I don't show up for class on Monday? I hadn't thought of that. I should have told Darcy to tell them—something. Would they buy the cover story? Maybe it doesn't matter because my school days look like they are over anyway.*

At least I have Orson, Valerie thought. *Good old Orson, the Cheshire Cat. Or is he? Lately, it seems like he's more down the rabbit hole with Corell than he is with me.*

Valerie lifted Orson from the chair, put him on the bed, and got in. As Orson rubbed up against her, Valerie laid her head on the pillow and closed her eyes. The day's events paraded past in her mind. The things Corell told her of his long life, his father, and the rings were amazing. But what he told her about herself was an earth-shaking revelation. Much of it would require time for her to reconcile. Sleep took her quickly as she yearned for her friends, family, and home in Arlington.

———————————

Lace curtains glowed with the morning's light. Valerie had slept past eight until a barking dog startled her awake. She went to the window to see what the commotion was about and was surprised to find Corell playing fetch with a huge, long-haired dog. From her vantage point in the second-floor window, she watched him throw a tennis ball. The big dog chased it, barking excitedly all the way there, then returned with it. When he dropped it at Corell's feet, the big dog was raring to have another go at it.

Corell took a knee, ruffling the big dog's thick fur, its thick ears flopping from side-to-side all the while. He hurled the ball again, which immediately sent the dog chasing after it, barking wildly as if the game was something entirely new.

In the distance, Valerie saw the tiny figure of an armed guard strolling the perimeter fence, reminding her of why she was there and the ever-present need for security. She guessed the guard must be half of a mile distant. Since the clearing appeared to be square, she estimated the clearing to encompass at least one square mile.

The guard shack at the end of the road was also visible from her window, its blue metal roof gleaming in the bright morning light. A second guard and dog patrolled the perimeter on the opposite side of the property. The grounds around the house were reasonably level. Rolling hills forested with a combination of Pine, Oak, and Madrona trees were visible, transitioning into high-peaked mountains beyond.

Even with guards everywhere, the scene from the bedroom window was intoxicating. The warm morning air was bright and clean. A few wispy clouds were visible on the eastern horizon. Some of the trees' size was striking, many of which were immense, towering old-growth Pines and Cedars. She had seen old-growth trees before, but only in National Parks while on vacation with her family.

By the time Valerie had showered and was ready for the day, it was after 9 AM, so she had low expectations about having company at breakfast. Concerned that Orson might become disoriented by the new location and run off, she left him sleeping on the bed and closed the bedroom door behind her. When she entered the kitchen area, she was surprised to find the dining room well-occupied so late in the morning.

The pleasant sounds and smells of food cooking in the kitchen greeted her from the top of the stairs. The house was an open floor plan with high ceilings, airy, bright, and welcoming. The house had the feel of a mountain lodge or resort hotel. The dining area was intended to be the focal point. Her first impression was that it was the kind of room that seemed to invite one to sit and stay awhile.

Valerie's eyes were then drawn to the twelve-place dining table surrounded by four stuffed leather chairs, a pair of matching couches complemented by an assortment of tables and lamps. A floor-to-ceiling bookcase filled with a mixture of books, knick-knacks, and decorations separated the dining room from a lounge. Bright morning light entering through large wood-framed windows warmed the room.

People sat together in groups of three and four, talking among themselves, sipping from coffee mugs, or eating at the big table. As Valerie entered, she recognized April, moving through the room with a coffee pot.

The large black dog she had seen with Corell jumped off the couch to greet her. As she embraced the friendly animal, Corell stood and welcomed her with a hug. The unexpected hug made Valerie blush.

"Everyone," announced Corell to the group, "meet my granddaughter, Valerie. She's going to be staying with us."

Valerie could not help but notice he did not add "for a while," which she found intriguing. She took that to mean the term of her stay was open-ended; she could stay as long as she wanted, making her feel welcome.

Corell continued. "Valerie is visiting from Arlington, which is up north of Seattle." Several people stood briefly, while others simply smiled and waved a welcome. Corell walked her to one of the leather couches then sat beside her. The dog joined them on the couch, taking up more space than both humans combined.

"I see you've met Comet."

"He's *huge!*" Valerie said affectionately. "What breed is he?"

"He's a Newfie, a Newfoundland."

"Comet, that's cute! Why Comet, though?" she asked, petting the big dog.

"You'll find out soon enough—he is all about food. You will not want to leave your plate unattended. He will have it in a flash! That is how he got the name Comet. When he was a pup, he would clean a plate as if it had been scrubbed with cleanser. Thus— Comet."

Valerie laughed warmly at the origin of the name, petting the affable dog softly. Comet responded by rolling onto his back, exposing a triangle of white fur on his chest.

"He loves to have his chest rubbed," Corell offered.

"I can see that," she said, smiling brightly as she continued rubbing Comet's soft black fur.

"I am so impressed with your home, Corell. It seems so welcoming!" Valerie gushed, then asked, "Are the people here your friends, family, or employees?"

"Friends *and* employees. But you are the only family I have here," Corell admitted. "We have two dining rooms here on the farm, and food is available 24/7. The kitchens are always open because our employees work so many different shifts. We call this a farm because we produce a good share of the food we eat.

"The farm also legitimizes us locally. We don't want people thinking we are a commune or religious cult," he elaborated.

"How large is it—the farm, I mean?"

"Five thousand seven-hundred and sixty acres, or nine square miles. But only about six hundred acres are farmed. The rest is a natural buffer zone."

"I love it here; it's so beautiful. From my bedroom window, I could see the old-growth forest! How long have you been here?"

Corell looked around the room, contemplating his answer before speaking. "Perhaps another time," he whispered, then added, "privately."

Valerie nodded, worried that she was asking too many questions. *Everything is such a big secret. And I am supposed to act as if it's alright and not freak out after being told there's another Valerie Dunne somewhere in the future!* An awkward silence passed between them for a moment. A waitress interrupted the silence by asking them if they would like to order something to eat. Corell ordered oatmeal and wheat toast. Not wanting to seem over-familiar, Valerie ordered the same.

"I don't mind answering your questions," he assured, noticing her unease. "I'm sure you have plenty more. Ask away," he invited.

"Okay," Valerie nodded. She did have more questions, one that had been nagging at her since she arrived. Valerie leaned in close to him and whispered, "I've seen a lot of armed guards. Why so many?"

"Good question," he commended her. "Security is important here. Remember what I told you last night." Then his eyes moved to his ring hand. Corell lowered his voice. "Only you and I know about the round thing here. Never mention it to anyone—*ever*."

"I understand. I wouldn't. Do that, I mean," Valerie stammered nervously.

"Sorry, I had to say it," he whispered. Valerie nodded. Then Corell continued.

"I have important friends and acquaintances, businesspeople, politicians, even a president or two. I have been around for a while, so I've accumulated wealth, and with it comes influence. No one with wealth or power questions the need for security these days. When we're done here, I will show you around."

After breakfast, Corell gave Valerie a house tour, introducing her to the staff, friends, and employees, confirming that the place was as much of a hotel as it was a home.

"All told, the home and farm employ over sixty people," Corell explained. "Housing for employees is located on the property, outside the main compound. My office is in an outbuilding immediately behind the house. But since it is Saturday, the business office is closed for the weekend. Now would be a good time to have a confidential discussion if you are interested."

Valerie nodded her agreement, then followed Corell through French doors onto a sundeck, through a garden with a gazebo, and on to an office building behind the house. Corell entered a code on a glass panel that unlocked the door then switched on the lights. Valerie followed dutifully to the back of the building and into his private office.

"This is my personal study," Corell gestured as he wound his way through a maze of books and boxes stacked on the floor. Corell seated himself in a high-backed red leather chair next to a window. Valerie assumed the big chair was a favorite reading place with books overflowing the table and onto the floor.

Awestruck and open-jawed, Valerie turned in a complete circle taking it all in. *This place is more of a museum than an office,* she thought. *If ever I doubted Corell's authenticity, this disproves it!*

Look at all the books! Artifacts, curiosities, paintings everywhere! There are not six square inches of empty wall space and barely enough room to walk. And look at these old weapons, knives, swords, and guns—some pretty cool statues and busts, too.

And yet, Valerie felt right at home in this cluttered environment. She craved knowledge, loved history, and respected wisdom, all of which surrounded her. Now she was compelled to be Corell's student more than ever, eager to learn from him.

From last night, Valerie recalled Corell's words when he said, "old people know stuff." Now that she had seen this study and saw first-hand what Corell Paris considered important, those words carried far more weight. Valerie smiled, marveling at the understatement.

Corell watched the girl with a combination of amusement and appreciation as her eyes darted about the room excitedly, inspecting items of interest one by one. He was pleased when she lingered over his Gutenberg Bible, his prized possession. For one so young, her intelligence and adaptability impressed him. He considered these traits key to her success in the challenging business that lay ahead.

The girl has metal, Corell thought. Still, he wondered if she could become the woman she had been forty-five hundred years earlier when she turned the Hesauronic rings over to their ancestors. *She has a lot of growing to do before she can be ready to face her enemies. But that responsibility falls on my shoulders. Only I can help her prepare for what lies ahead. If she is to win her battles, she must understand what is at stake and be made ready for the fight of her life. But I am thrilled at the opportunity.*

"*Eamon Dunne,*" Corell whispered to himself, *you are finally looking at what you have waited so long for—Valerie Dunne, the original Ring Bearer has reappeared as promised! What a sight for these old eyes. She is so beautiful, and doesn't know it! I just wish my father could be here to see her, too.*

She is just getting started—but this means I am finished. What have I got left—a year, maybe two at the most? I have sacrificed a lot in thirteen hundred years, but seeing her here and now makes it all worthwhile.

Corell marveled at the girl as she wandered around his study, doe-eyed, mesmerized by his collection of antiques and old books. *Soon, very soon, this girl must be able to do the impossible; complete the time loop she set in motion thousands of years earlier when she reset her timeline.*

The clock is ticking. It is time for her to merge with her future self, which I hope will happen when she is reunited with the Hesaurun Ring. But nothing is certain, he thought. *What if I am wrong? What if we were all wrong? What if what we all expected never happened?*

Those doubts had troubled him for as long as he could remember. Corell remembered his father voicing similar doubts and anxieties. Such misgivings were nothing new to him either. Even so, he wondered if he would witness the transformation of Valerie Dunne, the teenage girl, into Valerie Dunne, master of the Five Rings of Hesaurun. What could he expect to see? Would she be transformed in some way? Or would it be something indiscernible? Only time would tell.

Chapter 7

Egan Seamus Stone— November 1938 CE

Stone expected to be a busy man for the foreseeable future. He needed to tail Evers, keep an eye on Mayor Langley, as well as the mayor's girlfriend, the mystery woman. He also had to figure out who wrote the extortion letter—but he was already reasonably sure who was behind that.

Transportation was going to be a problem. Taxis, his usual mode of transportation, was not going to do for this job. Stone would need a car if he hoped to keep up with all these people.

He checked his watch, which read 11:41 AM, leaving plenty of time to deposit Evers' check and get enough dough to buy a used car. Stone liked watches, liked carrying a thick bankroll in his pocket, and telling people he only dealt in cash. It just felt right saying it.

A cab dropped him off at a used car dealer on Stewart Street with five-hundred dollars in hand. The black 1934 V8 Ford sedan in the front row caught his eye. It was perfect for what he had in mind, new enough to be reliable yet unremarkable, easily forgettable in traffic.

Three-hundred and forty dollars bought the car. After gassing it up, he returned to the Vista Hotel to stock the vehicle with surveillance supplies and equipment. Business always came first, so he stowed his loaded 1911 Colt Government .45, a box of cartridges, and a Ka-bar knife in the glovebox. Then he tossed a pair of black leather gloves and binoculars on the passenger seat. A wool blanket and pillow went on the back seat in case the need arose to stake out in the car overnight. His toolbox outfitted with a lock pick set, rope, piano wire, and pliers went in the trunk. One never knew when those items would come in handy.

Since he knew little about the mayor or even what he looked like, he would need to learn fast, so Stone drove to the public library. Public records and the phonebook provided him with everything he needed to know, including photographs and the mayor's home address.

Stone tore the pages he needed out of books and newspapers and shoved them in his pockets. With that, he had everything he needed to go to work that afternoon.

Chad Evers, Deputy Mayor, left his City Hall office that evening walking along Second Avenue toward his Pioneer Square apartment, a solitary figure among the busy streets at rush hour. The sky was already black, a drizzle dampening the pavement and sidewalks. Reflections from the surrounding buildings and streetlights glimmered where the rain had puddled. The sound of motor traffic mixed with the sweet smell of Chinese food filled the air as he approached his apartment in the Otterman Building.

Parked directly across the street sat a black Ford sedan with its V8 motor idling quietly. The large man dressed entirely in black was perched behind the steering wheel, watching the faces of passersby and chain-smoking Lucky Strike cigarettes.

Stone eyed Evers with a blank stare. The car was filled with a blue-gray haze. He didn't care about smoking with the windows rolled up and was oblivious to the fact that the ashtray was already over full. He had more important things to think about, such as how Chad Evers knew his full name, which galled him to no end. Once that spark started, it just kept on smoldering under the surface. It was only a matter of time before it ignited into a full-blown firestorm.

Evers' address was certain; Stone was sure about that. He was looking for patterns in the man's movements and habits. When he saw the man enter the Otterman Building and disappear behind the big glass doors, Stone nodded and pursed his lips with satisfaction. "Five-nineteen," he breathed as he stubbed out a spent cigarette in the ashtray. Then he put the car in gear and drove away. For the moment, he had what he needed from Chad Evers, so he headed to his next stop, Mayor Langley's Alki Beach address in West Seattle.

Fifteen minutes later, the black Ford sedan pulled off the road into a turnout and parked. Half a block away, the Langley home sat on the high bank above Alki Beach. Stone was close enough to observe any vehicles entering or leaving the driveway. The turnout was part of a well-maintained beach access area featuring grass, trees, picnic tables, and a phone booth. Seattle's picturesque skyline sparkled in the evening mist across Elliot Bay. The city lights reflected off the low-hanging clouds.

From his vantage point, Stone had an unobstructed view of the house. The place was well-lit; it seemed that every light in the house was on, although he was not close enough to make out any details inside. Familiarizing himself with the mayor's movements would take time, so he pushed his seat back and made himself comfortable. He hoped to learn when the man came and went, how he dressed, and what his family looked like so Langley could be properly identified. Stone did not want any mistakes.

Seeing the phone booth gave him an idea. He still had the crumpled page in his pocket he had torn from the phonebook with Langley's address and phone number. Since he had the phone number, it would be simple enough to call the house to see if he was at home. He liked the idea, so he decided to run with it.

Stone went to the phone booth, shoved a nickel in the slot, dialed the number, then waited for the call to connect. A woman answered after three rings.

"Hello," she said, a statement rather than a question.

"Good evening," Stone said, using the friendliest voice and good manners he could muster. "This is Mr. Gordon with City Hall. Mayor Langley is scheduled to attend a council meeting here at five this evening, but we have not seen him. Can you confirm that he is on the way?"

"Yes, he is here. Would you like me to remind him?"

"Yes, please," Stone said, then added, "for the record, may I ask who I am speaking to?"

"Of course, this is Mrs. Langley."

"Thank you, Mrs. Langley."

Stone hung up the phone. "Bingo," he whispered, satisfied the ruse had worked.

A few minutes later, a yellow late-model Oldsmobile sedan drove down the driveway, rounded the corner, then turned toward downtown Seattle. As it passed by, he noticed the driver wore a tan fedora and matching overcoat, but it would not matter much; that big yellow car would be hard to miss. The Ford fired up, then followed from a distance before the headlights came on.

The big Oldsmobile parked in the gated lot behind the City-County Building, home to both city and county governments and the courts. Knowing there was no city council meeting, Stone did not expect Langley to stay long, so he slid into a space opposite the parking lot, leaving the motor running with the lights off.

Sure enough, a few minutes later, Langley's car reappeared at the gate. The attendant waved Langley through—but rather than turning south toward Alki Beach, the vehicle continued east and then north on Fourth Avenue. Finally, Langley's car pulled into the drive in front of the Olympic Hotel. Stone idled slowly by as the man in the tan overcoat and matching hat climbed out of the car. He watched as the mayor turned the keys over to the parking attendant and strolled inside. Langley was a regular, so he knew no one would question his presence there on a Friday evening.

Stone circled the block once then parked his Ford on the street. Once inside, he had a pretty good idea of where to find Langley. By the time he entered the lobby, Langley was just leaving the Garden Room with a good-looking blond on his arm. Thinking quick, Stone threw himself into an out-of-the-way chair and watched from a distance as the couple approached the concierge station rather than the front desk as expected, presumably to avoid attention.

After warmly welcoming the couple, the prim attendant, a small man in a black uniform, went to the front desk and retrieved a room key. The concierge handed the key to Langley with a nod, and Langley slipped him a tip. As the couple ascended the stairs to the balcony where the elevators were located, Stone concluded the concierge was in cahoots with Langley. He considered that a good thing because he intended to strong-arm the twerp for information and knew right where to find him.

Stone moved the Ford to the hotel employees' parking lot then waited by the door smoking while watching for the concierge to get off work. A few minutes after 9 PM, the concierge came out of the door wearing casual clothes with a garment bag over his shoulder. Stone stuck his foot out as the concierge passed, tripping him, which sent him sprawling face-down on the concrete walkway.

Stone pounced on the little man like an angry grizzly. In one swift motion, he slammed a knee into his spine and twisted an arm behind his back. A big hand covered his mouth to muffle the cries of pain. As he pushed his weight into the man's spine and twisted the arm, the muffled screams were barely audible through Stone's thick hand.

"Quiet now," Stone breathed in the man's ear as he let the pressure off the distorted arm. Presently, the concierge became silent, other than the sound of heaving breaths and gurgling taken through a bleeding nose.

"That's a good boy," Stone soothed. "I am going to move my hand from your mouth, and when I do, you are going to tell me the name of the woman who was with Langley tonight. If you yell or I do not get the right answer from you, I am going to pull your arm off and shove it down your throat with my foot. Understood?"

The concierge whimpered, then nodded eagerly. Stone cautiously loosened his grip from over the concierge's mouth, then out came the right answer.

"Sylvia Moretti, Sylvia Moretti!" repeated the panicked concierge.

"And what else?"

"Attorney. For the city, I think."

"You better be right because you don't want me to make another visit—do you?" Stone hissed.

"No!" the man mumbled, shaking his head vigorously.

"Now, you have not seen me, have you? And you want to keep it that way— right?"

"Yes!" the concierge cried, nodding enthusiastically.

"You are catching on. That's good," Stone commended. "I'm going to leave now, but if I get the slightest idea, you moved a muscle before I am long gone, I'm going to come back, and you aren't going to like it if I do. Got it?"

Stone drove away in the Ford without looking back at the concierge lying face-down at the back of the big hotel. There was no need for confirmation that he had frightened the little man enough that he would stay that way long after he was gone.

As Stone headed toward the Vista Hotel, he began planning for tomorrow, seeing no reason to tell Evers anything he learned that day, other than he had tailed the mayor and learned nothing. The next day promised to be an interesting one.

Like most any other, the day began for Stone with breakfast at the Market Diner. Although he now had a car, he chose to walk rather than drive the short distance and then have to fight to find a parking place near Pike Market on a busy Saturday morning. Stone left the Vista Hotel at precisely 8 AM, walking briskly. With a clear sky, the temperature was just above freezing. The crisp salt air had the faint smell of fresh fish drifting in from the market. Checking his watch as he arrived at the diner, Stone saw he was two minutes ahead of schedule. He liked that and commended himself for making good time.

After breakfast, a second visit to the library yielded him the information he was looking for on Sylvia Moretti. According to public records, she earned her law degree at USC. Sylvia Elena Moretti began her career in the LA County Planning Department. In 1937, she was hired by the City of Seattle Legal Department. She was single, thirty-one years old, and lived in a downtown apartment. Sylvia's address and phone numbers were published in the phone book.

Stone decided to have a gander at Moretti's apartment building on First Hill, a ten-minute drive from the library. After circling the block a few times to familiarize himself with the area, he parked and watched the building for an hour. The recently built two-story brownstone was in a good neighborhood with various shops and restaurants lining the street. He judged the place to be a sensible choice for a single female professional. At 11:10 AM, Sylvia could be anywhere, so he decided to move. He could not wait all day for her to appear. He did not see her as being a key player anyway.

The next stop would be Evers' apartment, but Stone did not expect to learn much there since it was a weekend. But he wanted to cover his bases and did not want to miss anything. Just as he finished parking, Stone was stunned to see Chad Evers and Sylvia Moretti leaving the Otterman Building walking arm-in-arm. "Bingo!" he exclaimed at the sight of them strolling together.

Stone laughed hard, pounding on the steering wheel as the two love birds walked in lockstep as if strolling down the aisle to the tune of the wedding march. He had gotten lucky with this sweet little tidbit. A few moments later, he would have missed it entirely. The telling scene had answered a lot of questions, including who was trying to blackmail the mayor and why. This was going to be a good day; Stone could feel it.

Stone's suspicion that Evers was a devious political climber had just been proven beyond all doubt. Didn't that make him the perfect candidate for any public office? Stone laughed at his little joke, but he also believed it. Chad Evers had a gift for politics; the man could go far.

Yet Stone was stumped. So many questions were answered by this one swing of the bat that he didn't know what to do next. He certainly did not want to derail the Chad Evers money train, either. Riding it was just too lucrative. Not yet anyway. He had the answers he needed, so he saw no point in following Evers around town anymore. Maybe it was time to take a more direct approach.

Chad and Sylvia returned carrying grocery bags, which surprised Stone. As they disappeared inside the Otterman

Building, he wondered what it meant—if anything. Were they simply shopping together, or were they cohabitating?

Thirty-three minutes later, Sylvia answered that question when she exited the building alone, flagged down a cab, and left in it. Stone liked to keep track of how much time people spent on things. For instance, time said a lot about what people were doing when they were out of sight. Thirty-three minutes was enough time to ride an elevator, put away groceries, chat with a lover, and show up back on the curb. But thirty-three minutes was not enough time to engage in a proper tryst. No self-respecting woman of Sylvia Moretti's caliber would respect that.

At 3 PM, Stone decided he had enough of sitting in the car, so he walked to a nearby newsstand, bought a newspaper and a coke, then sat on a bench with one eye on the paper, the other on the front door of the Otterman Building.

Chad Evers' seven-room view apartment on the Otterman Building's top floor was in a prime location, within walking distance of almost anything anyone could possibly want or need. Restaurants, shops, and businesses of nearly every type and ethnicity catered to the residents and sightseers of Pioneer Square. All one had to do was walk out the front door, walk half a block, and everything was right there for the picking.

The luxury suite featured hardwood floors covered in thick throw rugs, complementing the sumptuous leather sofa, matching chairs, tables, and lamps. Coordinated wallpaper, all planned, purchased, delivered and installed by a downtown interior design firm.

The large picture window provided an excellent view of Elliot Bay, the islands in the background, and the Olympic Mountains. The late afternoon sun showed through the shades, producing a labyrinth of lines throughout the room like the lines on a legal pad. A jazz quartet played on the radio.

Chad Evers opened the hall closet and hung his coat on a hangar. Then he knelt, pulled a large black metal lunchbox and a softball-sized rock from the closet floor, then set them on the wooden coffee table with a thud. Chad took a moment to prepare himself, but this was something he had done countless times. He knew what to do. He held out his right hand, and when he was ready, spread his fingers, exposing a copper-colored ring. Chad gathered his thoughts, then uttered the word, "Gold."

The air quivered about him, much like a desert mirage. Instantly the rock was transformed into solid gold, shining in the afternoon light. Chad grinned a lopsided grin of approval, then wrapped the now-huge golden nugget in a newspaper and placed it in the lunchbox. After stuffing the box with wadded-up newspapers to keep the big chunk of gold from rolling around, he carefully buckled down the lid. Once done, Chad dialed a well-used phone number from memory.

"Ace Loan & Pawn," a raspy voice proclaimed.

"Good afternoon, Chad Evers here," he announced politely," I have another nugget to sell. Are you available today, sir?"

"I'll be here 'til six."

"Very good, sir. I'll see you in fifteen minutes then. Goodbye."

Stone spotted Evers when he left the Otterman Building, his eyes immediately drawn to the big black lunchbox cradled under one arm. The sight of it immediately caught his attention. In his mind, there was no universe in which Chad Evers, the effeminate politician, and the steel lunchbox went together. Something was afoot, and he knew it. It was a good day indeed!

Stone shook his head at what he considered a cockeyed spectacle, marveling at Evers's unique talent for irritating him. Whatever the occasion, he always seemed to be overdressed, over-sincere, and too-well mannered. His tan slacks, blue wool coat, matching fedora, and polished leather shoes, combined with the lunchbox, were living proof. *The man was dressed as if he might be on his way for tea with the Queen.* Stone chuckled to himself, *but with a big black workman's metal lunchbox in hand! Who did Evers think he was fooling?*

Evers walked at a brisk pace headed south toward Pioneer Square. Stone checked his watch, jumped out of the Ford, then hurried to get on Evers' tail. Keeping his distance and enough people between them prevented him from being recognized should Evers look back.

Stone noticed something odd. The lunchbox looked heavy, and something about how Evers carried it bothered him. Rather than using the handle, Evers cradled it like a football, a very heavy football, and kept changing from one arm to the other for relief. Whatever he had in the box had to be very heavy. But what, a cannonball?

After four blocks, Evers turned right on Jackson Street then entered a pawn shop. Stone crossed the street to be in a good position to follow without being seen when Evers left the shop. Ten minutes later, Evers exited, again with the lunchbox, although now it was held by the handle. There was no question the lunchbox was now empty, and whatever was inside it had been sold to the pawnbroker.

Blasted Evers did it again! Stone's mind rumbled. *Infuriating me in his own special way!* Stone thought he had seen everything until this. *What in the world would make a neat-nick politician decide to carry something heavy in a metal lunchbox, then sell whatever it was to a pawnbroker?* He could think of nothing, but he was confident of one thing—the lunchbox was Evers' not-so-clever attempt to fit in among the work-a-day pedestrians.

No doubt about it, decided Stone. *Evers had hauled something valuable in that lunchbox and wanted to draw as little attention as possible. What could be more natural than a man carrying his lunchbox? But what he was too dim to realize was that he stuck out like a sore thumb dressed like a Hollywood elite and lugging a lunchbox like a football. Any mugger worth his salt that saw that would have thumped his melon and lifted that lunchbox in a New York minute!*

While Chad Evers headed toward home, Stone followed, wondering if what he had just witnessed was the Chad Evers money train in action. *What else could it be?* Evers seemed to be made of money, but other than his job with the city, he didn't appear to have anything else going. It was obvious he had just sold something, but what? Lead sandwiches?

Not knowing what was in the box burned Stone. Clenching his teeth in rage, he balled his fists and stopped where he stood, glowering. Anger overtook him searching for an outlet. Instant satisfaction might come from strangling Evers, but he couldn't do that, not yet, not without getting some answers first. No, that could wait—until later.

Steaming like a boiler about to burst, Stone set his jaw, turned heel, and stomped back down the hill toward the Ace Loan & Pawn. *Perhaps a little persuasion would loosen some lips— or a few teeth,* he reasoned.

Before entering the pawnshop, the big man peeked in the front window to see if the store was occupied. It wasn't. The place was empty other than a small bald man seated behind the counter—the owner, he guessed. Before pulling the door open, Stone took a cleansing breath and did his best to look like a shopper. Once inside, he made a scene of searching the shelves for something interesting.

"Do you have any watches?" he called to the bald man as he approached the counter.

"Yes, sir, we have watches—right here in this case. I'm Steve," the little man added, "let me show you."

The moment Stone came within arm's reach, he wrapped one of his big hands around Steve's skinny neck and pulled him across the counter until their eyes met. Steve's eyes were wide as saucers, but Stone's were the eyes of an enraged bull. Then without forethought or warning, Stone slammed the little man's face into the hardwood countertop with a sickening crunch as wood splintered and bones shattered.

"The man with the lunchbox. What did he sell you?" Stone roared, but the bloody mess that was Steve's face offered no response. Furious now, he shook the limp body.

The head flopped freely from side to side, spraying blood and splattering gore over all the countertop and in Stone's face. Disgusted, he dropped the body, leaving it hanging over the display case, and wiped the blood from his face with his sleeve.

Still raging, Stone hoisted the big brass cash register over his head and slammed it down on Steve's already-ruined skull with a *whump*, crushing it flat as a pancake. Blood and brain matter splattered everywhere as coins scattered across the wooden floor.

"Cha-*ching!*" Stone laughed. "Beggar won't be buying any more lead sandwiches from Evers." He gloated, then turned away and began poking around for evidence of what might have been in the lunchbox.

The quick search revealed nothing promising until he found a safe behind the sales counter. The safe was locked, but he discovered a key chain hanging from Steve's belt. After trying a few keys, he found the right one and turned it. The door swung open, revealing documents, cash, jewelry, and one grapefruit-sized gold nugget.

"Bingo!" exclaimed Stone, as he laid eyes on the big nugget—or was it? Something about the massive chunk of gold seemed off. He wasn't sure what but guessed it didn't matter as long as it was the real McCoy. He picked it up, marveling at its size and weight, estimating it to be about twenty-five pounds. *Not bad,* he thought.

"No wonder Evers got tired of carrying it—the wimp," Stone muttered.

Then it hit him. He had seen plenty of gold nuggets, and everything about this one was wrong—other than there was no question about its authenticity. *It is gold alright,* he surmised, *but gold nuggets are rough, with plenty of holes and creases in them. They are never smooth, rounded symmetrical shapes like this.* This one was both smooth and symmetrical, just like a river rock. *Not that it makes any difference*, Stone decided. *It spends just the same.*

This must be what Evers sold to the pawnshop owner! He thought, eyes scouring the shop. *Nothing else here fits the bill. A chunk of gold the size of this thing must be extremely valuable and heavy. Now carrying it in a lunchbox made sense, notwithstanding Chad Evers.* With the riddle of the contents of the lunch pail solved, the only questions remaining were where Evers got it and did he have more of them?

Chunks of gold this large must be rare, he reasoned. Did Evers own a gold mine? Was there more where this came from? *Yes, there must be more, lots more, and I intend to get the rest of it while the getting is good. I am on the Chad Evers money train, and I'm not getting off until it reaches the station!*

What had just transpired was murder, so Stone knew he had to make it look like a burglary. When the police investigated, they would consider the scene a robbery as long as they found the safe empty. So why not make it one?

Wasting no time, Stone rummaged around the shop, unearthed a carpetbag, and stuffed it with everything from the safe: documents, currency, gold, and jewelry. Now Stone was feeling pretty good after turning off the lights and locking the door. It was Saturday night, he reasoned; the pawnshop was effectively closed for the weekend. It could be days before anyone found the body, and when they did, he would be long gone.

The adrenaline rush powered Stone's steps as he hurried through the crowded streets toward his parked car. When he checked the time, 4:47 PM, he remembered the glass case full of wristwatches he had left behind at the Ace Loan & Pawn and cursed himself for overlooking it. He thought about turning around but decided it was too risky.

A lot of things crossed his mind as he walked up the hill to Second Avenue, but never for a moment did he feel the slightest bit of remorse for what he had done to poor Steve, the shop owner, for leaving him the way he did, nor for his friends or family. For Stone, it was nothing more than business as usual.

Ten minutes later, he arrived at his parked car. After stowing the carpetbag in the trunk, he set about gathering the tools of his trade for what he had in mind next. The Colt Government .45, Ka-bar knife, and lock picks would be needed, all of which went into the pockets of his big black overcoat. Just that fast, he was ready for the next round of business.

Moments later, Stone entered the lobby of the Otterman Building. A schedule of tenant addresses was conveniently posted on the wall by the elevator. There he found the name C. *Evers* listed as being in apartment 4B. To keep from being seen by tenants, he took the stairs to the fourth floor, then cracked the door for a moment to be sure it was clear before stepping into the empty hallway.

The fourth floor looked and sounded unoccupied, and the building was silent as he quietly crept to 4B. Listening at the door revealed no sound or movement from within the apartment. When he was satisfied no one was present, Stone picked the lock then slid silently inside.

With the lights off and shades drawn, the apartment was dark. Stone switched on a lamp, then checked his watch—

5:35 PM—then began looking around. He found six rooms, two of them bedrooms, all clean and tidy. What else would one expect of Chad Evers? Once he had confirmed the apartment was unoccupied, he began looking deeper. His goal was to find that lunchbox and, hopefully with it, more gold.

Stone methodically searched and hunted through each room. The kitchen yielded nothing of interest, nor did any other rooms. As a last resort, he opened the closet door in the entryway. There he found a stack of round river rocks on the floor beside a black metal lunchbox.

Stone was puzzled. He expected to find the lunchbox somewhere in the apartment, but the pile of stones surprised and confused him. Each rock seemed to be roughly the size and shape of the gold nugget he had liberated from the pawnshop. Was Evers painting rocks gold and selling them to pawn shops? Surely, he was not that stupid, and neither were the buyers. Plus, the big gold rock from the lunchbox looked and felt exactly right.

Stone froze as he felt rather than heard footsteps outside the door. The hallway was carpeted, which silenced footfalls, but someone was there, and he knew it. The closet was inches from the door; he was in trouble if Evers had returned home. It was too late to retreat, and there was no time to hide. Stone held his breath, sure the door would open, but when a copy of the Seattle Post-Intelligencer newspaper slid under the door, he began breathing again.

Stone held his laughter behind his hands. He had what he had come for. Now it was time to look inside the lunchbox. But the moment he touched it, he realized it was empty. Disappointed, he cracked the box open and peered inside, instantly aware it was a waste of time. Other than wadded newspapers, the lunchbox was empty. His gaze flashed around the room, then returned to the neat stack of river rocks, puzzled by their presence. Maybe they hid gold, so he dismantled the pile but found nothing but stones.

Still, something about the rocks captivated him. Each one of them was about the same size and shape as the gold nugget sitting in the trunk of his car. The answer lay in these stones; he knew there was a connection — but what? Had Evers found a way to turn them into gold? Had he mastered alchemy?

On a hunch, Stone began going through the bedroom closets again, ransacking the coats and jackets and checking each pocket for anything hidden, but again found nothing of interest and not a single clue. Exasperated, he looked down at the neat row of shoes lined up on the closet floor and gave them a frustrated kick. As the shoes scattered, he noticed a barely visible cut-out of the hardwood flooring with a nail hole at its center. The cutout was well hidden with the shoes present, but now it was impossible to miss.

Dropping to his knees for a better look, Stone confirmed the cut-out. He found a nail on top of the baseboard, strategically placed to appear random. But it wasn't there by chance; instead, it was used to lift the panel from the floor. The nail fit into the hole perfectly, and with patience, Stone was able to remove the floor panel.

"Bingo," he burst out and clapped his hands together. A small safe with a brass face and recessed key lock mechanism was built into the floor. The safe looked professionally installed and securely strapped to the floor joists. No one would be busting this safe open or packing it off without a chainsaw and sledgehammer. But he had come prepared, and his lock pick made quick work of the padlock.

Once opened, he found nothing inside other than one small leather-bound notebook, about the size of a diary secured by a rubber band. He opened the book but was disappointed to see it was just that, a book. He expected something more: gold, a checkbook, or a map to a gold mine, something valuable that needed to be protected. However, as he flipped through the pages, he was disappointed to find nothing of value. He judged it to be a typewritten journal, nothing more.

Frustrated by the lack of results, he scowled then began putting the lid back on the safe when he realized that if Evers went to so much trouble to hide the little book, there must be something of value inside. Why else would he conceal it in a safe? There had to be more to it than what appeared on the surface, so the little book went in his coat pocket, intending to read it later.

Stone went to work replacing everything, putting it all back the way he found it. After turning out the lights, he quietly made his way out of the building. It was 6:08 PM when he landed at the bottom of the staircase.

Stone left the Otterman Building feeling like he had an exceptionally good day, even if he had not found out where the boss stashed his gold. Between what Evers had already paid and what he netted out of the pawnshop, he was a rich man, having earned several years' pay in just three days. Working for Chad Evers was looking pretty good just then.

When Sunday morning rolled around, Stone walked to the Market Café for breakfast as usual. Once seated, he found the leather-bound notebook still in his coat pocket, where it had been hastily stashed the previous day. Over eggs and bacon, he opened it and began reading.

To: Aedan Dunne

From: Valerie Dunne

Date: August 3, 2409, BCE

Dear Aedan,

If you are reading this, it is because I am gone. My journey may be over, but I can assure you that coming to know you and your family has made this the happiest and most fulfilling part of my life.

You have grown, learned, and accomplished so much in such a short time. You should be proud of yourself! You have worked hard; your English, reading, and writing skills are excellent. Please do not allow those skills to deteriorate. Continue reading the books I left you and using your knowledge and skills to benefit yourself and those that follow you. Passing those skills on to your descendants is a lifeline to their future.

You have done a wonderful job supporting your wife and raising your children. Moreover, you and your family took me in and made us, Orson and I, part of your family when many others would not have been so hospitable or gracious. I want you to know how much I appreciate your love and consideration.

Aedan, you are now a Dunne. Please consider this book and accompanying ring as my gifts to you for your loyalty and support. You know how important it is to me that these precious things are protected and passed on to your worthy family members. The plan I have set in motion is now entirely in the hands of you and your family. I have confidence knowing you will not fail me in this.

Love, Valerie.

NOTICE: If your name is not Dunne, or you are not a blood relative of a Dunne, you should assume you are not the rightful owner of this book and its accompanying ring, and these items have been lost or stolen. Again, if you are not a Dunne, you must consider it your sacred duty to return these items to the rightful owner immediately.

Stone read the first page, which seemed to be a deathbed letter, then brooded over it. *Everything about it is cockeyed,* he thought. *First off, the date is all wrong.* He huffed at that because it seemed impossible any book could last over 4,000 years. *How could it have been written in modern English even if it was that old? Impossible!* he reasoned. Plus, the little book looked brand new. *This thing is some sort of joke!*

Filled with skepticism, he flipped through the pages shaking his head disbelievingly. At first, he discounted everything about it, then realized the book itself deserved further scrutiny. The materials, including the leather cover, paper, and print quality, appeared fresh and new, which troubled him. Those materials were not in as-new condition; they were *better* than new. A *lot* better than new. They were *perfect.*

On close examination, Stone found the paper to be virtually indestructible. They sprang back to their original shape when the corners were folded over without leaving a crease. The material was flexible but resisted his efforts to wrinkle or tear it. The typewritten print was in English, but the print quality seemed almost three-dimensional. Furthermore, the text was far more precise than anything he had ever seen; it seemed to jump off the page.

Stone pondered this. Evers had gone to a lot of trouble to hide the little book where it wouldn't be found. That meant it was precious to him. If Evers valued it that highly, it had to be very important. Suddenly he felt uncomfortable about being seen reading it in public. After all, it was the stolen property of a local politician. So, he returned the little book to his coat pocket, promising himself to have a closer look at it in privacy.

While walking back to the Vista Hotel, Stone thought about Chad Evers. A lot of questions popped up. *Did that mean the book was stolen if his name wasn't Dunne? And what about this ring? Where was it? Surely, he was not wearing it. Why wasn't this highly valued ring with the book? Why did Evers hide the book so carefully?*

When Stone returned to his room, he made a pot of coffee then sat down to finish reading the journal. It was small, taking less than an hour to read. When he finished reading, he remained skeptical; the story seemed too farfetched to be true. But his gut didn't entirely agree. He decided there must be *some* truth or value to it, or it would not have been kept under lock and key.

The booklet told the fantastic story of a superior being having gifted five rings, one ring each to five Dunne family members. Accordingly, those five rings were supposed to be passed down through this Dunne family for generations. Each ring gave its wearer a unique ability, but no force in the galaxy could stand against them when the five were combined. It claimed that aliens would attempt to enslave humanity in the future, then destroy Earth, but only by the five rings' collective power could humankind be effectively defended.

The whole thing is some sort of joke or a comic, Stone thought. *What a goofy story! It's too far-fetched to be true!* Still, one sentence captivated him so much that he reread it several times: *"Ring wearers' lives are increased tenfold, which improves continuity of purpose."* Stone took that to mean a ring wearer could live as much as one thousand years. Although he scoffed at that, he was unable to forget about it. *Could one of these rings really make someone live a thousand years?*

When Stone laid the book down, he was convinced the ring, book, and Evers' gold were all somehow connected. He didn't know how, but he intended to find out. If it turned out that Evers possessed one of those Hesaurun Rings, he didn't think it would be that hard to separate him from it. Then he would find out for himself if the story was a comic or not.

Stone stared at the big chunk of solid gold on the table, eyeing it lustfully. He had never seen or heard of such a large nugget. Hefting it in his hands, he wondered at the possibilities. But he needed more information and a plan. After all, if Evers had a magic ring, he couldn't just club him on the head and run off with it. Or could he? His brain began to burn with all the possibilities. Gold fever had Seamus Egan Stone firmly in its grasp.

Stone placed the hunk of gold back on the table and sunk further back in his chair. The thought of living for hundreds of years seemed ridiculous. Yet the possibility of living for hundreds of years—and with the benefit of enormous wealth—was electrifying. He was beginning to see it as a life-changing opportunity he wasn't about to miss, and at that moment, he was determined to make it happen. If Evers had a magic ring—and Stone was beginning to believe he might—he would have it, and no one would get in his way.

The big man spent the remainder of the weekend holed up in his shabby room at the Vista Hotel dreaming of what he could do with a thousand years and all the gold he could conjure. By Sunday night, he was giddy—and more convinced than ever Chad Evers had a magic ring.

As with most Monday mornings, Stone sat in the Market Diner, eating his pre-breakfast snack of doughnuts and coffee. However, he was not his usual non-verbal self. It was a happy day, and he was ready to share the cheer he felt with everyone he met.

"Thanks," he commended the waiter, then dealt him a rare smile. The waiter stopped and stared as if confounded by the unexpected remark. *What—can't a man smile?* Stone thought.

The waiter scratched his head with a puzzled look, then checked the table number as if confused about which table he had just waited on. *Maybe he does not understand anything but "the usual" and "more doughnuts,"* thought Stone, as the puzzled waiter wandered away.

Stone was riding high in the saddle, feeling like his life had taken a sudden turn for the better in the past few days. For once, the dice were rolling in his favor. The thick roll of cash in his coat pocket was all the evidence needed. He liked the feeling carrying a lot of cash gave him. The sensation made him feel important, influential, and uncommonly cheerful.

Then he looked at his old wristwatch and regarded it with contempt. The bookies and loan sharks he collected for wore expensive wristwatches. Tough guys and bigshots like those guys always wore plenty of gold. He was unsure why, but watches had always intrigued him and made him feel good about himself. Stone wanted to be like the bosses and have a big fat gold wristwatch. Then he would show up with one and act like it was nothing special. But he would know better and would make sure they saw it, too.

Stone decided he would go to a jewelry store right away and choose the most expensive watch in the place—and pay for it with cash on the barrelhead. The thought excited him, and he grinned through a mouthful of bacon. He liked cash, and he liked watches. Buying a new watch would make him feel real good.

That worm Evers had a nice watch, Stone recalled; he had seen it. The thought of Chad Evers owning a fancy watch galled him, and his mood sank. He figured Evers was sitting on a pile of cash. *Must be in a bank,* he guessed, *because it wasn't hidden in his apartment;* He had made sure of that yesterday. While cash was a good thing to have, what generated it was far more important than having it. After all, wasn't the goose that laid the golden egg more important than the egg?

The game had changed the moment Stone closed the door on the Ace Loan & Pawn. He smirked, pleased with himself, knowing Evers would have to find some other way to exchange his gold for cash. He intended to watch every move Evers made with a magnifying glass, and when the time was right, he would have Evers' magic ring for himself. He nodded his head, confident it was just a matter of time before it would be his. Then he could buy any watch he wanted and carry a thick roll of cash wherever he went.

Stone imagined the look on Evers's face when he found out the Ace Loan & Pawn had been hit and hit hard. He imagined the prim politician toting his little lunchbox from shop to shop, trying to pawn softball-size gold nuggets. *That I would like to see,* he mused.

Pawning gold was a ridiculous idea anyway. Why didn't the dimwit simply melt it into a bar and take it to the assayer's office? Then he could sell it above-board like every other gold miner in the country. Stone shook his head at the glaring lack of common sense. For all his pretensions, he guessed that Chad Evers was actually dumb as a bag of hammers.

Four doughnuts, bacon, four eggs, toast, and a pot of coffee later, Stone was satisfied. He left the diner stepping into the soft morning light. The cloudless sky was crystal clear, the morning air stinging cold. He lit a cigarette before turning toward his hotel room. The sounds of the city, voices, and the rumble of delivery trucks unloading their goods echoed off the buildings. As he rounded the corner onto First Avenue, he melded into the sea of men moving purposefully about their Monday morning business.

Stone tramped through the streets with a Lucky Strike smoldering in the corner of his mouth, imagining the watches he would buy. The notion quickly became a fixation, and he decided to shop for one as soon as the jewelry stores opened. His eyes weren't what they used to be, so he'd make sure the clock face was easy enough to read.

Thoughts of his declining health brought a scowl to Stone's lips. Now in his mid-forties, streaks of gray in his long hair testified to his advancing age. The stiffness in his back and uneven stride became more distinct with each passing year. And as the weather turned colder, the pain and stiffness intensified, increasing his irritability.

Thus far, his surly nature had been a factor that played in his favor; his employers kept him working while younger men sat idle. But knocking heads and breaking legs for bookies couldn't last forever. No one had to tell him that no matter how big or mean he was, it was only a matter of time before he would be incapable of doing the job effectively.

In truth, he was no longer fast enough to run down a deadbeat gambler. Stone stayed in the game through malice, guile, and brutality. It worked, and it would continue working for a while longer, but it became more of a challenge as every day passed. His was a young man's game. Before long, he would be forced to fold.

The recent streak of good luck he'd stumbled onto was more than timely; it was an unexpected blessing that eased the anxiety Stone felt about his age and employment prospects. Then he remembered what he should be doing, shadowing Evers rather than daydreaming about glitter, rainbows, and unicorns. He scolded himself for that and refocused his thoughts on the business at hand: finding that ring and making it his own. That ring was his future because his would be a very long and happy life once he scored it.

Stone jumped in the Ford, fired it up, then set off toward Pioneer Square and the Otterman Building. It was still early, 7:36 AM, which left plenty of time to catch Evers before leaving for work. As difficult as it might be, he decided to put off his plan to buy a big watch that morning.

Chad Evers didn't own a car and didn't drive. He usually walked the short distance to City Hall or hailed a cab on rainy days. Before leaving his car, Stone took stock of the tools of his trade. The Ka-bar knife went in his sock, the Government .45, and a length of piano wire was stuffed in his overcoat pockets— just in case the opportunity arose to explain matters to his new friend.

Watching the Otterman Building's front door from a park bench behind his strategically-parked car provided the perfect cover. He didn't have long to wait before his quarry appeared. Much to his surprise, Chad Evers had one arm wrapped around Sylvia Moretti's waist. Stone stared as the conjugal couple headed south together on First Street.

Following from a discreet distance, Stone watched as Chad and Sylvia strode side-by-side on First Avenue down the hill toward Pioneer Square until they ducked into a coffee shop. Stone stopped in a dark alleyway smoking, patiently watching, and waiting for them to reappear.

Stone pulled off his hat and scratched his head, mystified at the sight of two prominent professionals displaying affection for each other so publicly. Was he wrong about Moretti and Evers blackmailing the mayor? If they were, surely they were not so bold that they would allow themselves to be seen walking together so near to City Hall. Stone shook his head in wonder.

While it didn't make sense, he decided it didn't matter anymore because, so far as he was concerned, his business with Evers was kaput. He didn't care if Evers paid him for the job or not. He no longer needed the money, and he couldn't give a toot about who, if anyone for that matter, was blackmailing the mayor.

At that moment, he became determined to stop pussyfooting around and get it over with quickly. Since the only thing that really mattered to him was separating Evers from his magic ring, why not simply thump his melon, take it, and disappear? What would he do about it? Cry to the police that some guy stole his magic ring? Stone didn't think so. But the thought of the prissy politician crying to the cops that someone stole his magic ring brought a wicked smile to his lips.

And why not go someplace where the weather was better? A place where the cold didn't make his backache so much. A place with palm trees would be nice, he mused. With the ring, he could buy a paradise island in the Caribbean! The thought made him smile as he stamped out a cigarette on the sidewalk. Stone was smiling a lot this cold November morning.

Moments later, Evers and Moretti exited the coffee shop, spoke together for a moment, then went separate ways. To Stone's surprise, Evers turned north back toward his apartment rather than proceeding down the street toward City Hall as expected.

Sensing the opportunity to jump Evers from the dark alleyway had just presented itself, Stone began preparing himself for the hit. With only seconds to spare, he surveyed his surroundings. It looked good; no one was around, and foot traffic had died down. In the dim light of the alleyway, he was nearly invisible in his black overcoat and hat. What did he have? The Ka-bar, the Government Colt, and the piano wire. He decided on the Colt, choosing to use it as a club. One good knock on the head with the heavy piece could do a man in, making it the right choice.

As Chad Evers neared, he noticed Stone appear from the shadows. Recognizing him immediately, he was at once irritated. What was the idiot doing? he wondered. The last time they had spoken, hadn't he made it absolutely clear the thug shouldn't contact him without an invitation? This insolence had to stop. Chad Evers marched forward purposefully, determined to give the overgrown dullard a piece of his mind.

Stone waved the naive politician into the alley without saying a word, doing his best to give him the impression he had vital information to share. Evers took the bait hook, line, and sinker, unsuspectingly following Stone into the darkness of the alley.

The big man whirled around on Evers in an instant. The butt of the .45 struck him hard across the bridge of his nose. Evers spun, then went down hard, landing face down on the pavement. The impact of his head slamming the ground made the sound of knocking on wood.

Without wasting a moment, Stone made sure Evers could not rat on him by pulling the Ka-Bar from his sock and thrusting it in the side of the man's neck. Stone finished the job by twisting it hard to be sure he bled out quickly. A thick stream of steaming blood erupted from Chad's neck as Stone yanked the knife out. The killer stood to see if anyone had witnessed what was happening in the dark alley. No one saw any part of it. The coast was clear.

After wiping the bloody knife off on the back of Evers' coat, the Ka-Bar was safely returned to his sock. Following that, he flipped the body over. Horror-stricken eyes stared back at him accusingly, but that didn't bother him in the least. This was business, he reasoned, and Evers should have known that.

Stone found what he was looking for on the third finger of the right hand. He pulled, twisted, and tugged, but the ring would not budge. Frustrated, he pulled the knife back out of his sock and then sawed the finger off. With the finger separated, the bloody ring slid off easily. Once the ring was safely in his coat pocket, the finger was tossed over his shoulder as if it was no concern. *Mister Prissy won't be needing it anyway,* he chuckled.

Aware that the police would investigate the murder, he did his best to make it look like a robbery by digging through all the pockets and turning them inside out. He took cash out of the wallet then dropped it on the ground with everything else.

As he turned to leave, he stared back at Chad Evers' body, which was lying face-up with arms and legs spread as if he was making a snow angel in the alley. The neck wound continued bleeding, but less furiously now. Stone grinned, thinking the chump was now light one nose, a finger, a gallon of blood, and one golden goose of a magic ring.

"Bingo," he whispered as he whirled away and began to make his way back up the hill toward his car. Then he began singing: "B-I-N-G-O, B-I-N-G-O, B-I-N-G-O, B-I-N-G-O, and Bingo was his name-oh!"

Egan Seamus Stone, you have it made in the shade, he told himself. He was elated, eager to get back to his hotel room where he could try the ring out and make some gold for himself. He knew Evers had chosen to use rocks but wondered if he could turn bricks into gold or maybe something more substantial than rocks. Was there a limit to what could be turned into gold? What about other metals? Were there limitations to what he could change into gold? He didn't know but intended to find out as soon as he got back to his room.

Then he recalled his earlier plans to buy himself a fancy watch, so he began watching for jewelry stores as he drove.

When he saw the big sign for Fineman's Jewelry, he parked and went inside. A tiny bell tinkled as he entered.

The time was just after 9 AM, so he was the shop's first customer of the day. Fineman's store was small but modern and nicely decorated. Wood plank floors creaked and groaned under his weight as he entered. The lone salesman stood behind a counter next to an ornate Seymour cash register. Stone eyed it mischievously. Behind the man, a blue curtain blocked patrons' view to a back room.

"Good morning, sir, my name is Fineman," the salesman welcomed Stone warmly. "How can I help you?" Fineman looked polite, but Stone noticed he seemed worried the moment he laid eyes on the rough-looking character. Stone limited his response to his standard-issue characteristic grunt. The well-stocked store had glass showcases lining the walls with an island at its center. Soft violin music played on the radio.

Fineman eyed Stone suspiciously as he moved from one display case to the next, searching their contents. Fineman was always wary of rough-looking men coming into his store, and this one fit that category perfectly. Having been robbed more times than he liked to admit, he pressed a hidden button under the countertop that switched on a red light in the backroom. The light alerted Felstein, his minor partner and part-time bookkeeper, that potential trouble had just entered the shop.

The instant the light went on, Felstien's heart thumped. He jumped up, grabbed the Remington Model 10 pump-action shotgun hanging on hooks over his desk, and moved silently to the doorway. Felstien, a veteran of the Great War from the Somme to Cantigny, peeked cautiously through the curtain gap. Knowing Felstein had his back, Fineman was reassured, aware that his partner was prepared to shoot first and ask questions later if things were to go south. The bookkeeper watched with the gun held close to his chest as the big man circled the room, eyeing each display case's contents.

"Why don't you have prices on these watches?" the big man growled, squinting as he struggled to focus on price tags.

"We do, sir," Fineman assured him, his throat tightening, "but the tags are small. Which one are you interested in?"

"How much for that one?" the big man said, pointing to an elegant gold wristwatch with a broad face and glow-in-the-dark numbers.

"Ah, an Elgin. Top of the line, sir, excellent choice. That one is 24-carat gold. The price is $149.99." Fineman pointed to the shelf below, assuming he spoke to a man of modest means. "We have much less expensive watches here, sir."

"I'll take it," the rough-looking man said eagerly.

Fineman was taken back by the ease of the sale. But he still had not seen the color of the man's money, so he remained guarded. When the big man lumbered through the door looking like a shabbily dressed bouncer, Fineman assumed his time would be wasted, or worse, a robbery. The selection of such an ornate watch in no way suited the customer, so he decided to ask a few discreet qualifying questions before unlocking the display case.

"Yes, sir. Will you want to have it gift wrapped?"

"I'll wear it," the man growled.

"And how will you be paying for it, sir?"

"Folding money," he burst out, then dug deep into his coat pocket, pulling out a thick roll of greenbacks. Thumbing through them one at a time, he flipped past the hundred-dollar bills, found what he was looking for—seven twenties and one ten—then laid them out side-by-side on the countertop. Then Stone slammed his hand down on top of them with a bang for emphasis.

In the backroom, behind the blue curtain, Felstein sighed. Seeing the bankroll, he returned the Remington to its hooks and went back to work.

Fineman's eyes focused intently on the big man's bankroll, startled at its size and by the large denominations there. He had seen many things in his time but never once had a customer come into his shop toting such a large roll of cash.

"Will there be anything else, sir?" Fineman managed to croak as the big man shoved the bankroll back in his coat pocket.

Stone held out his hand, eagerly waiting for the watch to land there. Although Fineman, ever the meticulous businessman, landed Stone's change there instead. Stone stared dumbly at the penny for a long moment.

"Your change, sir," reminded Fineman, then handed over the watch.

Stone unceremoniously grabbed it, put it on, then stomped toward the door without another word. With one hand on the doorknob, an idea struck him that stopped him in his tracks. He thought for a moment, then returned to the still-speechless Fineman.

"I'm a miner. Do you buy gold?"

"Certainly, sir," Fineman stammered. "We pay top dollar, too. Do you have gold for sale?"

"Yeah, lots of it," Stone muttered. Then for good measure, added, "It's a big mine—up in Alaska."

"I see. Is your gold raw or refined?" Fineman asked. "We can refine here; we deal with other miners too," he assured his new business prospect.

Stone was stumped for an answer. In truth, he knew next to nothing about how gold was mined, sold, or refined, but it was apparent he needed to learn fast if he was going to be in the business of selling gold. He had no idea if Evers' gold was raw or refined, so he decided to evade the question rather than tip his hand.

"I'll bring you a sample later today. We'll talk business then," he promised. With that, he turned and left the building, slamming the door behind him hard enough for the little bell to fall to the floor with a clatter.

Fineman was even more puzzled as he watched the big man leave his store.

"Hey, Felstien," he called to his partner in the back room. "You hear that?"

"I did," Felstien admitted. "Odd character that one! He had me worried at first."

"Me, too," Fineman agreed. "It will be interesting to see what he brings in, though."

Stone drove the Ford with one eye on the road and the other on the big Elgin wristwatch. The golden timepiece captivated him in a way he could not comprehend; he could not pull his eyes away from it. He always dreamed of having such a watch as this one. He loved the way it felt on his arm, heavy but not uncomfortable, and with it an unexpected sense of power, prestige, and privilege. For the first time in his adult life, Egan Seamus Stone felt complete.

As he pulled his car into the Vista Hotel parking lot, he stared contemptuously at the old building. Built before the turn of the century, the four-story brick hotel had seen better days—much better. Its twenty-one rooms had been electrified twenty years earlier after the building had been sold to a younger, more progressive owner. The antiquated structure offered nothing in the way of amenities, no insulation, no elevator, and was without a laundry. But it did have electricity, steam heat, telephones, and bathrooms in each room, making life at the Vista basic but tolerable.

Stone was no longer content living in the old hotel with his newfound wealth. He could now afford to do better or buy a place of his own. Moving into a more modern hotel crossed his mind briefly, but he discarded the idea when he recognized what he really needed was privacy. He had more than enough money to buy a place in the suburbs, but the suburbs didn't offer the kind of seclusion he had in mind. If he was going to be dealing in gold, security and privacy must be prioritized.

Stone mapped out his future while strumming his fingers on the steering wheel. One thing he was certain of was that the Vista Hotel was no place for gold conjuring activities. Something much more secure than a hotel room was required for that. Staying local and buying acreage in the country, or moving to where the weather was better, seemed to be his most logical choices. He could not decide, so he lit a cigarette and ruminated on it for a while.

Remembering his prize, he dug into his coat pocket and pulled out the bloody ring, and tried it on the index finger of his right hand. Although it fit, it felt uncomfortable, as if it did not belong there. The same was true of his middle finger. Oddly enough, the ring fit snugly on each finger, but none felt right until he put it on his ring finger. He didn't know why but a sense of calm came over him with it there. It just felt right, so he left it where it was.

Stone got a good look at the bloodied ring for the first time. He was surprised to find it was a simple thing, a dingy brown band with five insignias pressed into its face. It looked like cheap dime-store jewelry, the sort of cheesy junk one might expect to win at a fair for guessing the weight of the fat lady. He judged it to be the sort of thing no one would ever buy. It was just too cheap looking to spend cash money on. But he guessed none of that mattered, as long as it did what it was supposed to do; turn river rocks into big fat gold nuggets.

Stone climbed the stairs to his room, feeling the stiffness in his lower back with each step. By the time he reached his room on the fourth floor, he was cursing the Vista Hotel's entire existence. It was then he recalled the good weather he knew growing up as a boy in California. With unlimited funds, why shouldn't he find a private place somewhere on the Southern California coast? They had palm trees there, didn't they?

Stone scanned the dingy three-room suite from the open doorway. He hung his head, realizing for the first time the grimy world that was the Vista had sucked his life away, turning him into the boogeyman, and he was the shell of the man he once was. At that moment, he determined to change that. There was nothing here for him anymore. His belongings were meager: a few clothes, old books, kitchen, and bath items. Everything he actually needed was already in his car or on his person. With the decision to move on from here made, he closed the door and turned away from the room, knowing he would never miss anything left behind at the Vista Hotel.

Chapter 8

Amon— January 2431 BCE

F our hours past sundown, Pearse, Tierney, and Valerie continued their trek through the snow guided by a beacon of light that shone atop a ridge. That light was produced by Lauryn's bonfire to help Pearse and Tierney find their way home. Still, more than a mile away, Valerie's solar torches provided more than enough light to make the journey safely through the woods and deep snow of the river valley.

As they approached the little homestead on the edge of the forest, Pearse called out Lauryn's name to prevent her from being startled by their approach. But she had seen the lights of their torches and was waiting for them. As they broke out into the clearing, Lauryn ran to her husband, eager to put her arms around him. Puzzled at the unexpected sight of the strange torches they carried and the old woman trailing them, she stopped short.

Lauryn took Pearse's arm, guiding her husband to the fire. Once they were gathered around and enjoying the badly needed warmth, Lauryn leaned in close to Pearse and whispered, "Why did you bring that old woman to our home? Is she dead?" Lauryn's intense expression revealed her concern.

"That old woman is not dead," Pearse explained. "She is a traveler, a healer from a land far away. Do not worry; the old woman just looks dead," Pearse explained.

Valerie overheard the conversation and smiled. Then Pearse, who was always eager to tell a story, began relating his version of the day's events.

"When we reached a hill with a good view, all the trees were lying down in rows, as if a mighty hand had carefully laid them down! Not one of them was missing or out of place. But that is not all." Pearse met every eye but lingered on the impressionable children he knew loved his stories. With the firelight playing on his face, Pearse continued.

"That mighty hand had swept the ground so clean—so clean that even the smallest pebble was thrown into a pile surrounding the great glass fish. That pile was so big that it was a mountain—we had to climb over it! And as we got closer, we could see that that fish was made of glass!"

"Glass?" squeaked a little voice. Saoirse, Pearse's smallest one, wanted to know more.

"Daughter, you remember glass; we saw a man selling glass at the summer gathering in Erlin. That man had black and white glass, but the great glass fish shines like a new silver coin. Since it is shaped like a fish, we decided to call it a glass fish even though we know it really is not a glass fish. We just did not know what else to name it."

"If it is not a glass fish, what is it?" Lauryn asked, wide-eyed.

Pearse's voice lowered to a whisper, peering into the night sky with arms spread wide. "The glass fish is a great flying boat," he proclaimed, "that fell from the heavens! And we all saw it—did we not?"

Lauryn and the children all nodded and smiled as one, caught up in the story. Valerie paid rapt attention as Pearse wove his verbal description of the *Dreamer* lying at the crater's center. She remained silent though, listening intently, patiently waiting for an invitation to talk, but had to stifle a laugh at Pearse's dramatic description of how the ship fell from the heavens.

Pearse went on, the firelight playing on his face adding to the drama. "We approached the glass fish cautiously, careful not to frighten it—"

This time, Valerie could not help herself, laughing so hard she choked and went into a coughing fit, which narrowly saved her from embarrassment or insulting Pearse. She stopped for a moment as everyone turned to see what was wrong with the strange old woman with the dead eyes.

Is this old woman so near death that she is dying? Lauryn wondered.

"—and when I reached out to touch it," Pearse continued, "the glass fish bit me so hard I fell asleep as if dead! Tierney took care of me and kept me warm, but I could not move. I was a dead man until this old woman came from the glassfish to heal me. I would not be here unless she healed me," he assured everyone.

Lauryn gasped, horrified to learn that her husband had been seriously injured, and she hung on to him tightly. But now she understood why her husband had brought the old woman with him and was thankful for the healer. Lauryn showed Valerie her appreciation with a nod and a smile.

"How?" Lauryn insisted. "How were you healed?"

Pearse gazed at Valerie for a long moment before answering. "Her eyes. She healed me with the magic of her eyes."

"She is a witch then?" Lauryn asked cautiously.

"I thought so at first," he admitted, "but then she made me understand she is a healer, not a witch, and I knew I had to bring her with us. She wants to help us," Pearse assured. "She told me she is a gift from the people of the glass fish."

Lauryn eyed the old woman warily, wondering if what Pearse said was true, but said nothing more about it. If her husband was convinced she was a healer, then that is how she intended to treat the old woman.

"Father, tell them about the others from the ship," Tierney broke in.

"What is a ship?" asked Lauryn, the word being unfamiliar to her.

"The healer told us to call the glass fish that," Pearse explained. "She said the ship is like a flying boat that carries people in the sky. I would not believe it myself if we did not all see it this morning. That ship is what caused the great sound we heard."

"They came from the sky?" Lauryn asked, dumbfounded.

"You saw it yourself."

"There were other people?"

"Yes, and besides the old woman, there were three soldiers, and one of them was *yellow!*" Pearse exclaimed.

"Yellow—and hairless!" Tierney added.

"Husband, these people are very strange. Are you sure they are safe?" Lauryn said, her voice betraying the fear she felt of the dark-eyed stranger. "Why did they come here in that—*ship*?"

"I didn't have time to ask; we were in a hurry to leave. I think she was worried the people of the ship wanted to keep her."

"But I can tell you this," Pearse assured his wife. "The woman—Valyri—may be old, but she is a strong healer. So, I welcomed her to come with us. Our people can use such a good healer."

Lauryn agreed with a nod, then snuck a wary peek at the strange visitor. Pearse and Tierney had nothing but praise for the old woman who had saved her husband, a fact not lost on her. Regardless of the older woman's appearance, having a powerful healer around had a definite appeal.

"Welcome, Valyri," Lauryn said warmly.

The fire provided enough light for Valerie to make out some details of her surroundings, most noticeably a modest but well-built stone structure she assumed to be the family home. She saw a barn with fenced paddocks and a woodshed, all made of shale stones. While the house was of a simple design, she was impressed with its pitched roof, also covered in stone shingles. Square-cut window openings with wooden shutters hung beside each window, no doubt to keep the cold out. The wood plank door looked solid.

"Valyri," called Pearse, offering his hand welcomingly. "Come meet Lauryn and the children."

As they came together around the fire, he praised her generously, saying, "Without her help, I might not have walked again. This woman saved me with her eyes. Now she has come to live with us; she will be one of our family," he pronounced, his voice firm, leaving no room for argument. Valerie was pleased by that. She had gained these people's trust through actions rather than words.

That night, Lauryn prepared a place inside the little stone house for Valerie and the old woman's strange pet—an *Orson*, she called it. The children had never seen a pet Orson, so they took turns holding it. Orson responded to their friendliness by nestling into their arms and purring loudly. The bedding was laid out on the stone floor, but Valerie was comfortable enough in the wool blankets.

Valerie contemplated her prospects for life in this realm. She considered herself to be more than seven thousand years in the past. While the supplies she brought with her were well thought out, they were meager, consisting of two cloth bags and a backpack.

Aside from a few personal items, the only concessions she had made to tech included the three torches, an ion generator, a tablet containing the accumulated knowledge of humanity, and some printing materials, which were carefully chosen for practicality and durability. She assumed they would have to last for hundreds of years or until her death, whichever came first. There was comfort in knowing she had made quality, not quantity, her priority. She was fully aware that any one of these items could change the future if lost or stolen and was determined to destroy them before that could ever happen.

Aside from the rings, her most prized possession was an ancient booklet kept securely hidden within her undergarments. Back when she was a teenager, her mentor

Corell Paris had given it to her, along with the fifth ring of Hesaurun. With his tutelage, she learned the five rings had been passed down through her family line for generations.

That booklet contained priceless information about the five rings, in addition to guiding, motivating, and providing her with a purpose in life for more than three thousand years.

Initially, each ring was paired with a booklet. Since no two rings are alike, each booklet was unique, highlighting each corresponding ring's attributes. The first thing Valerie did whenever she reclaimed a ring was destroy the book that came with it to protect herself. She could not risk anyone discovering the secrets it held. Other than the one she retained for sentimental reasons, she ensured none of the other booklets would ever be used against her.

All but the fifth ring had been stolen from the rightful owner at one time or another. Narcissistic people bent on grabbing power and riches for themselves used their rings for selfish reasons, often to the detriment of humankind rather than their benefit. The rings' master, Osomarío of Hesaurun, intended for them to be used to help humans evolve into a mature society, preparing them for integration into the greater community of sentient beings in the galaxy.

Unfortunately, Osomarío's well-intentioned plan had backfired, and humankind's progress was delayed rather than accelerated. Even he could not control time and unforeseen circumstances, so Osomarío used his gift of the cat, Orson, as a surrogate to monitor the situation for him on Earth.

The realization that she had authored the books herself was a startling epiphany for Valerie, one that drastically altered her life's trajectory. Valerie had known for centuries the timeline must be reset. There was no other way to right the wrongs of the past. She was confident it was possible, but she would have to live out the remainder of her life in the distant past to make the necessary corrections to the timeline.

A time loop was the only way to accomplish her goals. Sure, she would meet her end here in this realm, but time would continue marching inexorably forward like it always has. Then in the twenty-first century she would be born, just like she had been the first go-around. Once again, Corell Paris would be there, waiting diligently for her appearance, and she would have a second shot at achieving her goals.

Valerie remembered the hard work and the careful preparations. She had traveled to this time period on multiple occasions, scouting out pre-historical societies and individuals she not only suspected of being her forebearers but felt were worthy candidates of being so. *And now, the circle was complete,* she told herself. She had successfully inserted herself back at the starting line and intended to prove that do-overs were possible.

For the first time in human history, she had the exclusive prospect of selecting her own ancestors. No one had to tell her she must choose well if she wanted to retain her core self, which had now become within her power to manipulate. The responsibility she had assigned herself was weighty, considering the dangers she faced.

All it would take is one bad choice to upset the cart, She thought. *Influence the past too much, or in the wrong way, and I could diminish myself in some unknown or unexpected way. Or worse, unwittingly erase me from existence, producing a paradox that changes the timeline in a way that has devastating repercussions. I must be careful because I am playing with fire!*

The long-term plan was for each member of Pearse's family to eventually receive one of her five rings, but before doing so, Valerie would have to teach them what it meant to be a ring bearer and what would be expected of them. Each ring possessed a unique ability, so everyone would need to be schooled separately.

Above all else, Valerie knew the burden rested squarely on her shoulders to instill in these people an unyielding resolve to protect their rings from loss to thieves and tyrants who would take them for their own advantage. She had seen first-hand what happens when they fall into the hands of selfish or ambitious individuals. She had dedicated her life to the classic struggle of good versus evil, and she intended to win.

Pearse and his family were not Neanderthals; these were intelligent, sophisticated people. That knowledge helped ease Valerie's anxiety over the radical decision to leave her former life behind, abandoning everything and everyone she knew. Making a clean break from her life without notifying family, friends, or colleagues was by no means easy. She had made the difficult choice of selecting a one-way ticket to nowhere—or was it no-when?

Valerie was determined to make this her last jump in time, no matter the consequences. She regarded the time and people she had seen grown old with great affection. Still, now she must consider them dead to her because they existed only in memory, no different from the generations of people she had outlived in her more than three-thousand-year lifetime.

Sleep took its time carrying her away that night as she worked on the long list of challenges she would face in the morning. But when she began remembering the people she left behind, sleep took her within moments.

The next day Valerie began implementing her plan for the future in earnest. Her goal for the day would be to give Pearse and his family sound reason to believe in her. Valerie intended to put on a demonstration of power they would not soon forget. She wanted lives forever changed by what they would witness. She planned to play the healer trump card to the hilt but knew she could not go too far with it. If she did, she stood a chance of scaring them off.

Valerie helped the family with the morning chores, and once everyone had eaten and was gathered around the warmth of the roasting pit, the same one used for the previous night's bonfire, Valerie spoke.

"Friends," she began, "I want to tell you how much I appreciate being allowed into your home and into your lives. Thank you. I am your healer now," she said graciously with a polite head bow, then paused, allowing a moment for her words to settle before continuing.

"I have important news to tell you that you need to know and understand." She focused on each family member individually, knowing that would add weight to what she was about to say and do.

"Please know that I now consider myself part of your family. As long as I am welcome, I intend to stay here with you. Do you consider me a member of your family?" Pearse, Lauryn, and the children nodded their heads, although with a hint of reservation. By all accounts, she was a newcomer who carried with her the lingering suspicion of being the *Cailleach Bhéara*. Depending on what she said and did next, her status could shift back to a witch in a flash.

"I was sent to you as a gift from my people—the people of the ship that arrived yesterday. We saw that you people need a good healer. Pearse was dying, so they sent me to help him, which I did. Now I am your healer. Do you accept this gift?"

"Yes," they answered as one, this time with less hesitation. Valerie saw that she was making progress and continued.

"Alright. You have already seen that I am a powerful healer, but more than that. I am also a teacher and a warrior. I can teach you many things that will make your lives better, and I can protect you. I may be old, but I think you will be impressed when you see my power for yourselves. But, you must promise never to share what I do or say with anyone. Ever. This is very important! Do you promise?"

Once again, the family nodded, but now eagerly.

"These five rings," Valerie said, "make me strong. With them, I am a strong healer and a warrior, but without them, I am weak," she admitted, holding her right hand up for all to see. Would you like me to show you what the rings can do?"

This time Pearse and his family stared blankly at Valerie, their eyes filled with a combination of wonder and apprehension.

Valerie held out her right hand and sent a log into the roasting pit with the command, "Into the fire pit!" All eyes followed the log as it floated lazily through the air and landed in the fire pit, unleashing a shower of sparks high into the sky.

"You *are* a witch!" Pearse exclaimed, jumping to his feet. Clearly afraid, he picked up little Saoirse and backed away. Lauryn and the boys jumped up and joined him.

"I am a *healer*, not a witch," Valerie reasoned, her voice serene. "I can do nothing except through the rings. The rings are a tool, nothing more. Using them does not make me a witch."

The family stared at her doubtfully, Lauryn clutching the children, her face a mask of horror.

"Pearse, listen," Valerie called, singling him out. "When you ride a horse, are you a witch because you move so much faster than a man on foot? Is the horse a witch? No! The horse is only a tool you use to move faster than the man on foot. Do you understand?"

Although skeptical, Pearse nodded. Valerie had anticipated that she would be seen as a witch, so she was well prepared to defend herself against the inevitable accusation.

Valerie stood. "Let me show you. Please watch," she said, then removed the rings one after another. As she did so, she said, "watch my eyes." Instantly her eyes were transformed from the ominous dark orbs they feared so much to her far-less-threatening natural pale blue.

Around her, Pearse and his family seemed to relax. With that, Valerie returned to her seat smiling widely, knowing she had made her point and won the inevitable "witch" argument. But she still had one more bombshell to deliver.

"Tierney, do you want to be a warrior? Pearse, would you like to be able to do what I did with that log? Lauryn, will you be a healer, too? You can be," Valerie assured, then remained silent as they drifted back to the roasting pit. Only when they were all seated again did she continue.

"I am here to give these rings to you. They will be yours. You will use them as I do," she promised. "But first, *you must learn how to use them.* I will be your teacher. You need to know how to use them without hurting yourself or your loved ones. You could hit someone in the head with a log!" They laughed together, then Valerie continued. "It is important that no one is hurt," she exclaimed, "and you do not have to worry about becoming witches because you can see I am not a witch."

Silently the little family nodded. The crisis passed, Valerie stopped wearing her rings for the next two days, feeling it was necessary for her bonding experience with Pearse and his kin. She wanted them to see her as a friend, a mentor, a family member with the more familiar blue eyes than the blackness her eyes took on when wearing them. It worked.

Valerie, Pearse, and Lauryn planned together during this time, discussing the need to build an additional home on the ridge for Valerie. In addition to serving as her personal dwelling place, she intended to use the new building as a schoolhouse and library.

On the third day, about midday, the ground began to shake. The sound of thunder resonated as the *Dreamer's* engines engaged. Valerie sighed as the craft clawed its way into the sky above the valley.

Valerie dug into her robe, returned the rings to her right hand, then sent the ship on its way into the future when it came from. With everyone's eyes fixed intently on the ship, no one noticed what she had done. It was a bittersweet moment for her, knowing she had just cut the final cord to her former life.

The hunting party pursued the healer and her friends through the deep snow. Tracking them was easy; their footprints left a clear path for the hunters to follow, but an alarm was raised when the solar torches were ignited.

"What are those—*lamps?*" said one.

"I do not know. It is not like any lantern I have seen," observed another.

Amon did not know what to make of them, but those strange flames concerned him, fearing they could be weapons. He did not want to find out the hard way that they were weapons, so he decided on caution, holding his men back rather than allowing them to close the distance.

"We must be cautious—" he began, but Jotham cut him off mid-sentence.

"The old woman is a witch, the *Cailleach Bhéara!*" he exclaimed wide-eyed, pointing in the direction she had gone.

"Keep your voice down—idiot!" Amon whispered.

Jotham was not in a mood to be insulted. In his mind, there was no question about it, and his opinion was non-negotiable. That healer is a witch and must be destroyed immediately to prevent bad luck.

"You...*you* are the idiot, old man! That woman is a *witch!*" Jotham burst out angrily. Then he boasted, "I will kill *you* now—then I will kill that witch—and her friends!"

Jotham dropped his pack and drew his knife in a flash. With his weapon in hand and teeth bared, he lunged at Amon, who averted the strike by throwing his pack at his attacker, ducking, and rolling to one side. By the time Amon was back on his feet, he had his own knife in hand and was prepared to fight.

Free of their burdens, the men slashed at one another with their knives. The other men backed off to get out of the way.

Although older and more experienced, Amon was no longer fast enough to keep pace with Jotham, who was swift and strong. Aware the younger man was less experienced, he retreated a few steps allowing his opponent to believe he had the advantage.

Not one to miss an opportunity, Jotham lunged at Amon, attempting an undercut to the abdomen. Amon kicked snow in Jotham's face with perfect timing, temporarily blinding him. Jotham was thrown off balance just long enough for Amon to close the gap between them. As Jotham wiped snow from his eyes, Amon swung his big hunting knife, slicing Amon's throat, severing his windpipe.

Jotham dropped to his knees, gurgling, clutching his throat with both hands in an instinctive attempt to stem the flow of blood. With horror-filled eyes, Jotham sunk to his knees; his blank gaze remained fixed on his opponent until he collapsed from loss of blood face-down in the snow. In one swift movement, the fight was over, and with it the question of who was going to lead and who was going to die.

Although Amon never liked Jotham, he was considered a clan member in good standing. Jotham had a reputation as being reliable and a hard worker with strong hunting skills. But he was also known to be reckless, argumentative, and troublesome at times. *None of that will matter if an avenger of blood comes after me,* Amon worried.

A panicked glance at the other hunters told Amon all he needed to know. The clan had a strong sense of justice, with an elder body that could be called upon to judge adultery, property disputes, thefts, and murders. When the council made judgments of guilt, reparations were ordered. In the case of murders, death sentences might be issued.

Amon was thankful he had two witnesses who saw Jotham attack first and that he had acted in self-defense. His companions were honest men he could count on to tell the truth. But establishing those facts with them now would be a wise move. Amon didn't want trouble with the elders or from Jotham's family.

"Hethe," he called, "tell me what you saw. Tell me now!" Amon demanded.

Hethe knew just what Amon was getting at. "Jotham was angry; he attacked you. He tried to kill you, but you defended yourself, and you won," Hethe shot back without hesitation. "As you said, he was stupid."

"Very good," Amon agreed with a nod. "I do not want any trouble over this. Our stories must agree, or the elders will see murder."

Amon turned to the other hunter. "Abiah, did you see a murder?"

"No!" exclaimed Abiah with a hard stare. "I saw Jotham's attack. You defended yourself."

Amon rubbed his neck and furrowed his brow. Clan tradition required the men to return with their dead for burial, so the three remaining hunters prepared the body for transport by wrapping it in skins and fashioning a sling that would allow them to pull the body through the snow rather than carry it. Within minutes the hunters had returned to the snow trail left by the now-distant party they set out to follow.

As night set in, the three hunters continued on the path with the body of their fellow hunter trailing behind them by a length of braided hide. At a rise in the valley floor, they spotted a beacon of firelight on a distant ridge. The path they followed would lead them directly to it. Earlier, Amon had noticed two sets of old footprints leading toward the crater and three sets of more recent prints heading straight for the firelight on the hill. Logic told him the source of the signal fire must be home for those he followed.

As Amon focused on the signal fire, uncertainty set in as he realized he recognized this valley. He discovered this was an area he hunted yearly, not far from his own home in Erlin. Then his blood froze as the truth raged in his mind. He was nearly home. Beyond the ridge that looked so familiar was *his* home, too.

Amon stared, speechless. The people he followed with intent to kill if necessary and whose family had built a signal fire to light their way home were members of his own clan! The people the hunter intended to kill so they could steal the healer were his clan brothers! Even worse, he might know them, and that changed everything. If what he suspected was true and was sure it was, he would have to reconsider everything, including following them any further. But he still had to make certain of their identity, now more than ever.

"Hethe, Abiah, let's talk for a moment," Amon called, then squatted in the snow track to rest. The men pulling their grim package let go of their burden and joined him.

"Do you recognize this place?"

Hethe and Abiah looked puzzled. Abiah glanced around, then said, "There is nothing to recognize. It is too dark!"

Steadily Amon searched his two friends' faces. "Erlin is only a day's walk from here. And that fire is a beacon intended to light the way home for the people we are following. They must be of our clan. If true, we do not have to take the healer for ourselves; we already have her. Do you understand?"

"What makes you think we are close to home? The sky is black, and I can barely see the trail," said Abiah skeptically.

"Were you asleep when we left?" Amon fired back. "This valley is less than a day's journey south of Erlin. We are in the River Nore basin, and that is the Bearnán Éile ridge. I have had many good hunts here."

"You are right; I know the valley you speak of well but not coming from the south. I know it from the east. We never cross the twin rivers here because they are too muddy."

"That is true, but now the river is frozen, so it should be an easy crossing. I have been hunting this valley for years. I know where I am. Erlin is less than a day's walk. That fire is one hour from where we stand. Our people made that fire; you know what that means, right?"

"What do you want to do?" wondered Hethe.

Amon took a moment analyzing everything they had seen that strange day, thinking about why they set out after these people. The woman they were following resurrected that man. She had commanded soldiers, which troubled him, reasoning that this healer must be very special or rank highly to control those men. Did the men dislike being ordered by a woman? It didn't, which puzzled him even more.

But none of those concerns had anything to do with why he thought they should claim the healer for themselves. Now he was beginning to feel like it might be a bad idea to take the woman. Indeed, his people needed a good healer. Healing the dead was unheard of, but he and his men had seen it themselves. Perhaps that was why the woman led soldiers, because of her high value as a healer. Amon could not know, but he was sure he needed to learn where she was going and with whom.

Amon stood and spoke. "That woman is a powerful healer. She healed the dead man; we all saw it," he said, resisting the urge to refer to the woman as the *Cailleach Bhéara*, a witch. "We need to keep on following, so we know who she travels with and how to find her. But be careful. We cannot allow ourselves to be seen," he cautioned, and the men knew why.

The hunters plodded forward, following the snow trail and the beacon of firelight in the night. As they approached Pearse's farm, they left their packs and Jotham's body behind, then crouching low, crept close enough on hands and knees to hear the family's conversation with the woman without being detected.

As soon as Amon laid eyes on Pearse, he recognized the man as a clan member and someone he had seen trading in Erlin, his hometown. The healer stood silently by the fire as Pearse spoke to his family. Amon could not hear everything said, but he was aware they discussed the woman's presence there. The man told his wife the healer's name, but it was unfamiliar to Amon. Was it Valyri? He was not sure but made a mental note of it.

When Pearse called the healer to him, she turned to where Amon could see her face for the first time. *The woman's eyes!* he thought. The sight of her eyes turned his gut to stone. Black and lifeless as chunks of coal. Then he recalled what Jotham said about her being a witch. *It seems he was right after all*, Amon thought. Those lifeless witch eyes changed everything for him in an instant.

But Amon was not alone. The other men saw it too and thought the same thing: Jotham had been right about the healer. Only a witch could have eyes black as coal. Although Amon's gaze remained fixed on the people around the fire, he could feel the accusing eyes of his companions on him, judging him harshly. Remorse for killing the boy struck his heart like a dagger.

At that moment, Amon decided to send Hethe and Abiah home to Erlin with Jotham's body. But Amon felt like there was more to learn about this strange woman, so he chose to stay behind. Amon made a cold camp at the edge of the woods that night, staying low, looking, listening, and alone with his own thoughts until long after everyone had gone to sleep and the fire was ashes.

Mid-morning, Hethe returned and sat silently beside Amon. The two hunters shared a meager meal of dried meat and burdock in silence. Amon was the first to speak.

"Did you return Jotham to his family last night?" he whispered.

"We did, and it did not go well," admitted Hethe with a sideways glance. "Riordan, Jotham's father, accused you of murder. He wants your blood."

Amon's back stiffened, his eyes frozen in a downcast gaze. "What did you tell them?"

"I told them the truth. I said Jotham became angry and attacked you. You only defended yourself. Abiah backed my story. Jotham had a reputation for hot-headedness, and anyone that knew him saw it. You are innocent of murder, but you need to watch out for Riordan and his sons."

238 — PETER HARRETT

"What did you say about me not returning with you?"

"I told them you camped in the woods waiting for news of their response to Jotham's death. I said you wanted to avoid trouble with his family. But the elders want to talk to you about what happened. I said I would bring you the news and that you would return with me."

Amon looked away as he considered Hethe's report. When he turned his gaze to Hethe, his expression was warm, and he put a hand on his friend's shoulder. "You did well," Amon thanked his friend. "I will go with you, but let us sit and watch a while longer. There is more to learn here—I can feel it."

"What happened while I was gone? Did you learn anything more about that healer?" Hethe asked.

"Nothing yet, but I have a hunch that is going to change, and soon."

"The elders can wait," Hethe said with a note of finality, then settled in beside Amon with a grunt.

Amon breathed a sigh, then rubbed the back of his neck. It seemed that his worries multiplied by the minute. The shock of learning the healer was indeed a witch, combined with grief over killing the boy, was wearing on his nerves. Now he had the added burden of Riordan and his sons, who had a reputation for being troublesome.

The morning watch passed slowly for the two hunters as they lay in wait, watching and listening for anything that would help them learn more about the witch. Hethe wanted to see her dead eyes, but more than that. Both men were eager to know what a witch was doing in their land, living among them, and what it meant for their families and people.

As the morning passed, Pearse and his family came and went as they performed their everyday chores. The women drew water from the river, the children fed the animals, while the man and his boy cut firewood—but the healer never came close enough for Hethe to see the blackness in her eyes. However, mid-day, that abruptly changed.

The spies watched as the man and the boy slaughtered a goat and skinned it while the women and children carried armloads of firewood to the roasting pit. The witch worked with them, eventually coming close enough to provide Hethe with his first unobstructed view of the woman's eyes. Just as expected, Hethe found those hideous, lifeless pools of darkness terrifying. Only a witch could possess such numbingly cold eyes!

Hethe stiffened at the sight as a wave of dread had him gnashing his teeth. For a moment running away crossed his mind, but he suppressed the urge as his hunter's instinct took over. "Never give your position away unnecessarily," his father taught him at an early age. Only that kept the man from fleeing.

"Stay down," whispered Amon, who sensed his friend's trepidation.

Then it occurred to Amon; the witches' dead eyes did not seem to bother the children, who walked with her hand-in-hand. Even the smallest child seemed comfortable in her presence. *Was she working her magic on them? Did she plan to kill the children and eat them? And if the witch did intend to harm the children, what would he do about it? What power could he have against a witch?*

The hunters brooded as a bonfire was made in the roasting pit then allowed to burn down to coals. The roasting pit was close to where they were hidden, so they had a clear view and heard much of what was said. A mutual sigh of relief passed between the two men when they understood the goat was about to be roasted rather than the children.

Once a good bed of coals was established, the meat was buried in the pit and covered with soil. An hour before dusk, the meat was removed from the pit, and the family gathered for a feast of roasted goat that smelled delicious. As they ate and talked around the warm fire, the hungry hunters shivered and salivated in their snowy stakeout.

With the evening meal out of the way, the spies watched in wonder as the hag stood taking center stage to speak to the man and his family. The witch's face illuminated in flickering firelight added a strong sense of drama to the strange scene. Captivated by the witch as she spoke, the huntsmen tensed, focused hard, straining to hear every word.

Although they could not understand everything said, the gist of the message was unmistakable: the information she was about to reveal was important. The healer began by calling her audience "friends," thanking them for their hospitality, and announcing she had important news and gifts for all of them. She claimed to be a traveler from a distant land, and they should accept the gift she offered—the scene bordered on surreal with the witch speaking with absolute authority.

Then as if revealing a secret, her voice softened, becoming unintelligible to the onlookers in the snow. However, one word was unmistakable: *magic*. And with it, the spies' pulses quickened.

The hag raised her voice, held out her right-hand high for everyone to see, then ordered a log into the air with a command that sent it into the fire without anyone ever laying a hand on it. The log landed among the embers, releasing a shower of sparks high into the night air.

"You *are* a witch!" cried the clansmen's voice as he jumped to his feet. With that, Amon and Hethe had seen all the proof they needed; this old woman was unarguably the *Cailleach Bhéara*— a witch. Without a word, it was mutually decided it was time for Amon and Hethe to leave. Quickly gathering their things together, the huntsmen backed away on hands and knees into the safety of the darkened woods.

With everyone working together, Valerie's new home rapidly took shape. The women and children hauled red shale stones from a nearby landslide in a wagon pulled by a cow while Pearse and Tierney prepared the building site. Relative uniformity in thickness made the flat shale stones a suitable building material. The brittle nature of shale made breaking them into desired widths and lengths manageable. Mud was dug out of the river for use as mortar, and timbers cut for beams and sheeting boards. Thin slabs of shale were used as shingles.

Working together, they would complete the new home in a little over a week. Valerie was pleased with the results. She judged it to be the equivalent of many homes built as late as the nineteenth century. It was sturdy with straight walls, a pitched roof, with a wooden door secured to the opening by thick leather straps. Window openings framed in wood, a wooden shutter secured by leather straps, hung above each

window opening. Shale stone floors would keep the dust down in the dry season.

Pearse's home had a fire pit built into the center of the room for cooking. Although it worked, the house was always cold and smoky. Since Valerie saw no harm in introducing fireplace flue and chimney technology to the world, she explained what she wanted and made the fire pit obsolete in a day. When Pearse and Lauryn saw how nicely it worked, they wasted no time adding a fireplace to their own home.

Pearse's dwelling was nearly void of furniture, so Valerie was pleasantly surprised by the quality of the furniture he crafted for her. With Tierney's help, he produced a good solid table with four chairs in under a week. A desk and storage cabinet made according to her dimensions came soon after. The house was warm, secure, and comfortable. It was more than she had hoped for.

At first, Valerie had no choice other than to stay with Pearse and his family, but she felt a great sense of relief with the project completed. Standing back to look at it, she was genuinely pleased. The little house was soundly built, clean, and solved her privacy issues. The feeling of being a visitor rather than a resident in this new world would never leave her until she had her own secure space. Safety from snoopers, thieves, and wild animals would be excellent in the little stone house.

Considering the self-imposed mission she had assigned herself, Valerie feared failure more than anything else. As she saw it, everything, including the future of humankind, depended on the success of her time gambit. The responsibility of going it alone was a heavy burden to bear, but she saw no viable alternative.

Then there was the unrelenting fear of creating a time paradox. That, more than anything else, kept her awake at night. *What if I died before I could successfully transfer the rings to my new family? Would I fail to reappear in the future timeline? Would anyone I have known and loved ever come to be? What if I have already altered the future in a way I cannot perceive?* Those questions haunted her from the first day she seriously began planning her escape from the future.

In her mind, the nature of her dilemma was just that; any problem-solving decision or judgment made rested on her own shoulders. She had no one else to consult or rely upon for a second opinion, which left Valerie feeling hollow inside. The fear of failure followed like a lost dog; it just would not go away.

Recently, Valerie began second-guessing her decision to leave Hafian Tohm behind. *I am lonely for intelligent conversation,* she brooded. *Pearse and his people are by no means stupid, but that does not make up for the seven-thousand-year developmental gap separating us. That disparity hinders the type of interaction to which I am accustomed. If only I had brought Hafian with me!*

Although Hafian was never Valerie's lover, he was at the heart of her inner circle of friends, her closest companion, and confidant. Hafian Tohm was the nearest thing to a mate she had had for centuries. Leaving him behind had turned out to be more difficult than she could have imagined. She remembered how her association with Hafian began when he was assigned as a mentee. It wasn't long before they developed an affinity for one another and were inseparable.

Thinking of Hafian, Valerie's face paled. *I knew he would have jumped at the chance to come with me. But that doesn't make*

it any easier because I couldn't allow it. Removing two people from
the timeline doubled the chances of a paradox. In the end, I was
forced to leave him behind. I had no choice. It was simply too risky
to include him.

As planning for the adventure began in earnest, hiding
her true intentions from Hafian became increasingly difficult.
Aware he suspected she was concealing something from him
only heightened the sense that she had betrayed her friend's
trust. She hated herself for the supposed transgression,
purposely moving the timetable forward searching for relief.
She just wanted to get on with it, in a sense running from the
hurt and guilt. Even so, she had underestimated the impact
that feeling forever alone would have on her, and now she
was paying the price.

But this was the reality Valerie had chosen for herself,
and it was too late for second guesses. She had done due
diligence and steeled herself for the challenge. With
construction completed on her new house, it was time to
move forward. The house provided her with a new level of
security and privacy. It was time to implement the next stage
of her plan, educating Pearse and his family.

Since the family was illiterate, she would need to change
that if they would learn everything she intended to teach
them and retain that knowledge for future generations.
Thinking of this made Valerie chuckle. In addition to serving
as her home, the little house would now become the world's
first and only schoolhouse run by a three-thousand-year-old
teacher.

The River Nore snaked through the fertile basin surrounded by wooded highlands. Situated below a mountain pass at a crossroads made the settlement of Erlin a convenient place for travelers to find lodging and resupply before moving on. An arched stone bridge where the two roads intersected gave the village a sense of permanence, providing the enclave with its sole landmark.

Eager to share what they learned, Amon and Hethe made their first stop in Erlin at Abiah's home. They were able to confirm the healer they had observed for more than a day was in fact, a witch. Both men were eyewitnesses: they saw the death in her eyes first-hand, as well as the magic the woman employed. Although unspoken among them, the truth of Jotham's death hung above Amon's head like a sword hanging by a hair.

Abiah reported the elder council had already organized an inquest into Jotham's death and was scheduled to be held in seven days. The three hunters would be required to make a statement about what happened. Abiah warned Jotham's father, Riordan, had formally accused Amon of blood guilt in the matter. Jotham's brothers could be touchy, but with Riordan provoking them, they were downright dangerous. The three men agreed to be on-guard if Riordan or his sons attempted to avenge the blood.

Days of travel and nights spent in the snow had sapped Amon's strength. He went home that night with a stiff body and downcast spirit. Ill at ease about the inquest, the fear of avengers weighed heavily on him. After lighting a lamp, he decided it was too late to start a fire, so he went straight to bed. He heard a knock at the door and groaned as he laid among the warm woolen blankets considering his testimony for the inquest. The last thing he needed was a visitor—or worse, for Riordan or his sons to show up.

Amon put his big hunting knife in his belt, ready to defend himself if necessary. Slowly, carefully, he opened the door. To his surprise, he found the witch wrapped in a blanket. Startled by the unexpected visitor, his first instinct was to slam the door and hide behind it, although instinct also told him the witch was not going to be stopped by a door if she really wanted in. But what surprised him most was the color of her eyes. No longer were they the foreboding black orbs he remembered from the cold camp, but rather pale blue, without a hint of threat.

What kind of witch's trick is this? Amon wondered. *Just hours ago,* the *Cailleach Bhéara* was an old hag with the eyes of the dead. But now she is more you*thful with blue eyes? Do not believe your eyes; you know what she is!*

Amon struggled to make sense of it, feeling like he was being pulled in two separate directions. On the one hand, there was no question as to what he saw; a magic-wielding witch with the eyes of the dead. *A witch who resurrected the dead! Who could do such things but a powerful witch?* But on the other hand, there was a harmless-looking woman at his door. *What do I do?* he thought.

Gazing at the unexpected visitor at his door, Amon trembled, and his heart pounded. Up close and in person, the witch did not look to be nearly as old as he remembered nor as menacing. Amon saw no threat from her in the thin light, which puzzled him. In his estimation, she appeared to be in her mid-to-late forties, roughly his own age, which did not seem to match up with what he thought he saw from his hiding place in the woods.

But none of that mattered. Too many questions remained demanding answers. What was this woman doing on his doorstep? How did she find him? And most troubling was the question: how did she know he had been watching her?

"I would like to speak to you, Amon. Is that possible?" the witch inquired, a disarming smile pulling at her lips. Amon stared at her in wonder for a long moment, not knowing what to say or do. Then he recalled the log she had thrown into the fire and knew that if she really wanted in or to cause harm, he could not stop her. Reluctantly, Amon stepped aside, silently inviting the woman into his home with a welcoming hand.

"Sit," Amon gestured to a bench in front of his fire pit. "It is cold. I will light a fire."

The witch did not object, sitting in silence as Amon started a fire, maintaining a wary eye on the witch as he moved about the room. Amon sat across from the late-night visitor once the fire was up, his brows furrowed, his eyes guarded in the flickering firelight.

"How did you find me? And why are you here?" Amon asked directly.

The healer countered, evading the question by shifting the topic. "Next week, there will be an inquest, a trial for the murder of your fellow hunter. Is that true?"

"Yes," Amon nodded, wondering how she knew these things. That this old woman seemed to know more about him than he knew about her was not lost on him. Somehow the hag knew his name, occupation, and where to find him. *More witch's tricks!* he thought.

"I will be there with you," she said convincingly, still smiling.

Amon's eyes narrowed. "Why?"

"It will not be safe for you. There will be a fight. I can help you."

Amon tensed. He did not like what she said but knew she was probably right. *I know Riordan and his sons well enough to know they may never forgive the death of one of their own. Jotham's death was unavoidable, he got what he deserved, but that changed nothing with those people.*

I cannot fight them all by myself; there are too many and too strong. Nor can I expect help from Hethe and Abiah; they know what would happen to them if they were to fight beside me. Riordan and his men would make quick work of all of us. The truth is, I am on my own and probably doomed!

"Why would you want to help me?"

Now it was the witch's pale blue eyes that narrowed. "I want you to return the favor by helping me afterward. Also, it will not be safe for you here any longer." Then she added, "And I think you know why." But now, the smile was gone, replaced by a mask of foreboding.

Amon looked away as he considered her words. *I cannot argue with her,* he thought. *It would probably be better for everyone if I walked away now and just kept going. Jotham's family is not going to care about the truth. They will want to avenge the blood and not stop until they have it. Although, having a witch at my side has a certain appeal.* Amon brightened at the possibility.

"What do you want from me?"

"You and I, we have the same problem; neither of us is safe. Although, we could keep each other safe—in different ways."

"You are the *Cailleach Bhéara*—a witch. Your magic will keep *you* safe," Amon scoffed.

"I am not a witch," she fired back, her brow furrowing. "But, I cannot help what others think of me. In some places, they burn witches. Don't you see? I cannot stay awake all the time—and I don't have eyes in the back of my head! We can help each other by working together."

"I think you *are* a witch," Amon huffed, avoiding admitting he had seen her magic just hours before her unexpected arrival at his door.

"It's easy to call someone a witch when you don't understand them," she objected. "Is the wind the work of witches? You cannot see it or touch it, but you see and feel its power, and yet you do not blame the wind on the work of witches. Do you?"

Amon remained silent, listening and thinking as Valerie went on. His eyes searched her features, exploring her eyes for signs of sorcery but finding no visual or verbal queues.

Valerie continued. "What force pulls you to Earth when you fall? Can you see what pulled you down? When you hit the ground, do you blame the fall on witches?

"Those powers are invisible, you cannot see them, but you know what they can do," she reasoned. "You do not understand them, but you do not deny they exist nor call them the work of the spirits, do you? Maybe you saw something I did and did not understand it, so you call me a witch. Do you call everything you don't understand the work of witches?"

Amon winced as he considered her argument. Her words cut deeply, made him feel stupid, but he saw her point. *Maybe I was too quick to call her a witch,* he thought and felt a twinge of guilt for it. She was also right about his safety. Right or wrong, innocent, or guilty, none of that would matter when Jotham's brothers came after him in force. And they might never stop coming until they decided Jotham's death had been properly avenged. His gut told him that was more likely to occur than not. Amon felt cornered with no way out.

Stories of witches being hunted and killed were commonplace. He supposed she must also be right about her own safety. He did not have to look far for an example, either. Jotham was ready to kill the woman based merely on suspicion until he put an end to it. Amon decided to take a chance and throw his lot in with the woman.

"Enough. What would you have me do?" he said, frustration evident in his tone.

"Protect me. You protect me, and I will protect you, then we both can be safe."

"I see, and if Jotham's brothers surround us?"

"I nuke all of them."

Amon looked puzzled. "What is 'nuke'?"

"Sorry. I meant I would destroy them if necessary."

"You can do that?"

"If necessary, yes," the witch said calmly, her hands working swiftly under the blanket. Suddenly her eyes were black as obsidian, reflecting flames from the fire like a pair of oval mirrors.

"I must see this 'nuke'—show me!" Amon cried as he pulled the big hunting knife from his belt and, in one swift motion, threw it straight at the witch's heart. The knife flew true but stopped inches from her upraised hand—the right hand, the one wearing five dull copper rings on all four fingers and a thumb. And then the knife dropped safely to the floor with a clatter.

Amon gasped, his mouth hanging open. "I see," he said, his eyes fixed on the big knife. "I needed to know if what you say is true."

"Consider yourself nuked," the witch laughed.

"How did you know I would do that?"

"Your heart spoke to me, and I heard it. Healers do that; we listen to hearts. Do you understand?"

"I understand that you would make a valuable partner, and you just proved it."

The witch's hands moved under the blanket again, then the blackness in her gaze dissolved and was blue once more. Although Amon had agreed to work with her, he wondered what he was getting himself into. Would the arrangement she proposed be more than a simple security partnership between them?

Then it occurred to him; the woman lived more than an hour distant from Erlin. Would relocation be required? Logic told him that he would be forced to abandon his home if he went with her, so he did not ask. If escaping Jotham's brothers meant leaving Erlin behind, he would be forced to go with her.

"I believe Jotham's brothers will fight me to avenge the death even if I am judged innocent of bloodguilt by the council. That means I cannot stay here after the trial. I will be an easy target here in my own home. Together we will 'nuke' our enemies—yes?"

"Good, I will see you next week then," Valerie said, standing and rubbing her palms together, pleased with herself.

"You are leaving?" Amon asked as he stood with her. "It's too cold and dark for you to travel. Stay here tonight; I have more blankets," he offered, genuinely concerned for her safety.

"It's alright. I have lodging nearby," Valerie lied as she continued moving for the door. "I will see you at the inquest," she promised as she pulled the door closed behind her.

"Wait!" Amon called. "One question before you go."

"Alright, what is it?"

"What do I call you?"

"Call me Valerie," she said with a slight smile pulling at her lips, her blue eyes lingering on the man's chiseled features.

"Valyri," he repeated, seemingly pleased.

"I saw your eyes, they were black, but now they are blue. Why?"

"Magic," she said with a coy smile, then pulled the door shut. Amon was left puzzled, dissatisfied by her response. Had the woman mocked him?

—————————————————

Valerie shivered in the frosty night air, then, pulling the blanket tightly around herself, ran silently on the cobblestone road. She ran with no specific direction in mind; after all, it didn't matter which way she went. She merely needed to gain distance from Amon's house as quickly as possible.

The road and stone buildings about her were perceptible only as murky shadows. Stars in the moonless sky provided just enough light to navigate the village streets. The chill stung her lungs. Breaths came as puffs of white mist in the night.

Good, she thought, panting, *I got what I came for, Amon's allegiance, and without being noticed. Loved seeing the look on his face when he realized I knew he was watching us. Wonder if he realizes I just saved his life?*

Turning at the first corner, she stopped and held herself against the stone wall, breathing hard. With her senses on high alert, she waited for any sign of being followed.

Another successful jump. Things are coming together nicely. We need him. When the time comes, having Amon on our side will make things a lot more manageable, she reasoned.

A cautious peek around the corner revealed nothing; the way she had come remained deserted. Nothing moved in the frozen village. No lights were visible, no sound was heard, even the night air seemed abandoned. The time traveler was nothing more than a shadowy figure on a deserted street.

When she felt sure she was alone and unobserved, Valerie pulled the fifth ring from inside her inner garment. When it was on her thumb, she imagined herself in her home in the twenty-fourth century. If anyone had witnessed it, they would have said they saw a woman's form glimmer for an instant and then extinguished like a flame blown out by the wind.

Chapter 9

Valerie Dunne— June Present-Day

Corell Paris waited patiently, answering Valerie's questions as she took her time moving through his study, inspecting each item, seeing everything, missing nothing. Once she had examined everything, and with her curiosity satisfied, she dropped into the big leather chair across from Corell as if exhausted.

"I couldn't find the Ark of the Covenant in your collection, but it is nice to know the Holy Grail is in good hands," She joked.

They laughed together, then Corell fired back, "Do you want to see it?" He moved to the edge of his chair as if he were about to show it to her.

"Really?" she asked, taking the bait, excitement in her eyes, tilting the eyeglasses on her nose for a better view.

"Naw, just kidding," he admitted, settling back into the chair. Corell was pleased the girl took such a keen interest in things he considered important, feeling that it boded well for their relationship.

"Seriously, you have an amazing collection!" Valerie gushed. "I love the paintings and sculptures. When we vacationed in Washington DC, we saw a Gutenberg Bible at the Library of Congress. They are extremely rare, so I was surprised to see you have one. It's amazing!" she said enthusiastically.

"I've had a while to accumulate them," he conceded.

"There is a question I have meant to ask."

"Ask away."

"Surely people notice you don't age as others do. How do you deal with that?"

Corell's gaze detached from her as if she had pulled the cord on a curtain, allowing him to see into his past, evoking repressed memories long buried. The images of a hundred lives, the faces of a thousand family and friends, flashed before him, driving an invisible spear through his heart.

Valerie couldn't help but notice the remorse in his eyes. He looked down. At that moment, she regretted asking and wished she could take it back. Just as quickly as that spear stabbed at his heart, it struck at hers. They shared the pain in a way she could not comprehend. She saw the accumulation of sorrows amassed by more than a millennium of abandoning loved ones, deserting cherished friends, standing by as they grew old and died. Far more was said in that brief silence than if he had read the book for her.

"Oh my," she gasped, struggling to make her voice sound normal, readjusting her glasses which had slipped down. "I felt that. It *hurt!*" she exclaimed, taking a deep breath as tears welled in her eyes. Valerie held her hands to her heart as if trying to protect it from further harm. "I'm so sorry for you, Corell," she sobbed.

Corell cleared his throat. "The rings connect us," he explained. "It is a telepathic bond that will only intensify as you grow closer to me and connect with the rings. The same thing happened to me when I came of age and began feeling my father's pain. I watched him perish," he said, a hitch in his voice. "He outlived—he had to desert many families, too. But I was able to stay by his side because I was the heir to the fifth ring. Leaving the people we love behind is by far the most difficult burden we must bear. I pray you can find a way to deal with it or somehow avoid it."

For a moment, Corell glanced at the wall, clenching his jaw, his face a mask of unspoken pain. "This life is something that requires planning ahead," he said sadly. "I have always kept a backup identity in a second location. Every fifty years or so, the time comes for me to move, so I move and assume the next identity. I've been here longer than I should, but I think this place will be my last stand." He smiled, attempting to put a positive spin on what troubled him most in life.

"What do you mean—the last stand?"

"I mean, I've had my time," Corell admitted with light in his eyes. "You are here; you have arrived—*it's your turn now.*"

Valerie nodded, looking at her hands.

"When I turn the ring over to you, I will begin aging again at a normal rate. I plan to make this my last home. I've had plenty of time to prepare, so I am good with it," Corell assured.

Valerie understood the import of everything Corell told her, and it made sense. But what he said about watching his father perish troubled her deeply. She wasn't sure why it bothered her so much. Perhaps it was his use of the word *perish.* Is that what was in store for her, just to watch him perish, to slowly fade away? Had Corell been forced to watch his father wither and die? What could she expect to happen when Corell turned his ring over to her? Valerie needed to know more.

"You said you watched Bede *perish,* which is an odd choice of words. What happened to him?"

"He um, my father deteriorated quickly—he was gone in about six months." Corell shifted uncomfortably in his chair, still grieving for the loss of his father after more than a millennium. After a silent moment, he continued.

"I expect the same will be true for me," he admitted, then immediately brightened, slapping Valerie on the knee encouragingly. "The important thing is you are finally here. I've waited my entire life for this, so I hope you can appreciate how excited I am."

Corell became very serious now. "Valerie— you need to understand you have a lot to learn and no time to spare. We need to get busy, work hard, and get you up to speed so you can reach your full potential. Only then can you defend yourself well enough to seek out the other rings. That is what this is all about. You need to shut everything else out of your life until you have all five rings. Do you understand?"

Valerie nodded enthusiastically, showing she was all-in. The excitement was building in both of them.

"Once you have all five of them in your possession, you will be complete. Eventually, you will be on your own, but until then, I will be here for you," Corell promised, smiling.

Valerie stared at the ring on Corell's hand, coveting it shamelessly, visualizing wearing it and feeling its power for the very first time. She wondered what it would be like, then remembered it had been her ring in another life. *Did that matter now?* What if something unexpected happened to her when she reclaimed it? Would she become that other person—that other Valerie Dunne? Those disquieting thoughts troubled her but decided she would have to wait and see, so she pushed anxiety aside for now.

"When do we start?" she muttered, never moving her eyes from the ring.

"Immediately. We should begin tomorrow, but not here at the farm. We are going to need privacy for what I have planned for you. We have a safe house nearby, so we'll go there."

"I can't help but wonder how many people know about this—about the ring, I mean."

"Other than you, no one here at the farm," Corell assured her. "A few on the outside, though. It is a well-kept secret. Those who know about the rings keep their mouths shut for fear of generating their own competition. That and being thought of as being crazy," he laughed.

Since she first arrived here, Valerie wondered who knew Corell's secret. *He surrounded himself with so many people,* she thought, *and yet not one of them is aware of it, not even April?* That was hard for her to believe. Perhaps April was not as close to him as she thought.

How did he hide the truth from so many people for thirteen hundred years? That could not have been easy. She could not imagine living with the constant fear of being unmasked. But the fact that Corell had anticipated her arrival for centuries was even more sobering. Was it any wonder why he was so excited to see her in the here and now?

Valerie admired his tenacity and dedication to the cause he had embraced. Corell Paris had become relatable, and he mattered to her. Moreover, she saw him as family— immediate family. But thinking of him that way troubled her.

She did not want to see him as a grandson or a grandfather, but wasn't he one of those? *What if—he was both?* She thought with a sudden shiver. It was all just too weird to think about, so she changed mental gears and asked:

"How long will we be there?"

Corell settled back in his chair before answering, making an arch with his fingertips as he worked the schedule out in his mind.

"I'd say about a week," he allowed. "More or less, depending on how it goes. It will be just the two of us. We will not have any help, so we will have to do our own cooking and cleaning, that sort of stuff. There is no food in the house, so we need to go shopping. We can go together this afternoon if you would like. Plus, it will give you a chance to look around Jacksonville."

"Sure, sounds good," Valerie agreed.

"Before we go, there's one small piece of business we still need to take care of. I need your phone." Corell then held out his hand, palm up, waiting for the phone to arrive there.

Valerie took her phone from her hip pocket and placed it in his hand without argument.

"I had time to think about it, and I'm okay with it," she confessed, then added, "I understand."

"Thank you. I am glad you see how important it is to conceal your whereabouts. Your life might depend on it. I hope you haven't made any calls or texts from here."

"The last time I texted was when we were still on the road."

"Good girl! Then let's get going. We're burning daylight."

Corell led the way from his office to the big garage next to the house. Unlike most large outbuildings she had seen back home, which were either steel or pole construction, this one was wood framed, sided, and finished to match the house. Concrete walkways surrounded the building giving it a businesslike appearance.

The garage was dark inside. Valerie realized the building was expansive, bigger than it looked from outside. The ceiling was high, and the concrete floor polished. The familiar scent of new automobiles mixed with the pungent odor of oil and rubber welcomed her as she stood in the light of the open doorway.

Corell flipped a switch, and the lights flickered to life. A showy display of strobing neon assaulted her senses all at once. Scores of lighted automobilia signs, antique gas pumps, jukeboxes, and collectibles seemed to jump from the walls, one after another filling the cavernous building in a blissful glow. The multitude of colors reminded her of Christmastime. The lounge was closest to the door with a bar, couch, chairs, and big screen TV.

The big garage was home to a massive collection of vehicles ranging from classic cars, trucks, motorcycles, and scooters of every size and shape. Some were current models, others antiques. Valerie guessed she saw twenty to thirty vehicles parked three-deep in places, not including the motorcycles.

"Follow me," Corell beckoned as he stepped away and began snaking his way through the maze of vehicles.

"Since we're going to the old farm today, we may as well take the old farm truck." He said it with a wry smile leading her to believe the old farm truck must be something special.

Her first guess was that it must be one of the many hot rods, but she was a bit deflated when she saw the well-used, scuffed-up old Ford truck.

"The old F-1 may be ugly but makes up for it by being uncomfortable and noisy," Corell joked as he swung the door open and jumped in. Once Valerie was seated, she began searching for a seatbelt. "Don't worry," he said, "this vintage didn't come with seatbelts. They weren't required back in the day. They didn't have power steering or air conditioning, so roll down the window and enjoy the ride. It's a beautiful day."

Corell pushed a button on a garage door opener, clipped to the sun visor, then turned the key, but nothing happened. Then to Valerie's surprise, he pushed a button on the floor with his foot, and the old truck fired to life with a cough as the garage door rolled up. Valerie stifled a giggle as he stirred the gearbox a couple of times, then the truck surged into motion with a grinding jerk that threw her head back. Soon the old pickup was rattling downhill toward Jacksonville, along the Applegate River.

"Jacksonville is about a twenty-minute drive because the road is pretty windy," Corell confessed over the rumble of the exhaust and whine of the manual transmission.

"Roll down the window," Corell encouraged, "you don't want to miss the scenery."

The spring day was warm, the sky clear, with the spicy scent of madrone and pine present. Late morning sunlight filtered through the canopy of trees producing a strobe effect as they rolled along the winding road beside the little river. As they rounded a bend, they passed a clearing with a small park where people were picnicking and swimming in the shallow water.

Mesmerizing, Valerie thought. *Corell was right. The beauty of the little river canyon is hypnotic, made all the better by the clunky old truck, and riding with an elbow sticking out the window. I've never seen such a beautiful place!* The winding two-lane road prevented the truck or any vehicle from moving very fast, which suited her perfectly. She could see why Corell chose the old road.

As the truck entered Jacksonville, she found the historic downtown had a late nineteenth-century Wild West feel. The architecture was a mixture of brick facades, clapboard-sided buildings, and wood plank sidewalks. Trendy shops and restaurants lined the main roads. Business was good that warm Sunday afternoon as tourists clogged the streets and shops.

The first stop was a supermarket where they shopped for groceries, stocking up with enough supplies to last for a week. From there, they went to the Big Y Sporting Goods store, which puzzled Valerie.

"Sporting goods? What do we need here?" she asked.

"Ammunition," he answered.

"Seriously? You have enough weapons and ammunition on your property to re-fight World War II and win. What do you need more ammunition for?"

"Specifically? We're here for bowling balls and arrows," Corell stated with a cocked eyebrow as he left the truck.

The absurdity of it froze Valerie in her tracks. Confronting Corell with hands on her hips, she exclaimed, "Let me get this straight. We're shopping for bowling balls and arrows, right? What are we going to do, practice fighting off invading Mongols from the castle walls?"

Corell stood his ground, crossed his arms, and locked his gaze defiantly on hers. A staring match ensued, which quickly became a contest of wills between two stubborn would-be bowling ball and arrow shoppers.

Evidently, taking one's eyes away from the other contestant was off-limits. With neither participant willing to look away or blink, the staring bout became a prolonged test of wills. With her eyes fastened on his, the girl stepped one pace closer to the man in a classic attempt at distraction. However, the move backfired miserably when the man countered by making one giant step forward, bringing them face-to-face and nose-to-nose. Desperate and out of options, the battle of wills that took place in the parking lot of the Big Y Sporting Goods store came to a draw when, with steely eyes, the girl whispered, "That's as messed up as a left-handed football bat."

That sent them both into hysterics, laughing until they cried, and their sides ached.

"Where did you ever hear that?" he crowed, laughing uncontrollably.

"A fisherman," she cried, bent over and holding her sides. "His reel broke—and the line unspooled all over him!" she said, coughing and wiping her eyes on her sleeve. "Went off like a hand grenade!"

That did it. Now Corell was doubled over in laughter, with Valerie laughing, coughing, and choking all at once.

Finally, still grinning like a couple of hyenas and wiping tears from their eyes, Corell and Valerie entered the sporting goods store, hugging each other like long-lost drinking buddies. In this single moment of silliness, an invisible wall between them buckled, crumbled, and fell, instantly replaced by an enduring bond.

Corell pushed a shopping cart ahead of them toward the back of the store with Valerie close at his side. When they reached the gun counter, the attendant behind the glass case, a large round-faced man in his forties, predictably asked if he could help them.

"Bowling balls and arrows," said Corell stiffly, his brow furrowed as he suppressed the urge to give in to more laughter. He glanced back at Valerie, who quickly turned away, holding her mouth with both hands.

"I need twenty-five target arrows and four bowling balls," Corell managed. "Can you direct me toward them?"

Sensing the humor in it, the clerk said with a sly grin, "Shooting skeet with bowling balls and arrows, eh? That's a new one."

The sales attendant helped them gather what they needed then checked them out. As they loaded everything in the truck, Valerie asked, "You never told me what you plan to do with this stuff."

"Shoot skeet, what else?" Corell shrugged, feigning innocence. Then he added, "I prefer to keep you guessing, but you'll see what I have in mind soon enough."

"Okay," she said with a roll of her eyes, guessing that whatever Corell had in store for her was worth the wait, so she let it go at that.

From the Jacksonville Big Y, the old truck turned toward home, heading back up the mountain toward the old farmhouse. Corell stopped at a cattle crossing and opened a gate leading to an access road. The road through the forest was a mile-long dirt track. Occasional washouts made the going slow. Soon the forest diminished, and the truck rolled onto pastureland, a farm with outbuildings became visible in the distance.

They passed a mature orchard of mixed fruit trees with evidence of recent pruning. Spring growth with flowers still adorned many of the trees. Cultivated fields beyond the grove stretched for what seemed like miles.

The dirt trail transitioned into a smooth concrete drive as they neared. The house was a mid-century bungalow, white with green accents, well maintained despite the remote location. When Valerie saw the attractive little house, she didn't need to ask to know the rough trail leading there was intended to discourage trespassers.

An impressive oak tree stood in front of the house with a tire swing hanging from a massive branch. Valerie stared wonderingly at the tire swing, its existence implying children had once played there. The knee-high field grass indicated the old tire swing had gone unused for a long time. Still, she had trouble taking her eyes away from it. Somehow it seemed that tire swing had called to her and touched her heart.

Corell parked in front of the two-car garage beside the house. A big red barn with matching cupolas on a high-pitched roof sat directly behind it. An attached lean-to sheltered tractors and farm implements. Beyond the barn, a livestock yard and old chicken coops had fallen into disrepair.

Corell unlocked the backdoor to the house but appeared hesitant to go inside, which puzzled Valerie. His mood had noticeably deteriorated since turning onto the road. Valerie followed his fleeting gaze as he seemed to be searching for something lost. He was distracted, but she didn't want to pry. Had the house been broken into? Momentarily, Corell cleared his throat, pulled the door open, and tentatively stepped inside.

"Let me show you around," he said unenthusiastically.

"Alright," she allowed.

Inside, there was no sign of a break-in; everything seemed to be in order. The air was stale, so Corell opened the screened front door to get the air moving. Not wanting to be left behind in a strange house, Valerie followed dutifully, with the old wooden floors creaking in protest every step of the way.

The house was old but in good condition. Antique free-standing lamps stood beside a couch and an easy chair. A coffee table and end tables topped by white lace doilies matched the white lace curtains filtering the warm afternoon sunlight as it played in the room. Firewood stacked on the hearth added its scent.

"When we purchased the property back in the 1920s, the house was already here," Corell reported. "But it has been updated a couple of times since then. It was the main farmhouse back then. Originally, we farmed one-hundred and twenty acres here, but that has increased quite a bit since then," he explained.

Corell continued the tour, leading the way. He showed her the downstairs office but simply pointed to the master bedroom, considering it improper to take the girl inside. Upstairs were two dormered bedrooms and a full bathroom situated between them.

"I'll be in the master bedroom," he explained, "so tomorrow, you will have your choice of either of the upstairs bedrooms."

With the tour out of the way, they set to work unloading the truck and stocking the kitchen cupboards and refrigerator. Once done, Corell locked the house back up, and they headed back down the rough road. By the time they arrived back at the farm, it was late afternoon. Lunch had been unintentionally overlooked, so Corell and Valerie were already thinking about dinner.

Valerie felt terrible about leaving Orson cooped up in her room all day, so she ran upstairs to check on him but found the door ajar with no cat in sight. *Oh no!* she thought and quickly checked under the bed. Nothing there, and a quick inspection of the room revealed no Orson. Panicked, she ran downstairs, calling his name—"Orson! Orson!?"—and was instantly relieved to see her beloved cat sprawled out on his back between Corell and April, enjoying a belly rub.

"Oh, there you are, you big lug," Valerie declared. Relieved, she sat at Corell's feet, rubbing the big tabby's furry head.

"How did he get out? I was so worried he might have run off!" Valerie confessed.

"After you left this morning, I went up to your room to feed him, but when I opened the door, Orson went through it like a shot," April explained. "Then I found him sitting in Corell's chair next to the fireplace, acting like he owned the place. He's fine," she assured Valerie. "Orson spent the day entertaining everyone. I don't think you need to worry about him running off."

Hearing this, Orson perked up his ears, his eyes glinting at April. "How can we spoil you if you run off?" April asked, speaking in baby-talk to the satisfied-looking cat, who purring loudly.

When Corell reached out to scratch under Orson's chin, the cat unexpectedly rolled over, sat up, then perched on his lap, staring him straight in the face with an unblinking gaze.

"What's he doing?" April exclaimed. "He looks like the Sphinx of Egypt!"

"I can't figure it out," Valerie shot back, her face a mask of bewilderment. "Ever since he first saw Corell, he's paid no attention to me at all. He seems to love Corell but ignores me entirely. I'm getting jealous!"

"Cats are strange," April observed. Then to comfort the girl, she added, "Don't worry, he'll be back to normal once he settles in. Won't you, Orson?" But this time, the baby-talk did not deter the animal's odd behavior. Neither did rubbing his ears have the desired effect. Orson perched stiffly, eyes fixed on Corell, unblinking and immovable until Corell spoke.

"Speaking of cats," he said, clearly amused. "Valerie and I are going to get away for a few days, maybe a week. I think we should leave Orson here. Would that be alright with you, April?"

Valerie could not believe her eyes when Orson's gaze left Corell and looked to her as if he expected her to reject the proposal. *How weird!* she thought—yet she had seen it before. The cat seemed to have an uncanny ability to follow a conversation, taking on that strange stiffened Sphinx-like stare whenever he acted that way. It was strange, but she didn't know what to do about it. Was there anything one could do or should do about an eavesdropping cat?

"Alright. We will have a good 'ole time, won't we, Orson?" April responded enthusiastically, speaking directly to Orson once again in baby-talk. Although Valerie appreciated April's enthusiasm and willingness to take care of Orson, the baby-talk was getting on her nerves.

"I'd like to take Orson with me if that's alright," Valerie said pointedly, locking eyes with the furry eavesdropper, daring him to look away now.

Valerie's eyes narrowed in a challenge to the animal, daring him to look away when Corell next spoke. Then, just as she suspected, the cat's eyes began drifting away from her just before he said: "No problem, bring him if you'd like." Then Corell nervously changed the subject. "I'm starving; what's for dinner?"

Valerie stared at Orson, her mind spinning. What she had just witnessed could not be explained away as happenstance. The darn cat had not only listened in on the conversation but correctly anticipated whose turn it was to speak. It was uncanny! Valerie viewed it as proof the cat was more than he seemed and that Corell Paris was in on it. She had seen Orson do it often enough to know she did not imagine it. Corell knew something about Orson he wasn't telling her. It was a thing, and she had caught them cold.

"We're having Southern fried chicken, mashed potatoes, corn on the cob, and apple pie," April reported. "Sandra has a wonderful recipe. I hope you like Southern fried chicken," she enthused. Then added, "In case no one explained it to you, dinners are served family-style."

"What do you mean—*family-style*?" Valerie inquired.

"Everyone sits down together at the table, and dinner is served in big bowls—just like home. There's no ordering from the menu. We all eat the same thing together as a family."

"Oh, nice," said Valerie, then related an experience. "One time, we went to a Basque restaurant, and they served dinner that way. There was no menu; we just sat down at a table with a bunch of strangers, and when the table was full, they served dinner. It turned out to be fun."

"Dinner is served at six, which is in twenty minutes. I know you missed lunch, so if you need something to hold you over, let me know so I can get you a snack," April offered kindly.

Valerie declined, preferring to wait. "I'm good, April, thank you."

"All this food talk has my stomach growling. I'm going to go wash up," Corell said, dropping Orson gently to the floor as he stood. The women watched curiously as the cat padded away right behind him.

The family-style dinner turned out to be unexpectedly enjoyable. Corell introduced Valerie to the group as his granddaughter and was warmly welcomed. After the big meal, everyone stayed for drinks and conversation; some drank coffee, others beer, or wine. The discussion was lively and often loud as they talked, told stories, and joked together.

Valerie was tired, so she excused herself early and went to her room. After climbing into bed and reflecting on the day's events, she logged it as one of the best ever and smiled, snuggling with Orson under the covers. She wasn't sure what part of the day she liked best: the drive along the Applegate River, the staring contest with Corell at the Big Y Sporting Goods store, or the family-style chicken dinner. It was all good, but remembering Corell trying to keep a straight face as he asked the clerk where he could find the bowling balls and arrows tickled her funny bone, eliciting a snicker.

But a sense of melancholy overcame her when her thoughts turned to the old farmhouse with the lonely tire swing hanging from the big tree. In a way, she felt connected to that empty swing, turning slightly in the unseen breeze. Imagining herself in it, swinging or merely dangling under the great Oak without a care in the world, gave her solace as the days' tension unwound.

Times changed, though, as times always do, and the swing laid empty. For how long? With the children gone, the grass had grown unimpeded under it, rising tall until the little children were hidden from view. That was why she couldn't see them. The grass was too tall, wasn't it? The children were still there, just hidden by the high grass. Weren't they?

Perhaps, like herself, the swing yearned for another time, an easier life, one without the fear of pointless violence and death. Her heart ached for a life where things were as they should be, where her parents had not died, and her family still lived together in their own home. That is the way it should have been, not sent away to live with others without a word to say about it.

Now the children were playing in the front yard under that big tree, and she was with them, swinging, running, and laughing without a single care in the world. These were her brothers and sisters. It was perfect. She loved them, and she thanked God for them. As Valerie Dunne drifted off to sleep cuddling Orson, these were her thoughts, and she began dreaming.

An endless number of doors paraded by as she walked a darkened hallway. Each wooden door, identical in appearance, contained a narrow slot for a window and polished steel latch. Beyond the murky pane lay a room consumed by menacing gloom so impenetrable, so dense no light could penetrate or escape.

I know this place, Valerie thought to herself; *it is familiar, yet I cannot remember why.* The feeling of belonging was present, just the same it troubled her knowing it was no longer true. This place was a part of the past. One final visit is all she wanted. Surely no one would deny her that. Like a moth drawn irresistibly to a flame, it was unavoidable.

Her friends were here, weren't they? Good times were had sitting at lunchroom tables, laughing and signing yearbooks. She wanted to see their faces again, but it was to no avail; they were all gone, every one of them. The hallways were silent and empty now. She was nothing more than an outsider looking in, reminiscing, no longer included or wanted here. The final frayed ties to this part of her life and this place were broken and swept away.

Being here was against the rules, but she didn't care about rules, not anymore. After all, it was just one last look, and there was no harm in that, right? So, she just kept walking as the hallway unwound in front of her. Stopping at each door, she looked inside, finding nothing there but shadows and gloom, so she kept on walking. One step, two steps, repeated until the next door came into play, repeatedly, until—a voice, deep and menacing, thundering out of the gloom called her name. "Valerie!" She heard her name explode off the walls of the hallway. She knew that voice, and no one had to tell her what was wanted. A spark ignited into a raging fireball, and all at once, she knew everything she needed to know—it was time to run!

Run for all your worth, escape, do not let anything get in your way, and whatever you do, don't look back! Then she heard it again, that dreadful voice calling her name. *"Valerie!"* She heard her name called over and over, like a sledgehammer beating on a steel drum.

"Valerie! Valerie!! Valerie!!!" And with each call, a long loud laugh; a growl tearing its way through the building, slamming into her as she ran. Stinging tears blurred her vision. A cold chill iced her veins.

"Give up. *You can't run from me!* Ah-hahaha!"

She knew what that man wanted and that he would surely kill to take it from her. What she had was far too important ever to let go, or allow to be stolen, especially by one so evil. *The ring,* she thought...*the ring must be protected above all else!* She wanted to stand and fight, but it was too late; she couldn't stop herself. Desperation and panic had her running wild.

Another voice called her name, but this one didn't threaten or laugh at her. This voice was there to help. She knew the voice. Her mentor was the master of the rings, who was always with her. *Stop running,* the voice told her, *turn and fight. You can win.*

A small spark of hope sputtered to life and began to expand. Just a feeble light at first, illuminating the void in her heart. But she could not do it alone, she needed help, and if he helped her, it meant she mattered. Valerie prayed it was a sign that everything would be alright. But as she looked over her shoulder and saw what she ran from, who she ran from, that spark of hope sizzled then extinguished.

The gloom stirred at the end of the hallway as a vague figure emerged from the shadows. A giant of a man stepped from obscurity as if he *were* the shadows. As she was about to turn and run, he raised his hand as if beckoning her.

With heart pounding in her chest like a runaway train, Valerie surged forward, moving with every ounce of energy she could muster. Then an overwhelming force grasped her, pulled on her, slowing her steps as if she were slogging through knee-deep mud. Before long, she was running in place, then slipping backward, sliding uncontrollably toward the fiend as if by magic.

Each feeble stride dragged her half a step nearer, which horrified her. Her arms and legs became heavy, steadily heavier until she could barely move. Desperation forced her to grab onto a door handle, which momentarily kept her from being pulled closer. But the force grew stronger until her feet came off the ground, and she hung sideways in the doorway.

"Valerie!" the big man snarled. "Give up. You can't win!"

The mocking voice reverberated mercilessly in her mind as the mysterious power pulled harder against her body. Her head spun as she tried to imagine a defense against it, but she found no answers. She was too afraid to think clearly. Focusing on her hands, she envisioned them as made of steel, part of the door handle itself. Then they *were* steel. For a moment it worked, but then the wooden door cracked and began separating from the frame.

Oh, no! This cannot be happening! Valerie thought. In a flash, the truth hit her; she had failed. She had wasted too much time running rather than fighting back. She cursed herself for thinking defensively rather than offensively.

Resisting the frightening man any further was futile. She had lost.

The door frame snapped and creaked. Then to her horror, it broke away, and the door swung open with a tremendous bang. Unable to hold on, she sailed through the air shrieking as if she had fallen off a cliff and into an abyss.

But Vallerie had no unrealistic expectations about what came next. And if this is what it felt like to die, she welcomed it. Because in death, there was no pain, no guilt, or caring, just nothingness. A part of her welcomed death because it meant she could finally rest with her parents. And in a way, she felt relieved.

Morning's merciless light burst into the upstairs room, scalding tired eyes, punishing an exhausted mind. The night had been a relentless combination of frightening dreams, panic, and spells of sleeplessness. When it finally came, sleep was too often interrupted by bouts of night sweats and hypnic jerks. In the end, she gave up trying.

Valerie sat on the bed's edge, massaging her head, coaxing blurry eyes back into service. Everything seemed to hurt. Her back and legs felt like she had run a marathon. Reaching out for Orson, she realized the cat was gone. Valerie rubbed her neck, confused. Dazed and confused, her thoughts returned to last night.

Sleep had come peacefully for the past few weeks. She hoped to have outgrown the dreams. But last night turned out to be a series of torments she would not soon forget.

Why would the nightmares stop abruptly, then return with a vengeance? It didn't make sense. Just when it seemed as if she had outgrown them, they returned more punishing than ever. She took a deep breath, then sighed at the realization that the dreadful apparitions of the night had merely taken an unexplainable holiday.

In one respect, last night's dreams were different. Unlike any previous dream, in this one, she had died. She heard that if you die in your dreams, you die in reality, your heart stops, and you simply never wake up. She didn't know if there was any truth in it, but she certainly felt close enough to death at that moment to make her wonder how close she had come to actually dying.

Thankfully, the hammering in her head was beginning to settle down as her eyes became more accustomed to the light. But the gut-wrenching memory of the frightful dreams she had endured that night felt like a block of ice inside her head.

And where was that darned cat anyway? *Probably sleeping with Corell,* she guessed and cussed Orson for leaving her alone when she needed him most. Valerie felt awful, nonfunctional, which disturbed her further, knowing this would be an important day.

Expectations were high, and much would be demanded of her. She needed to get moving, so reluctantly easing herself from the edge of the bed, she dragged herself into the bathroom, where she began putting herself back together.

Forty minutes later, Valerie left the bathroom showered, dressed in blue jeans, a long sleeve top, tennis shoes, and her raven black hair pulled back into a ponytail. Stopping to look at her image in the mirror from the bathroom door, she decided she did not look too bad, considering she had died in her sleep.

With her hands on her hips, she told herself to get over it, get on with the day, and make the best of it. The absurdity that she should get over dying in her sleep brought a smile to her face that lightened her mood. Bowling balls and arrows needed tending, so she headed downstairs to begin her day.

It was early. A digital clock on the wall indicated the time at 6:08 AM. She heard the cook chopping something in the kitchen, but she found herself alone in the great room. It was Sunday, so it made sense that no one else was there yet.

The coffee maker was on, so Valerie poured herself a mug then settled into an overstuffed chair while she waited for Corell or April to make an appearance. The coffee helped slow the pounding in her head.

Rubbing her eyes, Valerie squinted at the ceiling. She admired the way morning light warmed the wooden rafters overhead. The big timbers seemed to glow, enhancing the woodsy lodge theme to the place.

What April referred to as the library was, in actuality, a wall of shelves adjacent to the dining room filled with books and nick-nacks. She assumed an architect had skillfully created a contiguous gathering place with the addition. The room had an unobstructed garden view, which seemed like the perfect place to meditate. What did the room lack? *Just one big old tabby to pet,* Valerie sighed.

Then she noticed the lodge-like nick-knacks and decorations on the library shelves, and it all began to make sense. She had seen similar decorations at the old farmhouse. For the first time, she recognized these were his things,

Corell's belongings, objects that made *him* feel at home. She liked the style and felt at home, too.

These thoughts lead Valerie to wonder how long she would stay in this place. Could it ever become her home? She didn't see why it couldn't be. There was no way to know but concluded it felt right for her to be here. If it became necessary for her to stay, she found no reason to fight it. The only downside she could think of was the family and friends she left behind back in Arlington. That and her seemingly delayed or abandoned career aspirations.

After pouring herself another mug of coffee, her thoughts returned to Darcy and her friends back home. Tomorrow they would be going back to school without her. That stung. Valerie wondered if she would be missed and if the story they concocted about her running off to Montana with Grandpa would fly. The fact that she had left saying good-bye only in texts troubled her.

"Good morning!" April sang from in front of the big coffee maker. "You started early!" she observed, then eased herself into the chair opposite hers. The clock now recorded the time at 7:10 AM.

"Morning, April," Valerie returned, smiling as brightly as her haggard mind would allow.

"You look tired. Are you alright?"

Before she could answer, movement out of the corner of her eye caught Valerie's attention. Turning, she saw Corell enter the room, followed closely by Comet and Orson. As he poured himself a mug of coffee, the cat rubbed his fluffy body against Corell's legs then rolled on the floor at his feet. As Corell tried to step away, the big tabby made a nuisance of himself by batting his paws at Corell's feet. When a claw hooked on a pant leg, Corell had to put his cup down to free himself from the hooked claw.

"Orson!" Valerie scolded with an unmistakable note of irritation in her voice. "Don't be such a pest!"

Orson stopped pawing and clawing and peered up at her, an innocent look on his face.

"I'm sorry, Corell," Valerie apologized, "he's been such a pain since we left home."

"No, bother," Corell replied, sounding unconcerned as he took a seat next to hers.

Valerie's gut jumped as, for the first time, she realized more was going on between Corell and her cat than what met the eye. More than playfulness, she perceived; the familiarity between them was undeniable. Ever since Corell appeared, Orson had paid little or no attention to her but fawned all over him. For the first time she could remember, Orson hadn't slept all night on her bed. She had been abandoned for someone else. It just did not make sense that the cat would desert her for someone that, in essence, should be a virtual stranger.

Valerie said nothing about it because she wanted to avoid giving the impression she was jealous. But in truth, she *was very* jealous, and it really bothered her. Was she about to lose her pet, her lifelong companion? She didn't know what to make of it, so she classified the whole thing in the category of being thoroughly weird.

As the three of them settled in talking and sipping coffee, it occurred to her that April, Corell, and the animals had entered the room within moments of one another. That realization caused her to wonder if Corell and April were a couple. Were they sleeping together? While she felt it was none of her business, she also knew she needed to better understand the relationship. She did not want to come right out and ask; that might be uncomfortable for everyone. Instead, the best thing to do would be to watch for signals. Sooner or later, the truth would come out.

Others began filtering into the great room, and the dining hall became a hub of activity. Soon the place was filled with the din of the working kitchen, clinking tableware, and people talking.

When the conversation turned to the day's plans, Corell turned to Valerie. "If you plan to bring Orson along, I think I will bring Comet, too." His eyes moved between Valerie and April as if he were seeking their approval. But the ladies knew he was just being polite. His mind was made up, so neither woman objected.

After breakfast, April left to begin her workday. Valerie asked Corell when he planned to leave for the old farm with one eye on Orson.

"After lunch," he told her, "I have some loose ends to tie up first."

"I'll be ready and waiting here when you are ready to go," Valerie said, then grabbed Orson and carried him to her room. As Valerie petted Orson, he purred contentedly, and she was relieved he didn't seem to care about being abruptly separated from Corell. Nevertheless, her suspicion that a strange connection existed between the two would not leave her. She was unsure but suspected the ring had something to do with it.

Does the ring allow Corell to have some sort of control over animals? If it does, why Orson, and why bother? The notion seemed crazy. The feeling there was something Corell had not told her about his budding relationship with her cat continued scratching at her tired mind.

———————————

Corell worked alone at his desk, trying to catch up on the mound of paperwork piled up while he was away. He detested paperwork, putting it off whenever possible, or avoiding it altogether. But he was good at delegating, so the job got done regardless of his inattention. The office staff jokingly referred to his desktop as quicksand because whatever went in seemed to disappear, never to be seen again.

After signing a stack of checks, Corell answered emails and other messages. By the time he had whittled the pile down to a more manageable level, it was nearly noon. Exhaling a blast of air in relief, he kicked back in his chair and put his feet up on the desk to clear his mind before making an important phone call.

When he was ready, he pulled a fob from the top drawer of his desk then dialed a familiar number from memory. When the call connected, he pushed the button on the fob and waited. Moments later, he heard a *click.*

"Garrett on a secure line. How can I help you today, Mister Paris?"

"Hey, Cliff," Corell said easily. "What's going on?"

"Just keeping the boss grounded as usual. Ed can be a handful."

"That's a job I would pass on. Everyone hates the Chief of Staff, but I don't care what anyone says. I'm starting to like you—honest!"

"Yeah, it's a thankless job," Cliff laughed.

"When are we going to see you again?" Corell asked.

"Funny, we were just talking about that. Might be sooner than later."

"Really, what's up?"

"Can't say just now. But I will tell you that it is big, real big if it is what we think it is. In fact, it doesn't get any bigger."

"Now you have me worried. Are you going to bring me in on it?"

"If it pans out, you can count on it. We'll let you know."

"Alright."

"Why did you call?"

"Is Buchanan available?"

"He's over at STARCOM. Can I relay a message?"

"Tell Ed I got the girl. She is staying with me here in Jacksonville. You guys need to meet her sometime soon."

"Is it pressing?"

"No, but put it on the agenda, will you?"

"Will do."

"Oh, one more thing. We need to keep the station open in Arlington for the time being. Her parents could be a hostage risk."

"Got it," Cliff acknowledged.

"Keep me in the loop, will you?" Corell said, aware that regardless of whether they were on a secure line, there were limits to what Garrett could say. But it was easy enough to read between the lines. Something big was going down at STARCOM, or the President would not be there.

"Will do," Cliff promised, then the line went dead.

Corell fell back into his chair, holding his head. News that the President was at STARCOM had him worried.

Ed Buchanan is at Star Command? Corell thought. *That's Peterson Air Force Base in Colorado. They usually come to him, not the other way around. The President does not go to them unless there is a very good reason. Whatever they have going on must be, just as Cliff said, 'real big,' which does not sound good at all.*

Corell rubbed his temples. *Well, there is nothing I can do to help unless they decide to bring me in on it.* Then he felt a twinge: it was his ring, a whisper, just one word — *Valerie.'* That word made him wonder about the timing. *Could what was going on at Peterson AFB have anything to do with Valerie Dunne or the Boecki? Or was the ring simply nudging him to get on with her training?*

The Boecki seemed like a long shot, but Valerie had to come first. She needed his attention, so he changed mental gears and turned his thoughts toward Valerie and his plans for the day.

That afternoon they would be moving into the old farmhouse. The remote location was safe and secure, the perfect place to work with the girl. Corell could think of no better place to demonstrate the ring's power without distraction, interruption, or prying eyes. There they would be allowed to talk without reservation, and the barn would provide excellent cover for some of the more sensitive exercises he had in mind.

But deep down, he had mixed emotions about it, specifically about being there. Corell knew sleeping in the old house for a week or more would not be easy for him. He had not spent a night there in over sixty years, and although part of him was always eager to go back, another part of him dreaded it.

Other than yesterday, he could not recall precisely when he was last inside. He had driven out to it periodically, intending to go in, but found himself unable to open the door. Not long ago, he had parked out front but could not get out of the old truck, let alone go inside. His head said he should be able to go in, have a look around, and reminisce, but his heart would not let him through the door. While the place drew him to it like a magnet, it also repulsed him, pushing him away at the same time. Instead of going inside, he merely stared at his old home from a distance.

There was certainly no shortage of cherished memories there; that was not the problem. It had been a happy home for Corell, Laura, Mark, and Michelle for many years. The house itself had nothing to do with what prevented him from going inside. After seventy years, the loss of his entire family was still too painful to revisit. It was still too soon.

After being married in 1923 at the Jackson County Courthouse in nearby Medford, he and Laura remodeled the house themselves. The happy couple had two children: Michelle came first, soon followed by Mark. As the children grew, Michelle gravitated to her mother, preferring domestic life rather than the outdoors. Michelle, a studious girl who read voraciously, expressed interest in poetry and writing but had little interest in the farm or other outdoor activities. She loved animals but seldom ventured further than the front porch, preferring to watch the birds and squirrels from the rocking chair on the porch with Orson on her lap.

Unlike his sister, Mark was her exact opposite. He loved the farm and outdoor activities. The boy could hardly wait to get out the door in the morning, often staying outside until well after dark. As he grew, he and his father became exceptionally close, working the farm together, tending the animals, camping, fishing, and hunting.

Corell's thoughts returned to his son. He had hoped Mark would be his heir to the ring, but those hopes were long ago dashed. Driving home from town one day, he and Laura came upon their son's favorite horse. The saddled animal ran wild alongside the road, with Mark nowhere in sight. They found the boy lying dead in the street with the back of his head smashed. Corell and Laura were devastated; their son was only fifteen. Nine years later, Michelle was lost when the hospital ship she had been serving on went down in the Atlantic, sunk by a German U-boat.

In such a short time, the loss of both children destroyed Laura, who withdrew and began drinking heavily. Corell knew better than to try killing the pain with alcohol, having learned his lesson the hard way centuries earlier. Keeping Laura busy by traveling with her did not help, either. Twenty years of heavy drinking took its toll, and her liver began to fail. Corell tried using the power of his ring to support her health, but no matter how hard he tried, he could not heal his wife's broken spirit.

When Corell realized nothing he was doing helped, he took Laura to a psychologist in San Francisco. Sadly, she did not respond to professional help, either. As time progressed, Laura's alcoholism became acute, and she died in 1958, leaving Corell alone in the old farmhouse.

Corell batted away the sudden tears flooding his eyes. Life together as a family had been the happiest years of his long existence. Laura and the children would never know the truth about him and the ring because now they were forever lost to him. His secrets were safe, but the cost was nearly unbearable.

Laura would never know that he had taken the surname Paris the year she met him or that he had lived in the area for twenty years before meeting her. But the most burdensome secret he kept was that he had already outlived more families than he could count. His family, the people he loved, all died without ever knowing who he truly was or that he was thirteen hundred years old. Even worse, he was left alone without an heir to his ring. Despair threatened to ruin him.

Corell found himself disillusioned, weary of life, and with an altered outlook he could never have foreseen. The thought of remarrying and trying for another heir seemed unimaginable. Losing this family was simply one too many in a long line of too-familiar losses. Beginning the family process all over again would be a burden he just could not shoulder. The final worn ties to that life slipped away from him the day he walked away from the old farmhouse for the last time.

Once again, Corell was left alone in the world, a world he was pledged to help save. Was the world *worth* saving? He was not so sure. Based on what he'd seen of it in his lifetime, he had profound doubts.

So many centuries had passed since his father entrusted him with the ring, he often wondered why he carried on. In truth, it was an arduous responsibility, a constant weight grinding away at his resolve, testing his determination.

Resentment reared its ugly head, threatening to consume him. Believing that saddling him with the world's fate was in no way fair, he became disenchanted with the whole thing. Nevertheless, he carried on with the hope that it would work out in the end.

So Corell continued watching and waiting for the anticipated reappearance of Valerie Dunne. Years passed, but now without family obligations or distractions. Finding Valerie Dunne became his sole passion, his obsession.

The ring book was cleverly written, providing hints and allegations about when and where to watch for Valerie Dunne's reappearance. However, specifics were skillfully omitted, no doubt to protect the author. There was no question the season was ripe for her return; Corell just had to be diligent and patient. Believing the time was upon him, he began watching for her in earnest.

Determined to miss nothing, Corell read and reread Valerie's book until every word and letter was etched into memory. Even so, he still found certain passages riveting. As the story went, the future of human life on the planet rested on the five rings' successful transfer back to the book's author, Valerie Dunne, in the twenty-first century.

The writer explained that she had used the rings' power to travel far back in the past to escape aliens, preventing the five rings of Hesaurun from being stolen by off-worlders. These Boeckian aliens were intent on destroying Earth and enslaving humankind. Reunited with the rings and armed with a better understanding of future events, Valerie Dunne would use them to erase the deaths of millions of people at the hands of their enemies, the Boecki.

She wrote that the five rings were gifted to humans by their master, Osomarío, and his band of Boecki sympathizers. By doing so, those fugitives hoped to protect and preserve the inhabitants of Earth and neighboring star systems from annihilation.

Anticipating dire times ahead for Earth and its inhabitants, Osomarío arranged an ingenious way of monitoring Earth events by binding an animal to the fifth ring. Through that animal, a common household pet on Earth, he was allowed insight into the realm as well as the ring bearers themselves. But what Corell found most intriguing and what kept him grounded was the following text.

"*Osomarío, the renegade Boeckian, searched the cosmos for a worthy candidate to receive his rings. That search ended far sooner than expected when his probe revealed me, Valerie Dunne, an Earther, as the worthy recipient. Never had he expected to find dynamism in an individual equal to his own on the doomed planet he hoped to save.*

"*The day my parents were killed by Stone, Osomarío came to me and made sure I was safe. I didn't need his help, but he didn't know that—yet. He recognized the growing power within me and saw to it that I survived. He was there for me when I was most vulnerable. I fought and won a battle against a monster of a man empowered by his powerful Hesaurun ring, a ring that he had stolen from the rightful owner. He had a ring, I did not, I was only four, yet I prevailed.*

I wondered about his age, so I asked him, 'How old are you, and how long does the Boecki live?' His answer was succinct: 'I do not know. We do not concern ourselves with such asininity.' Osomarío went on to explain, 'The Boecki are not immortal, but will be extremely difficult to defeat because they are by far the most numerous species in the galaxy. We are so seldom harvested; our numbers increase at an exponential rate. By the time I reappear in the twenty-first century, the Boecki will outnumber all other sentient species combined by a factor of twelve.'

I was astounded by that number. It did not seem possible. I was unsure which word baffled me more, Osomarío's use of the word 'asininity' or 'harvested.' I had a bad feeling about what 'harvested' implied, so I saved 'asininity' for later. I asked, 'What do you mean — harvested?'

'Put to use,' he said. Then added, 'The Boecki waste nothing including their dead, which are recycled.' I found that somewhat disturbing but understood. Later I searched the word 'asininity' (stupidity) and came away impressed by his language skills and choice of words."

Seeking the reborn Valerie Dunne and returning his ring to her turned out to be the distraction Corell Paris needed to move on from losing his family. Focusing on this task single-mindedly pulled him away from the precipice and took his mind off the secret burden he carried. Once again, Corell's life had meaning.

Locating Colin Dunne, Valerie's father, had not been difficult because he knew when and where to watch for him. Once he was close, his ring did the rest. All he had to do was follow its lead.

But tracking this Stone character was another matter. Valerie's written recollections provided vivid images of his sadistic nature and atrocities but offered few if any clues on how to track him down. According to the author, this Stone, a former bookie's debt enforcer, happened onto one of the lesser rings, then made a fortune turning rocks into gold, but not before turning the streets of Seattle into a river of blood.

Corell understood it was only a matter of time before he and Stone crossed paths, and he was ready for it. The decision to burn Stone to the ground, at first sight, was cast in iron. If Stone turned up at Buckingham Palace sitting next to the Queen, Corell intended to light him up on the spot without a second thought. No-fuss, no-muss, no questions asked.

To make matters worse, rumor had it that Stone had added a second ring to his collection, no doubt at the cost of another life. Corell considered this to be terrible news. Every ring the brute obtained would multiply the power of his ring already by a factor of ten. Allowing Stone to get any more rings would make him an opponent to be reckoned with.

To have something Stone wanted would be a very bad idea. Getting in the way of obtaining something he wanted was an even worse proposition. And yet, this was the situation in which Corell found himself—in the way, and with something Stone wanted.

Stone had been hunting him for a long time, and Corell knew it. No physical evidence was required as confirmation because it was something felt rather than seen or heard, a persistent threat warning in his subconscious mind. As the time for action drew near, so did the intensity of the alarm raised. Just as one heeds approaching sirens in the distance, this forewarning of danger that lay ahead was impossible to deny or ignore.

What this ultimately meant for Valerie, he could only guess. But knowing she had already survived an attack by Stone, had won, and claimed his rings meant she should be able to do it again. That knowledge raised Corell's confidence, but she was just a girl with little or no experience right now. In a confrontation with Stone, that lack of experience might be the deciding factor when he came for her. And come for her he would; there was no doubting that. It was a matter not of *if* it would happen but *when*.

Fortunately, Valerie had a guardian she was unaware of in Osomarío and assets Corell was itching to share with her. He was excited for tomorrow, which couldn't come soon enough for him. This is what he had anticipated for longer than he could remember.

This time was exciting for Corell. He had survived long enough to witness the ages of Valerie's recurrence, rebirth, and awakening. But what intrigued him was something he could only make wild guesses at, the probability of a paradox.

As he saw it, three versions of Valerie Dunne had occurred, beginning with the original. That is the Valerie Dunne whom Corell craved to know. Valerie Dunne defeated her enemies and soared to unimaginable heights, eventually rising to command the Boeckian Resistance Union of Worlds. She accomplished the impossible by successfully traveling in time and staging her rebirth.

Possible paradox? Sure. If a contradiction in time initiated a reset of our reality, how would one ever know it happened? While he was ready for almost anything, Corell was determined to miss as little as possible.

"Well," he said aloud, pulling himself away from the desk. "Guess it's time to get after it. It's time for bowling balls and arrows!"

Chapter 10

Arlene Dunne— August 1947 CE

Her skin felt prickly. While not being entirely unfamiliar, the sensation was one Arlene Dunne felt only on rare occasions. Although there was no discomfort associated with it, it came as a faint twinge of apprehension, just enough so that it could not be dismissed as irrelevant.

The sensation persisted as she went about her work that morning. She thought she saw peripheral movement out of the corner of her eye, just beyond reach, but when she looked found nothing there. The phenomenon could be considered comparable to the feeling of being followed when walking down a dark street at night. Even though nothing or no one is there, instinct compels one to walk just a little faster than usual.

Arlene pushed her notes aside, stretched, and rubbed the back of her neck, hoping to relieve the stress. It didn't help, and she knew why. Whenever this feeling had ever visited her previously, another ring bearer was in the area. Hesauranaki in the vicinity could mean one thing—trouble. Her guard was up, and it would stay up until the feeling went away, or whoever it was showed themself.

The most obvious culprit would be Stone. Although she had never run into him, he was well-known among the small group of ring bearers as a Hesauranaki climber. Climbers are people outside the Dunne family line who pursue power by obtaining Hesaurun rings, more often than not by murder.

According to Corell Paris, also a Dunne whom she trusted, this Stone character was responsible for killing Chad Evers, also a climber, and stealing his ring. Reports of Stone's brutality frightened Arlene. But she was realistic. As she saw it, the problem lay with human nature. When someone learned what a ring could do or observed its power, they became obsessed with possessing it—stopping at nothing to get it. And if one ring was good—*two just has to be better!* Too much power is never enough. *That is just how it is with people,* Arlene thought.

Her observation was that people always seemed to want more, including what they didn't have or already possessed. Too much of a good thing was just enough to get by. Although ugly, these desires were virtually universal with humans. Arlene herself had felt it, the desire to have more power regardless of the cost or what it might take to obtain it. For the most part, she had been able to resist such unsavory urges and retain her objectivity and Dedication to the cause. But too many others had not, which was why, with few exceptions, ring bearers avoided one another like the plague.

The view from the lab window on the second floor of the Physics Building at Caltech Pasadena overlooked The Guggenheim, Dabney Hall, and several other picturesque buildings. Arlene looked down from that window as students and faculty moved between the Mission-style structures and walkways below. People stood together in small groups talking, but none of them seemed unusual or a threat. Probing body language and faces revealed nothing out of place. When she tired of it, Arlene returned to work. Still, the sensation continued distracting her.

Arlene's work involved medical research, led by Professors Pauling, Itano, and Singer, investigating disease-causing hemoglobin abnormalities at the molecular level. Early results were promising; she loved the team and had high expectations for success. But it was hard work requiring long hours and unrelenting concentration.

Arlene hated being interrupted when she was concentrating. "Not now, I'm in the zone," was all anyone on the second floor of the Physics Building needed to hear to know it was time to turn heel and run for safety. And it did not matter who it was; it could be Pauling, Singer, or Eleanor Roosevelt, for that matter. No one dared interrupt Arlene when she was trying to concentrate. Arlene Dunne had a reputation as a fighter. No one was brave enough to tangle with her.

They had all witnessed the soft lines around her blue eyes and mousy brown hair tied neatly in a bun disappear in an instant, transforming into the head of Medusa. After that happened, no one who knew Arlene underestimated the conservatively dressed, mild-mannered woman in comfortable shoes. Once was more than enough for anyone.

But Arlene's internal warning system would not allow her to focus that morning. Unable to concentrate, anxiety had her pacing the floor. Just before noon, she gave up, grabbed her bag, and signed out, making the excuse she was not feeling well and was going home for the day.

As she stepped out of the air-conditioned Downs Building, summer heat struck her in the face as if she had stepped into a furnace. In mid-August, the San Gabriel Valley had its own unique way of scalding one's eyes with intense mid-day glare. Instinctively, Arlene reached into her bag for sunglasses without missing a step. The warmth penetrated to the bone in a moment. Unlike many, she loved the sensation of the sun's rays penetrating deep into the core. The day was breezy, but otherwise, it was a beautiful day with the fresh scent of sage blowing in from the nearby mountains.

Although California Boulevard was just a short distance from the Downs Building, she remained alert, ever watchful of threats. At the curb, she hailed a cab which took her to her home in the nearby Bungalow Heaven neighborhood. She paid the driver then surveyed the area for trouble before approaching the house.

With shaking hands and nerves frayed, Arlene fumbled through her purse, unable to find her keys. Frustration mounted, absentmindedly patting herself, seeking pockets that weren't there, ignoring the fact that her summer dress had none. Cursing herself for losing her keys, she lifted a flowerpot on the porch, retrieved a backup key from under it, then let herself in.

Once inside, she dropped her purse onto an end table and collapsed into an easy chair. Relieved to be in the safety of her own home, Arlene breathed easy as she began unwinding. While relaxing, she closed her eyes, mentally retracing her movements that morning to recall the last time she remembered seeing the keychain. Remembering her habit was to turn the lock from the inside on her way out the door, automatically engaging it eliminated the possibility she left them at the lab. That left just one possibility: the keys were still in the house hanging on the hook in the kitchen.

Arlene was hungry anyway, so she got up to check for the keys and get herself something to eat. As she rounded the corner, she found herself staring squarely at the chest of a towering man dressed entirely in black. Before she could scream, a thick hand wrapped around her throat while the other pinned her right ring finger hand to her side as she was pushed roughly against the wall in one fluid motion. The notion that this brute knew precisely how to handle a ring bearer had not escaped her notice—nor had the stench of his sardine and cigarette smoke-infused breath. Stone had dropped in for a not-so-friendly visit.

Thrashing and kicking wildly, Arlene fought back with all her strength. But the more she lashed out, the tighter the vice-like grip clamped down on her throat. Instinctively she stopped struggling, and the crushing pain in her windpipe eased. Desperate for any opportunity to turn the odds in her favor, eyes darted left and right, fear-tainted sweat beaded on her forehead. But the building urgency in her lungs to take in air elevated to panic as the tall man bent down to meet her gaze. Dark eyes and scared features met her terrified gaze close-up. His eyes searched her face as if contemplating her future.

"Hello, Arlene," the big man rumbled, then smiled a twisted grin as he reveled at the terror in her eyes. Stone's sadistic unblinking stare bored into her soul, purposely taking his time studying her facial features, drinking in the fear.

"One wrong move, and I'll rip your throat out—understood?"

Unable to speak and frantic for oxygen, Arlene blinked away tears, nodding a desperate response. Immediately the grip on her throat eased up. With eyes bulging, nostrils flaring, and mouth open wide, Arlene gulped huge breaths of air, one after another in rapid succession. Once she began to recover, Stone leaned back in again, but now his merciless gaze had a death grip on her eyes, and there was no escape.

"Your book. Where is it?" Stone demanded, his voice hard, his face distorted in a frightening snarl. Rage welled inside Arlene at the mention of her ring book. Even if it meant her life, she had no intention of turning it over to this thug. She was determined to die rather than allow the likes of Stone to have it.

Pushing the panic back, Arlene considered her options, which she knew were few. She had already tried kicking him in the crotch, but she needed something more since that didn't work. With few alternatives, she decided to stay with the classics. "Want to see it?" she croaked while making her voice sound as natural as possible, then dug the thumb of her free hand into her attacker's bulging right eye with all her might, twisting as she put her weight into it.

As the thumb hit home, Stone let go a thunderous roar, releasing Arlene from his grasp. Holding the place where his eye had been, the huge man staggered backward, crashing across the room, smashing into the opposite wall, scattering furniture, and knocking pictures from the wall.

"What? Not what you had planned to see?" Arlene gloated.

Wasting no time, she stepped back, held her ring hand in front of her, then sent a gravitational wave at her assailant strong enough to divert an oncoming locomotive. Stone was thrown so violently against the wall the entire back of the house exploded with a BOOM, followed by the clatter of wrecked furniture, shattered plaster, and splintered lumber. The wall vanished as Stone sailed through it like it was made of glass. Arlene watched with satisfaction as the body rolled to a stop in the center of the backyard.

Arlene did not need to look back at her house to know the devastation she'd caused. The dining room wall had been removed from floor to ceiling as neatly as if a remodeling crew had taken it down. While Arlene was upset, she was not the type to sit and cry after such a life-threatening encounter. Having been there before, she was experienced—and tough enough to know the score and take care of herself. Evidence of that fact was now lying in a bloody heap in the backyard.

Satisfied that Stone was not going anywhere and most likely dead, she tottered to the sink, washed the blood off her hands, then took her time drying them. Once done, she picked up the phone to call the police, intending to claim an intruder had broken in and tried to rob her. But as she dialed, she glanced at the spot where her dining room wall had been, then dropped the phone.

The body she expected to see there was gone. The yard was empty.

Stunned beyond belief, Arlene stared slack-jawed, wondering what could have become of the dead man in her backyard. Gingerly stepping through the hole and over the pile of rubble, she searched for him. Still too weak to chase him down, it was a half-hearted pursuit. Since the property was not fenced, Stone had no barriers to go over other than a short hedge. He simply wasn't there anymore, and she had no idea which direction he might have fled.

Arlene sat on the pile of rubble that was now the back of her house, holding her head in her hands while replaying the days events. Why hadn't she realized an intruder had been in the house? A man Stone's size should be impossible to hide. She blamed herself for not being more alert and allowing herself to be so easily ambushed.

Now I know why my keys were missing this morning, she realized. *There is no mystery. Now it seems evident that somehow, someway, Stone got ahold of them and let himself in. It had to have happened this morning because I would have missed the keys soon enough. What if he still has them? I need to change the locks! But wait—why bother? Changing the locks isn't going to keep him out if he really wants in.*

More thoughts rattled around in Arlene's mind. *What about going somewhere more secure? But where? That's running. I am not going to run from him. I have made a life here, have a good job, and important work to do. Still, I need to do something. What about getting a guard dog? I have heard of people getting trained police dogs for personal security. I can defend myself well enough, but what I really need is an alarm—a dog alarm! A dog alarm would be just the ticket.*

By this time, neighbors began trickling from their homes, drawn by the sound of what they assumed must have been a nearby explosion. Arlene heard police sirens wailing in the distance. Clutches of looky-loos stood in the street, staring at the house with the massive hole in its side.

Mrs. Alice Devlin from next door broke from the crowd to check on her. The little woman was a housewife with a fastidious demeanor, a busybody by nature who fancied being referred to as "Mrs. Devlin" rather than by her first name. Arlene was sure it was to prevent anyone from ever

PETER HARRETT

forgetting her husband, Mark Devlin, a city prosecutor. Well-known as a gossip, Alice kept close tabs on the neighbors. If you wanted to know what was going on in the community, you asked Mrs. Devlin.

"Are you alright, dear?" she asked kindly enough, kneeling and taking Arlene's hands in hers.

"I'm alright, thank you, Mrs. Devlin," answered Arlene, then slowly came to her feet as a demonstration of her lack of injury and competence.

"*Tell me what happened!*" Mrs. Devlin inquired, her voice tactically sincere. But Arlene knew what she meant. As usual, Alice was foraging for gossip fodder.

"Must have been a gas leak, but I'm fine," Arlene said brightly, emphasizing the lie with a friendly nod. "Thank you for checking on me." Unwilling to get into an extended conversation with Alice about it, the latter was said with unmistakable finality. No one had to tell her that the less she said, the less her words would be embellished by Mrs. Devlin when she repeated them.

"Oh, I see," said Mrs. Devlin, her voice heavy with practiced insincerity.

"The police are coming; I have to go now," Arlene said, excusing herself, waving an arm in the direction of the front yard. "I need to talk to them. See you later!" she called as she whirled away.

"A gas leak that blew out one of your walls but none of the windows—and didn't start a fire? That seems mighty odd to me!" the little woman said, her eyes narrowing, then added, "*and by the way, who was that man I saw leaving your house?*"

That question stopped Arlene in her tracks. Spinning around to face the frigid fault finder, she knew she had to get this right; whatever she said was sure to be reported to the police, then throughout the neighborhood.

"What are you talking about?"

"I'm talking about the man I saw leaving your house right after the explosion. You know, dear—the very large man dressed in black." Since Mrs. Alice Devlin believed she had Arlene on the ropes, she allowed the false sincerity in her voice to show through. But it didn't work.

Arlene's first inclination was to give the meddling gossip a piece of her mind. But then, a better idea struck her. Why not put Alice to work doing what she did best, acting as the neighborhood watchdog she really was? Alice Devlin could be relentless when given the slightest hint of authority. She seemed to crave it. Putting her in charge of the neighborhood watch might be precisely what she needed. With Mrs. Devlin in charge, there was no way Stone could get to her without her catching him in the act and reporting it.

"Well, I haven't had any visitors today," Arlene lied, knowing the truth must be concealed. "If you saw a man in the neighborhood, he must have been a burglar. But if you see that big man in black again, call me immediately. You have my phone number, right?"

Arlene turned and hurried out to the street without waiting for an answer, which was now crowded with gawkers. Momentarily a black-and-white city police car rounded the corner, parting the crowd as it neared the house.

Arlene's encounter with the police was relatively short and uneventful. Since the officers didn't see evidence of a crime and no criminal complaint from her, they had little interest other than marveling at the destruction. The cops poked around for a few minutes, took Mrs. Devlin's expert eyewitness account of events, then left.

When things settled down, Arlene began calling contractors to repair the wall. The first few didn't answer the phone but had messaging services. She left messages and, a few minutes later, received a return call from a man identifying himself as Mister Morgan Beal with Beal Construction. Once she explained the extent of damage to her house, Morgan agreed to drop what he was doing. "I'll be there in fifteen minutes," he promised, much to Arlene's relief.

As promised, Beal arrived within a few minutes and went immediately to work. He assured Arlene he could have the mess out of the house and a temporary wall built with studs and tar paper the same day. Working together, they had the house cleaned up and sealed before sundown. Arrangements were made for Morgan to return to restore the damage entirely within a week. Morgan left Arlene feeling thankful to him for being so kind; she thought she had made a new friend.

That prickly sensation Arlene sensed the day before had left her entirely the following day. She felt more secure knowing Stone was unlikely to resurface again anytime soon, believing he must have been seriously injured; at a minimum, he had lost an eye.

By the time she realized Stone might have been hospitalized, it was late in the day. Scolding herself for not thinking of that possibility sooner, she made a few calls. Unfortunately, neither of the city's two major hospitals claimed to have admitted anyone by the name of Stone.

Hanging up the phone, Arlene closed her eyes for a moment, fingers rubbing frantically at the back of her neck. *Being assaulted in my own home is something I am not about to take lightly,* she raged. *Stone's attack was personal, and I need to be prepared to take the offensive. It's better to be the hunter than the hunted. I want revenge and am determined to get it one way or another. There will be a fight, and I will see to it he pays for what he did to me.*

Stone's goal was to kill me and steal my ring, but two can play that game. I am going to get him! What's good for the goose is good for the gander. If he cannot understand that concept, I will explain it to him the hard way!

Hatred for Stone, mixed with a healthy dose of resolve, flared up in Arlene, exploding to life like a wildfire in a windstorm. She was determined to get even if it took a hundred years, reasoning that killing him would be doing everyone a favor. Then she would have her just rights—and his ring for herself. With two rings on her hand, her power would be multiplied ten-fold. Then no one would dare cross her ever again. As yet, she had not realized that old nemesis, selfish greed for more power, had once again raised its ugly head.

Arlene understood Stone would be keeping an eye on her, literally seeking to get even with her for the loss of his eye. She guessed correctly that being beaten by a woman had him out of his mind with rage. *Rage often blinds people causing them to charge headlong into obvious danger, regardless of the consequences. Well, if he wasn't blind before, he is now, right?* She thought, enjoying her own joke.

She was confident that he would be back for round two when he was healthy enough. Arlene imagined Stone charging at her like a raging bull, and when he did, she would make sure his downfall would be fast to follow. She would see to that and make certain he did not get up again.

Arlene anticipated being followed everywhere she went. She expected Stone would be seeking patterns in her movements, looking for places to set her up for an ambush. When he broke into her house and throttled her in the kitchen, he demonstrated his preference for such tactics. Two could play that game, but she believed he was not smart enough to realize that. She would turn that tactic right back at him. Arlene decided to set a trap for Stone, then stand back and watch him hang himself.

Stone's recovery from his altercation with Arlene was confined to the eight-unit Cherry Motel on East Colorado Street in nearby Glendale. With the "C" on the neon roof sign burned out, the moniker appropriately identified itself to the world as the 'herry Motel.' Amenities included rooms for rent by the hour, an empty swimming pool half-filled with debris, and threadbare furnishings.

Going to the hospital was an option, but Stone wisely avoided police involvement. While hiding in one of Arlene's neighbor's garages, he had seen the crowd gathering in the street, so he stayed low and rested. The black-and-white cop car arrived, then left, but Stone stayed hidden until well after dark. When all was clear, he staggered two blocks to where he had parked his car in an elementary school parking lot. Then driving like a drunk, he happened onto the *herry Motel* and parked.

Stone stumbled out of the night and burst into the office like a towering apparition. The startled night attendant, Jerry, catapulted from his chair like he was on a hot seat. With the big man's clothes caked with dried blood and a dirty tee-shirt tied around his head, covering one eye, he looked like death warmed over. As Jerry opened his mouth to speak, the ghoulish man held a thick finger to his lips and shook his head.

"Uh-uh," grunted the tough-looking character. Jerry understood this as a clear warning: this customer had no interest in small talk. Then with shaking hands, Stone took his time laying out five one-hundred-dollar bills on the countertop. Awestruck, Jerry gaped at the big bills, silently anticipating instructions. The seventeen-year-old high school drop-out working for seventy-five cents an hour correctly judged the pile of cash as a get out of jail card—his ticket out of the *herry Motel*.

"Give me a room, shut up, and those are yours. Give me a week without a fuss along with three meals a day and a bottle of scotch, and you'll have five more—got it?" The barked orders left no room for discussion, and Jerry saw no need to question them. With that said, Stone reached out expectantly for a key, which Jerry instantly deposited into the big man's bloodstained hand.

"Yes, sir!" obliged Jerry. "You will be in number eight, sir. It's furthest from the road and the quietest unit we have. My name is Jerry; dial zero if you need anything more."

As Stone turned toward the door, he added, "Extra towels, a carton of Lucky Strikes, and a bottle of scotch. Hop to it, Jerry." Jerry beat Stone to the door, held it open for him, then dashed away into the night.

After a long shower, Stone stood in front of the narrow mirror, leaning on the sink assessing his injuries. His swollen head was the size of a basketball. The eye was too painful to touch, but he could still feel the eyeball moving below the lid. Hope remained that sight would return to it once the swelling went down. Blood continued weeping from a variety of nasty gashes and scrapes on his head, face, and shoulders, but none of them seemed to need stitches. Dark blue welts and bright red scuffs covered his body from head to foot. Remarkably, no bones appeared to be broken, which seemed to be the only good news of the day.

Anxious to kill the throbbing pain, Stone lay naked on the bed, smoking and chugging scotch from the bottle like a thirsty Bedouin. While he was in the bathroom, Jerry had left him a carton of smokes, a bottle of scotch, and a burger and fries, but the food remained untouched as Stone focused on the bottle. Once the bottle was empty, he didn't move again until long after the sun was up.

Timid knocks at the door, followed by a woman's soft call from outside, awakened Stone with a start. "I have breakfast for you, sir." At first, he was furious for being disturbed, then remembered that Jerry, as agreed, had arranged for food to be brought to him during the day.

"Leave it outside. I'll get it later," Stone grumbled, which he immediately regretted. Speaking produced pounding in his skull, to the degree that he saw multi-colored spots floating about the room like balloons released at a fair.

Stone cradled his aching head in agony. What seemed like a moment later, the soft knock returned to the door once more. This time the woman's voice reported, "I have lunch for you, sir." But this time Stone remained silent in self-defense.

He hadn't eaten or drank anything other than the scotch in more than twenty-four hours. Now he was dehydrated and hungry. Plus, his bladder felt like it was about to burst, so he knew he had to get up, take care of business and get some food and water into his body.

Gingerly rolling onto his side, Stone pushed himself up little by little into the sitting position at the edge of the bed. Stiff and sore, it was several minutes before he summoned the strength and resolve to stand. Once he was upright, he discovered the hard way that everything hurt, right down to the soles of his feet. Taking baby steps to the bathroom, he relieved himself, then downed several glasses of water in rapid succession, his head pounding with every movement.

Rejecting the blood-caked pile of ruined clothes on the floor where he had dropped them, he continued naked as he staggered back to the bed, then ate the stale burger and fries leftover from last night's food drop. He made quick work of that, then still unclothed, opened the door, and snatched the brown paper bag from the window ledge. Whoever had left it there had made a peanut butter and banana sandwich and included a couple of chocolate chip cookies, which he inhaled. It was good, but he wondered if Jerry knew men twice his size needed more than a peanut butter and banana sandwich and a couple of cookies for lunch. He would have complained, but that would hurt more than it was worth.

That afternoon Stone slept lightly, moaning in pain until more knocks at the door woke him from his dreams. This time he heard Jerry's voice at the door murmur, "I have the things you asked for, sir. I'll leave them by the door."

Rousing himself from slumber, Stone rubbed his head. *Starting to like that boy,* he thought. *Seems to know what side his bread is buttered on. Follows orders without question and never says anything more than he needs to. Eager to get ahead, too. I like that.*

The following day, Stone woke feeling stronger. Clear-headed enough to assess his situation, he began going through his things—which weren't much. His body was an accumulation of injuries and stabbing pains, but none severe enough to be worried about, other than the eye, which he guessed might require medical attention. He was healing alright, which he saw in the mirror. But he needed time, a few more days perhaps; and some clothes. Then he could head for home.

His clothes were ruined, but Stone trusted he could send Jerry out for new ones. There was no doubt in his mind the boy would jump at the chance to make more money, and he still had a thick roll of hundred-dollar bills, enough to keep him afloat for a month or more if necessary.

But when he noticed his big gold watch was smashed, Stone flew into a rage. He leaped from the bed, forgetting all about the pain, which produced sharp cramps and pangs in his back and shoulders. "Aww," he growled irritably, then hobbled about the tiny room, swearing and gesticulating like a sailor who'd slammed his thumb in a watertight door.

Laid up as he was, Stone had not thought much about Arlene Dunne in the last forty-eight hours, but with this outrage, the woman was on his mind full-time front and center. From that point forward, he thought of little else. *Forget the ring, what about the watch!* His foggy mind thundered. Seething with anger, Stone craved having his hands around Arlene's neck, slowly choking the life out of the woman that busted his favorite watch—the Elgin!

That afternoon Stone laid on the bed dozing lightly, dreaming of how he would make Arlene Dunne pay for what she had done to him. He would make her sorry—*real* sorry, sorry the hard way. The thing to do would be to disable her somehow, then get that ring without killing her. After that, he would give her time to stew about it for a while. And when the time was right, explain it to her, taking his sweet time about it too. It would be beautiful.

When he heard Jerry's voice at the door that evening, Stone called him in. "I need some new clothes, Jerry. Go get me some underwear, pants, and a shirt. Black, if possible. I wear 38x38-inch pants and a three-X shirt. You got enough money left for that?"

Jerry gulped. "No problem, sir. I'll have it here in an hour," he replied smartly as he darted out the door. Stone listened as the sound of the boy's footsteps faded. In three days, he hadn't heard Jerry utter a single word that didn't need saying. The kid was growing on him. He could use a boy like that.

Two hours later, Stone was freshly showered and dressed. The boy had done well, considering 38x38 pants were nearly impossible to find off the store shelf. He wondered how Jerry pulled off that neat little trick. He expected to be forced to wear 38x36 pants, which would do in an emergency but would be too short ever to wear twice. He reasoned there must be a big man's store in the area. Once again, the boy had done well, so he decided to leave Jerry a nice fat tip when he left.

The image in the motel mirror was much improved than what he saw the night he arrived. While the swelling around his eye was still significant, with black, blue, and yellow covering much of the left side of his face, the scrapes had stopped weeping and scabbed over. Now he simply looked like he had fallen down a flight of stairs rather than in a train wreck. He was making progress.

Stone stared at the proceeds of Jerry's last supply run with dismay. All he brought was a small box of Chinese food, a carton of Lucky Strikes, and a bottle of scotch. *If I don't get out of here soon, I am going to starve to death!* But he decided to eat the food, drink the scotch, and stay one more night. He was still barely able to walk, so there was no question that a little more undisturbed rest would do him good. Still, he determined to bail out of the Cherry Motel first thing in the morning. He had plans, unfinished business with Arlene to take care of, and was eager to get at it.

Aware that Jerry would not be at work in the morning, Stone decided to call him from the bedside phone. He dialed zero then waited for the boy to pick up. Jerry answered on the second ring. "Front desk, Jerry speaking."

"I'll be leaving in the morning," Stone announced. "Come here; I want to talk to you," he said flatly, then hung up the phone.

Moments later, there was a knock at the door. "Come on in," Stone called from the bed where he lay with his head propped up on the pillows. Jerry stepped into the room then stood silently with his hands folded in front of him, patiently waiting to hear what the big man had to say.

Stone took his time, thinking while he stubbed out a cigarette in the ashtray. "I'll be leaving in the morning," he repeated. "I've left you the money I promised on the table there," he said, pointing a thick finger at it. "You did well, so I also left you a tip. There's enough there to give you a good start. Spend it wisely."

"Yes, sir," Jerry said, then reached for the thick stack of one-hundred-dollar bills and put them in his hip pocket without comment. Stone marveled that the boy had not even thanked him, which was okay with him; he did not expect or desire to be thanked. What he expected was results, which Jerry had provided faultlessly. The boy had worked for the money and deserved to be rewarded, simple as that.

Jerry still hadn't asked any questions, nor had he uttered a single word more than needed. The boy also had not counted the money, which surprised and amused Stone. He looked the boy over as he stood stock-still as if waiting for further orders.

"You drive, boy?"

"Yes, sir. I have a license, but I don't have a car."

"What do you make here?"

"Nightshift pays seventy-five cents an hour."

"How would you like to get out of here and make five dollars an hour?"

Jerry sucked in air sharply, glanced around the room, and shifted his weight from one side to the other without answering. When he finally spoke, Stone began to think the boy was about to turn down the offer.

"Yes, sir," was his simple reply.

Stone grinned. "Where do you live?"

"Here—in number one, with my parents," Jerry said, then he added, "they own the place."

"I thought so. You probably don't need me telling you there's not much of a future for you here," said Stone, taking another long drag from his cigarette and exhaling it into the smoke-filled room. He considered the boy for a moment, then went on.

"I need an assistant, someone who knows how to get things done without asking a lot of questions. You seem to get things done without bothering me with your problems or talking too much. I don't like questions, I don't like problems, and I do not like most people. Do you have a problem with any of that?

"No, sir," was the boy's answer, which came immediately this time.

"Alright— you're hired."

"Thank you, sir. When do I start?"

"That's a lot of sirs, Jerry," Stone observed.

"My father was an Army Ranger, a Sergeant. He likes to be called sir."

"I see…You can call me Stone."

"Yes, sir," Jerry agreed. Then Jerry watched silently as Stone used the hot end of a short cigarette to light another.

"You want out of here, right?"

"*Yes, sir!*" Jerry repeated, although this time, with emphasis, saying it like he meant it. And he did. It was an exclamation of fact, leaving no room for doubt. After all, he most definitely did want out of the Cherry Motel and as far away as he could get from Sergeant Gerald Dunne, Army Ranger.

"I live in San Juan Capistrano. You know where that is?"

"No, sir."

"Call me Stone."

"Yes, sir."

"A couple of hours' drive south from here on the coast. It's a big place, with a room for you if you want it."

"That would be fine, s-s-s—uh, *Mr.* Stone," Jerry stammered.

"Alright…" said Stone, taking time to think about what he was about to say next. "I'll be leaving precisely at nine tomorrow morning. I like to be on time—see? I am still sore and can only see out of one eye, so if you are ready to go, then you're driving.

"Yes, sir, Mr. Stone. I'll be ready."

"Just *Stone*, Jerry. Just Stone. It is singular. You can lay off the sirs now. You're not in the Army anymore. You can consider yourself discharged, alright?" Stone half expected the boy to salute and bark out another *yes-sir* but knew the message had sunk in when Jerry answered, "Alright, Stone. I'll see you at nine then." Stone caught the boy's faint smile as he turned and left the room.

The following day, Stone closed the door to number eight precisely at 9 AM. He had nothing to carry because he brought nothing with him other than the ruined clothes he was wearing when he arrived. His old clothes were so stiff from dried blood they could've stood up and walked away by themselves. Disgusted with the smashed gold watch, he left that behind, too.

Stone found Jerry standing beside his black Ford sedan outside in the parking lot wearing a set of new clothes. A pair of new suitcases sat on the ground next to him. The boy was standing at attention as if he was about to be reviewed by a four-star general. Stone rolled his eyes, then said, "At ease, private." Jerry laughed at that, which surprised Stone, then he too laughed, which surprised them both.

"The trunk is unlocked, and keys are still in the ignition. Go ahead and stow your things in the trunk. You're driving," Stone declared, then took his time easing himself into the passenger seat with a painful groan.

Once they were underway, Stone directed Jerry to head west on East Colorado Street.

"When you hit Highway 99, head south. Also, I am going to need a new watch, so keep your eyes peeled for a jewelry store."

Jerry nodded. Stone loved the fact that Jerry had never once questioned him. Other than asking, *'When do I start?'* The boy had not asked a single question in three days. Surely the boy must wonder why he had shown up in the middle of the night beaten to a bloody pulp or why he carried so much cash. Unlike most people, the boy never tried to engage him in unnecessary conversation. Furthermore, he had performed every task given to him perfectly.

What's this kid's story? Stone wondered. For all Jerry knew, Stone might have been a bank robber on the run from the cops—and yet there was no hint of suspicion from him and no questions asked. Jerry had not involved his family either, other than to help him provide meals when he slept during the day. A lot of people would have taken one look at him and called the police, but not Jerry.

Impressive, thought Stone with a nod. *What a gem.* The kid was disciplined, brought up the right way, and knew how to get things done without whining about it. *This Sergeant Gerald—whatever, Army Ranger, his father, had done an excellent job raising the boy. What was his last name?* He could not remember, then decided it didn't matter anyway.

Until Jerry the Gem came along, Stone never realized how useful a helper could be. Upon reflection, he never considered bringing anyone into his life, let alone hiring someone. Still, the secrets Stone kept complicated matters. He could not have just anyone hanging around who might get in the way. While it was just a gut feeling, he had a notion that Jerry was not going to get in the way, cause problems, or question him about where the money came from. In just a few days, the kid had proved himself to be trustworthy, obedient, and did whatever he was asked to do, quickly and without asking a lot of questions—all of which combined to make Jerry the Gem too good of a catch to pass on. Stone wondered why others had not noticed the boy's potential and had already snatched him away from the dumpy motel.

"Sir, there's a jewelry store ahead on the right. Do you want me to pull over?"

"Alright," Stone agreed. Then an idea popped into his head that he put in motion without a second thought. A lot could be learned about the boy by sending him in to buy the watch for him, and if it worked out, great. If not, and Stone didn't like the watch, he could always find a better one elsewhere. And if Jerry skimmed some of the money, more would be learned. It was a good plan.

As Jerry was busy parallel-parking the Ford in front of the jewelry store, Stone counted out eleven one-hundred-dollar bills in his pocket without letting on what he was doing or what he had in mind.

"I'm still too sore to shop," he grunted. "Go in and get the biggest, most expensive gold watch they have in there.

Here are a thousand bucks. That ought to do it." Then Stone shoved the roll of cash at Jerry like he was glad to be rid of it.

Jerry returned a few minutes later with a small brown paper bag labeled "Parson Bros. Jewelry." Stone opened the bag to find a black velvet box, a receipt for $429.41, and a sealed envelope containing $670.59 in change. Inside the box was an elegant gold watch. Upon inspection, he noticed it was a Rolex. Stone's eyes lit up. Although the watch was of a type and style he had never seen, he was delighted with it.

As Jerry went about the business of entering traffic on Highway 99, Stone exclaimed, "Hey Jerry, the receipt and cash add up to eleven-hundred dollars, which is more than I gave you. What did you do, cheat old man Parson out of a hundred bucks?"

"No, sir. You gave me eleven one-hundred-dollar bills. A couple of them must have stuck together," he explained. Stone noticed the faint smile on Jerry's lips as he casually merged into traffic. He also saw the kid had not said he counted wrong. *The boy is sharp,* Stone thought, *and a keeper.*

Stone came away from his little experiment with three things learned. First, and perhaps foremost, the kid was life smart beyond his years. When asked about the watch receipt, his self-respect was readily apparent. No doubt, Jerry grasped that his honesty was being tested and received a passing grade for it, too. Second, Jerry was willing and able to do most anything asked of him and get it right the first time. Third, the boy wasn't afraid or hesitant to speak up when he needed to. He wasn't one inclined to timidity or to cower, traits Stone loathed—especially in men. Thus far, Jerry had aced every task assigned to him, and he felt good about bringing the boy aboard.

The three-bedroom ranch-style home outside of Capistrano was recent but relatively modest considering its location. At 320 acres, it was one of the last large tracts of undeveloped farmland on the bluff within ten miles either direction. The view from the ridge overlooking the Pacific Ocean was spectacular. In addition to Stone's ranch house, the original homestead was also situated near the bluff, although one-quarter of a mile south of the main house.

The mile-long tree-lined drive to the house was picturesque, with ancient Eucalyptus planted long ago by homesteaders. The enormous trunks towered high into the sky, creating long shadows. Slivers of intermittent sunlight strobed in the gaps as they rolled along the gravel road. Acres of undulant farmland fenced in barbed wire spoke of farm animals no longer present.

"Stay right," Stone commanded, "this is the old homestead. You will be staying there. My place is up the road a ways." Stone directed Jerry past the big red barn, a variety of smaller outbuildings, and an old farmhouse.

"I like my privacy. You can have the farmhouse to yourself. It's furnished, but you will need to get outfitted. Drop me off at my place, and then you can use the car to go shopping. I am going to need to rest a few more days, so I'll call you when I need you or the car back. My phone number is Olive-9-615. Can you remember that?"

"Got it, Olive-9-615," Jerry repeated.

Stone eased himself gingerly from the car, then abruptly slammed the door behind himself without a word or looking back. Nevertheless, Jerry remained parked watching his new boss hobble up the stairs, taking them slowly, one at a time, grunting and groaning with each painful step, until the big man was safely inside. Only then did Jerry pull away and head toward the drab-looking two-story farmhouse.

Jerry parked Stones' car in front of the farmhouse. Then gazing up at his new home, he concluded it wasn't too bad. *But battleship grey does nothing for the place,* he thought to himself. *Everything is grey, the siding, trim, window frames — everything. I wonder if the boss will let me brighten things up someday.*

Stairs led to a covered porch and the main entry. Large picture windows faced the ocean view. A pair of matching deck chairs with thick cushions were strategically placed to take advantage of the sunsets. Jerry wondered if Stone had put them there or if he ever used them. He doubted it, though. Stone did not seem like the decorative type.

Fifty yards out, rolling hills sloped sharply toward the beach, the ocean, and beyond. The expansive view of the water seemed to stretch into a barely perceptible haze at the horizon. Once Jerry had pulled himself away from the view, he found the door unlocked, let himself in, and did a quick walk-through. He was surprised to find the house and furnishings better than the old house's dated gray exterior suggested. Evidence of updates was everywhere, including contemporary furniture and drapes, but nothing smelled fresh enough to be considered brand-new. Everything appeared to be new but unused.

Jerry saw no reason why he should not use the master bedroom, so he unpacked his things in there then went to the kitchen to check the cupboards, which also proved to be new and unused. The closet, cabinets, drawers, refrigerator — everything was empty and showed no evidence of ever being used. *Stone was right; I will need to go shopping, and soon,* he thought. *The day is still young. I'll go now.*

Once in downtown San Juan Capistrano, Jerry's first stop was the Western Auto Store, where he picked up some cookware, a teakettle, dishes, silverware, towels, and toiletries. He also found a couple of paperback novels and a newspaper to read. After that, he stocked up on groceries at the Piggly-Wiggly Market. By the time he was done, the Ford's trunk and the back seat was so full there was no room for anything more. It was time to head for home.

Near the edge of town, Jerry saw a Studebaker dealer and pulled over to look at the new cars. Even after shopping, he still had over fifteen hundred dollars in his pocket, so while he didn't know if he had enough to purchase a new car, he was sure there was more than enough to buy a used one.

The moment the door closed on Stone's Ford, and before he made it to the sidewalk, an overweight salesman with a bad case of belly overhang rushed at him from the sales shack. The redheaded man nearly ran to greet him, with his tie flapping in the wind like a flag.

"Hi son, I'm Andy!" declared the red-faced man with a toothy grin and voice dripping with put-on enthusiasm. Andy grabbed Jerry's hand unexpectedly and pumped it considerably harder and longer than necessary. "Are you ready to trade in that Ford in on a brand-new Studebaker today?" Andy fired the words at Jerry as if he had the most exciting notion ever conceived.

"No, sir, that's not my car," Jerry admitted honestly. "I've borrowed it from my employer for the day. I'm just looking today," he confessed, then added, "but I am wondering about the cost of a new car."

"Well, let me show you around then!" Andy announced, delighted, keeping one eye on the boy and the other on the salesmen's shack in the center of the lot where the sales manager watched from a window.

Andy did his best to appear thrilled at the prospect of spending his day showing pimply-faced teenager's cars they could not afford. He reasoned the boy was probably truant, likely lying about having a job, and did not own a car himself. And to add insult to injury, the adolescent pimple farmer was wasting his valuable time. Despite that, Andy was thrilled to have a job, and jobs for overweight men in their fifties could be hard to find.

Entertaining dreamers and kids with their heads in the clouds was standard duty for Andy. He hated it, it went on day after day, but with the boss watching his every move, he had no choice but to make a show of it. The kid looked like he couldn't afford a new pair of roller skates, let alone a new Studebaker. Nevertheless, Andy continued with the charade humoring the boy. He'd like to tell the kid to take a long walk off a short pier—but that was not possible with the boss watching, so Andy continued playing the part.

"The new 1947 Studebakers are fabulous!" Andy bellowed with put-on enthusiasm as he snaked the two of them through the car lot. "Studebaker redesigned the entire product line from the ground up for 1947. We're talking double-dropped frames, clean fender lines, and more interior room than ever. And get this, mattering on which model you choose, you can have up to 94 horsepower! Do you like horsepower, boy?"

Andy was well-aware that young men liked horsepower—they all did, didn't they? He always asked the boys that question because it never failed to get them excited about the product. "Let me show you the Champion Six, which starts at $1,378. And this here blue one is a real creampuff!" And with that, Andy had Jerry's complete attention.

"Wah-one-thousand-three-hundred-seventy-eight-da-dollars?" Jerry stuttered, almost choking on his tongue. At $1,378, he had more than enough money in his pocket to buy the car.

Andy smiled. "Now, this Champion Six model here," he went on, "is a five-passenger coupé riding on a 112-inch wheelbase. Do you know what that means? Think comfort with a smooth ride, son." Andy raised his hand, emulating a car floating on air. "This car is a real crowd pleaser too, and the ladies love it! You like the girls, doncha?" Andy said with a wink, a toothy grin, and a nudge of his elbow. Andy always asked the boys that question too, and it worked like a charm.

Andy opened the driver's door to the sporty blue coupé, then stepped aside, motioning for Jerry to have a look inside. It was hard for Jerry not to like what he saw there. The car was stylish, the dashboard looked like a spaceship, and the cloth interior was soft and comfortable. It was affordable. It just seemed right, so he decided to see if he could chisel on Andy.

"I don't know," Jerry said, rubbing his chin, sounding as disinterested as possible. "$1,378 seems pretty high. I think I can get a Ford for less."

For a moment, Andy looked like his face was melting. "Hey kid, did you see the multi-pane wraparound rear window?" he asked, attempting to change the subject away from the price. "First time I saw it, I said to myself: which way is that car going anyway? Looks like it's driving in reverse! Do you know what that's called? That's called aerodynamic styling. You won't see that on a Ford!"

Jerry knew a sales pitch when he heard it, but that didn't matter; he liked the car and had enough money to buy it. The freedom that came with owning one's own car was undeniable. He did not want to be tethered to the boss's car any longer than necessary. And it was time to have a little fun at Andy's expense.

"Deliver it for me, and I'll give you $1,200 cash for it," he said.

Andy's eyes became wide as saucers as he heard the word "cash" exiting the boy's mouth. He knew he had a sale at that moment, believing that if the boy had anywhere near that much money on him, he could get him to pay more to close the deal. Plus, with a big down payment, the boss would in-house finance the difference if necessary. So, Andy put on his sad-sack face and muttered disappointedly, "Oh, I'm sorry, son, The boss is pretty firm. These new Champions are selling like cold beer on a hot day at a baseball game. We can get our price for them."

"Alright," Jerry responded as he got out of the car, then reached out and shook the salesman's hand with a wide smile.

"Great!" Andy burst out, slapping Jerry on the back. "Come on inside, and we'll write 'er up."

"Oh, I'm sorry, Andy. I think you misunderstood," said Jerry, his voice heavy with mock disappointment. "I'm going to the Ford dealer. I'm sure I can buy a new Ford for $1,200." Then he turned and began walking away.

Andy's eyes bulged in terror. "Wait!" he cried out, grabbing Jerry by the collar to prevent him from leaving. "I said the boss is *pretty firm*, but that doesn't mean I can't get you a cash discount!"

Jerry smiled. Taken by the arm, he was half-walked, half-carried into the salesmen's shack, where he was abruptly deposited into a chair in front of a metal desk. Andy seated himself on the opposite side of the desk then asked, "Do you have $1,200 in cash to put down?"

"I might."

Andy stiffened. "What do you mean—you *might?*" His face darkened, visibly upset by the snarky response. "Either you have it, or you do not, right? "

"I mean, I *might* have $1,200 on me if it buys that blue Champion 6. If it doesn't, then maybe I don't. But I'll bet $1,200 would buy a new Ford. What do you think, Andy? Do I have $1,200 on me or not?" Jerry said with a puzzled look pulling at his features.

Jerry waited, hiding his amusement as Andy's face turned bright red, and his chubby fingers dug into the desktop turning his fat knuckles white. Twenty years in, the veteran salesman had never seen anyone work him over like this kid was doing to him. At that moment, if it had been his car lot, he would have tossed the smart-aleck kid out on his ear. But it wasn't his business, and he needed the sale, so he fought to contain his temper. Taking a deep breath, Andy swallowed his pride and said, "Let me ask the boss. I'll be back in a moment."

Twenty gut-churning minutes later, Andy stomped back into the room, carrying a wrinkled sales order that landed with a smack on the desk in front of Jerry. Sweat glistened on the salesman's beet-red face. Dark sweat stains soaked his white shirt as he leaned over the desk, towering over the still-seated boy. The salesman's eyes bored into Jerry like red-hot branding irons.

"I got the boss to split the difference with you. Your price is $1,289, plus $26.63 for tax and license makes the total $1,305.63," which Andy said while tapping a chubby finger repeatedly on the documents.

Raising his eyes from the disturbing papers, he gave Jerry a hard look that said, *"You better have it, boy!* Then he asked emphatically, *"Do-you-have $1,305.63?"*

"Let's see," Jerry said, then stood. He took his time pulling out a thick roll of cash from the front pocket of his blue jeans. The relief on Andy's face at seeing the cash was unmistakable. Relieved, he leaned back in his chair, watching as the boy took his time counting out the exact amount down to the penny: thirteen one-hundred-dollar bills, one five, and sixty-three cents. With the exact amount fanned out across the desktop, Jerry returned to his seat and folded his hands on his lap.

"You can deliver the car this afternoon—right?"

"No problem," Andy mumbled grudgingly. "Sign that, and I'll go get the title for you."

While the salesman was getting the title, Jerry signed the sales order and added Stone's address. A few minutes later, Andy returned with an envelope containing the paperwork. After adding a carbon copy of the sales order, he handed it over to Jerry.

However, it was readily apparent Andy had enough of Jerry. He simply stood there with his arms folded across his chest, glaring, resisting the urge to point at the door and yell,

GET OUT! It was apparent there would not be a pleasant handshake or a "Thank you for your business" coming from Andy anytime soon. Jerry left the salesman's shack, feeling the heat of Andy's angry gaze on his back. Had he had been too hard on poor Andy? *Naw,* he thought, patting the hood of his brand-new car as he strolled from the lot.

Soon after returning to the farmhouse, Jerry unloaded his things from the Ford and left it parked in front of Stone's place. As he closed the door on the big black sedan, he saw the blue Champion roll down the road, followed by a black pickup truck. He wasn't surprised that neither of the men appeared to be Andy. Before he could walk the distance between the houses, the delivery men were gone.

Jerry walked around the futuristically styled coupé admiring its smooth lines and chrome trim. Soon he was rolling down the road for a test drive. Studebaker had a good reputation for quality, and the car was just as Andy described, a real crowd pleaser with a smooth ride. He loved everything about it and was eager to show it off.

Stone was still recovering from his injuries, so Jerry decided not to bother him with it. Showing the new car to his parents crossed his mind, but he decided against it, reasoning they might ask too many questions about where the money came from. It would be better to wait a month or two working for Stone. That would give him time to show income before presenting the new car to his folks, Gerald and Paula Dunne.

Two days later, Stone emerged from the ranch house and walked the distance to the homestead. Entering unannounced and without knocking, he found Jerry at the kitchen table, reading a newspaper, a teapot, and a cup in front of him. Also, without invitation, Stone sat himself down at the table opposite Jerry, made himself comfortable, and lit a Lucky Strike.

"I see you've got yourself outfitted here," Stone observed, exhaling smoke from his nose. "You like it?" he asked, looking around the room at the changes Jerry had made. Jerry thought he noticed a twinkle in his eye.

"It's great! And the view is incredible here!" Jerry gushed, pointing at the picture window overlooking the ocean view. Then, seeing that the boss was looking much improved, added, "You look a lot better."

"Feel better, too," Stone admitted. "Might have to go to the doctor about the eye, though. That your Studebaker parked out front?"

"It is," Jerry conceded, unable to hide his pride.

"Good choice. Studebaker makes a good car. You make good decisions, Jerry. That's one reason why I hired you," Stone commended between long drags on the Lucky Strike.

"Thank you, sir," Jerry accepted graciously. "Speaking of why you hired me, can you give me a job description? I would like to get to work as soon as possible."

"I don't know anything about a job description," Stone claimed bluntly, guessing correctly that a job description might be something formal as a document provided by an employer listing specific duties. Stone, however, wanted no part of such nonsense.

"I've never hired anyone before," he admitted, "but what I need is someone to help me take care of things around here. You have already proved that I can count on you to get things done."

Stone mulled his next words as he flicked cigarette ash in Jerry's empty teacup, then added, "I have investments and personal business I could use help with, too."

Stone smiled, tapping his cigarette nervously on Jerry's teacup. Stone left unsaid that he planned to use Jerry to help him bushwhack Arlene Dunne. Spying on her would be a crucial part of making that happen, so he couldn't help but wonder how that might sit with the boy. Would he object? Stone had no way of knowing but hoped he did not alienate the kid in the process. Meanwhile, he figured that overpaying him and giving him free rent might help keep him in line.

This was something Stone intended to put in motion sooner than later. Tomorrow would not be soon enough, but Stone also realized he needed to give Jerry something to do around the place to keep him busy. Making the boy feel needed and important would be the key to success. The old farm was getting dilapidated and overgrown, so he decided to keep the boy busy cleaning things up.

"The property needs a lot of maintenance—fields mowed, fences mended, and outbuildings repaired. Sometimes I might need you to help me with personal business, but we can talk about that later. Just take care of the place and be there when I need you, and you will have earned your pay.

"Speaking of that," Stone said, "we talked about $5.00 per hour, which would be hard to keep track of. Why don't we make it $750 per month and call it a day?"

"Sounds good to me," Jerry responded, well-aware that he had just received a $50 per month cut in pay, which is what a lot of people paid for rent. However, he knew $750 per month was still ridiculously high, considering he had already received sixteen hundred for doing next to nothing. It made sense as a business decision, so he graciously accepted.

"You like tractors?" Stone asked.

"Don't know, I've never had the opportunity to use one," Jerry admitted.

"Well, you can learn. If we had a tractor, we could get a lot of work done around here. It's a farm; we're going to need a tractor. You could get the barn cleaned up and store it in there. You can handle that. Go get one."

"Okay, but how would I pay for it?"

Stone took a moment to think about it, smoking while considering his options. "Let's go to a bank and get you a checking account. I will set you up with enough to get you outfitted. As long as you keep receipts, you are covered. If I do that, you're not going to run off with the money, are you?"

"No way," Jerry said emphatically. "Have you seen the view here? You'll have to fire me to get rid of me." Jerry laughed.

"Alright then, let's go to the bank and get started," Stone said with a note of finality. "Afterwards, we can go look at tractors. You're driving the Stude, right?"

"Right again, boss," Jerry said with an excited grin.

Jerry drove the Stude, as his new boss referred to it, with the windows down. The summer day was cloudless and warm as they navigated the winding road toward Dana Point. Along the way, they talked about tractors, work on the farm, and painting the homestead house. Then unexpectedly, Stone said, "You know, I haven't talked so much in—*forever*," he stammered but felt right for admitting it. Jerry took it as a sign that Stone, who was dour most of the time, might be allowing himself to lighten up a little bit. Jerry hoped he was right.

After opening the checking account for Jerry, with Stone as a co-signer, they drove to a Massey-Ferguson tractor dealer near Dana Point. They bought a red thirty-horsepower M-F tractor with several implements for it. Delivery was scheduled for the following day. Since Stone's objective was to keep Jerry as busy as possible, he made operating lessons part of the deal.

Jerry let his new boss do the talking but noticed that Stone did not negotiate prices at all. He simply paid the asking price in cash. It was not his money; nevertheless, Jerry hated seeing money left on the table. Jerry guessed that he could have saved at least ten percent on the deal with all the implements involved. It bothered him that Stone never seemed to care about the cost of things.

A flatbed truck drove down the lane loaded with the tractor and implements the following day. The driver, a mechanic from the Massy-Ferguson dealer, unloaded, then spent two hours tutoring Jerry on the big tractor's proper operation and maintenance. That afternoon, Jerry put the machine to work cleaning out the barn, ridding it of ancient hay, scrap building materials, and other junk. Anything burnable got piled high then set afire, which still left a significant amount of rusty metal and other junk needing disposal.

Jerry realized if he was going to accomplish his goal of returning the property to a working farm, the place needed a pickup truck. As he saw it, there was no need for anything new, just a set of wheels with a bed for hauling things to the dump—like that mound of junk piled next to the barn. The following day, Jerry returned to the Studebaker dealership to look for a suitable pickup.

Aware that Andy would not be happy to see him again so soon compelled Jerry to seek him out. Galling the big red-faced man was just too much fun to pass on. Sure enough, Jerry found Andy hiding in the salesmen's shack. Jerry was pleased when he saw the bulbous salesman alone, which prevented him from claiming he was too busy to help. Andy's face darkened the moment he laid eyes on Jerry.

"Something wrong with the Champion, kid?" Andy snapped, with bitterness written all over his face.

"Hi, Andy," chirped Jerry cheerfully from the doorway. "No, there's nothing wrong; I'm back looking for a used pickup truck. Let's take a look at what you have."

Andy sat for a moment staring back at the boy blankly, trying to come up with a reason why he could not help him, then remembered the thick roll of cash he carried the last time he was here. Sure, dealing with the boy was a pain in the neck, but he didn't detest him so much that he was willing to pass on another commission. Crestfallen, Andy forced his bulk from behind the desk and followed Jerry out onto the sales lot.

Andy answered Jerry's questions, but only grudgingly. Three of the used trucks caught Jerry's interest, although two were more than ten years old, making reliability suspect in his opinion. The other was a black 1940 Ford with just over twenty-thousand miles showing on the odometer. The little truck had the big 95 horsepower flathead V8, which he considered a big plus. This one seemed to have plenty of life left in it, so he decided it would do.

The words SALE and $595 painted in white shoe polish on the windshield established a benchmark for negotiations to commence. Jerry decided to begin with an offer of about fifteen percent off the sale price. Recalling Andy's sales approach had been a rapid-fire verbal barrage of memorized facts and statistics about the new Studebakers, he decided to have a little fun at the big man's expense. Turning that tactic around on him seemed like a sure bet to get under Andy's skin.

"Since we're friends now," Jerry said with rapidity, "I can tell you honestly, I like this truck a lot. I like that it only has twenty-thousand miles on it—and it is the right color. Fords should all be black, right? But that big flathead V8 probably eats gas like there's no tomorrow, which is a big negative. After all, I would be using it on the farm, and I don't want to have to keep coming to town every five minutes to fill it with gas. The four-cylinder engine gets a lot better mileage, which would save me time and money on running back and forth to the gas station. If it had the more economical four-banger in it, I would probably be willing to pay your sales price for it. But—hey, time is money, right? Now since I see SALE painted on the windshield, my guess is you wouldn't be having a sale on it if it was going to sell itself, know what I mean? Now I'm not even going to mention that this is a Ford, and there is a Ford dealer in town that probably has twice as many used Ford trucks as you do. So, what do you say we agree on $520 and shake hands on the deal right now?"

Jerry thrust his hand out to shake hands on the proposal, but Andy left him hanging as expected. But all that did was give Jerry further opportunity to goad the big guy, whose face had steadily reddened as he spoke. Knowing it wouldn't take much more to push Andy over the edge, he decided to go for beet-red.

Andy rolled his eyes, then stared at his feet for a long moment as he resisted the urge to tell Jerry to take a long walk off a short pier.

With his proposal left unanswered, Jerry continued to hold his hand out for a shake on the deal as he continued. "You know, that big flathead has a bigger engine with more horsepower than my new Studebaker? Do you know what that means, Andy? Think lower gas mileage, that's what, and I just don't need it on a farm. If I need horsepower, I can always get in the Studebaker and—"

"ALRIGHT!" Andy bellowed, cutting Jerry off mid-sentence, his face now just one shade short of the beet-red Jerry had been shooting for. "I'll take your offer to the boss. Wait in my office, and I'll let you know what he says." Then Andy whipped around and stormed off.

Ten minutes later, Andy returned to the salesmen's shack to find Jerry behind his desk reclining *in his chair* with his feet up on the desktop. With eyes narrowed and mouth agape, "Son of a..." escaped Andy's mouth, thinking this kid was awfully good at getting under his skin.

Andy's first inclination was to demand that the boy get the heck out of his chair. But then he correctly concluded that the kid was toying with him, so rather than continue trying to go toe to toe with the sharp-witted youngster, he decided to play along and see what happened.

For the first time, Andy recognized the boy was a lot more than a pain in his rear; he was intelligent and resourceful. More than likely, the money was coming from someone that trusted him. Whoever it was had given him a lot of line for one so young, and probably for a good reason. He couldn't guess who, but he imagined whoever was paying the bills considered the boy capable and dependable. Unfortunately, he had let Jerry get under his skin, which he now regretted. Now that he understood him better, he decided to see if he could make amends.

Andy plopped down in the customer's chair across the desk from Jerry, who continued leaning back in the chair with his eyes closed as if he were relaxing in a hammock under a shade tree.

"I hate to wake you, Jerry, but I have an offer for you," Andy said mildly. Jerry opened one eye but didn't respond; he was in a state of shock. The angry red face he was used to dealing with had been replaced by one pleasant with a multitude of freckles.

"The boss," informed Andy, "agreed to split the difference with you again, making it $557.50. I have a sales order prepared for you with the adjusted amount. With tax and license, the total is $574.81. Will that work for you?

Not expecting that much of a discount without a couple of go-arounds with "the boss," Jerry took his feet off the desk and sat up, scratching his head. Evidently, the game had been called for the day.

"Can I see it?" Jerry asked, referring to the sales order. Andy handed the document over then watched calmly as Jerry reviewed the figures. All seemed to be in order, so without looking up at the salesman, Jerry signed it and handed it back with a smile.

"Is a check alright?"

"Of course, Jerry, your check is always good here," Andy responded warmly, smiling. Jerry looked at Andy suspiciously, wondering what was going on with him. What had changed? Had he paid too much? After writing the check and handing it to Andy, Jerry was at a loss for words.

"Thank you for your business, Jerry," Andy said with genuine appreciation, then stood presenting his big paw for his customer to shake. As they shook hands, a truce was called, and the war ended without a shot ever having been fired.

"If you would like, we can make the delivery later this afternoon. Enjoy your new truck, Jerry; it's a nice one. And if you ever need anything else, just ask. I'll be right here."

"Ummm…yes, alright. That would be great. Ummm, thank you, Andy." Jerry offered a hesitant half-wave, then ambled out, scratching his head, wondering what had just happened.

The next day, Saturday, was a busy one for Jerry. The old farmstead had been neglected for decades, which he intended to remedy. He drove the truck to town, picked up some hand tools and a lawnmower, then made a couple of runs to the dump. The truck was handy, and he liked driving it. The more he looked at it, the more he drove it, the better he liked it. By the end of the day, he felt like it would be his first choice for short runs, although the Champion would still be the better choice for highway driving.

That evening Stone barged into Jerry's house, again unannounced and without knocking. The boss informed him that he would be called on to help with the "personal business" in Pasadena he had mentioned earlier.

"This might take a few days," Stone advised. Since they would be staying at least a couple of nights, Jerry would need to make reservations for two rooms at a hotel. He should also have his bag packed and be ready to go first thing Monday morning. Stone would explain more on the way there.

Jerry was concerned that he was spending too much money, especially with the pickup truck's unauthorized purchase. The tools, truck, tractor, and implements added up to a significant sum of money. The truck was parked in the driveway, which was impossible to miss. And yet, Stone had not mentioned it, which led Jerry to believe he didn't care about it. When he handed the boss an envelope full of receipts, Stone simply grunted and shoved the envelope in his hip pocket without looking at them.

The fact that his expenditures had gone unquestioned did not sit well with Jerry. He didn't know what to think. Jerry was accustomed to being held accountable for even the most insignificant expense. He had been taught to be diligent about comparing price and quality with every purchase he made. The records and receipts were all there. Believing the boss would scrutinize the receipts privately bothered him, too. He felt like he was being relieved of the opportunity to defend his expenditures.

Jerry wanted to sit down and discuss his plans for the farm. He hoped to have the opportunity to explain related expenses in detail. However, when he invited Stone to sit down with him and discuss his plans, Stone simply said: "You have the ball. Run with it," then left without further discussion on the subject.

Aware the boss was a man of few words, Jerry knew he should not expect lengthy conservations with him on any subject. But didn't everyone care about what things cost, regardless of how much money they had? Sure, the boss was wealthy, but Jerry felt like it was his obligation to conduct himself in a businesslike manner. But how could he do that without the worry of being second-guessed when he wasn't allowed to explain expenditures in person?

Jerry found himself confounded by Stone's lack of diligence. The situation was, without a doubt, different than anything he could have imagined. In less than two weeks, this man had turned his life upside-down. Perhaps, he reasoned, this was simply the nature of working for a man like Stone. *Maybe I should just roll with it,* he thought. *Why fight it if the boss is okay with it?*

But could he get used to it? Could he really be so lucky to have been rescued from the Cherry Motel and Sargent Gerald Dunne by a super-rich benefactor who simply did not care what things cost? It seemed too good to be true! And what appeared to be too good to be true was most likely just that—too good to be true.

Chapter 11

Amon— February 2431 BCE

E rlin's conclave lodge was a recent addition to the growing hamlet. Built on the local clan's traditional summer gathering grounds, it was an edifice that marked the settlement's ascension from a no-account wide spot in the road to relevance as a town. The conclave hall, built of river rock and massive timbers, dominated the river's south side beyond the stone bridge.

The council had decided its construction should be made the focus point of the summer gathering grounds, solidifying their claim to both sides of the river. Focusing growth beyond the bridge also made strategic sense if they were ever forced to defend the vital bridge and village from invaders.

While the conclave hall was nearly large enough to hold the entire population of Erlin, the elder council room was a late addition used for civic and judicial purposes. Unfortunately, the council room was only large enough to comfortably hold twenty to thirty people. On the morning of the inquest into Jotham's death, over one hundred people were pressed together in the small room. A gallery of interested ones overflowed the council chamber into the street.

When Amon entered the council chamber, all heads turned, and the room fell instantly silent. At that moment, the sensation of nakedness hit Amon hard, as if he were some sort of curious seldom-seen creature, shaved, and put on display for the very first time. The heat of a hundred sets of eyes boring into his soul stripped him of his resolve. But the malice in Riordan's burning gaze was what cut the deepest because Amon was unable to dissuade his heart from condemning himself for robbing the old man of his youngest son.

Amon joined Hethe and Abiah, who already had taken their place before a five-elders council seated behind a long wooden table. Elymas, also a council member, would hear the arguments, judge the matter, and render a binding decision. The judgment seat was situated at a right angle to the council, providing an unobstructed view of the councilmen and the litigants. An impressive iron lantern hung from the timbers above, lighting the room with a yellow glow.

The raucous crowd filled the room far beyond its intended capacity. With hundreds talking at once and pressing in on one another from outside, no one heard when Stren, chief of the elder council, called the meeting to order. When that did not affect the crowd, Stren climbed on the tabletop and repeatedly shouted, "QUIET!" until the racket subsided. By the time the din died down, the red-faced Stren was furious. He attempted to speak only after his face had returned to its usual color.

"This inquest has been called by Councilman Riordan regarding the death of his son Jotham, a huntsman," declared Stren. "This afternoon, we will hear the testimony of the eyewitnesses here." He held out his hand, motioning to the three hunters facing him. "Then the council will make a recommendation to the judge in this matter. Before we begin, we ask all onlookers to remain silent. *Do not comment* unless you are called on by name. Any interference from spectators will be dealt with severely," he warned.

Stren motioned to the doorway upon completing the announcement, where a pair of well-armed men stood beside the open door. Nothing more needed to be said about why the soldiers were present.

"Councilman Riordan," he said, retaking his seat, "you may begin."

The Erlin court had strict rules that few had dared to break. Unruly onlookers could be fined for speaking out of turn. On occasion, unruly observers had been ejected and beaten by the guards for disorderly conduct. One time, a defendant was publicly whipped for threatening a council member. Since then, no one dared speak once the council had been called to order.

Seeing as there was no rule against murmuring, the citizens of Erlin considered it their sacred duty to exercise that privilege at every opportunity. While murmuring was deemed to be the standard operating procedure, *oohs, ahhs,* and snickers were frowned upon, although grudgingly tolerated.

Amon didn't need anyone to tell him Riordan wanted him dead. *That was evident from the moment I entered the building,* he told himself. He cocked an eye at Riordan, saw the councilman spying on him, grinding his teeth in anger, so Amon turned quickly away. The old man never took his eyes from him; his gaze was unyielding, his watery eyes a mixture of contempt and condemnation. So, Amon was not surprised when the old man ignored his fellow hunters and concentrated on indicting him.

"Amon, you are a hunter?" Riordan spat the word "hunter" as if he was a low-born gutter rat. Nevertheless, Amon was not about to allow the old man to discredit him for his chosen occupation.

"Yes, as was your son Jotham," Amon snapped.

"Alright, tell me how you murdered my son—Jotham," Riordan fired back.

A cry arose from the onlookers, which Stren instantly silenced. Dismayed by the crowd's reaction, Amon looked at them with eyes wide. Such a pointed question caught him off-guard, and he reacted as if struck by a tremendous blow. It hurt, but Riordan's question implied malicious intent from the outset. *Of course, I killed Jotham,* he thought, *but there was nothing vengeful or deliberate about it!* Admitting murdering the boy in this context would be damning. Amon was desperate for the truth to be known.

"I didn't *murder* Jotham," he responded. "He attacked me with a knife, without warning, and while I was unarmed. I used my knife to defend myself. If he—"

Amon was cut off mid-sentence by Riordan, who bellowed, "Did you *hear?* This—*hunter* admits to murdering my son! And he confessed to using his own knife to commit murder! This butcher should be beheaded!"

Murmuring from the crowd reverberated so loud that Stren had to stand to silence the onlookers. "If spectators cannot remain silent," he bellowed, "we will close the doors and make this session private! Is that understood?"

Instantly the room grew silent. Riordan continued without pause. "We have two witnesses here to the murder—

Hethe, and Abiah, both of whom are Amon's friends. Hethe, tell us, did you witness Amon murder Jotham?"

Hethe gulped, and eyes widened. "I was there and saw everyth—"

Riordan interrupted: "This man saw Amon commit the murder!" he roared, waving his arms, playing to the crowd.

"But it was not *murder!*" Hethe tried to explain. "Jotham attacked Amon with his knife while Amon was still unarmed. He was forced to defend himself!"

"Oh, I *see*," Riordan slyly nodded, taking his time, pacing in front of the council table. "And who killed Jotham?" he whispered.

"Amon won the knife fight in self-defense," Hethe insisted.

"So, you are saying Amon killed Jotham, am I correct?" Riordan asked, a little louder now. After a pause, Hethe answered. "Yes. But it was—"

Riordan drowned his answer out as he thundered, "Did you *hear it?* This man witnessed the murder! Amon's own friend admits he committed *murder!*" Murmuring once again threatened to bring Stren to his feet, but his harsh expression quieted the room, this time without a word.

Amon gasped for air as if kicked in the chest. His heart sank as he listened to Riordan distort Hethe's words at will. The accuser turned everything Hethe said into an accusation. Amon bit his lip as his friend did his best to defend him, only to have his words used as an impeachment. Riordan continued his attack.

"Abiah! Tell me what you saw. Who killed Jotham?"

Abiah gaped at Amon. The young man had witnessed the way Riordan twisted first Amon's words and then

Hethe's. No doubt, the old man was skilled at twisting the truth to meet his own needs. Thus far, the councilman had succeeded in making the fight seem like something it was not. He wanted to avoid the trap into which his friends had fallen. Cleverness would be required on his part to prevent his own words from suffering the same fate.

Abiah knew the truth meant nothing to Riordan. However, the truth meant everything to his friend on trial for his life. The accuser was biased, and vengeance was his only goal; there was no doubt about that. Abiah saw how effectively Riordan defeated the opposition, seeking ways to turn that around on him.

Abiah set his jaw tight, his mind deep in thought. *Amon had simply defended himself,* he thought. *No question about it.* Moreover, Amon was fortunate to have survived since he was unarmed when Jotham lunged at him with the knife. Simply claiming Amon won the fight in self-defense might not be enough to convince the judge of his fellow hunter's innocence, so Abiah chose his words carefully.

"It all happened very quickly. Jotham—"

Now raging, Riordan spoke over him, drowning his words away. "That is *not* what I asked you! Answer the question!" he screamed directly into the boy's face. "I'll ask you again. DID - YOU - SEE - AMON - KILL - JOTHAM? That is the question I asked you, and I expect you to answer that question directly!"

The words caused Abiah to set his jaw even tighter. "Why am I here?" He shouted, angrily glaring over Riordan's shoulder at the councilmen while holding his hands up in a gesture of bewilderment. Then he took a step back to make breathing room and spoke to Riordan.

"It seems to me you want to ask the questions then answer them yourself. Maybe I should ask *you* the questions, so you can give yourself the answers you want to hear! Would you be satisfied then?"

The room broke into uncontrolled laughter, interspersed by whoops and catcalls. Riordan turned to face his fellow councilmen. "I will not be insulted by this—*hunter!*" he shouted, spitting the word *hunter* as if a bug had just flown into his mouth. "I demand this man be removed and beaten for his disrespect!"

Chief Councilman Stren lifted himself from his chair, his weary expression betraying his lack of patience. Holding a hand up to silence the murmuring crowd, Stren effectively blocked Riordan from further comment.

"Thank you, Councilman Riordan. Your time is up. I will take over questioning now."

"You will *not!* I am not finished with these witnesses! I will tell you when I have completed questioning them!" Riordan barked.

"Councilman Riordan, I am ordering you to sit down. *You are finished,*" Stren said calmly. "Do it now, or I will have you removed," he warned.

"Are you insane? This man has insulted this council, he has insulted me personally, and you want to have *me* removed? And this man," he said, pointing a shaking finger at Amon, "is a murderer, and I will see that he is beheaded!"

The word *beheaded* made Amon swallow hard. Inadvertently his hand went to his throat. Yet hope swelled in Amon as Stren challenged his wily accuser, effectively putting a stop to Riordan's ruthless interrogation. But when Riordan accused Stren, Chief of the Council, of being insane, he knew the old man had crossed a line from which there was no return. Now the man who had accused him so harshly would pay a heavy price for his insubordination, while Amon was about to be a free man.

"Guards!" called Stren, motioning the guards forward. "Remove Councilman Riordan and put him in the guardhouse. Hold him there for two days."

The crowd was so stunned they forgot to murmur. Wide eyes and mouths agape ruled the moment. As the guards approached the humiliated councilman, the crowd silently parted, making way for them. Riordan struggled and shouted threats and obscenities at Stren and the council as the guards seized him. "You dogs, idiots! You *are* insane; I will not stand for this!" he roared as he was dragged away.

Once outside, a commotion erupted in the street as Riordan's sons and supporters attacked the guards attempting to wrestle the old man free. Knives flashed around the badly outnumbered men, forcing them to draw their swords. A defensive perimeter was created by swinging their weapons and circling. The attackers backed away but took turns lunging and stabbing at them. But when several of those men had received nasty sword wounds from the capable fighters, they backed off. As numbers thinned, the guards were able to back safely away with Riordan in tow.

Unaware of what had happened in the street, Stren took over, questioning Abiah. "Son, what did you see? What happened?" he said kindly.

"Thank you, sir," Abiah responded, then took a moment to gather his thoughts.

"I saw Jotham attack Amon with his knife. Amon was unaware and unarmed, so he used his pack as a shield.

Jotham stabbed at him but missed because of the pack. Jotham would surely have killed Amon at that moment if he had not used the pack to defend himself. Amon rolled, then came up with a knife of his own. They fought; it looked as if Jotham was winning, but then Amon kicked snow in Jotham's face. That is when it happened. Amon came in and cut his throat."

"I see," Stren responded, rubbing his chin. "Hethe, is that what you saw?"

Hethe nodded. "Exactly what I saw, sir."

"Amon, does what Abiah say correctly represent what happened?"

"It does. Just as I remember it."

"Thank you," said Stren, turning to address the council. "See how easy that was?" he said, gesturing with his palms up. This time, the crowd remembered to do their job, murmuring with renewed enthusiasm.

Once the onlookers settled down, Stren went on. "There was no need to beat the truth out of these men. In my opinion, we have all the information needed to send a recommendation of innocence to Judge Elymas. Are there any arguments?" Stren looked to each council member individually for confirmation. "No?" He waited a moment longer, then continued, "Let us vote on it then. All in favor of innocence?"

Amon teetered, his heart thudding in his chest. All five of the councilmen raised their hands, including Stren. Then turning to Elymas, the judge, Stren said, "You have our recommendation. What do you say?"

"I judge this man, Amon, blameless," Elymas said without hesitation, then rose from his seat. "Today, Riordan demonstrated a serious lack of impartiality," he announced. "I have serious doubts about the councilman's moral character. In my opinion, he does not appear to have the best interests of the people of Erlin in mind. I order that Riordan be removed from the elder council immediately. His replacement can be considered in our next session."

"This council session is closed," Stren proclaimed.

Blameless! Amon thought as a wave of relief coursed through his veins. With the council concluded, the crowd began talking all at once, the many voices echoing loudly in the chamber. A throng of well-wishers pressed in on the three hunters congratulating them on the favorable outcome. Amon smiled and thanked them but said little, preferring to let Abiah and Hethe do the talking. He was looking for a way out as quickly as possible. If there had been a rock to crawl under, he would have already disappeared under it.

Although cleared of the murder charge, Amon felt ashamed and humiliated by Riordan's accusations. *The old man's words hit home,* he thought, *regardless of the trial's outcome. "This hunter admits to murdering my son and confessed to using his own knife!"* Those words echoed in Amon's consciousness. However, Riordan's words: "This butcher should be beheaded!" stabbed repeatedly at his heart.

Who but me is responsible for what happened on the trail that day? I insulted the boy! He reasoned that none of this would have happened if I had not done that. And Riordan's words had an undeniable ring of truth in them—I killed Jotham, which never would have happened if I had not disrespected him.*

The commotion diminished as the crowd filed out of the hall and into the street. As the last few people separated and went different ways, Amon noticed a woman standing alone in the shadows. *The healer!* He had forgotten about her during the inquest and the promise made to be here for him.

Amon remembered the woman's words. "It will not be safe for you. There will be a fight; I can help you—I will nuke them." But she was wrong about that. *There is not a fight,* Amon thought. *Most people have already left. Everyone is going home. The streets are empty, so why is she here?*

The healer had placed herself in a narrow gap between two buildings, where she was barely visible from the street. Amon recognized her immediately but did not have time to acknowledge her as a mob suddenly rounded the corner, heading straight for him. *What now?* He wondered. Many bore clubs and stones in their hands, leaving no doubt about their intention. Amon immediately recognized the gang was there to serve up Riordan's sick version of justice.

Realizing he was in serious trouble, his heart dumped adrenaline into his veins. The air suddenly was heavy against his skin as the mob approached, and the pressure mounted. Amon's first inclination was to make a run for it, but he realized that he wasn't likely to stay ahead of them for long at his age.

Recognizing the odds were impossible, his eyes darted hopefully to the alleyway where the woman remained concealed in the shadows between the stone walls. Was she there to watch Riordan's thugs beat him to a bloody pulp, or would she intervene? Would she nuke them as promised? Believing she could help if she chose to was not enough to encourage Amon, although her presence did present an option other than running. There was no time to spare, she would have to do something quickly, or it would be too late for him.

With the mob just steps away, the throng abruptly fell silent, frozen in place as if they had been turned to stone. Amon had not seen or heard anything happen; the crowd had been silenced and stopped moving all at once. Amon's mind raced—*What is going on?* he wondered. It seemed some were caught mid-stride, while others were suspended in the air with one or even two feet off the ground. A thrown stone hovered in the air as if hung by a wire. *Impossible!*

Amon stared at the strange scene, bewildered, trying to make sense of it —and then a voice called out.

"Come with me if you want to live," the woman called to Amon from her hiding place between the buildings. "Hurry!"

Amon did indeed hurry, and with every ounce of adrenaline e-charged energy, he had. His mind raced, his heart pounded, his lungs sucked in air, and his nervous system attempted to jolt his body into action. But it was no good; his feet remained anchored to the ground as if they were cemented in place. Paralyzed by what he faced just an arm's length away, panic held him in an unbreakable grip.

"Hurry!" the woman cried out again.

Still, Amon could not move. *What is happening?!* Suddenly an invisible hand wrapped him in its grip, pressing in from all sides, and he was roughly hauled into the air, carried away, and deposited at the woman's feet. Disoriented and confused, Amon stared up at her questioningly.

"Do you think you can move now, or must I carry you?" Valerie said mockingly. "I can't keep those thugs still forever! Well, actually, I *could*, but that would really bother some people I used to know," she said with a chuckle.

"Get up, and let's get out of here!" She ordered as she turned and began walking away. Amon's head spun as if caught in a whirlpool, but he struggled to his feet and stumbled after her.

Moments later, the sound of the mob clamoring from behind raised goosebumps on the back of Amon's neck. But this time, the sound was far different. He heard confusion and fear rather than the sound of an angry mob bearing down on him. A quick glance over his shoulder revealed a crowd alright, but now they fought for sanity rather than Riordan's brand of distorted justice.

"You were right," Amon admitted. "I am no longer safe here. I will go with you, but I need to return home to get my things. I'll need my weapons, clothes, and a few personal things."

"I understand. But keep your eyes open. You must realize there is still danger here—I cannot foretell the future! Remember, I don't have eyes in the back of my head. We must work together for our mutual protection."

"No eyes in the back of your head," Amon said, laughing at the unusual expression. "You said that last time."

"What do you mean last time?" Valerie said, puzzled, then stopped to face him with hands-on-hips.

"You do not remember saying that?"

"No, but that's alright," Valerie admitted after a moment of reflection. The truth was she only had vague recollections of visiting Amon in the distant past and could not recall the conversation for more years than she could count had passed by in her timeline.

Amon noticed how much older the woman appeared than she had looked, which puzzled him as they stopped to speak. *Perhaps,* he thought, *the firelight had played tricks on his eyes. I would have guessed her age to be in the late thirties, but now she must be at least fifty, maybe sixty.* Nevertheless, he saw her as an attractive woman when her eyes were blue.

In his experience, this woman was taller than most, with the uncommon combination of raven black hair and blue eyes. He judged her facial features and appearance to be unremarkable, although easy to look at despite the scar that marked her jaw. Amon did not remember seeing the streaks of grey in her hair or the laugh lines and wrinkles at the corners of the eyes. The softness of her voice quelled his fear of being so close to a witch. *Perhaps witches are not so terrifying after all,* he supposed. At that moment, Amon felt foolish for ever being afraid of her.

As they made their way toward his house, Amon remembered the chill he felt at first sight of the blackness in her eyes. The woman's magic was without question, and what he had just witnessed dispelled any doubts about her abilities. He would not have escaped Riordan's supporters if she had not shown up at the inquest as promised. That alone proved her to be a reliable ally, which obligated him to "return the favor," as she had put it.

Then it occurred to him that partnering with a powerful witch, or healer as she preferred to be called, might be just what he needed. While he enjoyed hunting, the long days of hiking, hauling heavy loads of meat, and long nights in the cold had taken a toll on his body. Aware he could not continue hunting forever, he considered the possibility that he might be due for a change. He decided that having a powerful partner such as this witch might be a good thing.

Once they reached the vicinity of his house, Amon and his new partner concealed themselves behind a stone fence for a few minutes, watching for signs of trouble. Then Amon felt a sudden shift—a shift in what, though? And he felt disoriented for a moment, along with a strong sense of déjà vu but dismissed it as the after-effects of Valerie's magic.

"Amon, we need to move fast and travel light. Only bring what you truly need."

"Do not worry about that," Amon assured her. "I just need my weapons, tools, some clothing, and bedding. Can you carry a pack?"

"No problem, Amon," she whispered from behind the wall.

"How do you know my name?"

"Shhhh! I'll tell you later," she whispered, knowing she wasn't about to broach the subject of time travel with him at this, or perhaps at any time.

They watched the street diligently for threats, but there was little movement in the area. A woman carried buckets of water to her garden, a dog ambled down the road, a pair of crows landed, then picked at something dead, but nothing else moved. The street was still and silent.

"Alright, Valyri." Amon agreed. "Let's go."

"Val-er-ee," she annunciated.

"Yes," he said. "Let's go Valyri."

Valerie rolled her eyes. "I give," she exclaimed.

Once inside, they worked together, gathering the things Amon considered essential, stuffing them into packs, and strapping them to their backs. No one in the vicinity noticed them enter or leave the little stone house. Soon the outlaw was away with the witch and without a hitch.

Two hours later, the pair entered the clearing that was home to Pearse's farm. Amon was not sure why, but he was sure something had changed. Having spent a day and a night looking at the place, he was convinced something was different. But what? Then the obvious struck him; there had been one house last week, now there were two. Houses are not built in a week—how could a second house appear so quickly?

"Where did that other house come from?" Amon blurted without thinking, then realized he had just betrayed himself.

"How did you know that? About the second house being new?"

Amon's stomach flipped. Had she seen him watching from the woods? At a loss for words, he looked at his feet and shook his head. When he looked up again, Valerie faced him with hands on her hips and a knowing smile. "You knew I was here, didn't you?" Amon admitted.

"Of course, I did," Valerie conceded.

"So how did the second house get here so quickly? Did you do that?"

"We built it two weeks ago."

"That is impossible. It wasn't here last week."

"That's right. But neither were you." The moment the words left her tongue, she regretted it. How would she ever explain this gaff away?

"If I wasn't here—*where was I?*" Amon said suspiciously, aware she was trying to keep the whole truth from him.

Uh-oh. Valerie thought. *I set myself up for this one, and now there is no escape. Amon guessed correctly that the building's appearance involved time manipulation and that I did it. The man might be a simple hunter, but he is no dummy.* She admired

Amon's intuition, but she had painted herself into a corner. Although reluctant to bring Amon up to speed on her use of time as a tool, she gave in, deciding she could not hide the truth from him.

"Alright— two weeks ago, the day of the hearing, Riordan's men were lying in wait for you outside your house. We needed to avoid them. I had to do something, so I jumped us two weeks into the future. It worked! That is why no one was there this morning. Two weeks have passed since the inquest. Do you understand?"

Amon, deep in thought, looked away, stroking his beard as his eyes set on something distant. While Valerie waited for his response, she thought back to how afraid of her appearance Amon and Hethe had been. She understood far better than Amon would ever know because she felt their presence long before she ever saw them. She also felt the terror the blackness of her eyes generated in these otherwise intrepid huntsmen.

Rubbing the back of his neck, Amon admitted: "No. I do not understand. But I think that was a good idea because it seems to have worked."

"I'm glad you understand, Amon—but please do not repeat what I told you." Then Valerie put her hand on his shoulder. "Don't you see? I already have enough trouble with people thinking of me as a witch." But when she felt the hard muscles of Amon's shoulders, her eyes moved to where her hand rested, then darted back to Amon's deep-set brown eyes as she realized she had been caught admiring the man and was uncomfortably close. Valerie flushed, then pulled her hand away and backed up a step. Amon saw it, smiled warmly but said nothing as the moment passed.

PETER HARRETT

Valerie had expected pushback at the notion of altering time, but Amon seemed to accept the concept. When he said nothing more about it, she breathed a sigh of relief. Now that it was out there, she had no doubt the subject would come up again and hoped to be better prepared the next time.

Shadows had grown long, and the late afternoon air had already begun to chill as the winter sun sank below the tree line. Amon looked to the sky to gauge the weather. Wispy clouds scudded across the bright blue expanse, releasing occasional snowflakes in their wake. The night would be long and cold on the ridge, and Amon expected another cold camp in the snow.

"Let's put your things in my house for now," Valerie suggested. "You can stay with me until we find a place for you to stay. But first, I want to introduce you to my family."

"I'm a hunter; I can camp outside." Amon countered.

Valerie gauged the man as she considered his words. *I'll bet you could,* she thought, then decided to press him further on the subject. "It's too cold for you to be out here; you are staying inside with me— I insist."

Amon raised his eyebrows in wonder. He considered it his place, his duty to camp under the stars. Didn't someone need to stay on the watch during the night? But he didn't dispute the fact that the clear sky overhead meant the night was bound to be bitterly cold. Still, he meant what he said; he was accustomed to cold camping and didn't want to inconvenience anyone.

As they approached the house, Pearse threw open the door. When he saw Amon, his eyes narrowed warily. *Pearse doesn't recognize the man I am with!* Valerie realized. Quickly she assured Pearse that Amon was a friend. Pearse beckoned them inside with a welcoming gesture. Before entering, the travelers set their bundles beside the door. Once inside, the young family welcomed them, and Pearse offered a seat by the fireplace. Lauryn had a meal of deer shank and boiled vegetables prepared and offered them a share.

This is nice, Amon thought. He observed the domestic scene, the likes of which he had never witnessed. The family of five was seated around a table rather than lounging on floor cushions by a fire pit. The seats were knee-high with seatbacks allowing them to sit comfortably upright around the table facing one another. Across the room, a pair of raised pallets held bedding above the stone floor. But the most exciting feature was the fireplace, chimney, and hearth, which he found captivating. Amon marveled at how the stone firebox was raised above the floor and built into the exterior wall freeing up floor space. As Amon stared at the dancing flames, he noticed how smoke was drawn up the chimney, keeping the room smoke-free.

As they sat beside the fireplace, warming themselves, Valerie recounted the trial and Riordan's twisted interrogation of the witnesses in vivid detail. Then she described the dangerous mob and their escape from Erlin. Without holding back on her part in the event, she revealed how she stopped time for the mob as they came upon Amon to murder him.

Without understanding Valerie's reference to "stopped time," Amon added that from his perspective, it seemed as if the crowd was suddenly turned to stone. Pearse and his family were fascinated as they recounted the day's events.

Valerie was aware Amon needed to be sold as a valuable newcomer to the group, so she set about painting him as a professional hunter, leader of men, and a capable fighter. Amon remained silent as she portrayed him as a protector and someone they could count on to bring in meat. Pearse and Lauryn nodded, agreeing that adding another capable man to the group would be beneficial, although they could not help noticing how she looked at the hunter and shared a knowing glance.

Valerie conceded that her first contact with people typically provoked accusations of being a witch. One look at her eyes was all one needed to confirm the fact. Pearse and Lauryn were well aware of Valerie's uneasiness regarding her personal security, having mentioned it to them repeatedly during the conversation. That she needed protection was undeniable.

Moreover, Amon had been driven from his home in Erlin, so he would not be able to return anytime soon. In essence, the man was in exile. If he did not stay here now, he would be forced to move on, and his valuable skillset would be lost to them. The problem of security would remain unresolved. That line of reasoning was hard to dispute, so it was agreed; Amon was in.

As the conversation moved on to other things, Lauryn served the evening meal. Afterward, the subject of additional housing came up. If Amon was to make the Bearnán Éile ridge his home, permanent lodging would be required. With spring on the way, wintertime would be the best time to get the work done. So, it was agreed they would all work together to build a third house, and with Amon's help, they could get it done quickly.

With seven people working together, they had the new house built in ten days. The new structure was identical to

Valerie's in form and function. However, with most of the red shale already used on Valerie's home, this one was predominately grey.

Amon felt like he fit in well with the group, marveling at how they worked tirelessly together. Not a complaint was heard right down to Saoirse, the smallest of the three children. He liked how they did everything as a unit, working, eating, relaxing, and sleeping as one.

A lifetime of associating with hunters taught him that modesty was a rare commodity. Amon had grown weary of the never-ending squabbling and wrangling for dominance that came with hunters. But what he detested most was the foolish one-upmanship. That sort of pointless nonsense got men killed.

Much to his relief and pleasure, he had seen none of that sort of folly with this group. Valerie had referred to Pearse's family as *her family,* even though she had arrived just days ago. Amon found Valerie's modesty remarkable, considering her talents. She set an excellent example working beside the others and never attempted to assert her will or dominance over them, even though no one doubted they could not stop her if she did.

A lot had happened since Valerie arrived. Amon saw that she had come with companions and that they followed her lead, not by compulsion but willingly. Then, when she left them behind to go with Pearse and Tierney, those people were visibly upset by her departure. There was no doubt in his mind as to why. He had seen her heal Pearse, levitate the log into the fire, stop time to save him from the mob in Erlin, and today erase two weeks from his life without his knowledge. The woman radiated power, yet everything she did was done for others' benefit and with discretion.

Things were good here, but maybe too good. Amon had the nagging feeling it might be too good to be true. An unease in his gut told him to beware of trouble from Erlin. The hole in his gut said they were never going to let him go. Sooner or later, they would come; they would find him and kill him. Until now, listening to that little voice had kept him alive, but this time he had ignored it. Why? Was it because he was happy here with these people? No one had to tell him that within days these people had become *his* family faster than he could have imagined. Had the happiness he felt clouded his senses, or was he ignoring the truth?

Amon spent the first night in his new home settling in, once again happy to have his own space. With the new fireplace providing the only light, he sat staring at the hypnotic flames for a long while. A sense of warmth beyond heat from the flickering firelight filled him with satisfaction as shadows danced on the walls. A knock at the door woke him from the hypnotic spell.

He was surprised to find Valerie, Pearse, and Lauryn waiting outside at the door. The moment he laid eyes on their anxious faces, he knew there was serious trouble. His very first visitors stepped into his new house with their eyes downcast, as if they were stepping into a funeral. Once they were all seated around the fireplace, Pearse spoke.

"We had a visitor a few minutes ago," he said uneasily. "Padraig, our nearest neighbor to the west, came to inform us that fighting men from Erlin paid a visit to his farm today. He said they were searching for a hunter named Amon, demanding to know if they had seen the man. Padraig told us he and his family knew nothing, but those men asked many hard questions and were rough with him and his family. The warning was clear: if they saw this man Amon or hid him without reporting it to Riordan in Erlin, they would be back to teach them a lesson."

All eyes were fixed on Amon as they waited for him to come to terms with this startling news. *How could I have ever believed Riordan's men would give up searching for me?* he thought. Deep down, he knew better than to think the danger had passed and ignore the threat. And now his new friends' lives were at stake. Amon shook his head in grief.

"Riordan will never call them off until the clan has had its revenge," he mumbled. "I will have to leave tomorrow. My being here endangers all of you," he said sullenly. His words echoed in the dark, followed by another lengthy silence. No one wanted to speak first.

"You can't run forever. Neither can we. We need to find another way."

Amon raised his eyes to meet Valerie's. "There is no other way," he said. "I cannot allow them to find me here. If they do, we all may die. And what of the children?" he asked, gesturing at Lauryn and Pearse. "I cannot let that happen. I will leave tomorrow."

"I won't let anything happen to the children or anyone else here," Valerie assured him. "Maybe you forgot about what happened in Erlin. That crowd never stood a chance at getting to you while I was there." Then she added, "And don't forget you and I have an agreement. You protect me, and I will protect you. Together we are strong. How can you help me if you leave? Your promise is good, isn't it?" Valerie said with a knowing smile.

Amon could not help but notice how the firelight played on the dark orbs of her eyes as if they held their own fires within. Recently he had become so comfortable with them that he seldom noticed or remembered to fear them. And it was always a treat when she decided they should be blue.

Knowing she could choose to make them blue whenever she wanted helped. *Perhaps the firelight is playing tricks on my eyes!* Then he realized he felt differently about Valerie. The attraction was real. He had feelings for her and did not want to leave. But was the interest mutual? He couldn't be sure but also couldn't help wondering. Her eagerness to help him, combined with her steadfast determination to keep him from leaving, hinted that there might be more than what met that unknowable gaze. Then Amon wished her eyes could be blue once again, if only for a moment.

The age difference between the two did not deter his interest in her in the slightest. He guessed she might be ten years older than he, but she was capable, fit, and had a healthy glow. It seemed to him her greying hair aged her more than it should. Her black eyebrows contrasted with her lush head of silver, betraying its former pigmentation.

Intuition told him Valerie was right when she said she did not have eyes in the back of her head, but if she had someone like him looking out for her, they were all stronger. Amon decided that he could trust her without endangering Pearse and his young family.

Valerie continued. "We are stronger as a team than we are alone. Stay with us, and we will fight them together."

Hearing this, Pearse and Lauryn nodded their agreement.

"Alright, you have a point," admitted Amon," I hope you are right. I will stay, but we need to be prepared for Riordan's men. They could come anytime."

For a long moment Amon considered the possibilities. "I have an idea," he said. "Hunting dogs would warn us of danger day or night. I know a man who sells good dogs. I can go see him tomorrow."

"I think that is a good idea, Amon," Pearse said with enthusiasm. "But I should be the one to go. You should not allow yourself to be seen by anyone right now."

"Agreed," Valerie said, while Lauryn simply nodded again. "Amon, can you tell me how to find this man?"

"I can," he said. "His place is easy to find. Lochlan has a farm on the road to Erlin, halfway between Locarno and the Erlin bridge. You can be there from here in one hour. He is proud of his dogs, though. He will not sell them unless he likes you, and his price will be high. Do not bargain. Pay his asking price," Amon advised.

"I have gold. I will pay for the dog," offered Valerie.

"Pearse, I suggest that you buy two dogs," Amon insisted. "Raiders have been known to kill a dog before striking. More than one dog would give us more warning and make it even more difficult for intruders to surprise us. Ask Lochlan if he will sell you a mated pair. That would be best. We can breed them, so we have more in the future."

"Where I come from, we call them watchdogs," Valerie added.

"Watch-dogs? I like that," Amon said. "The dogs can be the eyes you do not have in the back of your head!" They laughed together at that, although the joke fell flat with

Pearse and Lauryn since they were not present when she claimed she did not have eyes in the back of her head.

Pearse and Tierney set out on foot for Lochlan's farm just after dawn. Valerie supplied them with a pouch of golden pebbles, far more than it seemed necessary. But since he could not know the price of trained hunting dogs, Pearse didn't want to object to the amount she offered.

As they came off the ridge heading toward Erlin, Pearse noticed the scent of spring in the air. Behind him, the ridge was still heavy with snow, although he saw that most of the snow had melted off as they descended, revealing green grass in the pastures and fields. The blue sky was crystal-clear above, but the valley below was a sea of thick clouds that were just beginning to burn off. Birdsong was everywhere, while squirrels ran to-and-fro in the underbrush indicating spring was imminent.

Approaching Lochlan's farm, they spied a man in the distance tending to his animals. Before turning on the trail to the house, dogs began barking, announcing their presence on the road. The man they assumed to be Lochlan looked up from his work as soon as the dogs barked, which brought a knowing smile to Pearse's face.

"See how the dogs warn their owner?" Pearse said to Tierney, with a hand on his son's shoulder. "That is the warning we need."

Amon was right about hunting dogs, Pearse decided. Sounding an early alarm to approaching visitors would protect them. As they turned to walk down the lane, the man named Lochlan whistled to his dogs, instantly ending the commotion, then scolded one dog that ran at the visitors with its head down. Another whistle turned the dog turned obediently back to him with its tail between its legs.

"Make sure you say nothing about where we live or that we have a hunter," Pearse whispered. "Lochlan has probably heard about Amon from Riordan's men. We need to be careful." The boy nodded obediently.

Once he was face-to-face with Lochlan, Pearse introduced himself and his son, then explained he had heard that he sold good dogs from some hunters. If that was true, he and the boy were there to see about purchasing a pair of hunting dogs from him.

"Who were these hunters?" Lochlan asked, his brows furrowed, his voice filled with suspicion. No doubt the man was concerned one of those hunters the visitor spoke of might be the one sought by Riordan's men.

Aware that he could not provide any names, especially Amon's, Pearse thought fast to come up with a plausible story. "A group of hunters came onto our farm a few weeks ago. They came upon us without warning, which made me uneasy. I was worried for my family. We want a pair of hunting dogs that are also good watchdogs."

"Watchdogs—what does that mean?" Lochlan asked, puzzled by the unfamiliar term.

"Hunting dogs can tell us when visitors approach, just like your dogs did when they saw us on the road. They watch out for us, which makes them watchdogs."

"I see," Lochlan said, his mood lightening. "That's right, they do."

"How many dogs do you keep?" asked Pearse.

"A few," the man said evasively.

Pearse could see and hear several dogs tussling, whining, and fussing beyond a fence behind the house. "Do you have a pair of dogs for sale?"

"I might, but a breeding pair of these dogs are worth their weight in coin. My dogs are trained for hunting, not *watching*."

Pearse flashed an understanding smile. "I planned to hunt with them, too. We live on the ridge; I have small children and want them to be safe from intruders and wild animals." With Pearse's reference to children and living on the ridge where wild animals were known to prowl, Lochlan's suspicious attitude evaporated all at once.

"Let me show you what a good pair of hunting dogs can do," Lochlan offered.

Pearse and Tierney looked on as Lochlan turned and disappeared behind the house. At the same time, a commotion ensued as anxious animals maneuvered for position to receive his attention. They heard Lochlan muttering to the animals as they whined and scuffled over one another.

Lochlan reappeared with a pair of medium-sized dogs, one at each side of him wagging their tails, looking up at him, eager for his attention. The shorthair dogs were predominately brown with white spots on the face and hindquarters. Lochlan whistled once, which sent the excited animals sprinting together into the open field. The pair worked together for a few minutes running and sniffing at the ground picking up scents. When he let loose with two loud whistles, the animals returned then sat at his feet, staring expectantly up at him. Lochlan knelt on one knee as he patted, rubbed, and commended the dogs for their "good work."

The display of his animals' obedience deeply impressed Tierney, who pulled on his father's arm, exclaiming excitedly, "Did you see that? Will they do that for us?"

Lochlan answered for Pearse. "Certainly," he assured the boy, then added, "but you need to learn the commands and always be consistent with them, or they will not respect you."

"Is this pair of dogs for sale?" Pearse asked, attempting to begin bargaining for them.

"Yes, I will let you have them for ten silver coin— each."

Never having used gold for trading, Pearse was unfamiliar with comparing the value of gold nuggets to silver coin, and had not thought of asking anyone before leaving that morning. So, with the hope that Lochlan had a better knowledge of comparable values, he simply stated, "I have gold."

"Oh," Lochlan said, standing. "That's alright. That would be about three gold coin then."

"Twenty silver coin is too high." Pearse sighed. "You have very nice dogs, but I could buy the Erlin bridge for that much! I think ten coin in silver would be a fair price."

"I know a man in Erlin who would sell that bridge, too," laughed Lochlan. "But you do not have silver, so I guess he will have to keep his bridge," Lochlan joked.

"Can we agree to the equivalent of two gold coin?"

"What do you mean when you say 'equivalent' to two gold coin?" Lochlan said, once again suspicious.

"I have gold nuggets, but they spend just as well as coin. Let me show you." Pearse reached into his bag of gold stones and picked out three pebbles the approximate size of coins, then handed them over. Lochlan spent a moment inspecting them intently, then took his knife out and dug at one of them to check the quality.

"It *is* gold, and there appears to be more than two coin in these nuggets, so it is good. The dogs are yours."

"Can you tell me how to make them obey me as they do for you?" Pearse asked.

"Can you whistle?"

"I whistle the same as you did when you sent the dogs out."

"These dogs have been trained to work as a team, obey whistles, and simple voice commands. When you want them to come, go, stop, hunt, or go home, simply say what you want them to do in one or two words. More than that will confuse them. Say it as a command, and they will do it for you.

"These dogs obey whistles," he continued, "just as you have seen. One whistle means go, and two whistles mean to stop or return. Three means work harder or attack. It is all the same to them. You want to be careful when you whistle three times, he warned. When a stranger is nearby, they might attack if they are working. If that were to happen, just remember that you can call them off with two whistles."

Lochlan gave the boy Tierney a hard stare. "These dogs just want to please you, so they will work for you until they drop. Remember that!" Lochlan said, pointing a finger in Tierney's direction. "Never forget to tell them when they are done working and to commend them when they do a good job for you. You are their master, so they love pleasing you."

Tierney nodded, his eyes eager.

"Boy— do you want to try commanding the dogs?"

Unsure of himself but excited at the opportunity, Tierney asked, "What should I say?"

"Pet them first. Talk to them, so they can get to know you. When you think they are ready to work for you, stand, point at the field, and order them to *hunt!* Or whistle once. Make your voice strong, so they know you have commanded them."

Lochlan took a few steps back to give the boy space with the dogs, then put his hands on his hips while he watched and waited. Anticipation built as Tierney took his time petting, talking, and reassuring the animals. The dogs soaked up the boy's attention, squirming and rolling over so he could rub their bellies. When Tierney felt the time was right, he stood, pointed at the same field they had run in previously, and commanded them. *"Hunt!"* cried Tierney. To his delight, the dogs were up and racing away like an arrow shot.

Threats from Riordan's supporters had forced Amon to leave his home and most of his belongings behind in Erlin. He was limited to what he and Valerie could carry on their backs. Since he was a hunted man, returning was out of the question. Unfortunately, that left him without the supplies and raw materials needed to repair his equipment and outfit himself for hunting.

Upon his arrival at Pearse's farm, his entire list of personal belongings included his two best bows, the bulk of his store of arrows, knives and axes, a tent, camping gear, hand tools, and the clothes on his back. The only personal item he truly cared about was his father's sword, which was the first thing retrieved. Unfortunately, most of his clothes and household goods had to be left behind.

While Pearse and Tierney were off buying dogs, Amon set out that morning to hunt for suitable leather to rebuild his stores. He needed skins, leather, sinews, and bone, all must-have raw materials for a hunter. Those supplies allowed him to repair and replace the tools of his trade on demand.

The women and children spent the morning dying wool in a copper pot in the men's absence. Working together, they built a fire in the roasting pit, filled the pot with water, mixed the dye as the water heated to a boil, and took turns stirring it with a wooden paddle. While the women were hanging the newly colored material to dry, four horsemen riding hard appeared out of the morning mist.

Lauryn heard the riders before she saw them. The little woman stiffened, gasped, then screamed. Startled by the unexpected intrusion, the children cried and clamored for the safety of their mother as the horsemen rode up on them. "Shush, don't be afraid," Lauryn whispered in an attempt to hush the little ones.

The instant Valerie heard Lauryn's scream, she looked up from her work and heard the hoofbeats too. Before she could see them, she turned quickly away and removed her thumb ring, hiding it in her inner garment to prevent them from seeing the blackness of her eyes. By the time she turned around, her eyes had already returned to their natural pale blue color.

Without stopping or dismounting, the horsemen rode to within an arm's length of the women and children, grinning and laughing as they slowly backed them up against the fire pit. Armed with a combination of swords, knives, bows, and arrows, these men were experienced intimidators. No doubt these were Riordan's men, the very same ones their neighbor Padraig had reported seeing the previous day.

"Where are your men?" the lead rider demanded to know from the whimpering children, ignoring the women as though they did not exist. "Where is your father?" he demanded. When the children did not respond, his eyes fell on the women, his gaze moving rapidly between them, sneering with a mixture of condescension and disgust.

"Well? Are you going to tell me where your men are?" he whispered, this time with his eyebrows raised as if he were a beggar imploring them for a piece of bread. "You two are surely the ugliest pair of skirts I've ever laid eyes on! But— I'll wager you do have men here— ALTHOUGH YOUR MEN ARE AFRAID TO SHOW THEMSELVES!" He crowed the last words over his shoulder, drawing howls of laughter from his fellow riders.

Not one to be intimidated, Valerie bristled at the intrusion. "State your reason for being here so we can be rid of you. We don't like trash blowing through our yard."

Whatever the riders found amusing evaporated instantly, replaced by angry stares and rage that threatened violence. The leader, a short but sturdily built man, leaped off his horse, placing himself face-to-face, nose-to-nose with the older woman, his shoulders tense and fists balled, ready to strike. But he was half a head shorter than Valerie, which forced him to look up at the much taller unblinking steadfast woman.

Fearing for her safety and for the safety of her children, Lauryn attempted to defuse the situation by answering the man's initial question. "Our husbands are on a hunt." Although she lied, it seemed like a plausible excuse as any.

"No, they're *not* hunting," Valerie spat out, staring down the lead rider. "Here's what's happening," she exclaimed, loud enough for everyone to hear. "You idiots were making so much noise that our men heard you coming fifteen minutes ago. They took their bows and hid. Right now, you are surrounded. One wrong move and you will be eating arrows for breakfast. Now tell us why you are here while you can still leave in one piece. I suggest saying it loud enough so that they can hear you, or you may not live to regret it."

Valerie saw it in the lead rider's eyes first. His confidence melted away abruptly, replaced by dread. As he backed off a step, his face carried the apprehension he felt. It was obvious he believed Valerie's ruse. As the riders still on horseback shifted their weight, searching for hidden archers, the horses snorted nervously and stomped their feet.

"Now— tell us why you are here. What do you want!" shouted Valerie angrily.

"We are looking for a hunter named Amon," the lead man stated, loud enough to be heard at a distance. Valerie knew she had won the test of wills when the lead rider's eyes darted toward the woods on either side of him.

"We don't know any hunter named Amon. Now *leave!*" Valerie stormed, pointing in the direction from which the riders had come. She continued pointing as the humiliated man turned and mounted his horse. Once saddled, the man fired an angry finger back at her with a threat of his own.

"Be warned, woman," he seethed. "If you have hidden the hunter Amon or know of his whereabouts without reporting it to my father, Councilman Riordan, in Erlin, we will be back with a lot more men. Then I will see you die slowly for your lies." His hissing glare left no doubt that he meant what he said. With those words hanging heavy, the men turned their horses and rode away at a gallop.

Chapter 12

Valerie Dunne— June Present-Day

*A*sgardian was the only word Valerie could conjure that came close to describing the dream she had that night. All other names and descriptions fell short. It was readily apparent to her that whatever person, power, or entity that had generated this dream was the same one that had been disturbing her sleep since she was a child. But this dream, she *liked!*

Previous dreams had a consistency to them that had become so disturbing, so maddeningly predictable that she hated to sleep. It was as if a video player had been hammered into her head with a mallet, then stuck in an endless playback loop. She suffered the same fate, night after night, for fourteen years. Although frightening, the repetition of those dreams had long ago become mundane. Valerie was tired of being tired of them.

However, this unique and wonderful dream changed everything. Unlike most mornings, she was well-rested and excited to start the new day. She hoped she had dreamed her last nightmare, that this vision of the night would be her new reality, and that she no longer needed to dread falling asleep.

Valerie saw herself in an elegant spaceship crewed by aliens of every size, shape, and form imaginable in this dream. They traveled to a world where a massive palace stood, with stunning parapets, sky bridges, and spires. Upon her arrival, she and her entourage were treated as conquering heroes or royalty wielding tremendous authority.

She stepped onto a free-floating transport with two of her shipmates. The vehicle carried them past row after row of soldiers and dignitaries lined up along the promenade. These statuesque alien creatures waited patiently for her review — innumerable brigades adorned in impressive uniforms, polished armor, and fine regalia.

In the distance sat an arena, a theater with a grand throne platform at its center. Nobilities gathered around waiting on her arrival. As they drew near the throne, one could be seen seated, presumably an emperor, wearing shining armor, symbols of his authority, and a scepter held in one of his four hands. As she stepped down from the transport, the one seated on the throne rose, then knelt prostrating himself at her feet. The king remained there until she beckoned for him to rise, which he did — towering over her by several feet.

"Valerie of Earth, my dominion is yours," announced the bronze monarch, his stony voice repeatedly echoing over the immense parade grounds. The deposed ruler turned aside, gesturing for her to take his throne. Once she had assumed the seat of rulership, her companions took positions beside her, acting as her first and second.

When the emperor handed his scepter over to Valerie, she noticed the cold chill it generated in her core. Regarding it as a manifestation of evil that needed to be done away with, she planned its destruction. Still, as a symbol of the transfer of power, the scepter was an irreplaceable image at that critical moment, so she held it high for all to see. As she did so, the gathered masses bowed to her authority. Then she and her companions were ceremoniously adorned in fine robes, fitted with extravagant jewelry, and offered exotic morsels to nibble on.

All the while the humiliated despot stood aside, stoically awaiting her judgment and his destiny. He was hers to be judged; his future rested in her hands. How would she decide the fate of this defeated tyrant? Surely retribution was in order. Few would argue this one deserved whatever fate she deemed justifiable. Clemency was not called for, nor was it expected.

Seated on a throne that now represented the entire galaxy's populated worlds, few believed Valerie would allow the tyrant more than moments to live. Certainly, she had the authority, the power, and more than enough reason to execute the monarch. But she had no desire for thrones, rulership, or power. She never wanted anything other than security for her people and their allies, which is what drove her actions. She considered this ceremony more than a formality—this was a once-in-a-lifetime opportunity to correct millennia of injustices. Peace and security for her people and her allies were her sole obligation.

When she rose from the throne to address the emperor, the thousands in attendance held their collective breath in anticipation. Absolute silence ruled as they awaited her pronouncement with keen interest.

"Now there will be Peace!" she declared, allowing those words to hang in the air as they returned in echo. "Peace in this galaxy and security for all peoples has been established.

This peace *will be aggressively defended*, ensuring that it endures for generations to come. No longer will conflict or conquest be allowed. With this promise, I return this man to you, your King, so you people can govern yourselves. His fate is for you to determine. Choose wisely."

The dream concluded with an image of the emperor's scepter floating in space as it tumbled toward the Boeckian home world's star.

Upon awakening, Valerie recalled every moment of the lucid dream in vivid detail. But, with no way to interpret the dream's meaning or implications, she was left speculating. Although, one thing she was sure of: this was more than a dream. This new vision was much too realistic and detailed to be random. The cold sting of the ruler's scepter on her hand was unforgettable. She could not help but regard it as prophetic. Was it a portent of what her future held and what she would become? No other conclusion she could conceive of made sense.

Nice dream, Valerie thought as she crawled out of bed. *I could do that all day! I wouldn't mind staying in bed and doing that one over and over again. If I thought I could get away with it, I would, too. It was that great. But it must be more than that because no dream is ever that realistic. The cold sting of that scepter is something I will not soon forget. Was it a dream—or a vision?* She wondered. *If it returns tonight, maybe I'll find out then. Interesting that it coincides with my stay here with Corell...*

The kitchen table in the old farmhouse would serve as the setting for Valerie's first formal lesson. It consisted primarily of a history lesson interspersed with affirmations, discoveries, and eye-opening revelations. Corell felt it imperative that she understand what her predecessors went through to bring her to this moment in time. Corell paced the room as he spoke.

"For more than four thousand years, good people made enormous sacrifices to help you fulfill your destiny. My first duty is to help you understand and appreciate the sacrifices made on your behalf."

"Think of it—dedicated people, people you will never know or meet, spent their lives safeguarding the Hesaurun Rings so they could be returned to you! Those people had such great faith in your story that *they sacrificed their lives*, knowing they would never live to see you reunited with your rings. Theirs was a noble sacrifice made by people you will never know, for what they considered a worthy cause—I think that is pretty amazing!"

Corell stood there a moment, disappointed by the disconnected look on Valerie's face. He needed confidence that she was up to the challenge before surrendering his Hesaurun Ring. He considered helping the girl comprehend and appreciate the sacrifices made by Pearse, Lauryn, the others, and their children to be critical to his success as her mentor. The chain of events set in motion by The Ring Bearer thousands of years prior was about to culminate. As he saw it, what happened next either saved the world or sentenced it to oblivion. Failure was never an option.

Corell continued pacing, then stopped, turned to face Valerie, and wagged a finger at her. "Do you realize that everything rests on your success as master of the five rings of Hesaurun? Once the fifth ring is yours, your work, your sacrifices have just begun. According to the ring journals, your journey will last for centuries, even millennia. The responsibilities you assigned *yourself* ages ago include a lifetime of commitment, struggle, and sacrifice. I can help you get going in the right direction, but I will not be around forever. You need to be prepared mentally, physically, and emotionally for what lies ahead..."

"The Ring Bearer did such an extraordinary job of engendering a lasting belief in the alien threat that her legacy is strong today," he said, pacing again. "Those journals really worked! They laid down a compelling narrative that stood the test of time. People who had never met her bought into her crusade, based on faith alone, which is remarkable in itself. That faith was strong enough to outlive her by thousands of years."

"You can forget whatever life planning you had for yourself—everything's different now. There will never be medical school or work as a doctor in your future. You must consider those plans *kaput!* For the foreseeable future, you need to forget about all that stuff and concentrate on getting all five rings! I am going to show you—"

Corell stopped mid-sentence when he realized he had lost Valerie's attention. She appeared to have checked out entirely, gazing out the window, paying no attention to her very first lesson. *And I have only been talking for fifteen minutes!* He wondered if she heard anything he said. Corell sat down next to her realizing he had gotten himself worked up, gone off on a tangent, and alienated his audience. The girl looked glassy-eyed, bored, rejecting everything said.

"Valerie—are you alright?" Corell asked, concerned.

"I'm sorry," she said. "I am just—over-communicated, that's all."

"Well, I got excited and digressed," he admitted. "Sorry about that."

"It's okay; I'm just not sure I can do this," she admitted nervously.

"Don't worry; you will be fine," Corell assured her. "It's my fault. I am just excited to be with you and finally able to talk to someone about it. You know, I have been holding this in for a very long time."

Valerie nodded and smiled. "It just seems like—a lot, that's all."

"I get it. It *is* a lot," Corell admitted. "But you can do it. Hang in there, alright?"

As he watched, Valerie's smile faded. *The burden being handed to her is a heavy one,* Corell thought. *More profound than anyone so young should ever be asked to bear. Nevertheless, that very same burden was one she mastered in another life.* Corell reasoned that since she had done it once, she could do it again. *Inexperience is her biggest challenge right now, but there is no question she has it within her to succeed. She just needs to believe in herself and make it happen.*

Valerie listened intently now as he related to her the oral tradition of the rings he had memorized as a child. She seemed content hearing how she had started a family in the distant past and what happened to them through the ages.

"You do understand that this is *your* story, right?" Corell emphasized. "What I have been telling you is *your* story, as told by none other than *yourself,* then passed back down to *you* through your kin." Valerie's eyebrows raised, clearly puzzled. Corell swallowed his disappointment, aware that he was not getting through to her.

In his opinion, she needed to embrace this truth because lives were at stake. Corell was uneasy about what he planned to talk about next, namely the rings and their powers. As he attempted to explain that the rings' power was transmitted through Osomarío of Hesaurun, the girl began blocking it out, rejecting the narrative. She crossed her arms once again and looked out the window.

Corell stared at her, frustrated. He was wading into water that was getting deeper by the moment. When he attempted explaining that Orson, her cat, served as the alien's window into our dimension, he stepped into a hole that put water over his head. Valerie rejected the notion outright.

"What?" she cried angrily, standing and waving her arms. "How do you expect me to believe my cat is an alien? I have had him since I was four years old! Don't you think that's something I would have noticed by now?"

"Well," Corell said, flustered, "Orson's really more *my* cat than he is yours. I mean mine more than the present you, not including the *other* you, I mean you *later*. Know what I mean?" Seeing the confused look on her face, he admitted, "Heck, I don't even understand what I am saying. I'm sorry, this whole thing must sound like nonsense to you."

"You're right. It sounds like nonsense!" Valerie shot back irritably, scowling with arms crossed. "Try again. I am listening. What are you trying to tell me about Orson?" No one was more aware than Valerie that there was more to that darn cat than met the eye. She wanted to know more, so she encouraged Corell to continue.

"What I meant to say is Orson was *your* cat originally. You took him with you when you went into the past." Corell turned away for a moment, and then he breathed a long sigh filled with sentiment. After regaining his composure, he continued.

"You see, father passed him down to me when I was a boy. You were four when I gave him to you. I had Orson for thirteen hundred years. You have had him for fourteen. That is what I was trying to say to you when I said he is more *my* cat than he is yours, but not the *old you* because the old you had him for a long time too. I am just talking about the *new you*—the you that's *now*, I mean. God! I'm doing it again, aren't I?!" he finally blurted out, throwing up his hands in frustration.

"Alright, I get it!" Valerie exclaimed with a hint of a smile and sparkle in her eye. "My cat is an immortal alien! *But* he isn't actually my cat anyway, because he's really more *your* cat than he ever was my cat—I mean the *here and now me*, not the other me. See? I can do that too!"

Both laughed at that, which relieved the tension between them. "Yes, Valerie, you could say your cat is an immortal alien. Semi-immortal anyway." Corell said incredulously, holding his forehead with his palm. "But he is still a cat, so he isn't an alien. Think of it this way— Orson is a cat who has been empowered by an alien so he can keep track of how we are doing here on Earth—*that or it is the work of the Hesaurun rings*. Orson allows the alien to observe and step into this realm and help us when needed. That darn cat, or DC as you often call him, does seem to be immortal and is connected to Osomarío in a way that's hard for us to understand."

Valerie thought for a moment, weighing the concept in her mind. The idea of a house cat somehow being connected to an alien in another world or alternate dimension seemed far-fetched. But wasn't that true of the entire story? And that was the problem as she saw it; the story was just too fantastic not to be true. But that did not nullify the need for some sort of verification either.

"How do you know that? I did not see anything like that in her journal. Do you have any proof?"

Frustration at the nature of her question raised Corell's hackles. "Valerie, you—*you* are the only proof I have," he contended. "Have you forgotten about your dreams? I think you will find the answers you are looking for in them—I did. Now that you know more about what's actually happening, I think you just need time to make sense of it, you know, connect the dots."

Valerie's eyes lit up. "*You* did? *You had dreams too?*"

"Sure. I have experienced plenty of dreams similar to what you describe. Over the years, I have come to grips with them and feel like I understand them."

Valerie looked like she had just seen a ghost. "I never thought of that!" she whispered. "I never stopped to think you might have had similar dreams!"

"In my dreams," Valerie went on, "there's always this— shadowy figure present. I couldn't know who it was or why he was there, but I always knew he wanted to help me. I always felt like he was on my side, but the fact that he never intervened puzzled me. He just watched. I have often wondered who that was, why he was there. Why do you think he never did anything to help? Do you think it might be him? This Osomarío?"

"Valerie, only *you* can know. But I can tell you this; I have seen it, too. Many of my dreams have had an obscure figure lying back in the shadows watching. I used to be worried about that until I realized he was more of an observer than anything else and never a threat. I also got the feeling he wanted to help but was holding back. Why? I have no idea. But I cannot imagine who other than Osomarío would fit the description."

"What makes you think Orson is Osomarío's window to our world?"

"It just adds up. I noticed a long time ago that I only have those dreams when Orson is with me. I never had one when he wasn't with me, and until last night, I haven't had one in fourteen years. What do you think that means?"

Fascinated, Valerie moved to the edge of her chair. "You had a dream last night?"

"Yes, and it was a doozy, too. Different from anything I have ever seen before. I suspect the difference is you. Your being here with me has changed things somehow. I often thought there might be an event of some kind when you are reunited with your rings. That makes this a very exciting time for me."

"Event? What kind of event?"

Corell scratched his head, unsure how to put his theory into words, pacing the room as he gathered his thoughts, aware it was an abstract concept that would be difficult to put into words that she could relate to. After all, he had centuries to meditate on the subject, consider it from every angle, weigh every possible outcome. Now he spoke to a young girl who knew nothing about it until a couple of days ago. There was only one way to find out if she could understand, and that was to charge forward and hope for the best.

"Think about it. Essentially, there are three Valerie's — you, here in the present, the elder you, and the one who existed in your past. Here is the problem; how can you exist in the past, present, *and* future? It doesn't seem possible, but here you are." Corell let that concept sink in for a moment before continuing.

"What gives me goosebumps is that by existing in three realities, you have become your own forebearer, your grandmother, and at the same time your own grandchild. A paradox is an inconsistency, a contradiction. A time paradox is an impossibility tied to the timeline. Have you ever heard of the multiverse or parallel universes?"

Valerie simply shook her head, a blank look on her face, never having heard those terms.

"The multiverse," he explained, "is the theory that there is a vast array of universes in which we exist. There are several versions of the concept, but the two that seem the most plausible to me are repeating universes and parallel universes."

"The repeating universe theory of multiverses is based on the premise that space-time is infinite. Since it is infinite, eventually the arrangement of particles will repeat themselves, so if you were to travel far enough, sooner or later you would encounter another Earth and ultimately another you."

Now Valerie's eyes were locked on his, her interest piqued, Corell continued.

"The parallel multiverse theory is the belief that the universe we perceive isn't all there is. There are more, an infinite number of them and dimensions beyond the three spatial dimensions we perceive, plus time. We co-exist in other three-dimensions and space acting as parallel universes."

"Here's what intrigues me; according to some theories, universes can intersect or collide. So, what would be the outcome if that were to happen to you? I suspect we are about to find out because I believe there is a high probability you are about to cause that to happen. I think you are about to collide with another version of yourself, and when that occurs, anything can happen."

Corell smiled at Valerie, and Valerie smiled back, although uncertainly. "By reappearing twice in our universe," he continued, "you already may have altered the space-time continuum in a way we cannot perceive. In other words, you may have already altered our reality, creating another universe without us being aware of it. Or maybe nothing happened—or is ever going to happen. We may never know."

"So," Corell continued, "the eight-hundred-pound gorilla in the room is this: what happens when you are reunited with your rings? Will something happen that we can see and feel? And if it does, will we even be aware that our reality has been altered? Will sparks fly when universes collide? Since I was a boy, I have wondered what happens when I hand you this ring. This is the single most fascinating moment of my entire life! Do you understand now?"

"Uhm, I guess so," Valerie said, appearing overloaded with information. Corell needed a break, so he made a suggestion.

"I need to get some air. What do you say we go for a walk? And, there is something I'd like you to see,"

Valerie agreed, grabbed a power bar and a bottle of water from the kitchen, stuffed the bar in her hip pocket, and followed Paris out the door. As they made their way across the backyard toward a well-worn stockade fence, she perceived Corell was intimately familiar with these surroundings. As he led her through the gate, past the barn, and into an expansive field, he moved in a way that only one who had done so thousands of times could do. The morning was late, with the sun near its apex in the blue expanse. Although motionless, the air was filled with life as crickets chirped, grasshoppers jumped, and bees went about their usual business. Meadowlarks made their plaintive calls in the distance. As Valerie trailed behind Corell, she breathed in the scent of dry soil and wild grasses, which reminded her of camping trips made with her family.

The pace was leisurely as they followed an animal trail breaking into the hills. The knee-high grass was dry, the day's warmth already having long since burned away the dew. In the distance, perhaps half a mile beyond the edge of the field, the terrain rose into an undulating mixture of hills carpeted in wild grasses, punctuated by madrone and mature oaks.

Corell, who now led by several paces, turned and called to her, "It's just ahead," pointing toward a treeless knoll which by then was just a short distance away. When they finally stood atop the summit, they turned, standing side-by-side, enjoying the fruits of their labor.

From their vantage point, the entire Rogue River Valley spread out before them, a woven tapestry of colors and shapes. The view was an intricate mosaic of woodlands, farms, and pear orchards intermixed with roads and homes. Downhill, the farmhouse appeared as little more than a speck of white. Faraway, Medford lay in the shadow of Roxy Ann, a humpback mountain shimmering like an illusion in the midday sun.

"It's wonderful," Valerie gasped, a hitch in her voice, her eyes searching every piece of the puzzle that lay in front of her. "This is your special place," she said matter-of-factly. Corell's continued silence served as confirmation. Soon they were sitting side-by-side in the grass and had taken up the conversation they had left behind in the farmhouse.

"My son and I hiked up here many times," Corell said, his voice filled with melancholy. Then he added, "Mark loved it here," the emotion in his voice and in his expression, palpable.

"Where is Mark now?" Valerie asked, treading lightly, attempting to sidestep the apparent conclusion that somehow a father had the misfortune of losing a son.

A moment passed before he responded. "Mark has been gone for a long time." Then added solemnly, "He died in a riding accident."

"I'm sorry for your loss, Corell," Valerie offered.

"I'm sorry, too. I didn't mean to bring that up. I just wanted you to see this place," he whispered, then paused for a moment gathering his thoughts.

"This is a very special place; thank you for bringing me here," she assured him, her soft voice appreciative.

"Valerie, this morning, we were talking about the people who followed you in the past. I brought you here to show you what you left behind all those years ago."

She spun her head quickly to face him, her expression twisted in a quizzical mask. "What are you talking about?"

"I want you to understand and appreciate that while forty-five hundred years sounds like a long time ago, it really isn't when you realize that just five people lived in that span of time."

Holding up one hand, he counted them off on his fingers. "First there was you, then Pearse, Amos, Bede, and finally me —that's five. Now you have completed the circle. The time loop you set in motion has returned to you. Do you understand?"

Valerie nodded. Encouraged, Corell felt like he was making headway.

"Good. Now I want to show you the nature of this ring and what it can do. My father, Bede, was born about twenty-five hundred years ago. He knew Amos personally. Amos knew Pearse, who knew the elder you. Let me show them to you."

After pulling up a fistful of grass, Corell pushed himself to his feet. Then with a wave of his arm, he tossed the handful of grass into the air. But rather than returning to the ground as one would expect, the grass expanded and continued rising until the valley view disappeared entirely. The panorama was gone, replaced by what seemed to her like a shimmering dome of energy.

"Cool! What is that?" Valerie exclaimed, gaping at the fascinating effect that continued expanding as she watched.

"It's a time distortion," he pointed out. "Local time will continue as usual, but within this distortion zone, the time has temporarily halted. Now I can show you some things that will go unobserved by others. We cannot have anyone watching. More importantly, the distortion prevents any unwanted effects outside the field."

Valerie was fascinated. "Is it a force field like in Sci-Fi movies?"

Corell paused, contemplating the question for a moment before answering. "In a way," he said slowly. "But a force field wouldn't alter time as this effect does," he explained. "Keep in mind this is just one of many of the possible ways to apply the power of your Hesauronic ring. It is a tool that can be used in a variety of ways. Removing yourself or others from the timeline can be a potent defense in desperate times."

"Think of the ring as a lens that magnifies what is already within you," he said, pointing at his heart, tapping for emphasis. "When someone good uses a ring to help others, it intensifies their good qualities, and good things tend to happen to them. But when that ring is used selfishly or to hurt others, one becomes even more selfish and violent. That one is likely to withdraw from others, become unhappy, sadistic—dark."

Valerie nodded as he continued, acknowledging her agreement. "Like karma, right?"

"Exactly," Corell confirmed. "People don't realize how true that can be. The old adage, 'What goes around, comes around,' is more powerful than you can imagine. That's why you always want to use your ring to help others. If you are smart, you will only use it to help, not hurt. If you use it for good, you will never lack anything. It makes no sense to use your ring to make money or for selfish reasons because the rings bless goodness. You will have far more success in life if you use it strictly for charitable purposes. Never use your rings to take from someone else or to hurt others unnecessarily."

"Alright," said Corell, moving on to his next topic. "Let's say that a ring wearer attacks you, and you have only a moment to react. What do you do? You can use your ring to stop time within the distortion zone, allowing you to escape and live to fight another day."

"Or get the bad guy out of my hair for a few minutes while I save the world. Right?" Valerie joked.

"Absolutely," Corell agreed. "And who knows what you can do with all five rings!"

"Now, there's no reason to hide the fact that you have the power to do this. You should want your enemies to know your capabilities. You want the bad guys to think you could send him all the way back to the stone age if you choose to. Fear of reprisal is one of the best tools you have at your disposal."

"So, how do you do it? How do you make the ring work for you?"

"I already told you, it acts as a lens magnifying what is already within you."

Valerie felt frustration building within her, which drove her to her feet. She felt like she had asked the question every way she knew how to, without ever getting a direct answer.

"That doesn't answer the question," she snapped. "I want to know how you operate it. What do you do to make it work? Push a button, click your heels, wiggle your nose? What!" she pleaded.

The moment she said it, Valerie regretted the words. She didn't mean to snap. It just happened. She scolded herself for allowing frustration to build to the point she lost composure.

After all, she knew Corell was simply trying to help her. "I'm sorry, I'm just frustrated," she said, throwing her hands up before he had time to respond.

Corell took a cleansing breath, struggling to quell his own frustration. "I think I know what you are trying to say. Let me answer the question this way. Whenever I want to use the power of the ring to perform some kind of 'magic'—let's call it that—I picture it as happening in my mind. I believe it will happen; I see it happen; therefore, it happens! It's simple, which is why I said it comes from within you. That is how it was explained to me. My father described it to me in the same way. It isn't hard. The power is within you; it is already there. You just need to learn how to draw it out. Do you understand?"

"I guess so," Valerie nodded enthusiastically, but nothing about it felt exciting. She was faking it because she did not feel like she would ever be able to do such a thing as manipulate time. Hiding the truth about how she truly felt did not sit well with her, either. Resentment built in her for being put in the position to lie about it.

Valerie felt a twinge of guilt rush through her. She respected Corell, admired the man, considered him a friend, a mentor, so she considered lying to him as her failure to perform as expected. She had lied, so she had no one to blame but herself. But that didn't change the fact that she was tired of hearing about it and even more tired of thinking about it. She wanted to take Orson, go home, and be relieved of the whole thing once and for all. Reseating herself, she pretended to listen placidly while planning her escape.

Corell built a fire then served pizza and salad in the living room that evening. When he offered Valerie a beer, she gladly accepted and was thankful for it. She loved pizza and beer, feeling like it was the perfect combination of food and drink. Plus, the alcohol helped her unwind after a long day listening to Corell's tedious lectures.

He promised the following day would be bowling ball and arrow day and that it would be fun. He would show her how to shoot arrows without a bow and chuck bowling balls without touching them. Although it sounded like fun, Valerie's heart was not in it. Her thoughts were of home, her folks, and being with her friends, and she longed to have her phone back.

Both were tired, so they ate together on the sofa, only speaking occasionally. Valerie was relieved Corell seemed to want to separate leisure time from lecturing; she had had enough of that. While flipping through old National Geographics from the 1960s, she continued considering asking him to take her home tomorrow. Old magazines would usually interest her, but she was just too dispirited to care about much of anything that evening.

Valerie decided to wait until the morning to ask Corell to take her home. She knew it would upset him, expecting a confrontation, which would lead to yet another lecture. She was not looking forward to the drama, which was another good reason to put it off. There was no sense in upsetting Corell right before bedtime, so she said good night and went to her room, leaving him alone on the couch.

Valerie slept, but fitfully that night. Her mind refused to switch off. And when her thoughts slowed down enough to doze, her mind was filled with flashes of dreams past. But it was not a repeat of the same old nightmares. These were more like shards of those old nightmares. It was as if they had been pulled from her head, thrown on the floor, stomped into a million pieces, and the fragments shoved back in. Somehow, she knew those bad dreams were gone for good, never to return. She hoped to have seen the last of them, but forgetting them entirely was impossible. She tried to restart the amazing dream she had last night but was disappointed because she could not do anything more than remember it.

Chapter 13

Arlene Dunne— October 1947

After Stone's attack, Arlene planned her revenge in earnest. Obsessed with vengeance, she thought of little else. Just one thing would make things right again. Payback.

Arlene knew what Stone intended to do. He had made that clear enough when he told her he planned to take her ring and then kill her nice and slow. When he followed that with a laugh, she saw the glint in his eyes and knew he meant every word. *He would enjoy every second of it,* she thought. That is what really galled her. Arlene was not about to allow him to get away with coming into her house the way he did. She would make sure he paid for it with his life.

Hatred combined with steadfast resolve smoldered within her like white-hot coals. *I'll get my revenge if it takes a hundred years. Then I will have his ring rather than the other way around.* The more she thought about what it would feel like to have two rings, the more she desired Stone's ring. *That is why he came for me, right?*

Stone wanted her ring because he craved the warmth. The power was good, but the warmth was even better. No doubt he liked it, too. She understood well enough how those whispers warmed the soul, the irresistible craving that came from the thought of bringing two rings together. If one was good, two rings just had to be better—right? The intoxicating sensation Arlene experienced when she pleased her ring that's what it was all about. Too much of that was just enough.

Before she knew it, unrelenting greed to obtain a second ring had taken hold of Arlene. Adding Stone's ring to her hand had become an obsession so fast she never saw it coming. Unknowingly, the egotistical desire for more power had overtaken her desire for revenge without even realizing it. Now greed had her in a death-grip, clouding her thinking, distorting her priorities.

Arlene began planning by making personal security a priority. She became ever more observant of her surroundings, always vigilant of any sign of threat. Aware that predictability encouraged ambushes, she took a leave of absence from the University. Traveling to and from work five days a week was unavoidably predictable—and dangerous. So, she stayed in as much as possible.

When she did leave the house, every move she made was carefully planned, meticulously thought out in advance to avoid opportunities for entrapment. Varying her routes and modes of transportation made her movements impossible to predict. Sometimes she drove her own car or called a cab, alternating that by riding with a friend or neighbor. Knowing safety came in numbers, she avoided being alone and kept to public places.

As soon as Stone is healthy enough, he will strike again, she thought. *His style is unmistakable, like a leopard that attacks only when the prey least expects it. I can count on that*, she reasoned.

He proved that when he snuck into the house and bushwhacked me. But I won't allow that to happen twice. That inherent predictability will be his downfall. This time around, I will be on the offensive. I will be the hunter rather than the hunted. Round two with Stone is inevitable, but the knockout blow will come the moment the bell rings!

Arlene expected to be watched and followed. Stone would be watching, waiting, and seeking patterns in her movements. He would be looking for suitable places to set her up for a surprise attack. But two could play that game. All she had to do was turn that tactic around on him by setting a trap for him.

It wasn't long before she had a sound basis for her own bushwhack. The idea was to draw him out of the shadows where she would have the advantage. But first, the battleground would have to be established. Once she had chosen a suitable site, all she had to do was make that location part of her routine then the trap would be set. The big fish would bite so hard on the bait he would swallow it whole, never noticing the hook until it was too late, and he had already lost.

Although the sky was clear and the day warmer than expected, Morgan Beal noticed the sun's lower angle in the sky. By his reckoning, it was a reliable sign Summer was over, and Autumn had arrived in Southern California. The leaves had already turned their usual mixture of brown, yellow, and orange, but few had fallen. He expected that to change significantly and soon. The first rainstorm of the season would strip the trees bare in a matter of days.

It had been a busy Summer for his one-man remodeling company. Morgan had worked ten-to-twelve hours a day since the first of May, so he was looking forward to the rainy season when work would slow down, and he could take it easy for a while. Light construction and remodeling were hard but satisfying work. His reward was seeing a job well done and money in the bank.

From the time he worked his first job as a teenager, Morgan saved ten percent of his earnings. He was not cheap but avoided wasting money on things he considered frivolous. He made sure he would get by in retirement but was by no means a rich man.

Morgan Beal liked what he did for a living and preferred being his own boss. Accustomed to working hard, he was healthy; his body was tanned and lean. But at fifty-six, muscle aches, pains, and stiffness had become his daily reality.

Morgan was getting older and saw the end of the road approaching in the distance. He knew he would not be able to keep up the pace forever. Recently he had begun to think of what there would be for him when he retired. One day in the not-too-distant future, the one-man show at Beal Construction and Remodeling would close because the boss would fail to come to work anymore.

A few days after the work on Arlene Dunne's house was completed, she called him back to build a fence and doghouse in the backyard. Arlene explained she was concerned about her security and that a dog would make her feel safe. She wanted a police dog trained to defend its owner, she said. Beal understood her desire for safety but felt that buying a police dog was a bit over the top. Plus, corralling a big dog like that behind a fence seemed unfair to the animal.

Arlene explained she had gone to the Glendale Police Department for information about where she could buy a trained security dog. The receptionist recommended an academy in Pomona that sold trained police dogs. The academy informed her that owning a working dog was much more involved than merely paying for and bringing home an animal. They warned the dog could be dangerous under certain circumstances if not properly handled. Accordingly, the academy would require her to take owner training classes before she would be allowed to take delivery. So, three times a week for two weeks, Arlene dutifully took people training courses at the academy.

Morgan had the doghouse and fence completed when Arlene came home with her trained police dog. Since he was already in the yard when she released the big male Shepherd, he bonded with it immediately. Morgan sat with him, talking gently and scratching him behind its ears for an hour. By then, it was well into the evening, so Arlene invited Morgan to have a sandwich with her on the patio.

Morgan smiled broadly, accepting the invitation, pleased they were getting along together. He liked Arlene and was correct in assuming the invitation was a sign that she liked him. He worried that their apparent age difference might be a roadblock to any lasting relationship. While Arlene and Morgan talked, ate, and got to know one another, the big dog lay under the table, resting on Morgan's feet the entire time. Morgan never mentioned it to his host because it seemed the animal had unintentionally bonded more with him than it had with her.

The big police dog was magnificent, but at seventy pounds, Arlene decided he was just too large to have in the house. Morgan understood but did not like it. Having grown up on a farm where dogs had plenty of room to run, he felt sorry for his new friend. Seeing the Shepherd cooped up in the backyard bothered him, so he tried to stop by to visit the dog—and Arlene whenever he was in the area.

Two had passed, and Arlene still had not named her dog, which seemed like an unforgivable sin to Morgan, so he stuck to calling him *Buddy* during Arlene's period of indecision.

Eager to see the dog named, Morgan began offering name suggestions. The Shepherd had been a working police dog, so he suggested naming the dog *Sarge*, but Arlene rejected that recommendation outright.

On a whim, Morgan suggested naming him *Police*, thinking it would be funny to stand on the porch yelling *Police!* When calling him. They laughed at that. It was funny, but when she explained that it would drive her nosy next-door neighbor Mrs. Alice Devlin mad, it seemed like something she just had to do. Hitting on a sure-fire way to aggravate the tedious busy-body next door had instantly become a must-do.

But then Arlene realized that repeatedly hollering *Police!* Out the back door might cause someone in the neighborhood to call the police. If that were to happen and the police department responded to the call, she was pretty sure they would not be happy about it. The idea was fun, but Arlene decided that it would be going too far with a joke.

Yet a chord had been struck. The name's absurdity would not allow it to be easily forgotten. Then Morgan suggested naming the dog, *Dang it!* They both thought that was hilarious. Arlene agreed to give the name a try for a few days to see if she could make it work. Morgan was looking forward to standing on her porch, hollering *DANG IT!* repeatedly to call the dog. Surely it would drive Mrs. Alice Devlin bananas, making it a worthy endeavor.

On his next visit, Morgan learned Arlene had tried calling the dog *Dang It* a few times but decided it was just too silly to take seriously. A more traditional name was needed, so she had settled on naming the dog *King*. That seemed alright to Morgan, but he was disappointed. *King* would not be nearly as much fun as *Dang It!* But it was her dog, so *King* would have to do.

Subsequently, the big German Sheppard got bored and started digging. Once the big fella started digging, it quickly became an obsession. In a day, Arlene's pristine backyard was transformed into a moonscape. Within a couple of days, the once-immaculate landscaping was a total loss. Much to the dismay of Mrs. Alice Devlin, that is when Arlene found a good reason to forget all about calling the dog King. Along with an occasional expletive, her dog's name was now officially *Dang It!* Henceforth this was the big dog's designation, and Morgan could not be happier.

And so it went; Arlene, Morgan, and *Dang It!* became an item. Although Morgan and Dang It! were welcome additions to Arlene's inner circle, she was not about to allow those budding relationships to distract her from her favorite obsession—getting even with Stone and collecting her second ring. As intended, her new dog alarm improved security, made her feel safer, and was a good companion. Plus, it didn't hurt to have an able-bodied man like Morgan around the place.

Arlene had secrets to protect, which meant she could not let Morgan get too close. She had to keep him at arm's length, at least until she had relieved herself from the threat posed by Stone. To accomplish that, she needed to focus on the task at hand, setting a trap for her not-so-favorite Ring Bearer.

Then it occurred to her that Morgan just might be what she needed to help her set the trap. Morgan was not involved. He was innocent, so she felt compelled to protect him from harm. She considered any direct participation involving her new friend to be out of the question. Still, she saw no harm in putting him to use as part of the setup.

Reasoning that if she were to do the unthinkable by setting a pattern of meeting Morgan regularly, the trap would be set. Meeting for a late dinner on a particular day of the week seemed perfect for what she had in mind. A late dinner date would provide the cover of darkness, and at a specific time and day would provide the pattern she needed to draw Stone out of the shadows. All she had to do was figure out how to surprise him before she was expected to be there. And she knew just the place, which was just a ten-minute walk from home.

O'Brien's Diner, a twenty-four-hour café, had decent food and was less than fifteen minutes away on foot. Morgan was a simple man, so she doubted he would object to O'Brien's diner-style fare. Along the way, a highway underpass with thick concrete piers would provide excellent cover for a man to hide. At night, the area would be dark and free of pedestrians. Arlene guessed that Stone would be unable to resist trying to catch her in the darkness of the underpass.

Arlene scouted the area diligently. If the attacker expected her to approach from the direction of her home, which was east, that would leave the other direction, west, unobserved and undefended. If she snuck up on Stone from his blindside, she could make mincemeat out of him before he knew what hit him. It was the perfect plan. She could put the hit on Stone without getting dirty or missing her dinner date.

Arlene set the plan in motion with a phone call to Morgan, then walked to O'Brien's on the same day and time two weeks in a row. Anyone watching for repetition in her movements would have no trouble recognizing the pattern. How could Stone resist if all of her other movements were random and this was the one thing regularly scheduled?

But that left one nagging problem unsolved. How would she know if Stone was there or not? She needed to know if Stone was there before entering into the underpass's darkness for the plan to work. If she could find a way to know that, she could go around the block and attack Stone from the West.

But how could she spy on the underpass and be seen walking there at the same time? Since she could not be in two places at once, Arlene saw no other solution to the problem other than bringing someone in to spy on the underpass for her. But who? And how would they communicate? More importantly, how would she prevent that spy from witnessing what the police would surely identify as a murder? This issue proved to be a puzzle without a workable solution.

When the answer dawned on her, Arlene laughed at herself for missing such an obvious solution. It was right in front of her nose the whole time! Who did she know that loved to spy on people? There could be only one nominee for the role: one Mrs. Alice Devlin! The nosy, holier-than-thou next-door neighbor was incapable of minding her own business. Regardless, those shortcomings made her the perfect candidate. It was time to put Alice to work doing what she did best—being nosy and spying. All Arlene had to do was mention that she had seen the man that blew the back of her house off hanging around that underpass, and Mrs. Devlin would be on it like a hog on slop.

Arlene spent a day working on her story, making sure there were no holes in it. Alice was a pest, but she was not stupid. For the plan to work, the story had to be plausible. Since there is no substitute for the truth, Arlene settled on a relatively close version of what actually happened.

Early the following day, Arlene went to work preparing the scene. She made a pot of tea, set the picnic table for two, and put out some shortbread cookies. All that was left to do was get her nosy neighbor's attention. She did not figure that would be too difficult.

"*DANG IT!* Quit digging—you blasted mutt!" Arlene hollered out the back door. But the big dog paid no attention to Arlene's rant. Once the dog was headlong into a newly dug hole, nothing short of a hand grenade would dislodge him. She knew that, so she wasn't disappointed by *Dang-It's* failure to obey. Several *DANG IT'S!* more made certain Mrs. Devlin hadn't missed anything.

When Arlene was satisfied, she sat at the picnic table and waited. She didn't have to wait long. A moment later, she noticed the bedroom curtains next door move, which indicated she had achieved the goal of getting her neighbor's attention.

"Good morning, Mrs. Devlin," Arlene called to Alice sweetly. "Would you like to sit and have a cup of tea with me?" In a flash, the curtains parted, the window slid open, and Mrs. Devlin appeared looking disheveled but eager. It was early, so she wore a pink robe over pajamas with her hair in rollers.

"Oh dear, I am such a mess," Alice declared, fussing with her rollers. Then she added, "I'll be right there!" She mock whispered the words as if it was a great secret. Then the window slid shut with a bang.

Arlene guessed right that Mrs. Devlin would never miss an opportunity to restock her inventory of gossip fodder. The fact that she was still dressed in her house clothes wouldn't slow her down one bit. Arlene guessed correctly because Mrs. Devlin appeared out her back door in a moment without the slightest alteration to her appearance. The little woman had run through her house, quick-stepping in her fuzzy pink slippers, through the gate, onto Arlene's porch, and was seated at her table in less than one minute flat. Arlene was impressed.

To describe Alice Devlin as a small woman would be an understatement. Just a frog's hair over five feet and one-hundred-five pounds soaking wet, her children's size twelve outfits were loose-fitting. With her high-stacked bouffant hairdo in rollers, thick black framed cat-eyeglasses, and pink robe Alice was a sight to behold without makeup. Nevertheless, Arlene welcomed her warmly, stifling a smile while pouring her a cup of tea. After a bit of small talk centered around neighbors and local goings-on, Arlene turned the conversation to her intended goal.

"You would never guess who I saw hanging around the Santa Ana Street underpass last night," Arlene whispered, leaning forward with a confidential tone. This was a tidbit requiring a deft delivery. If she was going to suck Mrs. Devlin in on her scheme, she needed to make it sound as if this piece of information was a salacious bit of news. What is more, she had to be coy about it, making it seem as if Mrs. Devlin had dragged the information from her.

"Really? Who?" Mrs. Devlin demanded to know.

"Well, I'm not sure, really," said Arlene, doing her best to sound unsure of herself.

"Tell me—who!" Alice insisted.

Arlene hemmed and hawed, allowing tension to build. "You know—that man. The one in black," she whispered.

"The man in black?" asked Alice, not immediately making the connection.

"You know, the big man who attacked me in my home last month."

At this piece of news, Mrs. Devlin's eyes became wide as saucers as she recalled the big man in black she had witnessed staggering away from her neighbor's house that day. As the memory took shape in her mind, her teacup came down hard enough to knock cookies off the plate.

"No!" she gasped disbelievingly, holding both hands to her mouth in genuine shock. "I saw him leaving here, but I had no idea that man came into your home! Why didn't you tell me?" Alice scolded, then offered support by taking Arlene's hands in hers.

Arlene felt a twinge of guilt for dismissing her neighbor outright that day. Had she misjudged Alice, she wondered? Certainly her neighbor was a busy body, but perhaps she had been too dismissive.

"I didn't tell anyone in the neighborhood because I didn't want to cause them to be frightened."

"You poor sweetie! I'm so glad you weren't seriously hurt!" Alice said sympathetically. Although a moment later, the true Mrs. Alice Devlin reemerged as she began pressing Arlene for more information.

"But tell me, dear, what happened to your house? Did that man blow up your house? Is he a Communist?"

Arlene burst out laughing, unable to restrain herself. "I have no idea," she said dismissively. "Maybe it was a gas leak."

"Then what was that man doing in your house? Was he a burglar? Is he someone you know? Was he with the gas company?" Alice persisted, asking four questions with just one breath, a fact that had not escaped Arlene.

Alice bolted from her chair, knocking it over in the process. Slamming both hands down on the table, she cried, "Why—that man *raped you*, didn't he!" Now the little neighborhood sparkplug was right in Arlene's face. "And you didn't want anyone to know the truth!" she declared accusingly.

"Whoa, slow down, Alice!" Arlene said, holding her hands up in an attempt to get her to stop jumping to conclusions. But it was no use; Alice was a tiger when she latched onto something. The conversation had transformed into an interrogation so quickly Arlene never saw it coming.

She needed to think fast if she would turn the conversation back to the intended destination.

"No, that man isn't someone I know, and no, I wasn't raped," Arlene assured her. "But he *is* dangerous—he choked me, he is a burglar, and if he is still in the neighborhood we need to watch for—"

"He choked you?" Alice interrupted, clearly frightened as she eased herself back into her chair with her mouth agape. But the comment had the desired result: Alice listened again rather than ranting.

"He choked me," Arlene repeated, holding her hands to her neck for effect. "This is a dangerous man we're talking about, and he is still in the neighborhood. *We need to be on the watch for him.*"

She finally got it out there, and apparently with the desired effect. Behind the thick cat-eyeglasses and high stacked rollers, the gears were turning in Alice Devlin's head. Now that Arlene had admitted to having a burglar in the house who tried to strangle her, the gas explosion alibi seemed too farfetched to defend.

Arlene breathed a sigh of relief, thankful she had diverted Alice from the subject of how the house was damaged. She didn't have a believable story for what caused the destruction, other than claiming she didn't know or couldn't remember. But then, how could one not know what caused the back of their house to be blown off? Regardless, she had no choice other than to keep the little woman focused on the intruder rather than the damage.

"Mrs. Devlin, would you keep an eye out for that man for me? Promise me you will tell me immediately if you see him again, alright?" Arlene pleaded, then smiled inwardly, believing she had cast exactly the right bait at Mrs. Devlin. Now all she had to do was wait and see if she would bite.

"Oh, you can count on me!" Alice agreed all too eagerly, poking at her chest emphatically. "And when Mr. Devlin comes home from the office, you can be certain I will tell him all about it! Did you know my Alvin is our fair city's prosecutor? Everyone at City Hall just loves Alvin Devlin. Why my Alvin will have everyone in the police department hunting that scoundrel within hours. You can rest assured Alvin Devlin will not rest until he throws that terrible man in the pokey! And when—"

"*Alice!*" interrupted Arlene, startling her into silence. "Alice," she repeated, "will you help me watch out for that man?" All she needed was to suck Alice into her plan, and it would have legs.

"*Um, yeah, I can do that,*" Alice assured, nodding vigorously. "Should I call the police if I see him?" she said weakly, betraying the fact that Arlene had successfully gotten into her head.

"*Call me if you see him.* I need to know, and you know why," Arlene emphasized.

"Oh? Why do you need to know?" asked Alice suspiciously.

"I need to know, Alice, because Wednesday nights at eight, I walk over to O'Brien's Diner to meet my friend Morgan for dinner."

"Oh no, no, no, you can't do that!" Alice insisted, shaking her head. "What if he saw you walking there? It wouldn't be safe!"

"Well, I'm not going to worry about that," Arlene assured confidently. "I'm not going to live in fear—or alter my lifestyle."

Arlene knew that Alice would jump at the chance to spy for her given the opportunity. But if she thought she could spy and gain notoriety as someone who saved a life, she would be...what? Then it hit Arlene: she would be as famous as Alvin Devlin!

"Only if," Arlene sighed.

"What, dear?" Alice asked intently.

"Only if I had someone looking out for me. Then I would feel much safer," implored Arlene.

"Oh, I would *love* to look out for you!" Alice gushed. "What can I do to help?" she said, excitedly smiling, overly eager to be involved in what she considered to be something sensational.

"Well..." Arlene paused as if she were trying to think of something for Alice to do. "Oh, I know!" she exclaimed, "If you were to drive through the underpass on Wednesday night just before eight, that would be perfect. Then, if you saw him, you could tell me before I walked through there. Do you think you could do that for me?"

"Of course!" Alice agreed, bouncing in her chair excitedly. "Let's do it!"

"Alright," Arlene agreed. "Tomorrow night just before eight o'clock. I will be on the corner of Eleventh Avenue and Santa Ana Streets, waiting for your report. All you have to do is drive through a couple of times and let me know if you see anyone there. Okay?"

So, it was settled. Mrs. Devlin would be the spy Arlene needed to trap Stone. But what she did not tell her newly adopted co-conspirator was that tomorrow, Wednesday, would be her third walk through the underpass at precisely eight o'clock. The pattern had already been established, so there was a better than fair chance Stone would be their lying-in wait. And if he were not there, she was sure it wouldn't be long before he was.

The following night at precisely seven forty-five PM, Arlene left her house, walking three blocks to the corner of Eleventh and Santa Ana Streets. A moment later, she spotted Mrs. Devlin's green Plymouth business coupé pass her by. The car turned right, then disappeared down the incline to the underpass on Eleventh Avenue. Two minutes later, the green Plymouth returned, turned left, then parked next to where Arlene waited. Mrs. Devlin stopped the motor then rolled down the window.

"Did you see anyone?"

"Nope. No one is there," Alice assured her.

"Do you want to go around another time?"

"Sure," said Alice. "I'll go a couple more times. Should I blink my lights if I see someone?"

"Alright. But remember, that man was dressed all in black clothes that day. He might wear black all the time, and if he is wearing black again, he will be hard to see in the dark." Then she added, "If you don't blink your lights, I'll know it's safe to go. After that, you can go home. I will call you after dinner. Morgan will drive me back, so I'll be safe." Arlene thanked Alice warmly then she pulled the Plymouth away from the curb.

Alice passed by again without blinking the car's lights a few minutes later. Arlene waved her off, and then her gaze followed the green Plymouth as it turned toward home.

When it was gone, she turned and began walking toward the underpass, O'Brien's Diner, and her 8 PM dinner date with Morgan Beal.

As Arlene exited the underpass, she noticed a black Ford sedan parked at a closed service station across the street from the diner. The car was strategically parked to provide a clear view of the underpass. Although the vehicle was barely noticeable in the shadows, Arlene was able to make out a dark figure sitting behind the wheel. The recurrent red glow of a smoldering cigarette betrayed the drivers' presence. No one had to tell her who that driver was or why he was there.

Stone smiled with satisfaction as he stubbed out the cigarette in the overfull ashtray, then glanced at his gold watch to check the time. *Straight up eight o'clock, just as expected. Good,* he thought, *the skirt is a good timekeeper.* She was punctual, someone he could count on. He liked that about Arlene Dunne, but that precision would be her downfall; he would see to that.

This one is a fighter, he thought. *I like that in a woman. But that ring makes her a tough customer. She nearly gouged out my eye and threw me against the wall so hard I sailed right through it. I underestimated her that time, but I will not make that mistake twice.*

This time around, Stone intended to keep his dealings with Arlene short and sweet. There would be no time to play with her. Having to forgo the fun of choking Arlene Dunne, one that deserved it so much, was a disappointment. The prospect of toying with her was compelling, although this time, he would sacrifice the fun to accomplish his goal of getting her ring.

Three times he had observed Arlene Dunne walking to the diner on a Wednesday night at precisely eight o'clock. Each time she met the same guy at the diner. She sat across from him in a window booth as they talked, ate their meals, then talked some more. Then at about nine o'clock, they left together in his pickup truck. Nothing changed; it was all predictable. When they left together, he followed them from a safe distance, but it was always the same. The guy dropped her off at her house, and she went in alone. *Punctual as ever,* thought Stone. *That's good. She is both punctual and reliable.*

Stone's car rumbled past Jerry's house that night just before ten o'clock. Jerry had been reading a Zane Grey Western in bed, so he couldn't help but wonder why the boss was out so late. What could he be doing? He had been gone from dawn until after dusk seven days a week for the past two weeks. When Jerry asked if there was something he could help with, Stone brushed him off, saying he had personal business to take care of. Although he had a gut feeling the boss was up to no good, that didn't bother him.

And Jerry had good reason for being concerned. As Stone staggered out of the darkness and into the Cherry Motel that first night, Stone's condition raised questions that remained unanswered. Jerry paused to recall the night Stone came into his life. He guessed the big man had been in a terrible fight, but the evidence did not support that assumption.

Stone came in soaked in blood from head to foot. His body was a patchwork of nasty cuts, scrapes, and bruises. A shirt tied around his head covered an eye that remained swollen shut for a week. It was ugly, but Stone seemed to heal surprisingly fast, which raised even more questions. The man appeared as if he had survived an explosion enough that Jerry checked the newspapers for reports of one but found nothing. So, he wrote the entire episode off as a fight, although he still wondered what was true.

The thought of following Stone that night crossed Jerry's mind, but he decided doing so would be a breach of trust. And if the boss learned of it, the relationship might suffer irreparable damage. Jerry was taught to believe that sooner or later, the truth always reveals itself. All one has to do is be patient and let it happen.

As it turned out, the situation was entirely different the following day. Jerry was surprised when the boss didn't leave as he had every day for the last two weeks. He stayed in, and it was almost noon by the time he finally came out the front door. Jerry and Louis, a farmhand he had hired to help him around the farm, were just coming in for a lunch break. The two were riding together aboard the Massey-Ferguson tractor when Stone approached them.

"Hey Boss," Jerry called down to him as he came to a stop and shut down the engine.

"How is it going, Jerry?" Stone responded cheerfully. "Who do you have there?" he asked, referring to his helper.

"This is Luis. He's helping me blow stumps and build fences." Then Jerry added, "It's a two-man job. Luis doesn't speak much English, but he's a good worker and reliable."

"Well, that's good," Stone commended. "The place looks great, Jerry; you're doing a terrific job. Keep up the good work." Stone took a moment surveying the newly fenced pastures. "You've really taken charge, boy," he said with a broad smile. "Let me know if you need anything." With that, Stone slapped Jerry's knee affectionately, turned, and went back inside his house.

Jerry was dumbfounded. *Stone's mood is good—too good*, he thought. Then he realized that he had never seen the man smile. Not like that anyway. He was unsure what to make of it, but if the boss was happy, so was he. Jerry guessed that whatever the boss had been doing while he was out all day must have gone awfully right for him to be so good-humored. Since he had no way of knowing what Stone had been up to, Jerry was once again left wondering.

In the following days, Stone continued to be unusually cheerful. Jerry suspected that Stone was looking forward to something big but had no clue what that might be. Typically, getting Stone to say anything more than a few words was difficult as pulling teeth. Jerry had become so accustomed to having no one to talk to, so he resorted to carrying on lengthy conversations with Luis even though he did not understand enough English to order a hamburger.

But Jerry knew there was more to Stone than what met the eye. Sure, he could be ill-mannered, sullen, and brusque. More often than not, he had nothing to say beyond what was absolutely necessary. Too often, he was discourteously blunt and foul-mouthed. That, combined with being so tall and wearing black all the time, made Stone an intimidating character to behold.

More than anyone else, Jerry had been able to see past the moodiness, bluster, and bad manners. When Stone arrived at the Cherry Motel broken and bleeding, Jerry saw him as no other ever had, a pitiful creature in need of help. He had seen the big man helpless and hurting in a way that engendered an affinity between them that went beyond mercy. The kindness Jerry paid to Stone earned him dividends when Stone released him from the prison that was the Cherry Motel. Stone gave him the gifts of stability, responsibility, and the kind of trust Sergeant Gerald Dunne, Army Ranger, never could. Those badly needed gifts prompted Jerry's fierce loyalty to Stone.

When Stone got in his car and left without notice on Wednesday night at six-thirty, Jerry rushed to the window and watched him go in disbelief. Stone had been home every night for a week and was uncharacteristically happy and talkative the entire time. As Jerry watched the taillights of Stone's car in the evening light, he had a hollow feeling in his gut that something was not right.

The boss had nowhere to go on a Wednesday night; Jerry was sure of that. Besides, Stone would have called and asked him to run to town and fetch it for him if he needed something, which he would have gladly done. But Stone up and left without saying a word—and that was the only clue Jerry needed to know something was afoot. And whatever it was more likely than not meant trouble.

Without thinking twice, Jerry grabbed the gun Stone gave him, the keys to the pickup truck, and ran for it. It wasn't dark yet, so he would have no problem following Stone's car. Jerry reasoned that there were far more old Ford trucks on the road than sleek new Studebakers, making the truck a lot less likely to be spotted in a rearview mirror. Jerry followed Stone's black Ford sedan at a comfortable distance.

Forty minutes later, Stone pulled into the Flying A Gas Station parking lot opposite O'Brien's Diner. He was early, it was dusk, but he knew it would be dark by eight o'clock when he expected Arlene Dunne to appear. A glance at his watch told him it was seven-ten, which left him fifty minutes to spare.

Stone was anxious but confident, knowing that surprise would be the key to his success. He was reassured, knowing Arlene would be on foot because it made her an easy target. It would be dark by then, so all he had to do was conceal himself between the big concrete pillars of the underpass and lay in wait. His black clothes and the darkness of night would be all the camouflage he needed. The setup was perfect.

Stone's plan was simple. He had no need to carry a gun or a knife. The concrete pillars would serve as his only weapon; just grab the woman unawares and slam her head against one of the concrete pillars; it was that easy. The attack would catch her by surprise, so she would not have time to react. It would be quick, efficient, and best of all, silent.

Once the deed was done, all he had to do was lean the body against a post, slip the ring off Arlene's finger, then stroll away as if nothing at all had happened. The whole thing would only take a few seconds. It would be over, and no one would be the wiser. Even the police would be stumped. The woman would simply be discovered leaning against a post with her head bashed in. There would be no evidence of a robbery or of foul play. And without witnesses or evidence of a crime, they wouldn't have a clue what happened. Case closed as simple as that.

Stone sat in his car, counting down the minutes. Only the occasional car passed through the underpass. There were no pedestrians in the middle of the week and very little traffic at this time of night. As darkness descended, he replayed his attack strategy over and over in his mind, looking at it from every possible angle and every conceivable scenario. He couldn't imagine anything that could go wrong with it. His plan was flawless. He liked it.

Another look at his watch told him it was seven-forty — time to go. Stone took less than five minutes to cross the street and position himself between the pillars. He had merged into the darkness and was virtually invisible in a moment.

Once he was in place and set, he kept a watchful eye out for Arlene's approach from the direction of Santa Ana Street. As the minutes and seconds ticked off, Stone held his breath, anticipating Arlene's appearance. Even as eight o'clock approached and she had not yet appeared, he remained diligent, unmoving, barely breathing. So, when he heard a woman's voice from behind him say, *"Hello Stone,"* his heart skipped a beat, and his blood turned to ice. For the first time in his adult life, Egan Seamus Stone was scared to death.

What frightened him most was that the source of that voice was immediately recognizable as his intended prey, Arlene Dunne. The voice was familiar, as well as the power he expected her to unleash upon him. Somehow, she had gotten the drop on him. But how? Wasn't *he* the one with the perfect plan? Then the truth dawned on him; the entire thing was a setup! She must have orchestrated everything. Walking to the diner in the dark on a specific day and at the preordained time? He felt like a chump for falling for it and cursed himself for not seeing it for what it was—a trap.

Stone turned warily to face his rival and found her standing a reasonable distance away, perhaps ten paces, wisely well out of his reach. Like him, she wore a black overcoat and hat that made her close to invisible in the darkened gloom of the underpass.

"So, what are you doing hanging around here in the dark?" Arlene said, already enjoying the win. "Don't you know it could be dangerous here at night? My goodness," she went on, "there could be any sort of scoundrel lurking about, looking for trouble."

"Just trying to help improve security in the neighborhood. People like helpful neighbors," Stone said with a toothy grin laden with false sincerity.

"Well, isn't that ironic," Arlene quipped. "We're here for the same reason! I was planning on stomping a few gutter rats tonight, and then I found you—how convenient!"

"Amen!" Stone said, then lunged forward and went for her throat. He knew he had just one chance to save himself, so he put everything he had into closing the distance between them as quickly as humanly possible. He was quick for a big man but not quick enough this time. Arlene was ready. It was never a fair fight.

Arlene's ring generated a bolt of energy strong enough to blast Stone across the four-lane avenue. She watched with pleasure as the dark form slammed into the concrete abutment on the opposite side of the murky underpass. The broken man stuck to the wall for a long moment before slowly peeling away from it with a sucking noise, and his wet imprint remained on the wall marking the spot.

Arlene watched blissfully as the body slumped to the pavement with a soft thud, where it lay in a pile of seemingly tangled body parts. *For that to happen, every bone in the body would be pulverized,* she thought. *No one could survive that.* "Couldn't happen to a nicer guy," she gloated.

The fight was over by a knockout in the first round. All that was left to do was collect the bounty—the third Ring of Hesaurun. As Arlene walked into the street to inspect the mess that had been Stone and retrieve her new ring, she heard two shots ring out. The first bullet missed high; the second bullet grazed the right side of her neck, but the third struck her in the back of the head, exiting her forehead in an explosion of red mist. The shot Arlene never heard killed her instantly.

A hundred feet away, Jerry lowered the gun. Unfortunately, Arlene's body was lying in the middle of the street. Her body would be impossible to miss being seen by anyone in an oncoming car. Jerry ran into the street to retrieve the body, grabbed the woman by the arms, dragged her to the side of the road into the relative safety of the shadows, then unceremoniously tossed the body aside as he attended to the jellified mass that was his boss.

Expecting the worst, Jerry was surprised to find the broken man still breathing. But he had to act fast if he was going to save him. But he couldn't leave the woman's body behind, and he was worried that the gunshots were heard. Jerry had a lot of work to do and very little time. There was no time to waste; he was now a murderer. The woman's body

was evidence that had to be removed from the crime scene —
and fast if he wanted to live.

Jerry knew what he had to do; with the .45 Colt still in
hand, he dashed for the pickup truck. He had the truck in the
underpass next to where the bodies lay within a minute. Jerry
jumped out while it was still rolling and began dragging
Stone's body to the back of it. In addition to being incredibly
heavy, the body was slick with blood. Jerry pulled with all his
might, ignoring the jagged shards of broken ribs and bones
jutting from seemingly everywhere. Stone was too large to be
timid about it, so he pushed, pulled, shoved, and jammed the
big body into the truck bed. It was a struggle, but he got the
gruesome job done. The work was exhausting, leaving Jerry
panting. By the time it was done, he was spent, breathing
hard and covered from head to foot in sticky blood.

When Jerry returned for the woman, he found her to be
a fraction of Stone's size and much easier to move. Pulling
Arlene's body from the ground by the arm, he was able to
hoist the body onto his shoulder in a fireman's carry. Once he
had her up, Jerry was relieved. Unlike Stone, she was still in
one piece. Stone's body bent, sagged, and drooped
unnaturally in all sorts of inconvenient directions, making
loading the body by himself a herculean effort.

Running the woman's body as quickly as he could, he
tossed it next to Stone, slammed the tailgate, and latched it.
A quick look around told him no one had seen him loading
the bodies. Jerry let out a sigh of relief, but what about the
gunshots? Had anyone heard them?

Jerry presumed someone heard the shots and reported
them to the police. The neighborhood was residential, other
than the Flying A Gas Station and O'Brien's Diner. People

were at home, and nearby houses had lights on. He had to assume people were out right now looking for the shooter, that the police were on the way, and that if he had not already been seen, he soon would be.

As he saw it, at this point, acting natural was his only defense, so Jerry made a show of strolling casually to the truck's cab. He hopped in, turned the key, started the engine, but just as he put it in gear, a black-and-white police car rounded the corner directly ahead of him. Jerry instantly knew why: someone had indeed heard the gunshots and called the police. No doubt the cops would be looking for witnesses and evidence related to those shots.

Jerry froze as he realized he was in serious trouble with no way out. *So close,* he thought. *All I needed was a few more seconds, and I would have been long gone. With my truck being the only one in the area, I can count on being pulled over and questioned. There's no way to conceal the bodies; they are impossible to miss, and I am covered in blood. I am doomed!*

Beads of sweat broke out on Jerry's forehead as he watched the police car approach. Outrunning a police car in the old pickup was impossible. With moments left to do something, he remembered an old trick learned from Sergeant Gerald Dunne. *"Click-bang,"* Jerry said aloud. *"Got to do a click-bang!"*

Jerry turned off the ignition key, pumped the gas pedal three times, then held it to the floor while returning the key to the on-position. The resulting exhaust backfire sounded exactly like a gunshot in the echo chamber that was the underpass. A moment later, he repeated the deception. Much to his relief, a quick look in the rearview mirror revealed that the police had not bothered to follow him. The cops had their hands full. More gunshots were fired! However, the boy in the old Ford pickup truck had nothing to do with it.

Although free to go, Jerry was not home yet. Fear and stress had his heart hammering, each beat shaking him to the core. Numb from shock, the boy drove south, unaware of his direction or destination. Pulling that trigger had flipped a switch in Jerry's head. His actions were based on instinct rather than rational thought or reasoning from that point forward. Shaking hands gripped the steering wheel as if his life depended on it. Cold sweat ran into his eyes, blurred his vision, and soaked his clothes.

Nevertheless, the truck continued on its way, as if driving itself, all the while headed in the right direction and without disobeying traffic signals or speed limits. The vehicle stayed off the main roads and on the less traveled, poorly lit backroads. It was as if the old pickup had a mind of its own. Maybe it did because when Gerald Dunne Jr. was once again lucid, he found himself in the driver's seat with the keys in one hand and the parking brake handle in the other.

Jerry was taken aback when he realized he was parked in front of the homestead house with no memory of ever driving or arriving there. The last thing he remembered was pulling the trigger on Stone's Government .45, then watching the woman drop to the ground. After that, everything was a blur. But there was more, and he watched it unfold in front of his eyes in the moonlight.

Snippets of the night's events flashed in front of Jerry's eyes as if he were at a drive-in theater. From his vantage point parked on Eleventh Street, he had seen Stone leave his car then hide himself in the darkness of the underpass. That is when Jerry knew he had been right to follow. As he suspected, the boss was up to no good.

Moments later, a woman approached from the diner's direction, although she held back as if she was spying on Stone. The two people seemed to be looking out for one another. Why would two people hide from one another, knowing the other was there? None of it made any sense.

Jerry's gut churned, knowing he was now a murderer. He regretted that, but when he realized the woman was about to finish the boss off, he had no choice; he had to act. Besides, it appeared to him she had it coming. As he saw it, she had snuck up on Stone, surprised him, then unleashed some sort of violence on him he could not understand. But all the boss had done was fight back in self-defense. Jerry wondered what might have led up to such an encounter. Perhaps this was the "personal business" the boss claimed had to be taken care of. Was that woman that business? It certainly appeared to be so.

Whatever the woman had used against Stone was something he could not reconcile or explain. It seemed as if she had used some sort of explosive device. But what? What would blow a man the size of Stone across the road without affecting the woman? It was a horrific sight but unexplainable. Jerry didn't recall hearing an explosion or seeing any smoke. Or had he simply missed it? He guessed he must have been in shock; tragedy could cause memory loss. So that is how he resolved not hearing a report from the blast. It was just part of a very crazy night, he reasoned.

Then it hit him. The bodies! Two people were in the back of the truck, and one of them was alive! Jerry leaped out and inspected the grisly cargo. He was relieved to find Stone still breathing but unconscious. His color was decent, and the blood had stopped flowing. He marveled at the man's resilience. The big man was undeniably tough! He had seen him in similar condition back at the Cherry Motel, which gave Jerry hope. But there was no way of getting around it; those broken bones would need a doctor's attention—and soon.

Jerry feared he might have made the wrong decision about heading for the farm rather than straight to a hospital. Indecision tore at his conscience like an angry claw. But after reasoning on it, he decided he had made the right choice. Showing up at the hospital with the dead woman's body rolling around in the truck bed would have been suicide. After a speedy trial, he would inevitably end up in the gas chamber.

Then it occurred to him he could have dumped the woman's body somewhere, then taken the boss to a hospital for treatment. Surely they would ask questions he could not answer, which could lead in only one direction—calling the authorities. So that was not a risk-free option, either.

What if someone saw him ditching the woman's body? And if he did ditch it, wouldn't it be just a matter of time before someone found it? So many possibilities of failure came into his mind that he decided to forget about it, just hide the woman's body for now, and get Stone to a hospital.

By now, the woman had been dead for hours. The body had turned grey and cold, leaving no question about her status. He knew what he had to do. He had to get rid of the body and get the boss to a hospital as quickly as possible.

Jerry's next move was to lay out black plastic on the ground, deposit the woman's body on it, strip off his blood-soaked clothes, and wrap it all together in a tight package.

Naked now, Jerry carried the bundle to the barn and hid it among the bales of hay. He worried about Luis stumbling upon it in the morning, but it was the best he could do for now. After a quick shower and change of clothes, Jerry cleaned dried blood off the truck's seat and steering wheel, then headed for the largest medical facility in the region, Sacred Heart Hospital in San Juan Capistrano.

Jerry saw no need to mind traffic laws or the speed limit at that late hour. Not only were the country roads abandoned at night, but if he did get pulled over, that might be a blessing in disguise. Combined with the tall tale he planned to tell at the hospital, the police would provide him with an escort and a solid alibi.

Jerry drove as fast as he could push the old truck safely. When he pulled up at the emergency room entrance, he ran inside and hollered to the receptionist, "I have a badly injured man in my truck! Come quick!" Then he ran back outside to check on Stone. Relief washed over him as he found Stone still breathing. "You are one tough character," Jerry marveled, shaking his head.

However, that tough character was an unconscious, blood-soaked, busted-up mess. The man's limbs were bent at impossible angles. Splintered bone jutted from everywhere, and his head was cocked at a strange angle. Then there was the blood smeared over the carcass from head to foot. Jerry's stomach churned at the gruesome sight. But at least his friend was breathing, so there was still hope. A moment later, a trio of orderlies and a nurse clad entirely in white arrived, pushing a gurney. One look at his cargo had all four of them gasping in unison.

"My God!" the head nurse shrieked, grasping her hat with her hand as if it was about to fly away by itself. Surprise, shock, and amazement held the emergency room crew in a trance as they stood gaping open-jawed at the twisted man-shaped mess Jerry had just hauled in. Then one after the other turned their disapproving trance-like stares at Jerry as if to say, *What in God's name have you done?*

Jerry shuddered at that and then realized the emergency room crew hadn't done anything for Stone other than stare at him, which made him cross.

"What are you guys waiting for—a written invitation? *Get busy!*" Jerry demanded with hands on his hips. With that, the spell was broken, and the emergency room crew started moving. But Jerry couldn't help noticing how each one of them kept a wary eye on the enormous mass as if it might jump up and bite them without provocation.

The nurse checked the patient for a heartbeat, then scrunched her face and rubbed her forehead with the palm of her hand. "He has a pulse," she declared as if she disbelieved her own words. "He's alive alright. Let's get him inside."

"That...is *alive?*" declared one of the orderlies, pointing a shaky finger at the bloody heap lying on the gurney.

"For now," the nurse muttered. "I don't give him much of a chance, but let's get him inside and see if we can get him stabilized."

Hauling the immense limp body out of the truck and getting him lifted and secured to the gurney required the three-man crew's combined strength to accomplish. Grumbling as they struggled with the slippery mess, they were all sickened by the amount of blood. By the time it was done, the three orderlies were smeared in dark red gore.

Although they would never know it, their clean white uniforms were ruined from the blood of not one but two bodies. Still, Jerry felt safe, knowing there was no way they could ever prove that.

Before entering the emergency room, the orderlies took a white sheet and covered the body. Jerry recognized there were people with children in the lobby, so he didn't object. It was better to let them believe the man on the gurney was dead rather than let the truth be known.

Jerry followed the orderlies through the entrance but was rejected by a nurse at the operating room door. "Go get cleaned up, then take a seat," she instructed. "The bathroom is over there," she said, pointing to the men's room across the hall. "We'll call you when we know more."

Jerry obediently turned away, deflated and tired, but just as he was about to head for the men's room, the nurse reappeared in the doorway. "Look, son, it's late," she said. Then she continued with a sigh. "Frankly, your friend doesn't have much of a chance. You know that, right?" A long moment of silence passed between them as her eyes searched his sympathetically.

"Go get your friend checked in at the main desk, then go home and get some sleep. There's nothing more you can do here," she advised. "I'm Judy. I'll be here until 9 AM. Call me before then, alright?" The door closed behind her with a *click* leaving the young man feeling empty and alone.

Jerry agreed with nurse Judy; there was nothing for him to do here but wait, which served no purpose. So, after providing basic information to a nurse at the main counter, he reluctantly decided to follow Judy's recommendation to go home and try to get some sleep.

At half-past the midnight hour, the country roads seemed lonelier than ever. The threat of being convicted of murder hung over him like a sword dangling from a thread. But that is not what worried him most of all; his conscience topped that by a long shot. Jerry couldn't shake the feeling that he was blood guilty.

I don't like thinking of myself as a murderer, but isn't that the truth? He reasoned. *There is no getting around it; I am a murderer; I killed a woman and don't even know who she is. She must be someone's mother or wife. Is her family out looking for her right now? What am I going to do with the body? Should I turn it in somewhere? How can I do that without incriminating myself? I can't just leave it on the police department's doorstep without being caught.*

When Jerry pulled up to the house, the property seemed unnaturally dark and his home cold and empty. It just didn't seem the same anymore. With the boss living next door, the feeling of belonging and of family was strong. But with Stone gone, Jerry felt deserted. He had made this place his home and feared what would become of him if Stone didn't make it. It had been a while since he had prayed, but that night, Jerry poured his heart out to God in prayer.

Jerry awoke at 7 AM with only four hours of sleep. The first thing he did was call Judy at the hospital for a report on Stone's condition. He was filled with dread, believing the worst must be true. The degree of Stone's injuries was shocking, even to professionals. Although Stone's survival seemed to be against the odds, he continued to hope. As he waited for Judy to come to the phone, he steeled himself for the bad news he expected her to deliver. When her voice came on the line, he closed his eyes and held his head wearily.

"Judy Donaldson, may I help you?"

"Hi, Nurse Judy," he said gloomily. "This is Jerry from last night. Can you tell me Mister Stone's condition?"

"Certainly," she chirped, the bright tone of her voice providing immediate encouragement. "Once we got him stabilized, we scheduled surgery for this morning. The surgeons are already here and preparing to get started a few minutes from now."

"Really!" Jerry said, smiling, not expecting such good news.

"Mister Stone must be an exceptionally strong man," Judy observed. "No one here believed he would make it more than a few minutes after he arrived. But he seems to be getting stronger by the hour. It's pretty amazing, considering."

It sure is, Jerry thought, wondering what was keeping Stone alive. His heart pounded as Nurse Judy calmly explained, "We need you to come in and fill out some paperwork for us. Can you come in this morning?"

"Sure," Jerry said. "But I have something to take care of first. Would late morning be alright?"

"That would be fine, Jerry. But I will not be here, so you will want to ask for Mrs. Clark. She will be ready for you."

"Alright. Thank you, Judy," Jerry said brightly. Then he hung up the phone wearing a broad smile, thinking he should pray more often.

The *something he had to take care of* was the body of the woman he had hastily wrapped in plastic and stowed in the barn. The bundle was well hidden behind hay bales, but that had to be remedied—and fast. The need for a permanent solution was a priority, and Jerry needed it quickly before someone missed the woman and began searching for her. And he knew it would not be long before the body started putrefying. He hoped to have the body permanently laid to rest long before that happened. But he still had to decide on how to do it.

Luis, his helper, would show up for work within the hour, so Jerry decided to make a pot of coffee and think about it over a hot mug. When Luis showed up at his door, the solution came to him the moment he laid eyes on him. Jerry explained the boss was in the hospital and was expected to be there a while, then promised to call Luis back in a few days. Luis didn't understand a word but understood work was canceled for a while. Jerry gave him twenty dollars and sent him home for the week.

Of course, it was perfect! He and Luis had been blowing stumps with dynamite yesterday! There were at least a dozen craters where they had blown stumps and pulled them out with the tractor. Better yet, most of the holes still needed to be filled. Then another option came to mind: those stumps still needed to be burned. They already had a burn pile started, so now he had two choices: the body could either be buried or burnt.

Jerry considered burying a body on the property too creepy to do. Just knowing it was there would forever be an unwanted reminder of what he had done. He already felt guilty enough, so he wanted to avoid creating a constant reminder of it. He thought, *perhaps I won't feel that way if the body has been burned and then buried.* And with that, the decision was made. Burning and then burying the woman's remains seemed to be the least distasteful option available to him.

Jerry intended to find the largest hole, put the body in it, stack the stumps on top, pour on some diesel, and light it on fire. Burning stumps in a newly cleared field was as common as blasting them out of the ground with dynamite. Anyone who noticed would think nothing of it.

After loading the plastic-wrapped body in the tractor's bucket, Jerry set out for the burn pile in the south pasture. He selected the largest of the many stump holes and placed the plastic-wrapped package into the hole. Then moved to the burn pile and loaded a stump into the bucket, intending to drop it in the hole over the body. But just as he was ready to drop that first stump, he hesitated. Something seemed to be preventing him from pushing the lever forward. His hand hovered over the lever, but something deep inside said; *Stop! Go no further!* Jerry could not do it; his hand seemed held in place by an unseen force. Was it his conscience? He didn't think so.

Jerry stared at the plastic-wrapped body questioning his motives. *Come on! Get it over with,* he told himself but his conscience, he assumed, prevented him from dropping the stump on the woman's body. He didn't know why but it seemed as if something called to him from the pit saying, *come—you must take it for yourself,* and suddenly his heart was filled with overwhelming warmth. The voice was his heart, his conscience speaking to him, wasn't it? The message was loud and clear, one he could not ignore. It said something more needed to be done before unceremoniously burying the woman under a pile of stumps. That something moved him to turn the tractor's motor off. Jerry sat, staring absently into the hole, wondering what to do. He didn't know the woman but felt a duty to, at a minimum, say a prayer over her.

Then he realized he knew absolutely nothing about the woman he had killed. He didn't even know her name! Surely, she had friends and relatives who would miss her. Wouldn't they want to know what happened to her? Jerry hated the thought of them searching for their friend, wife, or mother but never finding her. Of course, he would never be able to tell them the truth. But maybe there would be some way to help ease the pain of their loss or help them sometime in the future. Since collecting her personal things and learning her identity seemed fitting, that is what he decided to do.

After backing the tractor away, Jerry jumped in the big hole with the body, then sat with it contemplating what to do next. He was not squeamish but certainly wasn't looking forward to unwrapping the body. Having already forgotten what the woman looked like, he preferred to keep it that way. The last thing he needed was a lasting image of his victim imprinted forever on his heart and mind. When he had steeled himself for the task at hand, he said aloud, "Let's get on with it, Jerry."

Once he had the body unwrapped, he avoided looking at the woman's face. But he could not help but notice the golf-ball-size hole made by the .45 caliber bullet exiting the forehead. Jerry cringed at that and shook his head regretfully. The woman was dressed all in black and still wore her hat. The hat caused him to wonder how it had remained in place after she was shot, carried around, transported in the back of a truck, and dumped into a hole. But there it was, right where she put it. *She must have had it screwed on real tight*, Jerry mused.

Jerry searched through the coat pockets, found a wallet, and set it aside. The woman wore no jewelry other than a wristwatch and an old copper ring on her right hand. After removing them, they were laid beside the wallet. Jerry was relieved not to find a wedding ring, which meant the woman wasn't married. At least she had not left a husband behind. He hoped there were no children either.

Thus far, the evidence he saw indicated she must have been a modest woman; both the ring and the watch were ordinary. But they were hers, and he intended to find a way to return those things to her family. That was the least he could do.

Slowly opening the wallet, he found her California driver's license, credit cards, pictures, and cash. It was all expected, but when he noticed the dead woman's name on the driver's license, his heart pounded, and throat tightened. Arlene Dunne's name startled him like seeing a scorpion climbing up a pant leg.

"*Dunne?*" he mumbled, barely able to believe his eyes. What was the chance that he and the dead woman shared the same last name? At that moment, he took a good long look at Arlene's features, scrutinizing her face, searching for clues. She didn't look familiar, but could this Arlene Dunne be an unknown relative? Dunne was a rare name of Irish descent, and her name was spelled the same as his. But since he did not remember anyone named Arlene in the family, he shrugged it off and went on with the unsavory business at hand.

Once he had put the contents of the wallet back together, he continued searching through Arlene Dunne's pockets. Just as he was about to give up, he felt something odd, a hard object, possibly another wallet or notebook, secured to the woman's waist. Then he decided whatever it was must be enclosed in a leather money belt or something similar because it did not appear to have a fastener anywhere he could find. Since he could not unbuckle it, he decided to cut it off with his pocketknife.

It took some work, but he had the black leather belt cut off after a few moments. Jerry examined it closely, turning over what he assumed to be a money belt in his hands. There wasn't any money, but he found a hidden flap containing a brown leather notebook, which he removed. As he flipped through the pages, he saw that it appeared to be an ordinary diary. That puzzled him considerably. He closed the book then turned it over and over in his hands, trying to decide why anyone would bother securing a journal to their waist in such a curious way.

Why hide a journal so securely? It made no sense. Although what did make sense was that Arlene Dunne had secrets to keep. After all, she attacked the boss, not the other way around. *Did Stone know something she didn't want to get out? Is that why she tried to kill him?*

Jerry was convinced the journal held secrets, or else why would the woman bother hiding it? So, he put it with the other things and decided to study it in detail when he had more time.

After rewrapping the body and gathering the personal possessions of Arlene Dunne together, Jerry hopped up on the tractor and started it. He had the stump pile moved to its new location an hour later and was ready to start the fire. After taking a moment to say a silent prayer for the woman he had killed, he poured diesel fuel on the pile, put a match to it, then stepped back and watched solemnly as the flames took hold. With most of the stumps being Eucalyptus wood, the fire spread quickly and burned hot. The fire would burn unaided for days.

Jerry cleaned himself up, made himself a sandwich, then drove the Studebaker to the hospital, arriving there at just before 11 AM. Believing that doctors would have already operated on the boss, he was eager to update his condition.

The emergency room was a hive of activity. People were lined up at the reception counter, so he fell in at the back of the line and waited patiently for his turn to talk to someone. It smelled as if somebody in line ahead of him had a bladder malfunction. Jerry guessed he was right about that and tried to think of something else.

Ten minutes later, he introduced himself to the desk attendant as Gerald Dunne Junior, Mister Stone's assistant, and that he had an appointment with Mrs. Clark. The attendant—Mrs. Newsom, according to her name tag, was a middle-aged woman dressed in a white nurse uniform. The moment she heard the name *Stone* she paused; all other activity behind the reception counter paused as heads turned to regard him. A shock of fear coursed through Jerry's veins. What did it mean? Had Stone died, he wondered? Or were the police waiting for him?

With half a dozen hospital staff gawking at him, Jerry shifted his weight nervously as his gut continued grinding away. Without responding, the staff exchanged knowing glances with each other, stepping up his anxiety another notch. What that meant, he could only guess. The worst-case scenario would be that Stone had died, and the police were waiting for him with an arrest warrant. Although he recognized those knowing looks could be interpreted as either good news or bad news. He had no choice other than wait to find out.

"Can you give me an update on Mister Stone's condition?" he asked timidly.

"Mister Stone is still in surgery," reported Nurse Newsom. Then with a smile, she whispered, "We haven't heard much, but the fact that they've been working on him for four hours is a good sign. No one here expected him to make it this far. Mister Stone must be very strong!" Then she added, "When you are finished with Mrs. Clark, you are welcome to have a seat here in the waiting room. We will let you know as soon as we hear something."

Nurse Newsom directed him to an office down the hall. "Look for the business office on the right, and you will find Mrs. Clark there," she assured Jerry with a kindly nod and a smile.

Jerry did as instructed and quickly found the business office with Mrs. Clark seated behind one of three desks. Although she was readily identifiable by the nameplate on her desk, he would have approached her regardless. The woman seemed to ooze business administration.

"Mrs. Clark," he said, "Nurse Judy asked me to come to see you. She said you would have some paperwork for me to fill out."

"You must be Gerald Dunne Junior," she said as she stood, although Mrs. Clark had not met his eyes, nor had she invited him to sit. Jerry expected she had risen from her chair to shake his hand, but she turned away instead to grab a file, which left him hanging. He saw Mrs. Clark was an attractive woman in her thirties, immaculately dressed, high heels, and long hair. Despite that, he judged her harshly, for she came off as inattentive and self-important. Behind the glasses, Mrs. Clark was all business and cold as a fish.

"I am he," Jerry stated solemnly, then added, "Gerald Dunne Junior. I am Mister Stone's assistant."

"Pleased to meet you, Mister Dunne," Mrs. Clark said mechanically as she thumbed through the file. "Please understand I know nothing of Mister Stone other than the name, that he is very ill, and that you are his assistant. I do not see how he intends to pay for this hospital's services. I need to know his full name, address, contact information, medical history, and method of payment."

"Here," Mrs. Clark said, thrusting a clipboard in Jerry's face. "Fill out these forms, and be sure to complete the insurance and payment information completely. You can sit over there," she said, finally meeting his gaze while pointing to a chair next to the door. Mrs. Clark's expression was a humorless mask, whose eyes said, *Move it, buddy!* At that moment, Jerry felt thankful he was not Mr. Clark.

The amount of information he was expected to provide was bewildering. The forms included a lot of questions he was unable to answer. Suddenly he realized how little he knew about Stone. It shocked him when he realized he had no idea whether Stone was the boss's first, middle, last name, or nickname. To that point, all he had written on the form was the word *Stone* and the address. He knew nothing of his medical history, his date of birth, or even his age. The man had never mentioned a place of birth or of ever having a career. Worse yet, Jerry had no idea how Stone intended to pay for the hospital stay. Sure, the boss carried plenty of cash around; he always had plenty of that. However, what was missing, what had always been missing, was the source of Stone's income.

All of this combined to drive home the point that Jerry was entirely in the dark about the man with whom he had attached himself. When he returned the clipboard to Mrs. Clark, he felt more than a little bit embarrassed by how little information he could provide. Jerry scolded himself. For months he had been selling himself as an assistant to a man he knew absolutely nothing about.

The inherent lack of substance related to Stone's identity, combined with the preceding day's events, caused him to question every decision he'd made since leaving the Cherry Motel. There was no question that Stone was up to no good, which is why Jerry had followed him to the Santa Ana Avenue underpass. Unquestionably Stone was there to bushwhack Arlene Dunne. Jerry knew it, so why had he been so quick to defend him? *I even killed for the man! How did I let it happen?*

Jerry felt like a fool and scolded himself for being so naive. Now it seemed everything he had accomplished for the past five months was done with his eyes wide shut. He was disappointed with himself for allowing it to happen and being so gullible. Suddenly rather than one finger pointing at Stone, he found four fingers pointed back at himself. The boss had not forced anything on him. Everything he had done was of his own free will.

Reluctantly, Jerry handed the clipboard back to Mrs. Clark. One glance at it, and she exclaimed, "Well, there's hardly anything here other than his name and address!"

"I am Mister Stone's employee, not his mother," was Jerry's terse reply. Then he added, "You will have to get the rest of that information from him." Mrs. Clark blinked incredulously at Jerry as he turned away and left the room without another word.

Jerry was distraught and had more than enough reason to feel that way. Even though he was not happy with Stone, he cared about him and hoped he would pull through. Having heard nothing more than "Mister Stone is still in surgery" was another thing that had him on edge. He was eager for real news on Stone's condition but knew he could not expect to hear anything of substance until the surgeons had completed their work.

The crowded emergency room lobby was a whirlwind of people coming, going, and waiting in line at the admittance counter. Only a few unoccupied chairs were left in the room, so he chose one as far away from the madness as possible. Hoping to unwind, he leaned back and closed his eyes in an attempt to shut out the din. But that did not last long. The emergency room was too chaotic for him to get any rest.

The hubbub was centered around the admissions counter. The sick, injured, and those with appointments waited in line, many none too patiently. A toddler ran in circles until it stumbled, fell, and cried loud enough to wake the dead or anyone trying to relax as Jerry was. Staff members were repeatedly hailed on the scratchy intercom, adding to the chaos. The noise had him on a precipice, but the commotion threatened to push him over the edge.

Through all that racket, Jerry's mind turned to the fire he had left burning back at the farm. He would have preferred to stay close enough to tend it, although doing so would be pointless. Fortunately, there was no chance of the fire spreading, with the fields being cultivated for hundreds of yards in every direction.

Envisioning the charred body at the bottom of the fire pit haunted him. Jerry was beginning to think that disturbing image would forever plague him. He was tired, and his brain ached. It felt like the top of his head was being pried open with a can opener. He could not take it any longer, so he decided to bolt. He knew someone at the hospital would call him when they had real news to report on Stone's condition. So, he left the hospital and headed home.

As expected, upon his return to the farm, Jerry found the stump fire burning hot and well within safety limits. He knew it would continue burning for days all by itself, so he felt comfortable leaving it unattended. By then, it was early afternoon. He was hungry, so he went inside, intending to get something to eat. But when he entered the kitchen, he found Arlene Dunne's things lying on the countertop where he left them.

Jerry stared at those things as if in a slow-motion dream. He had an odd feeling about them. As he made himself a sandwich and poured himself a glass of milk, he kept one eye on that little pile of possessions the entire time. He didn't know why but they seemed to call to him, to be talking to him; he could not take his eyes away. The feeling was strange, one he could not describe.

As Jerry ate, he stared vacantly at Arlene's things, then realized some of the items looked familiar. Particularly the ring and the diary. But how could that be? He couldn't know. Perhaps it was déjà vu. Nevertheless, the feeling persisted as Jerry struggled to reject these wild thoughts.

Lifting the thick wallet, he went through its contents again, this time emptying everything out entirely on the tabletop. Categorizing everything as he sorted through it, he ended with five piles. Then he began methodically laying them out piece by piece in rows.

Jerry had a neat stack of currency totaling sixty-seven dollars when he was finished. Beside it sat a row of business cards, a row of pictures, and a row of membership cards. He reserved the last pile for identification cards, including the driver's license, which he placed at the top of the row. Then, in descending order, Jerry laid out the identification cards. Those cards fascinated him.

Each identification card included picture identification with various stamps and official seals. These were a combination of government-issue, university, and other identification cards. All of them characterized Arlene Dunne as someone of significant importance. The final card in this line was the Caltech Physics Department Identification card, marked in red with LEVEL ONE ACCESS. Jerry studied that one diligently, his mind swirling.

It wasn't hard to guess what it added up to. In his estimation, it meant that Arlene Dunne worked with famous people, the likes of Linus Pauling and Albert Einstein. The newspapers and magazines regularly reported on such people. The Physics Department at Caltech was well-known, so he was familiar with the nuclear research done there. If Arlene Dunne worked in that department and with those people, he assumed it meant she was engaged in atomic research.

After studying the piles for twenty minutes, Jerry was bewildered. The conclusion? *Things have just gotten a lot worse for me. Yesterday I shot in the head—a woman with a top-secret clearance. Just this morning, I burned her dead body in my own backyard!* Apparently, this woman, a key player in the country's national security community, would not go without being missed for long. He imagined busloads of FBI and Secret Service agents circling the neighborhood at that very moment.

What a stupid thing to do! Jerry scolded himself. He cradled his head in his hands in dismay, wondering how he had gotten himself into such a mess. All he had intended to do was protect the boss, but it ended up in murder. *For all I know, Arlene Dune was Albert Einstein's girlfriend!* Now he was up to his neck in it, with no way out.

But then he remembered Stone had intended to bushwhack the woman. *Why would Stone want to do that?* He wondered. Jerry doubted government secrets had anything to do with Stone's actions. There had to be something more. Perhaps he would find the answer in Arlene's journal. He opened it and began reading and did not put it down until he'd read it twice from start to finish.

Jerry closed the journal, scrutinized it, turned it over in his hands before laying it down next to the little brown ring. His eyes moved from the book to the ring and back again before returning to the ring. *A cheap woman's ring without any decoration,* He observed. *Just dull metal with five hieroglyphs pressed into its face. It looks like something you win at the county fair for popping all the balloons!*

By his reckoning, the journal was more impressive than the ring. *The paper is unusually crisp, and there's something odd about the print too. The book looks brand new, but no way is it thousands of years old. I ought to throw it in the trash where it belongs!*

Jerry's mind kept going back to what he had just read. *The story seems impossible, absolutely absurd—but what if it is true? Aliens? The end of the world? Time travel to save the world? If true, and this Valerie Dunne really did what she says she did, then what? I guess it would change everything then.*

Arlene must have believed it, he realized, *or she would not have gone to such lengths to secure it to her waist. These magic rings would also explain what the woman did to Stone. Whatever it was, it blew him across the road like he was shot out of a cannon—minus the cannon!*

And what about Stone? He has one of these rings, and I'll bet one of these books, too. But he sure does not act like he is worried about aliens—or the end of the world. All he's concerned with is where his next carton of Lucky Strikes and bottle of Scotch whisky is coming from!

Jerry reached for the ring, held the unassuming little band up to the light, and noted how small it seemed. This was a woman's size ring he doubted would fit on any finger other than his pinky. Although, he was surprised when he tried it on and found it slid on easily without any trouble. Although it fit on his little finger, it was somewhat uncomfortable. Instinctively he tried it on his ring finger. It fit there as well, but again it did not feel quite right. *Surely,* he reasoned, *such a small ring would never go on my much-larger middle finger!* But to his surprise, it fit perfectly and felt comfortable as if it belonged there.

Then out of curiosity, Jerry tried it on his index finger and then the thumb. It fit them as well—although each time uncomfortably. So, Jerry returned the ring to his middle finger and was satisfied with it there.

Suddenly Jerry's skin felt prickly. An unfamiliar sensation struck without warning, like a chill biting at his skin. But he wasn't cold—no, it was not like that, and he could think of no explanation for it. The tingling began with his right hand then rapidly spread throughout the rest of his body. *Am I having a stroke?* He wondered. He didn't think so, but whatever he was experiencing was out of his control.

As the sensation continued spreading, it felt like a divergence, as if he were being led along a path, not his own. But he didn't fight it; strangely, it felt good and right and warmed him to the bone. Momentarily the skin of his scalp, upper body, torso, arms, and hands all tingled as if they had fallen asleep. Then as quickly as it began, the strange sensation was gone.

Jerry smiled as he considered what he had just experienced. Although the story seemed preposterous, the ring on his finger seemed empowered, just as the diary claimed it would be. He had witnessed it himself, so there was no doubt about it. The ring had just resized itself to fit each of his fingers! Even more curious, the ring had indicated which finger it belonged on. Then it let him know it was part of him, and he part of it—that they were one. There could be no other explanation, and though it defied all logic, Jerry knew it was true.

The journal and the ring provided enough evidence for Jerry, as crazy as it seemed, to believe what he had read about Valerie Dunne was true. No one had to tell him that this ring had just been passed on to another Dunne in a long line of Dunne's. *And I am one of them!* he realized. As he saw it, there was no chance of any of this being some sort of crazy coincidence.

Then Jerry realized he was right about something else: he had seen the ring before. Stone wore one just like it and never took it off. Jerry nodded his head at the realization. After reading the diary, it was all clear to him. If what the journal said was true—and he now assumed it was—there could be only one reason why Stone tried to bushwhack Arlene Dunne. He coveted her ring, the very ring he wore on his hand. Stone planned to steal it from her and add its power to his own, whatever that might be. Probably printing hundred-dollar bills, Jerry guessed.

And what of Arlene Dunne? What did her actions say about her? Was she any better than him? In truth, he did not know enough to make informed character judgments about either one of them. But it was readily apparent that both Arlene Dunne and Stone were on the same destructive path. Covetousness motivated their actions, which seldom works out for good. The confrontation between the two ring bearers culminated the only way it could: in their mutual ruin. As Jerry regarded the ring on his finger, he considered the conflict between them a life lesson.

Utterly mystified, Jerry stared at the journal. He found Valerie Dunne, the author, fascinating. As he studied the ring on his finger, he considered the fact that he, Arlene, and this Valerie Dunne all shared the same surname. And what of Stone? Was he a Dunne as well? Was he also of Irish descent? What a coincidence that would be! What if they were all related? Jerry hated to think he had killed a relative, even a distant one. Then it occurred to him that Stone never asked him his surname. Jerry had never offered it, but neither had

Stone. Arlene, Stone, and he could all be Irish Dunne's. *What an odd chain of events,* he marveled.

According to the narrative, each of the Hesaurun Rings possessed a unique individual ability, a force unto its own. And with all five possessed by the rightful owner, the power of the lot was greatly magnified. This "rightful owner," Valerie Dunne, would make her reemergence in the twenty-first century, reclaim the rings, and use them for their intended purpose; the defense of Earth.

Although the journal's story seemed improbable, Jerry knew what he had seen and witnessed. Less than twenty-four hours earlier, he watched as Arlene used her ring against Stone. From his perspective, the ring's power was formidable. But what sent chills down his spine was the journal's claim that these rings were gifted to humankind by a benevolent alien named Osomarío. The intended purpose was to help Earth defend itself from invading aliens, which could not happen until Valerie Dunne was reunited with all five rings in the twenty-first century. However, the twenty-first century was still a long way off. Jerry wondered if he would live long enough to see it.

Coincidently, Jerry just happened to know where two of these rings were and wondered about the other three. Who had them and where were they? He could not guess, but the prospect of finding them was compelling. This was a thrilling story, of which he was now a part. Although the tale had him bubbling with enthusiasm, it was also disturbing for various reasons and on multiple levels.

He had a multitude of questions to ask, but no one he knew of had answers other than Stone, whom he now considered suspect. Assuming Stone would recover from his injuries, Jerry had no choice but to consider the boss a potential enemy. Jerry did not doubt that as soon as Stone was healthy enough, he would come after him seeking Arlene's ring. Stone went after Arlene, and he would come at him for the very same reason. No doubt Stone coveted the power of the ring more than anything or anyone. Jerry was convinced Stone would stop at nothing until he got what he wanted.

Jerry estimated he had a day at the most before Stone recovered enough to wonder what happened to Arlene and her ring. His first thoughts would be about the ring and who possessed it. When that happened, Jerry would need to be ready with answers.

Or would he? Jerry began speculating about available options for the first time since leaving the Cherry Motel behind. As he did so, he realized he was free of Stone. His future was no longer dependent on his relationship with him. He could be independent if he chose to be. He had enough money saved to start a life of his own or travel the world if he wanted to. But that would be running, wouldn't it?

Getting out of town had a certain appeal, but that might not be as clear-cut as it seemed. What if the authorities connected his disappearance with Arlene's? Then there was the subject of what Stone would believe. All he would have to do is connect the dots to know that he was betrayed. Stone might even suspect he and Arlene had run off together! The last thing he needed was to have the big man after him on a blood vendetta. Spending the rest of his life looking over his shoulder was not what he had in mind for a future.

The most straightforward solution might be to simply act as if nothing happened, that he knew nothing about Arlene or her ring. Play dumb, then go about his business without the boss ever knowing the difference. After all, how could Stone ever know Arlene was gone. How could Stone ever know that he shot her and disposed of the body— unless he spilled the beans?

Running away was off the table. But staying did not sound so hot, either. With no viable options available, Jerry was tempted to walk into the hospital while Stone was still unconscious and relieve him of his ring. Then if he wanted to hit the road, it would be with the benefit of two rings. But he didn't see that working out. That smacked of the sort of thing Stone might do. And again, hitting the road would lead to living in fear of being followed, or worse, being found, and Jerry had no desire to live like that.

Killing Stone outright was the only other option that would solve the problem permanently and might not be too difficult if done soon enough. While that was an unsavory option to consider, the logic was inarguable. Doing so would give him control of two rings, which felt compelling. It also reduced the likelihood of living in fear of being hunted. But Jerry hated thinking of himself as a murderer.

Walking into a hospital and knocking a guy off—now that's murder! But most of all, Jerry knew he would not like what it would feel like when the deed was done. One murder was already more than enough weight on his conscience. Despite that, the murder option clearly had the most plusses to it, which made it the most tempting proposition he had considered that day.

By the time Jerry looked up at the wall clock, he was shocked to see that it was nearly four o'clock. The day had flown by. Surely the surgeons had finished their work and could tell him whether or not Stone was going to pull through. It was time to head back to the hospital to find out what they had to say. Jerry was eager to assess Stone's condition for himself. But before leaving the house, he reloaded the Government .45 and tucked it into his belt.

Chapter 14

Amon— August 2422 BCE

A few months after the trial for the murder of Jotham, former Councilman Riordan died in his sleep on a blustery April night. After his sons laid him to rest under a suitable burial mound, they moved on with their lives, never giving Amon a second thought. In truth, they had grown weary of the old man's badgering and harping on issues they considered long dead. "The boys," as he was fond of calling his four sons, had lives of their own to live. With the old man gone, they had the freedom to think for themselves for the first time in their lives. And that they did. Within weeks, the three eldest of "the boys" had departed Erlin for greener pastures, leaving the youngest behind to care for the widow.

The acquisition of Lochlan's trained hunting dogs had helped transform life for everyone on the Bearnán Éile ridge. In addition to improving security, they were great companions for Valerie when Amon was away hunting. Every year Bono and Ali had at least one litter, which kept Tierney busy training and selling the ones he did not intend to save for breeding stock.

Lochlan, a widower without an heir, took to Tierney straightaway and held nothing back regarding dog training. It wasn't long before the boy was soon referring to himself as a hunting dog trainer. As the years passed, Pearse and Tierney became close friends with Lochlan.

Amon's leadership, strategic thinking, and strength of character led to him becoming the de facto head of the growing family on the Bearnán Éile ridge. Soon his time was split between hunting and working with Pearse on the farm. He understood the true benefit of having trained dogs was the security they provided. The animals were never off duty, always on the watch, and eager to protect. There were plusses to having dogs, but for Amon, there were minuses too.

"Since we got the dogs, the predators have vanished," Amon observed." But so have the game animals. I think they smell the dogs."

Pearse, who was working on a chair for Tierney, looked up from his labors. "I haven't seen a bear or wolf in months," he observed.

"Neither have I. But hunting is not as good. Now I have to walk further to find the game, and then I have farther to pack the meat. Perhaps the dogs smell like wolves to the game animals. Or maybe I smell like wolves. What do you think?" Amon paused, then continued. "Now, I am away from the farm more often than I would like."

Standing, Pearse said, "Look around! We have plenty of meat right here. We have sheep, goats, and chickens. Now that we do not have to worry about predators, we have more than we can eat. I plan to sell some of them at the market in Erlin. We do not need you to hunt so often. Why don't you spend more time here?"

"You are right. Now that things have settled down, I think I will," agreed Amon, rubbing his shoulder. "I'm getting older. Packing meat in cold weather is hard on the body," he confessed.

"I don't know how you do it," Pearse admitted. "I cannot keep up with you, and I am half your age."

"Necessity," Amon chuckled.

Pearse considered his words carefully before continuing. "We need you here a lot more than we need more meat," he said finally. "There is plenty of work for you here. Tierney plans to take a wife soon, so he needs his own dwelling. I want to keep him close, so I want to get a house built for him soon. And with more mouths to feed, we are going to need another barn."

"We used the last of the shale stone when we built my house. What do you plan to use?"

"We have plenty of timber here," Pearse suggested. "Valyri told me she knows a way to make sawn lumber. You should ask her about it."

Amon did ask Valerie about the lumber, and when he did, she pointed out that the River Nore lay at the bottom of the ridge and that the waterway could be used to power a mill. Hydropower could be used to grind grain or saw lumber. Valerie told Amon they could build the mill, saw lumber for their own use, and then start selling lumber downriver in Erlin.

Valerie did a historical search of sawmilling techniques on her tablet. She learned that most water-driven sawmills used coping saws, straight-bladed saw blades operating on a rod or cam, which she saw as a relatively simple mechanism tied directly to the waterwheel. It all seemed straightforward, and she was sure they could get it done with the materials available.

"Although, finding someone to make sawblades for us might be a problem," Valerie cautioned. "Steel is available, but I haven't seen anything steel larger than a sword, and I don't think we will be going into the forge business anytime soon."

"I know a man in Bregia who has a forge," said Amon. "Tadhg makes swords, knives, and saws, of steel. He is trustworthy and does good work, but Bregia is a day's ride away."

"I would like to see one of Tadhg's saws," she said. "Would you go there and buy one from him so we can try it?"

"We could also use a good ax," Amon added. "If he has one, I would like to get it. Do you have enough gold left to buy a saw blade and an ax?"

"Don't worry about the gold, Amon," Valerie laughed. "We're not going to run out anytime soon."

Amon left for Bregia the following day, planning to return with a saw and an ax the day after. The straight sawblade was just over a foot long but looked promising other than being smaller than needed for sawmilling.

"The blade looks good," Valerie said. "Your friend Tadhg does good work. Let's give him an order for larger blades. I made a drawing, so he knows exactly what we need. Tell him what it's for, so he understands how we plan to use it."

"I already told Tadhg what we want to do," Amon assured her.

"We can speed things up by bringing Tadhg some things to improve the quality of his steel. If we add ten percent chromium and five percent manganese, we will get better results. But whatever you do, do not tell him what these ingredients are, only how to use them. That will be our secret. I'll have some for you before you leave in the morning."

"Where are we going to get it?" Amon wondered.

"Don't worry about that," Valerie promised with a sly look. Amon noticed the look but said nothing; he knew she had secrets, so he did not press her for more information.

Amon returned to Tadhg's forge the following day and presented him with the drawing. After Tadhg agreed, Amon produced the chromium, manganese, and more than enough gold to cover the expense of making a pair of matching straight steel sawblades, this time three feet in length. When Tadhg saw the pouch of golden pebbles Amon carried, any objections he may have had evaporated instantly. It also helped that Amon offered new ingredients to improve his steel-making techniques. Tadhg was eager to improve his steel but found it strange that both the gold and the ores Amon brought were oddly shaped—just like river rocks.

The Dunne family was operating their own water-powered sawmill on the River Nore by late summer. Within the first two weeks of operation, the mill had produced enough pine timbers and planks for Tierney's home and a new barn. Pearse, a skilled carpenter, understood logging, sawmilling, and woodworking, making him a natural to manage the sawmill. Pearse took on Lochlan as a partner, and with the help of Tierney and Hethe, Amon's former hunting partner, they were in business.

Valerie felt it essential for the Dunne name to have a reliably traceable past for her descendants to identify. However, people of the era and region didn't typically adopt a surname. When she asked Pearse to embrace her last name Dunne, he was glad to do it, and soon the name was adopted by everyone on the ridge—including Orson. From then on, the big tabby was a Dunne, whether he liked it or not.

Erlin was growing, and along with it, the demand for lumber. Business was good from the outset, but delivering that lumber to market was an ordeal. No road existed between the sawmill and Erlin, so the heavy green lumber had to be hauled up the riverbank by oxcart and overland to Erlin from there. The footpath to town became impassible when rain and increased traffic turned it into a quagmire. A quick solution was needed if the sawmill was to continue operating.

Again, it was Valerie who offered a workable solution to the transportation problem. She recommended rafting the wood downstream to Erlin. If the Dunne's were to establish a lumber yard in Erlin alongside the river, they would be able to bring it out of the water, air-dry it, and distribute seasoned lumber from their own lumber yard. Pearse tried it and found that the plan worked nicely. That summer, Dunne Lumber Company was born in Erlin. With a steady supply of quality building materials, the village of Erlin was rapidly becoming a small city.

Meanwhile, Valerie, Amon, Lauryn, and the children were tasked with building the new barn. Iron nails were available but were in short supply and expensive, so wood joinery was produced using mortise and tenon joints, wood pegs, and notching. The resulting structure was every bit as sound as modern construction methods. Once the framing was up, they enclosed it with board and batten siding.

Amon found Valerie to be intelligent and a tireless worker. Whenever a problem arose, she was always there and could be counted on to offer a quick solution. As Amon became more familiar with her, he no longer thought of her as the *Cailleach* but as an invaluable asset to the group. In time he began considering her as best friend and confidant. The feeling was mutual, and the pair started having eyes for one another.

Valerie was interested in taking the relationship to the next level, although Amon appeared to be holding back. She had seen the way he looked at her, which was the same way she looked at him. Still, he remained reticent. Valerie wanted to know why but was reluctant to ask.

One day, while working together building a paddock for the horses, Valerie removed her thumb ring and broached the subject of their relationship status.

"Amon," she asked casually, "how do you feel about me? Do you still see me as a witch, the *Cailleach*?"

Caught off-guard by the unexpected and personal nature of the question, Amon put down his mallet and faced her. The softness of her blue eyes took him aback. Off-balance, he nervously replied, "No...?" The fact that he said it as a question made her smile. She had known enough men to know that when cornered about their feelings, any sort of nonsense might follow.

"Is that a question or a statement?" she asked, pressing her finger into his chest, enjoying making him nervous a little bit more than she should have.

Amon looked down at her finger, then back at her quizzically. "I guess so," he blurted.

"You guess so, what?"

Amon was stumped. In his heart, he knew this might be a defining moment in their relationship, but he did not have much experience talking to women about his feelings. Now he was cornered by a woman asking how he felt about her and found himself at a complete loss for words. From an early age, Amon had spent most of his life among men who, for the most part, kept personal feelings to themselves.

Amon fidgeted with his long hair, then admitted, "No. I do not see you as a witch anymore."

Valerie liked the way Amon wore his greying hair long but shaved his beard daily. She found that most men, especially the hunters and farmers in this era, wore long unkempt beards, which she did not care for. Amon's clean-shaven face, flowing hair, and hard chiseled features combined to give him a masculine but civilized appearance. Soft brown eyes peered back at her questioningly but as always controlled, carefully measured, unyielding.

"Alright," she cooed, "but you didn't answer my question. How do you feel about me?"

"I like you," he responded, although his discomfort at the admission was palpable.

"I like you too, Amon," she admitted but felt somewhat deflated because she was eager to move their relationship past the 'friends' stage.

"A lot," Valerie added, searching his features hopefully.

Come on, Amon, help me out here, she thought anxiously. *I see what's behind those big brown eyes. There's more. I know it! Surely you can do better than 'I like you.' But if I have to drag the truth out of you, I will!*

Amon smiled but said nothing more. So rather than keeping Amon squirming, Valerie decided it was time to show how she truly felt about him.

"You stupid man," she stated, then pulled him close and kissed him hard. All the emotions she had hidden landed on Amon with shocking suddenness. His eyes widened, then he took her in his arms, and they kissed some more. Soon they found themselves sitting under an apple tree side-by-side, holding hands, talking, laughing, and flirting. They took turns laughing at themselves for taking so long to admit their mutual attraction to themselves, let alone one another.

"I was afraid you thought I was too old for you," she admitted.

"At first, I thought you were dangerous," Amon confessed. "But I got over that soon enough. And after that, I didn't think you could ever be interested in a simple hunter like me."

"There is nothing simple about you, Amon. You are amazing. But it's true, I am dangerous," laughed Valerie, "just not when it comes to you," she assured him.

He nodded and chuckled. "I am glad to hear that. I have seen what happens when you decide to be dangerous."

When Pearse and Lauryn saw Valerie and Amon sitting together and flirting, they turned to each other and simultaneously said, "I told you so!" The couple's mutual interest had been evident to everyone except themselves for a long time.

In the following weeks, Amon and Valerie were inseparable. Amon intimated that they should live together, but Valerie would not have it. If she was going to have a relationship with a man, she wanted a wedding.

"Amon and Valyri are planning to get married," Pearse whispered one day to Hethe.

"It's about time!" Hethe exclaimed when Pearse told him of the budding relationship.

"Pearse asked me to go get more of Tadhg's sawblades," Amon told Valerie over breakfast, "so I will leave in the morning and return the next day. Can you get some more chromium, manganese, and gold to pay for it?"

"Alright, I will have it for you this afternoon," she agreed.

Amon was curious about where Valerie was getting the gold. *I saw her go down to the river and come back with a bag, but that raised more questions than answers,* he thought. *I know that river as well as anyone, but I have never seen a speck of gold in it. But Valerie has her secrets, and if I know what is good for me, I should not question her about it.*

"Those sawblades do not last long," Amon exclaimed. "I think we should order more of them, so Pearse has them on hand when they are needed. He hit a rock today and ruined a blade."

"That's a good idea," agreed Valerie. "We should have an inventory of blades on hand. Tadhg is going to need more supplies than usual, so I will bring you more this time," she assured him.

"The gold nuggets raise a lot of suspicion," Amon said apprehensively. "We are overpaying for them, and Tadhg is aware of it. Changing to silver would solve that problem. Silver coin would be even better."

"Alright," Valerie agreed. "Silver it is."

"Can you get the silver in coins?"

"Sure," Valerie said simply.

Amon raised his eyebrows in wonder. "How are you going to do that? Rivers have gold in them but not silver. Silver is mined, so how are you going to get silver coins out of the river?" The moment the words left his mouth, he regretted saying them. He had exposed himself observing her trips to the river and returning with bags of precious metals. Nevertheless, he felt justified in asking about the coins.

"You know what?" Valerie fired back. "You're right. If we are going to be married, you need to know exactly who you are marrying and what you are getting yourself into. Come with me right now, and I'll show you."

Valerie went into her house and returned with a bag, then Amon followed her as she walked the path down to the river. Amon sat on the riverbank watching as she took off her shoes, pulled her dress up to her knees, then waded into the shallow water. Soon she had the bag filled with stones, approximately the same size he had previously seen.

Valerie emptied the bag of stones in front of Amon then began separating them into three piles, two separate mounds of the larger rocks and one of smaller pebbles. Then falling to her knees, she said, "Surely you guessed that I have been turning stones into metal."

"I did," Amon confessed. "But I didn't want to say so because I didn't want you to think that I still see you as a witch. I have learned that you are much more than that."

Pleased that Amon viewed her that way, she jumped up, embraced, and kissed him hard. Now sitting on his lap beaming, she said, "Are you still afraid?"

"Sometimes, yes." He laughed. "Not at the moment, although I do want to understand."

"Alright then, but you must promise never to tell anyone what I am about to show you. My safety—*our* safety depends on it," she said firmly.

"I promise," he assured her.

"Alright then, let me show you," she agreed, kneeling again.

"Observe," she proclaimed, then made a show of removing and replacing her thumb ring so Amon could see the effect on her eyes. Each time she pulled off the ring, her eyes were instantly transformed from black to blue.

"As I said to you many times, I am not a witch; the rings are a tool I use to make things happen. Do you understand?"

Amon nodded expectantly, then watched as Valerie returned the thumb ring, then hovered her hands over one of the piles of river rocks.

"Chromium ore," she said, her gaze fixed unblinkingly on Amon as the air around them wavered. The river rocks instantly changed into lustrous steel-grey chunks of ore. Valerie continued working in her mysterious way without ever taking her eyes off Amon. When her attention turned to the pile of pebbles, she said, "Silver coin," and it was done. Then Valerie waited wordlessly for Amon's response.

Although Amon knew what Valerie was doing, he was astounded by her demonstration of power. *Is there anything this woman cannot do?* Amon wondered. *She has one amazing idea after another, turns river rock into gold or silver, and makes it all look easy! I was not afraid of her a moment ago, but now I am not so sure. What if she decides to turn me into an ass?*

"Well?" Valerie asked. "What do you think?"

"I think that if I marry you, I had better keep you happy—or you will turn me into an ass," Amon exclaimed."

"Too late, dear, you accomplished that all by yourself!" Valerie laughed.

Amon rode away on his old mare at dawn, carrying the secret raw materials for making steel and a pouch of silver coins. Stars were still visible, but the sky was clear, and the summer day promised to be warm. If he didn't lose any time, he could be at Tadhg's forge by late afternoon. Since he now carried silver coins, he decided to treat himself to a hot meal and a night at an inn in Bregia rather than sleeping under the stars as he had on his first visit.

As he descended from the Bearnán Éile ridge, Amon made a brief stop to visit Lochlan, sharing some news with him, then followed the road to the bridge at Erlin. From there, he took the crossroad west toward Bregia. The August sun was intensely hot by late morning, so Amon took a break under a tree on the Nore Riverbank.

Amon relaxed with his back against the tree, watching peacefully as his horse waded into the shallow water to drink. He allowed his thoughts to wander lazily in the heat of the day, and then his thoughts returned to Valerie. Just yesterday, she had been seated on his lap talking and kissing him beside the bank of the same river he now watched flow by.

Amon realized he was happier than he had ever been, and it was all because of the strange woman he had let into his once-predictably ordinary life. As he saw it, she had changed his life in a way that he could never have imagined. Now life was full of surprises and new challenges. Admittedly he had exchanged mundanity for unpredictability but welcomed it, nevertheless.

Valerie has reawakened my thinking ability, he realized. *I am experiencing and doing things never conceived, like learning a new language, and reading and writing.* Sure, she was strange, but he had grown to love her for that. It seemed that no two days were ever the same; anything could happen with her around.

But do not forget, he told himself, *I am planning marriage to a woman who turns river rock into silver coins, levitates logs, and resurrects the dead. What is next?* he wondered. *What other surprises does she have in store for me?*

Amon ran his hand through his hair then massaged the stiffness out of his neck. Suddenly something spooked his horse, which broke and ran upstream at a gallop. Amon jumped up and called to it, but it was no good; the old mare was running wild as if her tail was on fire.

Amon stood in the shallow water watching in frustration as the animal disappeared upriver. Something had spooked the usually steady mare, but what? The grassy riverbank allowed a clear view of the valley floor for more than a mile in every direction. There were no wolves, bears, or anything else that would have scared the horse. *A water snake?* He wondered.

Then Amon felt rather than heard something odd, a raising tremor in the earth, and he knew that was what had scared the old mare. Searching the ground, he saw no reason for fear; other than the tremor, all seemed as it should be— and then the sky above Amon shuddered and broke with an audible shriek.

Amon raised his eyes, and his heart turned to stone. A streaking fireball appeared to be headed directly at him. Amon sunk to his knees in a combination of astonishment and horror, for surely, he was about to die.

The ear-piercing scream echoed through the river valley as the blazing mass approached. But as the ball of flames flashed overhead, he realized it was higher in the sky than initially thought and that it would pass safely above. A wave of relief washed over Amon as his eyes followed the object's trajectory and disappeared behind the hills.

A flash, immediately followed by a compression wave and a thunderous boom, stunned him. Once Amon gathered his senses, he stared as a dust cloud formed west of his position. Amon could not help but think of what might have happened to him had he continued toward Bregia instead of taking a break.

But Amon knew the area well and guessed that whatever it was that hit the ground was close, just over the hill, not more than a mile or two from where he stood. A sense of foreboding overcame him as he remembered the day he and his fellow hunters watched Valerie's ship *The Dreamer* rip through the atmosphere, then hammer itself into the ground in much the same way this object had done.

Fortunately, this thing was nowhere near as large as the Dreamer, nor was it nearly as destructive as when it fell to Earth. He was sure this thing, whatever it might be, was a much smaller sphere, whereas Valerie's ship was perhaps one-hundred times larger, rectangular, and with fin-like appendages. Although he did not know what might have fallen out of the sky in this instance, he guessed it was something entirely different than the Dreamer.

Amon was eager to see the object with his own eyes, but first, he had to catch the old mare, which still carried his weapons and the valuable supplies intended for Tadhg. Following the stream upriver, he found the mare grazing peacefully alongside the riverbank as if nothing had happened. Then muttering as he closed in on the animal so as not to startle it, he was able to recapture and remount her.

Hurrying, he turned his horse west and prodded it into a gallop. Soon Amon stood atop the hill surveying the impact site from a safe distance. A long furrow marked where the object first impacted then skidded to a stop at the base of a knoll. A smoking sphere rested at the bottom of a crater steaming and snapping as it cooled. But there was more: an otherworldly metallic thrumming sound emanated from the abyss.

Amon took a knee as he studied the site with the patience of an experienced hunter. He was in no hurry; there was no need to rush. In his experience, diligence always paid dividends when assessing a situation. Respect for one's enemy kept men alive, and Amon considered this thing as a potential enemy. It certainly did not look friendly.

Although more than an hour had passed since the event, the torn earth and surrounding debris smoldered still. The charred surface of the sphere shimmered in the midday sun. Other than the sphere's rhythmic thrumming sound, the site was silent, and nothing in the area moved.

That thrumming troubled him made him feel uneasy, and he considered it as a warning. What happened to Pearse when he touched Valerie's ship was still fresh enough in his mind that he knew better than to repeat the error. He had no intention of touching it. Pearse had touched something similar and almost cost him his life. Amon took pride in learning from others' mistakes, and he considered Pearse's error as a lesson well learned.

But Amon still wanted to have a closer look, so he walked his horse down the hill then tied it to a tree before going any closer; he did not want to take the chance of having to chase down a startled animal again. The site seemed peaceful enough — until he heard a loud clank and the sound of metal against metal. Suddenly the mare's eyes went wild, and the old horse began stamping her hooves and pulling away. Amon looked over his shoulder and was startled to see movement in the pit.

The sphere burst open like a broken egg, with the shell opening into four symmetric sections. Now the thrumming sound came much louder as something rose out of the fragmented casing. Amon watched in horror as the thing unfolded itself into the shape of a six-legged spider roughly the size of a man, then all at once flew directly at him. Without time to react, the thing was instantly upon him.

Amon was thrown roughly to the ground by the hovering, thrumming metallic creature. Panicked, he tried to escape its grasp, but the strange machine was too quick. Six dangling arms grasped him and pinned him down; he was immobile, no matter how hard he struggled. The bug-like thing hovered over him, shining lights in his face. Blinding white light scorched his eyes, then a hard stabbing pain on his neck, like a sting, and then he was abruptly released.

The assault was over in seconds. But the horrible flying spider was not finished yet. In a flash, the thing was on the old mare, its six legs wrapped firmly around her head, shining lights in her frightened bulging eyes threatening to drive the animal mad. He watched helplessly as she struggled against the attack, snorting, tossing her head, and bucking. But it was no use; she was unable to break away from the vile thing. Another arm unfolded from the beast's belly and stabbed at the horse's neck like a scorpion, sending the horse into a frenzy.

The instant the stabbing arm had done its work and was fully retracted, the machine released the horse and was instantly on a nearby tree branch. The poor old mare was wild now, crying, bucking, and kicking. Although firmly held to the tree by the rope, she could not escape. The machine repeated the procedure on the tree, the same as was done to him and the horse, and when it was done, it flew away at incredible speed, thrumming all the way.

Still flat on his back, Amon felt broken, too stunned to move. The attack came so fast, so overwhelming in its effectiveness, that he never had a chance to react. His defeat had been so swift and so thorough that he could not reconcile it in his mind. Wholly demoralized, Amon stared helplessly at the flying spider as it hovered over a bush, shined its blazing lights on it, then stabbed again with its scorpion-like stinger, then was on a rock.

Man, beast, rock, or vegetation made no difference to the machine. It treated them alike and then moved on without the slightest hesitation. It was done in seconds, then it raced away thrumming, incessantly thrumming, searching for its next victim. The thing stopped at a patch of tall grass, lights flashed, and it moved again, and again, and in a few moments, it was gone entirely and with it the upsetting thrumming sound.

Groaning, Amon rolled onto his knees and touched his neck where he was stung, then stared at his hand wonderingly. Although there was a trace of blood, he didn't find enough to be concerned about. The injury appeared to be slight, which surprised him. From what he could see of the horse, the same was true of her wound. Blood stained the animal's neck, but the wound was superficial like his own.

Amon held his head, struggling to understand what had happened. He had no words to describe it, no experience to fall back on, no information to help him make sense of it. This airborne iron scorpion moved so incredibly fast that it was impossible to avoid. *What moves like that? Nothing! What was it doing, and why? Why would anyone—or anything bother to tackle a man, sting him, then unceremoniously toss him aside like refuse? Even more curious is the fact that it treated the plants and animals the same way!*

He wished Valerie were here. *She would understand. She would know what to do—wouldn't she?* And yet intuition told him there must be a connection between this great iron insect and Valerie Dunne. He did not know what, but the logic was unavoidable. She needed to know, and he had to get to her as quickly as possible.

Amon untied the now-calmed mare from the tree, hopped on her back, and galloped east toward Erlin. When he arrived at Valerie's house, it was dark, the sun had already set, and lamps were lit inside. Valerie heard him coming and opened the door in time to see him leading the old mare to the barn. The horse was wet with sweat and needed to be cared for.

"Amon is that you already?" she called.

"I will be right there," Amon returned. "As soon as I take care of the horse." Amon unloaded the mare, brushed, fed, and watered her as quickly as he could, then rushed to Valerie's door. Since she was expecting him, he entered without knocking and seated himself at her table.

One look at Amon, and Valerie knew there was trouble. "Amon, what's wrong?" she cried, "you look like you saw a ghost!"

Amon, who was a master of understatement, replied, "Might have. Got anything to eat?"

"Amon, you tell me what's wrong right now!" Valerie insisted.

"It's a long story, and I am hungry."

Valerie turned and pitched a loaf of bread at him, which he caught one-handed. "Got any wine? I need some," he said, then with a full mouth of bread added, "really bad—and pour yourself one, you are going to need it."

After pouring two mugs of wine Valerie seated herself across from Amon expectantly. "So, what happened? Why didn't you go to Bregia?"

Amon stopped eating and stared hard at Valerie. Not sure where to begin or how to put his strange experience into words, he decided to start with the most significant part of the story.

"An iron spider knocked me down, then stung me on the neck. Then it flew up and stung the old mare—which I can assure you she was not happy about. After that, the ugly thing stung everything else in sight, trees, bushes, grass— even rocks!" he exclaimed.

Valerie laughed. "Yeah, well, some people have all the fun!"

Amon remained silent, without a hint of humor in his eyes, and Valerie realized that although he was a terrible storyteller, he was not joking and saw no humor in it. Something dreadful had happened to him on the road to Bregia; she just needed to draw it out of him. Amon showed her the welt on his neck where he had been stung, and Valerie's eyes widened in horror.

"Amon, please start from the beginning and tell me what happened."

Amon took a moment to gather his thoughts, picking at the bread with a desperate look on his face before beginning. When he met her gaze, Valerie saw that he considered what he was about to disclose extremely troubling.

"I was halfway between Erlin and Bregia when I decided to rest beside the river. The day was hot, and I was thirsty. The old mare was wading in the river when something startled it, and it ran. I spent an hour tracking her down."

"What was it? What startled the horse?"

"A fireball in the sky," Amon said with a definite edge to his voice.

"Was that at about midday?"

Amon nodded.

"I saw it in the west, heard it too," she said. "A meteor, right?"

"I don't know," Amon paused. "I don't know what it was, but it seemed to be heading straight for us. It flew overhead and hit the ground about a mile away, so after I caught the horse, I rode out there to see it."

"What was it? What did it look like?"

"A ball, a smoking metal ball."

"*Metal!*" Valerie exclaimed. "Are you sure?"

Amon nodded again. "A metal ball," he confirmed, "a metal ball that cracked open like an egg. And when it happened, an iron spider emerged."

Valerie's throat tightened. "Iron spider," she choked the words. "You mean a machine, right?"

"I guess so," Amon reluctantly confirmed, then added, "It wasn't a creature if that is what you mean. It was metal, maybe steel, and its eyes were like your solar torches."

Valerie was horrified, immediately recognizing what Amon described as a probe of some kind, perhaps even something from the future. Nothing else fit the description. *Who sent it? The Boecki? Or has the BRU sent a probe to find me?* She wondered.

She sighed, convinced she knew what Amon had seen. "Amon, describe the machine," she said, her voice filled with foreboding.

"It was metal, about the size of a man—bigger maybe. It had six dangling arms hanging from it and a hidden stinger. It flew at me so fast I could not dodge it; it knocked me down, shined bright lights in my eyes, then stung my neck. After stinging me, it was on the horse so fast, she couldn't avoid it either, believe me, she tried. I was proud of her for that; she fought like a wild cat!"

Amon smiled, then continued his account. "The machine got its legs wrapped around her head then stung her, too. And then the strangest thing happened; the machine went into a tree and did the same thing it did to the horse and me, like a bee moving from flower to flower. Then it was on a rock, a bush, and everything else it could find. It seemed to miss nothing; it shined its lights and stung everything, and then it was gone."

"Gone?" Valerie asked.

"Yes, gone. It flew away, probably looking for more things to sting."

"I see," Valerie said, rubbing her temples. "Amon, what color was it?"

"I am not sure. It was moving very fast," he said as a matter of fact. "Brown—Bronze, maybe. What do you think it is?" Amon wanted to know.

"That figures, I should have known better," she said, shaking her head in disgust—*a Boecki resource seeker drone, just what we needed. But this development is a good reminder of who is running the show. It is so easy to forget the Hesaurun Rings are sentient, that I am little more than arms and legs for them, merely a vassal. I was foolish ever to think it was my idea to come here. They knew the Boecki would send a seeker drone to Earth in this time period—and guess what? Here I am at the right time and place to intercept it.*

"What do you mean?" Amon wondered.

"Oh, don't worry, dear," she said, patting his hand. "The probe didn't sting you; it was just taking samples. It might have felt like a sting, but it did not intend to hurt you or the horse. It is a machine that's broken; it isn't working right. It was supposed to check—uhm, check to see if you are healthy. Yeah, that's it—that's all," Valerie lied, and badly.

Valerie watched Amon's face for a reaction. *For now, half-truths and outright lies will have to do,* she thought. *How can I tell him the truth when I barely have the strength to admit it to myself!*

"Samples? Samples of what?" Amon gulped, puzzled.

"Blood samples," Valerie admitted, as brightly as she could manage, but in truth, what she had learned was crushing, and she was horrified by it.

"The machine is a medical drone from the future, like me—I mean, it is from the future like I am, not that I am a drone myself. Know what I mean?" she explained, laughing nervously.

Amon just stared at her, more puzzled than ever.

"In the future," Valerie continued, "we take small blood samples that provide us with information about an individual's health. The machine is a medical drone that is supposed to help people, not scare them to death."

Valerie watched Amon's face for a reaction. She had no idea what he must be thinking. She felt his eyes on her, anxious and questioning, but the truth about the drone was just too frightening to explain. Instead, she just sighed and took his hand. "Why don't we go see if we can find it tomorrow? I am sure that by now it is safely back in its shell asleep."

Valerie smiled, came close, and ran her hand through his hair before he could say anything more. *Getting better at lying,* she thought. *But if it is what I think it is, I must find it—and fast!*

THE END OF BOOK ONE -

THE RINGS OF HESAURUN
BOOK 2
THE RING BEARER

(Excerpt)

Chapter 1

Valerie Dunne. June Present Day.

Young Valerie Dunne sat up with a start as she awoke. Something was different, but the room was too dark to offer any clue about what that might be. An impenetrable blackness surrounded her, and all was silent, so she had little to go on other than intuition. Staring hard into the darkness, straining to see, revealed nothing but more blackness. But she shuddered when a kaleidoscope of colors encroached on her peripheral vision, intruding at the edges of her consciousness like feathery clouds blown on a winter's night.

When what had been shimmering peripheral lights turned into throbbing pulsations of hot white energy, she cried out in fear and pain. So intense were they that she was forced to cover her eyes with her hands. Even so, she felt as if she was staring directly into the midday sun. Blinded by the intense explosions of color, her ears rang, and her mind swirled. Startled and confused by the painful experience, the girl fought to maintain her senses in what had abruptly become a trial of sensory stamina.

As quickly as the strange phenomena began, it dissipated, allowing her mind and senses to recover. But when she opened her eyes, she found herself not lying in bed as expected but standing. However, staying upright proved to be a Herculean task. Wobbling knees refused to cooperate while her feet seemed glued to the floor. More than that, her entire body felt as if gravity had suddenly doubled. *What's happening! Is gravity playing tricks on me?* Aside from gravity's cruel betrayal, her addled mind and impaired senses found no reliable explanation.

Struggling against the chaos, she fought to focus. Finally, she was able to make out the dark silhouette of an enormous stick figure standing directly before her. She recognized the form as humanoid, although she could not decide whether she looked at a sculpture, a being, or something else. The possibility of it being something else had her worried.

"Corell? Are you there? Corell? What happened? Where am I?" she managed to mumble weakly, her frayed voice sounding so desperate she hated the sound of it.

"Corell Paris cannot hear you, Valerie Dunne," the unfamiliar though kind voice assured her. "You are not in any danger. You have no reason to fear."

Although the voice she heard was not what she expected, it was soothing enough that it eased her worst fears. Her vision was still too blurry to make out details, but it seemed the bronze figure remained stationary, which eased her nerves. Since the voice came from the general direction of the silhouette, she anticipated movement, but none came. Nevertheless, logic told her that whatever was directly in front of her must have spoken. She just couldn't be sure.

"What's happening? Where is Corell?"

"Corell is right where you left him— of course."

"Of course," she agreed, now feeling foolish for asking such an obvious question. *No doubt Corell is exactly where I left him. Where else would he be? Maybe if I could see something, I wouldn't have to ask such dumb questions,* she reasoned.

"I'm sorry, I can't see you. It's my eyes..." Valerie said impatiently.

"Do not worry. Your vision will clear momentarily," the smooth voice reassured once more. "Please seat yourself while your sight recovers. Right behind you," the speaker advised.

A quick glance over her shoulder revealed the shape of a bench, so Valerie backed up a step guided by touch, then lowered herself carefully on the edge of the bench. Half-blinded and afraid of stumbling, she felt better being seated.

Then drawing a deep breath of relief, she blurted, "Who are you?"

"My name is Osomarío. I brought you here," proclaimed the pleasant voice, but she needed to know more.

"Wh-Where is... *here?*" she asked tentatively.

"The answer to that question might be difficult for you to understand. However, the precise answer is not so much where is here, as much as it is *when is here.*"

"Well," exclaimed Valerie, "one thing is certain: 'when is here' sure is hot! It must be over a hundred degrees!" No one had to remind her she was no longer in her air-conditioned room. Although dry, the heat was oppressive, as if she had stepped into a furnace.

"Osomarío, I am confused. I was in bed in Oregon a moment ago at Corell Paris' estate. Then I woke up and found myself here, fully dressed, half-blind, and in this— pressure cooker. I feel like I have been kidnapped. If you brought me here, tell me why."

"I saw that your time had come."

Frustrated, Valerie frowned and scratched her nose. Another cryptic answer delivered matter-of-factly, which wasn't what she had hoped for. *I need to know where I am and what I am doing here! I need facts!* Her host's voice was reassuring enough, but it also carried an undeniable note of authority with it, which made her nervous. Instinct told her she was speaking to someone that commanded her destiny. Although she didn't feel an immediate threat, she remained guarded.

"Time for what?" she asked, swallowing hard. Yet, Valerie felt a compelling sense of serenity from this strange brown man and this scorchingly hot place. She felt dry, but licking her lips did nothing; they felt dry as paper. The air was desert air, carrying with it wonderful fragrances, that of a garden she assumed. But if this was a garden, it was different than any she knew of because the scents were all wrong. While her focus cleared further, colors became more vivid, revealing every hue of the sunrise and sunset. Now her sight was returning quickly, just as her strange host had promised, and she felt more at ease.

"The time has come for you to know the truth about yourself. I will teach you." Osomario proclaimed.

Valerie furrowed her brows and squinted. With her vision clearing now, she realized that everything about this Osomarío was indeed bronze in color. *No wonder I thought he was a bronze statue,* she thought. The creature was exceptionally tall, perhaps seven feet or more in height, and startlingly lean. Valerie was taken aback as she noticed his broad shoulders supported, not two, but four long muscular arms of equal length. Each of those four arms ended in broad powerful-looking hands with three fingers and a thumb. The lean muscle definition of this obviously alien life form was accentuated by hairless, leathery skin, making for an imposing presence.

But the feature that set it apart from anything she had ever seen or imagined was the high forehead punctuated by a pair of large, deep-set eyes. And those eyes shone of darkness, obscure as obsidian, reflective as mirrors, incomprehensibly empty. Although unknowable and more than a little unnerving, those glistening orbs seemed to see everything— and yet nothing. So utterly black and featureless were they that it was impossible to tell if they moved, looked past or through her. Even as the creature turned its head, gestured, or spoke, those eyes did nothing other than mirror their surroundings. Seeing her own flawless image reflected in them caused a shudder.

Nevertheless, Osomarío's presence radiated serene intelligence, and in a strange way, undeniably beautiful. The creature's chiseled form and overall appearance confirmed her first impression: this Osomarío seemed to be more of an animated bronze sculpture than a living, breathing being. *What am I dealing with? A god? Perhaps.* The thought rattled her.

"So— you say I am here to learn the truth? About myself?"

How odd, Valerie observed. *The creature's clothing matches his skin color perfectly. Considering the heat, the loose-fitting shapeless robes make sense, but the robes, even his sandals, are all the color of bronze.* She reasoned this character had embraced his favorite color like no one ever had. Although she knew better, for an instant, she imagined the creature to be a man of metal, entirely of bronze from head to foot. A walking, talking four-armed metallic scarecrow.

"Yes. You are here to learn the truth about yourself, the Hesaurun rings, and how they should be used. I am Osomarío, your liaison to the five Hesaurun rings. I will teach you. I will be your guide."

Valerie's heart skipped a beat as she recalled the name *Osomarío* from Valerie Dunne's journal and conversations with Corell Paris. According to Corell, he had gifted the five rings to humankind. Now she found herself face-to-face with the master of the five rings, and she assumed, the source of their power.

Valerie thought of pinching herself to be sure she wasn't dreaming. For whatever reason, this Osomarío had chosen this time to bring her to him, which made her feel important. The warm glow of feeling needed and truly appreciated coursed through her veins. Moreover, now she knew it was this alien she had seen so many times working in the shadows of her dreams. He had always been there to help her, and now he had called her home to him.

"Osomarío," Valerie faltered, "I just realized I know you."

"Yes, you do. We know each other quite well, do we not?" Osomarío said, with a trace of mischief in his voice. A wide smile had formed there, producing deep creases in his leathery features. It seemed he enjoyed the admission as if it was something confidential, a special secret between them. At that moment, the tension Valerie felt evaporated, replaced by a sense of kinship with the strange alien.

"Almost every night for the past fourteen years," she confessed. But realizing what she had just said could easily be misconstrued, she laughed, embarrassed at the unintended double entendre.

"Quite true," her host responded, avoiding her verbal misstep. "We have a lot to talk about, do we not? But before that, allow me to show you my home," he welcomed, gesturing gracefully with a pair of open hands.

With her vision finally regained, Valerie looked beyond Osomarío for the first time and made a discovery that took her breath away. The scope and splendor that was Osomarío's home were almost indescribable. As she took in her surroundings, she was instantly reminded that she was no longer home— heaven perhaps, but definitely not home.

As she saw it, nothing compared to this place. No fantasy or a fairytale could compare. She was reminded of OZ, or perhaps Asgard. The hanging gardens of Babylon crossed her mind, but she found no comparative metaphor.

What Valerie saw seemed not to be a home at all, rather more of a domed indoor open-air botanical sanctuary. The place was a galleria of pillars and arches, with sculptures, fountains, and more exotic foliage than her eyes could assimilate. Light, colors, and textures converged within the immense airy space, producing a scene anyone could savor.

Referring to this palace merely as *home* would be a gross understatement. The entire structure appeared to be hewn of stone. A series of intricately engraved arched braces rose until they merged, producing an eloquent dome. Valerie didn't know much about rock or building materials but guessed she saw marble with meandering green, blue, and black veins.

Osomarío took the lead, and Valerie followed past what she assumed was the main entrance, where she had her first glimpse of the landscape outside the dome. One look told her she wasn't on Earth, or likely anywhere near it. A pair of suns, one yellow another red, hung in the cloudless gray sky as indisputable proof of that. The terrain was disturbingly jagged and torn with massive rocks thrown about. A valley visible in the distance helped her place the location high on a ridge or mountain. Deep gouges marked the valley floor without evidence of life or of habitation. Although she couldn't imagine how anyone would want to live in such a lifeless inferno, she resisted judging Osomarío adversely for choosing a desolate inferno as his home.

Valerie followed the creature past a courtyard adjacent to an aquatic garden. As they passed, something struck her hard from behind, on her hip. Valerie shrieked and spun around in time to see the head of a large red flower retreating with a power bar in its maw, munching voraciously on it, wrapper and all. Instinctively she reached for her hip pocket where she had put it before yesterday's hike with Correll but felt nothing; it was gone. The big flower swallowed the bar whole then loosed a resonant call similar to a baying goat. She watched bemused as the vine-like creature slunk back into its watery plot with a splash.

"What the—" Valerie exclaimed, pointing an accusing finger at the offender, that by the time Osomarío had caught up with her appeared to be as innocent as any house plant. Just then, a bubble escaped the surface, sounding suspiciously like a burp.

"You have to watch that one," Osomarío warned with a smile. "The Telygren is always looking for something to eat."

"Tel-ey-gren," Valerie repeated. "I'll remember that for sure."

Although the atmosphere was sweet with a luxuriant scent, it had an otherworldly tang she tasted and felt on her skin, similar to cooking Brussels sprouts in a sweltering kitchen. Everywhere she looked, she saw gardens, rockeries, and water plots with too many varieties to count. Each plant seemed unique, so different in appearance she guessed correctly that they were from disparate worlds, none of them familiar.

Osomarío led her past a stone staircase that spiraled to the highest levels before being swallowed by incoming light streaming in through the arched openings. Sunlight played on the steps in a mosaic of glowing illumination and shadow.

Osomarío waited patiently for the girl while she stood, staring wordlessly at the majestic scene.

"The staircase leads to an observatory," he explained.

"It's beautiful, your home is amazing, and I love all these plants!" Valerie gushed, then dutifully fell in behind her lanky four-armed tour guide.

Osomarío led the way to a fountain featuring a graceful four-armed figure cradling an earthen vessel pouring water into a pool filled with floating vegetation. The creature motioned toward a bench across from the fountain and seated himself. Valerie joined him feeling refreshed, the tour through Osomarío's gardens having calmed her previously frayed nerves.

Comfortable now in this strange place, she felt content focusing on the serene fountain, watching the water flow. Osomarío rested next to her in silence, with sixteen long fingers folded on his lap. The reality of having been involuntarily removed from the safety of her bed without consent crept into her consciousness. Tension built the more she thought about it. As she was about to ask again why she was brought here, Osomarío interrupted.

"Patience. Please. Valerie," the creature told her in clipped words, exasperation evident in his voice. "I am very aware of your feelings. You want to know why I brought you here."

That this alien knew precisely her thoughts and feelings took her by surprise. But then it began to make sense. After all, Osomarío had been in her head since she was a child, which meant he knew her intimately through dreams. And what of the first go around, the original Valerie Dunne? How well had he known her in that iteration of herself? She couldn't say for sure but guessed they must have had an intimate bond. Didn't that make a difference? She thought it did. Humbled by this realization, she made a mental note to avoid playing poker with Osomario.

"I am," she admitted. "I am eager to know more about why you brought me here," she said anxiously, seeing no reason to hide her feelings at this point. "Tell me." What she actually wanted to say was, *Just say it will you!?*

"Alright," Osomarío allowed. "Remember, I said, 'It is your time to learn the truth about yourself? You are here for that reason. I fear there may not be enough time for you to learn by trial and error. Time is limited. You have much to learn. I must teach you."

Teach me? Teach me what? Valerie wondered. Yet without saying the words aloud, Osomarío answered.

"Trouble is on the horizon. When the Boecki claim star systems, they take everything of value, like what happened here on Hesaurun. The population is enslaved, and everything of value is stripped away, including soil, minerals, water, plant, and animal life. Nothing of value is left behind. It is what they do; it is what they have always done. That is their way. Currently, they are in the Epsilon system. Once the Boecki has completed their harvest, Sol will be next. That is why I brought you here. You will stop them. I will teach you how."

The creature raised a pair of bronze hands, sweeping them across the room. "This sanctuary...." he said with a note of melancholy. "These life forms are all the last of their kind, brought from worlds harvested by the Boecki," now long dead. Then an emotional admission— "I do not want to see the remnants of Earth preserved here."

Valerie's heart sank. She wasn't sure which part of what she had just heard hit the hardest. Was it the fact that aliens were headed to Earth to destroy it? That she had just learned the beautiful indoor gardens were all that was left of untold worlds consumed by this 'Boecki Dominion'? Or that she was expected to do something about it? It was all so awful she lashed out defensively.

"Osomarío!" she cried, turning to face her host. "I don't understand why you need me; you said you are the master of the five rings! Why don't you do it yourself? Why on Earth...."

Realizing her poor choice of words, she stopped, searching for another way to express her feelings. After a cleansing breath, she rephrased. "What do you need *me* for?" she said, exasperated. Then added, "I'm just a girl from Arlington, Washington. Why does everyone want to hang this on me?"

A silent moment passed as the emotion of the moment receded.

"They know who we are, my companions and I," Osomarío admitted. "We cannot interfere with the Imperium directly. If we are going to sabotage their efforts, we must do so indirectly."

"I'm sorry, I still don't understand. What makes you think I could ever do anything to stop them?"

"You are more powerful than you realize, Valerie Dunne. And you are not Boecki!" Osomarío spat those words as if distasteful. "The Imperium does not expect effective resistance."

The untold truth hit her like a hammer blow to the chest. What was not said was stunning, so shocking she wanted to erase it from her mind. But this revelation was not something she could brush aside or easily forget. Willing herself to breathe, she struggled against the horror in an attempt to remain objective. But the truth was too horrible to suppress.

"Osomarío..." she erupted, seething, glaring at the creature, "you— you are one of them, aren't you. You are Boeckian!"

To be continued...

Made in United States
Troutdale, OR
06/25/2023